Out of Time

David Klass is the author of many critically acclaimed young adult novels and has also written more than forty feature screenplays for Hollywood studios, including *Kiss the Girls* (adapted from the novel by James Patterson). He has also written for *Law and Order: Criminal Intent* and currently runs the TV Writing concentration at Columbia University's Film School. *Out of Time* was inspired by conversations with his teenage daughter about climate change.

Out of Time

DAVID KLASS

MICHAEL JOSEPH
an imprint of
PENGUIN BOOKS

MICHAEL JOSEPH

UK | USA | Canada | Ireland | Australia
India | New Zealand | South Africa

Michael Joseph is part of the Penguin Random House group of companies
whose addresses can be found at global.penguinrandomhouse.com

First published in the United States of America by Dutton, 2020
First published in Great Britain by Michael Joseph, 2020
001

Set in 13.5/16 pt Garamond MT Std
Typeset by Jouve (UK), Milton Keynes
Printed and bound in Great Britain by Clays Ltd, Elcograf S.p.A.

A CIP catalogue record for this book is available from the British Library

ISBN: 978–0–241–45622–4

www.greenpenguin.co.uk

For Gabe and Maddy

1

The man lay in darkness near the cliff's edge, staring down through binoculars at the moonlit Snake River as it wound through the Idaho hills toward the dam. Despite the colorful nickname the media had given him, he was dressed in black from his boots to his hood, and the drone in front of him was also black, from its four propellers to its nine-kilogram payload. He had built the large quadcopter himself in his hunting shed over the course of three months from parts he'd scavenged. Now it perched on the cliff next to him like a spikey prehistoric bird ready to swoop down on unsuspecting prey.

He stroked the stubble on his cheek. He had not slept in a bed, had a shower, or talked to another person in four days. He had driven his van on back roads through seven states without carrying a cell phone or using credit cards, and he had not logged online since he had said goodbye to his wife and kids and pulled away from his house in Michigan. He had brought his own food, water, and gas with him because any store, no matter how small, might have a camera, and once an image was taken, it became data and could be accessed by those looking for him. He was wearing fleece and an outer shell layer of nylon to contain body heat, because he was less than a mile from a major soft target and they were searching for him with thermal-imaging satellites.

Below him the ancient Archean formations – the oldest

exposed rocks on the earth's surface – fell away steeply into a ravine through which the Snake River cut westward on its thousand-mile meandering journey toward Wyoming and the distant Pacific. Looking down at this vista in silvery moonlight, the man had the sense of peering back across the ages to a time when the earth was still innocent and pristine and mankind hadn't mucked things up.

For a moment he was overtaken by a great sadness and sense of futility, and he almost gave up and headed back to his tent. Contrary to the psychological portrait the FBI forensic profilers had drawn up and disseminated so widely that he had read it himself, he did not want to be caught. If they found him, they would lock him up for the rest of his life. He was not afraid of pain, but a lifetime of incarceration was a hell on earth that he desperately wanted to avoid. If they caught him, they would also destroy his family, which was beyond precious to him.

He was acutely aware that each time he struck, the odds of making a mistake increased. The Green Man Task Force now numbered more than three hundred dedicated federal agents, twice the number who had pursued the Unabomber. Eventually, he would blunder and give them the clue they needed to find him – it was a matter of time and luck, but if he continued striking targets, it would happen. If he stopped, they would only have whatever information they had now. There seemed no point in taking further risks – the world was far along on its suicidal course, and he profoundly doubted that anything he could do would reverse what had already been set in motion. The wise course would be to abandon his mission and spend precious time with his wife and kids. But then he saw the headlights of a Jeep blink on as a sentry on night

2

patrol drove across the parapet guard ledge, and the twin pinpricks of light moving atop the four-hundred-foot dam spurred him to action.

He took the transmitter out of his large black backpack but kept it enclosed in a three-sided fiberglass case to mask its thermal footprint. He switched it on, and soon the four rotors on the drone were whirling. He checked the payload one last time – the twenty sticks of closely packed plastic explosive lay snug against the blasting cap.

The drone lifted off the cliff, and the man expertly moved the two control sticks to correct for roll, pitch, yaw, and throttle. He steered it away from him, and the large UAV flew out above the ravine, the moonlit reservoir, and the massive dam. It hovered, slowly circling, a black spot against the full moon, and he kept it high enough so they would not see or hear it. It was a calm and cloudless night – a night when God seemed very much in his glorious heaven, and the man had a final moment to hesitate at the enormity of the destruction he was about to unleash and to regret the taking of innocent lives.

The profilers were wrong about that, too – he was not a sociopath; he was in fact highly empathic, and killing brought him no joy. Nor did he have any illusion that the people whose lives he was about to end held any responsibility for the dam's existence or purpose. Most of them hadn't been alive in 1970 when it was built, and it was just their bad luck to be around the night it was destroyed. He understood that the dam employees had most likely just taken the job for a steady paycheck. When he was fresh out of Yale and knocking around, he had taken several similar jobs. But there was no way to do what needed to be done without loss of life.

The man lowered his head and prayed. 'God, forgive me,' he whispered, and then his fingers moved on the right control stick, sending the drone into a steep, expertly controlled dive. He felt the stab of excitement that always came with the knowledge that it was really going to happen, coupled with the guilty pride of seeing his creation finally fly at its peak speed of sixty miles per hour. Every kilogram of weight made flight more difficult and curtailed speed, so it had taken years for him to learn to build something with such a heavy payload that could fly this fast.

The Jeep was halfway across the parapet when it stopped moving. Had the driver heard something? It was unlikely, and it was also too late, unless he was a sharpshooter with the presence of mind to bolt out and squeeze off a shot in two seconds. More likely the sentry had paused midway across to have a smoke and admire the same moonlit vista that the man was watching. Framed by the ravine, against the hulking, dark monolith of the vast concrete wall, a stream of silvery water burst from one spill-gate and cascaded four hundred feet to the gleaming reservoir below.

But nothing happened – time stood still – and the man felt sure that something must have gone wrong. If the explosive device didn't detonate, they would find the drone and the bomb intact. Despite all his care, they would have a great deal to work from. He panicked and thought of Sharon, Kim, and Gus and how their lives would be upended if he were caught. The kindest thing he could do for them would be to spare them the nightmare of a trial, so he carried a suicide pill with him wherever he went.

He saw the explosion before he heard it. A sheet of fire cloaked the downstream face of the dam from toe to crest. A concussive burst — a wave of violent sound — throbbed through the ravine. But the dam did not immediately crumble, nor did the man expect it to. The attack on the World Trade Center had demonstrated with terrifying clarity that it was not necessary for a blast to instantly demolish its target — it need only do sufficient structural damage for weight, pressure, and gravity to finish the destruction. The man was using the same concept here. The blast had only to undermine the structural integrity of the arched dam at a crucial spot. Thousands of tons of Snake River water would soon do the rest.

For several tantalizingly slow seconds, everything seemed as it was before. The cloak of fire folded back up into itself. The concussive blast reverberated to silence. Then the first tiny spigots seeped through cracks as if a dozen new spill-gates had simultaneously been opened above the reservoir.

The man did not wait for the river to punch through — he took no pleasure in destruction and death, even though he had planned this for months. He could already see lights going on and hear sirens. Choppers would be on site in less than twenty minutes. He gathered his things into his backpack, checked carefully to make sure he hadn't left even a single wire behind, climbed onto his motorcycle, and sped away into the night toward his van and the long roads that would take him home to the people he loved.

2

Tom arrived at the hotel bar five minutes early, but his father was already there, halfway through a glass of scotch, glancing at his watch. He didn't look up as Tom approached from behind, but he said, 'Figured maybe you had a hot date. Should have known better.'

Tom noted the thin strip of mirrored glass above the bar that gave his father a sweeping view of the room. The old man still saw everything. He sat down on the barstool next to his dad. 'How was your flight?' Tom asked, holding out his right hand. 'Dad, come on.'

The paternal handshake was firm and brief, not a gesture of intimacy but an acknowledgment of male protocol, akin to a salute. 'How the fuck do you think my flight was? Fat lady sitting next to me must have weighed three hundred pounds.'

'Well, fat people have to fly, too.'

His father grunted dubiously and took another big sip of scotch.

'How's Mom?'

'She says hello.'

'What's she up to?'

'She's got her book circle.'

'What are they reading these days?'

'I forgot to check.'

Tom waved at the bartender. 'It might be something you would find interesting, and then you'd have something to talk about with her.'

His father put down his scotch and looked at Tom full in the face, and Tom saw how much older he had gotten. The once thick, jet-black hair was almost entirely gone, and the few tufts that remained were wispy and more white than gray. The skin sagged from his cheekbones, and he had a new nervous habit of pinching loose folds and tugging them. It was the sour face of a miserable old man, unsatisfied with his life and not looking forward to his death. 'Are you trying to be funny?'

The bartender came over, and Tom ordered a craft beer.

'At least drink with me,' his father said.

'I am drinking with you. I just ordered a beer. For Christ's sake, Dad.'

'We don't have to do this.'

Tom forced himself to be calm. 'Listen, I don't want to fight. I'm glad to see you. And I'm glad you came to see me. I'm sorry I couldn't make it out to Florida for your birthday. You're looking great.'

'I didn't come to see you.'

'Fine. I'm glad we met by chance at this bar. How are you feeling? How's life with a pacemaker?'

'They let you wear your hair that way?'

The bartender brought the beer, and Tom thanked him with a nod and took a sip. 'It's not the marines, Dad.'

'You're lucky it's not,' the former Marine Corps captain said.

They were both quiet. There was a TV above the bar showing a mixed martial arts match, and one of the fighters got in a control position and began to ground and pound. 'I miss boxing,' his father finally said. 'This shit killed boxing.'

8

'They're highly skilled. Those elbow strikes are Muay Thai.'

'Give me Joe Frazier or Roberto Durán any day.' His dad finished his scotch and waved for a refill. 'So,' he said, 'how do you like it?'

'You mean the job?'

'I never would've figured you for it.'

'Thanks. I'm just starting out, but I like it fine so far.'

'Your mother says they put you on a big taskforce.'

'Just a week ago. That guy who's been blowing things up. Green Man.'

His father frowned as if he'd tasted something unpleasant. 'The liberal media calls him that.'

'Dad, everyone calls him that.'

'It's to make him a hero.'

'Even Brennan calls him that.'

'Mr Brennan to you.'

'No, Assistant Director Special Agent in Charge Taskforce Commander God Incarnate Brennan to me. He calls the guy Green Man.'

'Jim Brennan's a good man. Have you met him?'

'There are more than three hundred agents on the taskforce. He runs the big briefings. I sit in the back and try not to fart too loudly.'

'So he doesn't know who you are?'

'What are you really asking?'

The bartender poured Tom's father a generous refill, and he pulled a twenty out of his wallet and smoothed it down on the polished oak bar. 'I could put in a call.'

'No, sir.'

'There are lots of people in the world named Smith. He'd want to know –'

'You built your career. Let me build mine.'

His father nodded and glanced at his watch. 'Build your career. I got to get to bed soon. I'm leaving early tomorrow.'

'Mom said you were going to see an old friend.'

'Bill Monroe, if you remember him. Out in Mitchellville.'

'Sure. He used to throw lousy Christmas parties and dress up like Santa, and you and Mom would get drunk from the bourbon punch.'

'The party's over. He's got advanced prostate cancer. I'm saying goodbye.'

'Very sorry to hear it.'

'So, you got a motive?'

Tom glanced at his own watch. It felt like he had been controlling his temper for a half hour, but only five minutes had actually ticked by. 'For what?'

'Green Fuck.'

The craft beer was too sweet and not to Tom's liking, but he took a big swallow. 'The liberal media says he's an environmental activist who wants to call attention to the way we're destroying our own planet.'

'And you buy that?'

'Look, I know you don't agree with this, but I don't work from motive,' Tom said carefully. 'What I do is mostly about crunching data to find patterns. Having one prejudged motive in mind can be misleading if you're letting the data speak. I try not to impose myself and think about why. But I know we're different that way.'

'So you don't need to worry about motive?' His father finished his scotch and put down his glass on the bar. 'Or maybe the truth is you're really afraid to consider it?' Tom knew that they were almost done, and what his father was going to say next was going to be the old man's nastiest shot. 'You admire him, don't you?'

'Green Man?'

'Green Lantern. Superman. Batman. Green Man. He's a superhero to you.'

'That's tremendously insulting, and it's also not true.'

'You and your sister were always tree huggers. You don't want to save the world?'

'He's killed thirty-one people. Five children.'

'Saving the world's a bitch. The end justifies the means, doesn't it? If you have to kill five kids to save our planet, isn't that worth it? Come on, we both know you agree with him. You were out there in the streets marching for green this and green that. So Green Man's fighting your battle, and he's doing it well.'

'I'm gonna say good night, Dad. You've got an early drive out to Mitchellville . . .'

Tom started to stand, but then his father's heavy hand was on his shoulder, and the old man was speaking in a muted, confessional tone that Tom had never heard before. 'I've never said this to anybody, but there's a part of us that always admires them. We hunt them and we hate them, but on some level they're doing the forbidden things we want to do and getting away with it. They're smarter than we are until the day we arrest them, and they're having more fun than we are, and if we didn't have a bit of their dark side we couldn't understand them and we couldn't possibly catch them. Right?'

Tom was silent for several seconds. He was surprised at the depth and honesty of his father's admission. 'Okay, right,' he finally admitted. 'On some level I guess I admire his goals, even if –'

'I was bullshitting you,' the old man said, very pleased

11

with himself. 'You think I admired the serial killers and scumbag rapists I was hunting? That's the kind of horse manure FBI agents say in bad movies. There's not a bone in my body that wanted to be like them. Never. Not for one second. But now we've established that you admire the man you're hunting, and for that reason alone, you're never gonna catch him.'

Tom's hand clenched around the beer glass. 'I'll catch him,' he said softly.

'Why didn't you go to Silicon Valley, Tom? You interviewed. You went to all the fancy schools. You could be pulling in some big bucks.'

'I'm doing okay. Dad, I'm gonna go now.'

'Finish your beer. Was it to honor me? Because I don't have long left?'

'No, that's ridiculous.'

'You're damn right, it is ridiculous. Because – to be very frank – you never gave a flying fuck about what I did. And it's too late now. Live your life.'

Tom shrugged the hand off his shoulder and stood up to face his father. 'It wasn't to honor you. But maybe I'm doing it for the same reason you did. To catch bad guys. It's the family business, isn't it? Grandpa Vic. Uncle Will. You. And now me. And he's definitely one of the bad guys. There's no way to justify the killing of innocents, no matter the ultimate goal.'

His father stood also. They were almost the same height, but his dad still had him by half an inch. 'I suppose it is the family business. Good night, Tom. Go out on a date once in a while, try to get laid, and make your mother happy.'

But Tom was looking past him at the TV, where a newsflash had interrupted the third round of the MMA fight.

There was footage of a moonlit river winding through a dark and mountainous ravine and a wrecked dam and people being evacuated in ambulances and on helicopters. Tom glanced at his watch and then back at the TV. 'It's him.'

His father turned and studied the TV screen. 'Green Man? How can you tell?'

'The dams on the Snake River are perfect targets for an environmental terrorist. They stopped wild salmon runs, and there have been legal challenges to them for years. They're important infrastructure, but they're also deeply symbolic – exactly what he looks for.'

'You glanced at your watch,' his father said. 'Does he always strike at the same time?'

'No, he doesn't.'

'But the timing is important somehow? It's part of his signature?'

'I can't talk about that,' Tom said.

'You can't talk about it to me?' his father repeated, and suddenly there was rage in his voice. 'The fuck does that mean? Like I can't keep my mouth shut? Listen, you little asshole . . .'

But Tom wasn't listening to his father anymore. He had climbed up onto the bar and turned up the volume manually, and he listened as the newscaster mentioned the first casualty reports and how a family of six on a houseboat in the reservoir beneath the dam had drowned – including four young children.

3

'The explosive was precisely delivered by a large drone to a lower bulwark section of the Boon Dam deemed critical by our experts. A top structural engineer on a good day couldn't have picked a better spot.' Brennan paused to sip coffee and looked out at the three hundred agents in folding chairs, many of whom were taking notes on laptops. In the dim hall their screens gleamed and silhouetted their faces with a bluish tint so that they looked like an army of trolls. 'Arched dams are curved so the hydrostatic pressure from the river presses against the arch and actually strengthens the dam. But if compromised in the right way, that stress point creates a potential structural weakness, and Green Man exploited it perfectly.

'As many of you know – and this is not public information – he times his attacks to coincide with an environmental doomsday clock run by a radical environmental group based in Sweden. The Östersund Clock claims to take into account a variety of factors, including global warming, and is ticking down to what they term "midnight," when the harm to our planet will be irreversible. Their clock is now at eleven thirty P.M., and the explosion at the Boon Dam occurred at *exactly* the equivalent in Idaho Mountain Time.'

Slides came on the large screen behind Brennan that showed what was left of the dam, and he could feel the reaction in the room and even hear a few gasps. It was one thing to hear the details, but it was another to see two billion dollars of damage. 'In other words, he picked his target expertly, researched it thoroughly but somehow covertly, and he hit a bull's-eye at the exact second he wanted.'

The army of trolls felt their leader's anger, and the tension in the large hall amped up. 'We suspect a plastic explosive – probably Semtex. Given the damage, there must have been more than eight kilograms. It's extremely difficult to build a drone that can carry such a heavy payload and fly that precisely.' Photos came on the screen of several tiny black shards that had been extracted from the concrete or fished from the reservoir. 'So far only a few fragments of the drone have been recovered. It had what our bomb people call a suicide cap. The main charge of plastic explosives took out the dam, but there was a much smaller charge committed to destroying the drone itself, the blasting device, and all traces of the explosive. Every bomb maker has a distinctive signature, but the suicide cap erased whatever we could have learned about Green Man.'

'As in the previous five incidents, a hand-typed letter – sent through the mail – arrived at a major urban news outlet this morning addressed to a senior editor, taking credit for the attack and explaining his reasons for it. He varies the city, but this morning it was Manhattan and the *New York Times*. You can read his letter on your website of choice since it's exploding on the Internet. For reasons I can't go into, we're sure it's Green Man. It was written in the same logical, circumspect tone as the other letters, and it expresses his reasons for blowing up the dam and his conclusion that given the environmental threats to our

16

planet, active resistance is not only warranted but a moral imperative. Our forensics people are poring over the letter, the stamp, the typeface, the paper – so maybe we'll get a break, but we didn't from any of the other five. As in those other letters, he ends by apologizing for what he terms the "tragic collateral loss of life."'

Brennan's gruff voice softened, as it always did when he turned to the casualties. 'Three Idaho Power and Gas workers were killed outright, and two more dam staff are critical. The blast damaged the dam sufficiently so that the pressure from the Snake River cracked through. In the ensuing flood of spill-water into the reservoir below, two houseboats capsized and the families on them drowned. Total loss of life is now at twelve but expected to increase. Preliminary damage estimates are well over two billion dollars, and the Snake River in the Boon Canyon has largely resumed its normal course.'

Brennan waved a hand, and the overhead lights came on full. 'We have seventy agents on-site, and over two thousand local and state police and airport security folks are working with us, following up every lead. The manhunt is now national in scope and unparalleled in the number of agents and ancillary investigators and the combined and diverse expertise brought to bear. But bottom line, he struck again and he got away. Questions? Grant?'

A tall African-American agent in the front row stood. 'Sir, for the drone to have been steered into the target so precisely, Green Man must have had a ringside seat. He had to be close and also have a direct view of the dam's downstream face.'

'There are over thirty hills, mesas, and cliffs above the downstream side of the dam that would have given him the proximity and viewpoint he needed,' Brennan said. 'We have forensics teams on-site scouring them, but so far we haven't found anything. Many of them are hard-rock formations and wouldn't preserve prints, and all indications are that he wears special clothing and shoes and is methodical about not leaving anything behind. Yes, Dale?'

A wide-shouldered man in khakis and a blue jacket stood. 'The Boon Dam is one of the soft targets we monitor by satellite. Wouldn't he have left a thermal image, and wouldn't the transmitter of the drone have sent a heat plume?'

'We had a direct overflight. Our eye in the sky didn't pick up anything. He's finding some way to mask it. Hannah? What data can we get you?'

A middle-aged Asian woman stood and said in an unexpectedly booming voice, 'That part of northern Idaho is very rural. Only a handful of airports. Just a few interstates. Once he struck the dam, he had to get out fast. The more images we can get in the hours right after the blast from airport cameras, gas stations, tollbooth cameras –'

'He would never drive on an interstate,' a voice blurted out from the back.

Brennan held up his hand. He was a big man, and his upraised palm looked like a catcher's mitt. 'You, in the back, who just spoke out of turn. Stand up.'

Everyone in the room turned to look as a rail-thin, gangly young man with unkempt black hair, who looked like he should still be in college, stood awkwardly at the very back.

'I don't recognize you. What's your name?'

'Tom Smith, sir.'

'Did I call on you, Agent Smith?'

18

'No, sir.'

'Agent Lee was asking a question, wasn't she?'

'Yes, sir. Well, she wasn't exactly asking a question, but she was talking, sir.'

'But now you're talking. So go ahead and talk.'

'I meant no disrespect, sir. But Green Man doesn't take major highways. At least not when he's on a mission. He would never do that. He doesn't use airports. He probably carries his own gas with him.'

'Are you psychic, Agent Smith?'

'What, sir?'

'Are you clairvoyant?'

There were some laughs. 'No, sir. But I –'

'Too bad. Because if you *were* psychic, we wouldn't need to cover all the bases and painstakingly gather the information that eventually breaks these cases. Sit down and contain yourself. Hannah, we already have thousands of those images heading your way, but if we're missing any catch-points, please let me know.'

'Yes, sir,' she said, and sat down.

'We're done here,' Brennan announced. 'The media is already making a meal of this, and several news stations and websites are coming close to lionizing him for mass murder. They're highlighting that this may help bring back the Pacific salmon and barely mentioning that two families were killed. Their names haven't been released yet, but I know them.'

Brennan stepped forward, and his voice was now almost painfully soft. 'The Terry family from Boise. Fred Terry and his wife, Susan, and their six-year-old, Sam, found drowned in his tiger-striped pajamas. And the Shetley family from Riverton. Jack, a doctor. His wife, Mary, who

19

worked for the fire department. And their four kids, including their oldest child, Andy, thirteen, whose Facebook page says he wanted to be a first-responder hero like his mom. That's it. Go catch this bastard.'

Tom put his laptop in its case and stood up, not making eye contact with those around him. A mocking whisper from behind him asked, 'Hey, clairvoyant guy?' but he didn't turn around. 'Are the Redskins gonna win this weekend? Can you give me the score?'

There were hoots of laughter. Tom kept his head down and headed for the nearest exit.

Someone stepped in his way, and a voice said commandingly, 'Agent Smith.' It wasn't a question.

Tom looked up and saw the tall, African-American agent named Grant who had asked a question from the front row. 'Yes?'

'Commander Brennan wants to see you.'

'Sure,' Tom said. 'Whenever he's —'

'Now.'

4

Tom followed the tall agent out of the hall, down a long corridor, and out a side exit into the crisp Washington morning. A gleaming black sedan idled at the curb. 'Back seat,' Grant told him. 'If I were you, I'd keep my mouth shut.' Tom took a deep breath of cold October air, opened the rear car door, and climbed in.

Brennan reclined on the leather seat, checking his cell phone and eating roasted sunflower seeds from a brown paper bag. He was a large man – nearly six-foot-four and close to three hundred pounds – approaching seventy, and he sat in a lazy sprawl that took up most of the spacious back of the sedan. He made no gesture of welcome to Tom but said to the driver, 'Let's go, Don,' and the sedan pulled out into traffic. Tom waited silently as Brennan peered down through his reading glasses, finished typing a text and sent it, and finally lowered his phone and looked at him. 'Are you trying to commit career suicide before you have a career?'

'No, sir.'

'Do you know who Hannah Lee is?'

'Only by reputation. I've never met her. I've heard she's superb.'

'She does what you were hired to do, only she's been doing it for fifteen years and you'll be very lucky if you ever get to be half as good at it as she is.'

'I didn't mean to offend her or you, sir.'

'You didn't offend me, but it pisses me off when people

speak out of turn at my meetings. As for Hannah, she has a long memory and sharp elbows, and she's in your direct chain of command. I would apologize to her. Do you do meek?'

'When necessary.'

'Humbly and meekly, then.'

Tom looked at him and nodded. 'Yes, sir.'

The big man crunched a seed between his molars, and it was a little like a whale feeding on plankton. 'Tom Smith? Not exactly a memorable name.'

'Yes, sir. I mean, no, sir, I didn't choose it, sir.'

'I once knew a Warren Smith.'

Tom felt himself tense and kept silent.

'A hard man in many ways, but just about the best field agent I ever worked with, and I've worked with thousands. Any relation?'

Tom hesitated, but it was clear that Brennan knew everything. 'I asked my father not to get in touch with you.'

'What makes you think he did?'

'Because I asked him not to. I also assume he asked you not to tell me that he'd called you.'

Brennan smiled slightly. 'I never reveal intelligence sources. I can well understand that Warren probably wasn't the easiest father in the world. But his deductive instincts were uncanny, and he always told me the truth, and those are two qualities I value highly. Let's see if you can keep that family tradition alive. What exactly did you want to get across so badly that you blurted it out of turn today?'

Tom could smell the salt on the sunflower seeds. 'It doesn't take a clairvoyant to know that you're chasing somebody who's taking exactly the right precautions.'

'Yes, but how and why is he taking those precautions?

Don't hold back, Tom. Your father didn't edit, as I'm sure you know better than anyone.'

'It's clear that he understands your methods perfectly. If you continue to search for him in ways he can predict, you'll probably never catch him.'

'And just how does he come to have our playbook? Do you think he's an FBI agent?'

'Or he could work in some other area of law enforcement. Maybe he just watches a lot of crime shows on TV.'

'There are lots of *Law & Order* junkies out there. We have a pretty good record of catching them no matter what they watch or read or look up on the Internet. In fact, the more they think they understand how we're looking for them, the easier it usually is to catch them.'

'You wouldn't have gotten the Unabomber if his brother hadn't turned him in. This guy's much smarter than the Unabomber. You've had two years, and he's struck six times and sent you all his justifications, and you still don't know squat about him. Forgive my bluntness, sir.'

Brennan ground seeds between his molars and swallowed with a sour grimace. 'You do remind me of your father. Not many data analysts fresh out of grad school would tell me I don't know squat.' His cell beeped, and he glanced down at the screen and said: 'Don, Rayburn in five.' He tucked the phone away and said, 'I've got three hundred of my sharpest and most experienced agents searching in every possible way, and thousands more helping. You really think we won't catch him?' His blazing dark eyes were now trained on Tom.

Tom met the formidable gaze. 'He selects and researches his targets in ways that you don't understand and can't anticipate. Once chosen, he plans his missions meticulously

23

and builds his own explosives. He understands forensics and data, so he's not going to leave footprints or thermal plumes near a target or buy gas with a credit card or anything stupid like that. He engages with you on his own terms, and he's apparently very capable of sending those hand-typed letters without giving you any clues to his identity. He refuses to engage further or be drawn by your psychological experts into revealing anything else about himself. If you continue to search for him in conventional ways, I don't see this turning around, unless . . .'

'Unless he gets careless or we get lucky?'

'Eventually something will go wrong for Green Man, or he'll slip up and make a tiny mistake. But it could take years for either of those to happen. He may just decide to stop, or die a natural death, or retire and move to Florida to play golf, in which case you'll never catch him.'

There was a silence in the sedan, and they heard a jackhammer blasting away *rat-tat-tat* from nearby construction work. 'If memory serves,' Brennan said, speaking succinctly and projecting over the street noise, 'your father retired to Florida to play golf.'

'I wasn't referencing my dad.'

'Of course you were. You were ascribing a profile to our villain, and you chose two characteristics that exactly fit your father's situation.'

Tom looked back at him and admitted softly, 'Well, maybe you're right. Somehow I grew up in Virginia and Florida not liking golf much.'

Brennan nodded. 'I get that. But since we're now indirectly talking about your father, on that call I didn't have with him, he didn't tell me about your background. Computer science at Stanford. Grad work at Caltech. We don't usually see that profile around here, Tom. They head to Silicon Valley, and Google or Microsoft pays them five times what Uncle Sam could. What the hell are you doing here? Slumming?'

'The family business is catching bad guys.'

Brennan smiled appreciatively and glanced at his watch. 'Okay, Tom Smith, you've been pretty blunt about what we're doing wrong. I assume you've put some thought into what you would do differently to catch this particular bad guy?'

'A little, sir. But I know you've been doing this a lot longer than I have. I don't want to shoot my mouth off again. It didn't work so well for me the first time around.'

'The target range is now wide-open, and I'm ordering you to fire away. You have less than four minutes. These chances don't come around very often, so if I were you, I'd take my best shot.'

Tom saw that the sedan was rolling up Capitol Hill. He knew the Rayburn House Office Building was close. Because of the sudden time pressure, he uncharacteristically had trouble framing his thoughts, and his first few words came out almost painfully slow: 'As I mentioned, he's done a remarkable job of keeping one step ahead of you and not tipping his hand. You can use his understanding of your methods as his own weakness.'

'Speak up, Tom. That's a strength of his, not a weakness.'

'You can turn it to your advantage. It's clear he understands exactly how you're hunting him, and he's taking specific steps to avoid you. But by taking those steps, he's making himself vulnerable because he's establishing new and predictable data patterns.' Tom felt himself relax, and he began speaking more quickly. 'If he normally has a presence online but he stops during missions, if he customarily uses his cell phone but goes silent before strikes, if he stops using his credit cards, if he regularly favors highways but suddenly there's no record of his car because he's using back roads, we can search for that. The intentional avoidance of creating useful data is itself data. If you're searching for someone who doesn't leave fingerprints, then stop looking for fingerprints and look for someone wearing gloves.'

'Easier said than done,' Brennan grunted, but he was listening more closely now.

'Look, I know the kinds of broad-spectrum data searches I'm suggesting might come close to accessing private information that's protected by personal freedoms. The CIA or Homeland Security might be able to run those searches to catch an international terrorist, but crime fighters can't do it to catch domestic criminals.'

'I don't make those laws,' Brennan reminded him. 'You've got one more minute. Anything else? Fire away. Tom, I can see you editing. What are you afraid to tell me?'

Tom took a breath and let it out: 'Your profile sucks.'

Brennan didn't like that. 'Profiles are always easy to criticize, but we've got fifty years' experience creating them with great success. The best foreign law enforcement agencies come to study with our profilers.'

'That half century shows, sir. It's mostly recycled tropes about sociopathic serial killers and solo mass murderers who are alone, twisted, and angry. The motives you impute to Green Man are the same tired old ones of revenge and empowerment. Your profile doesn't consider any of the factors that make this case so unique. It dismisses Green Man as a cold-blooded loner sociopathic kook.'

'He's killed forty-three people. Would you mind telling me how he cannot be a cold-blooded loner sociopath kook?'

'Because this case is different from the other cases in your file. An argument can be made that what he's doing is justifiable and even necessary. In his letters, he's doing a pretty good job of making that argument. Not just hundreds or thousands but millions of people believe in his goals, if not his methods. Which may mean he's able to keep doing what he does because he's not alone. That could be how he's posting letters from different cities so close to when he's striking a target.'

'We've considered the possibility that he has a collaborator or partner. It's called a dyad. But there are also several ways he could be doing it all by himself.'

'I know what a dyad is, and I'm not talking about just one collaborator. He could operate with a small but sophisticated support structure that helps him do research and cover his movements. That might explain why he's so hard to track.'

Brennan shook his head. 'More than two people would be untenable. It would contradict virtually everything we've learned from past cases like this.'

'What I'm trying to tell you is that there are no past cases like this. If he has a few people helping him, they could completely throw you off. And it would also obliterate all your assumptions about him being a loner kook sociopath.'

'You really think he might be sane and capable of inspiring that kind of loyalty?'

'Absolutely,' Tom said. 'He could be sensitive, thoughtful, empathic, and well-adjusted. A devoted family man,

27

respected in his community. Possibly a successful academic whose students adore him. You're going to have to open yourself up to the possibility that he could be doing what he's doing not out of anger or a need for empowerment or some twisted, frustrated sexuality but out of a sincere love for mankind and the highest altruism. He has a cause he believes justifies his extreme actions. That's what his letters say, and maybe we should take him at his word.'

Brennan sat there drinking it down, but he clearly didn't like the taste. 'So what would you do to catch this paragon of virtue?'

'Well, for one thing, when it comes to profiling his background, you're going to have to get less politically correct and be a little more elitist.'

'Go as elitist as you want, Stanford man. You have twenty more seconds.'

Tom spoke in a burst, watching government buildings flash by. 'You said yourself an engineer couldn't have hit the Boon Dam at a better spot. The sabotage of the pipeline, the Mayfield Chemical bombing, the attack on the nuclear energy facility, the destruction of the nanotechnology lab, and the sinking of the ex-Secretary of the Interior's yacht all show an almost professional knowledge of structural engineering, chemical engineering, and computer engineering.'

'The possibility that he's a trained engineer is in our profile.'

'Not just an engineer but a brilliant engineer who can work across disciplines, presumably with an elite educational background. He probably studied at one of our best universities. Don't forget that the Unabomber went to Harvard.'

'And Ted Bundy, who had a genius IQ, went to the University of Puget Sound. Not sure I'm buying this. I went to Penn State, by the way. Not too much Ivy out there in Happy Valley, and I've done okay.'

'I didn't mean any disrespect. My point was –'

'You're projecting your own accomplishments as biases. That's a well-known profiling trap. Don, the side entrance.' The sedan turned off Independence Avenue onto South Capitol Street.

'Ted Bundy never showed any technical ability,' Tom pointed out. 'He had charm and street smarts, but what Green Man has done would take highly sophisticated training. I'm betting he's also sane, well-adjusted, and high-functioning but he believes – for good reasons – that without his violent intervention, we're going to destroy our planet. He's trying to save Earth in the only way he knows how.'

The limo rolled to a soft stop outside the marble office building. Brennan gave Tom a curious, probing look. 'Sometimes you sound like a member of his fan club.'

'No, sir. I want to catch the murderous bastard just as much as you do.'

'I doubt that,' Brennan said, 'but I'll think about what you've said. Your job now is to apologize to Hannah and eat a little crow.'

'Meekly and humbly. Thanks for opening the firing range up for me.' Tom hesitated and then said, 'I wish my father hadn't called you, but I also know most data analysts just starting out don't get a chance to shoot their mouths off in the back of your sedan.'

Brennan pulled on his suit jacket. 'Don will drop you off anywhere you want to go.'

29

'I can take the Metro.'

'When you're offered a ride in a warm car on a cold day, son, take the ride.'

The driver opened the door, and Brennan started to squeeze out. The big man had one leg outside when his phone beeped again. He glanced at the screen, read it closely, slowly sucked in a breath, and then climbed back into the sedan and closed the door. He looked at Tom, and his gravel voice was suddenly so low it was almost a whisper: 'Tom, I'm really very sorry.'

Tom looked back at him. 'What do you mean, sir?'

Brennan reached out and placed a big hand on Tom's shoulder. 'He was a tough man, but I liked him, and on some level I'm sure you did also.'

5

The police car flashed its lights at Green Man a little after ten in the morning as a two-lane road twisted outside a small town in Nebraska. He had been driving for eleven hours straight as he listened to news of the dam collapse. He avoided interstates because they sometimes had cameras that took photos of license plates, but local roads had their own hazards. He was positive he hadn't rolled through a stop sign or run a red. Even after a long night at the wheel, he didn't make those kinds of mistakes.

He switched off the radio and pulled over to the side and peered into his rearview mirror. It was a young cop driving solo, and he was already out of his police car and walking over, which was a very good thing. If he had paused to run the plate, or had a partner doing it, Green Man would have been forced to act. He felt the weight of the loaded pistol in his right jacket pocket as he leaned over slightly to operate the control to roll down his window. He knew what he would almost certainly have to do, but he desperately didn't want to do it.

The young cop ambled over to the black van. He was still in his twenties – a polite local boy with a buzz cut. Green Man guessed from his haircut and his walk that he had recently gotten out of the service. He smiled up from under his shiny police cap. 'Morning.'

'Good morning, Officer.'

'Do you know why I pulled you over?'

'Sorry, but I don't.'

'Your right brake light's out.'

Green Man had a second to appreciate the irony of it. He had meticulously planned this mission for months, built a sophisticated drone and a bomb that not one engineer in a hundred could have constructed, covertly and with some help researched the dam without tipping anyone off, taken incredible precautions to mask his identity during the thousand-mile trip, struck quickly and with surgical precision, and it had all gone flawlessly. But a tiny bulb had unpredictably burned out or become disconnected and now threatened it all.

A non-working taillight was a ticketable offense. If it came to that, he would have no choice. They were alone on a remote stretch of road. His gun and bullets were untraceable. A single shot, in the center of the forehead, and he might have an hour or two to get away before the dead cop was found.

'Very sorry to hear that,' he said. 'It must have just burned out. Or it could be a loose wire. I hit a bump back in Wyoming.' His throat was dry, but he somehow managed a chuckle. 'Felt like I rolled over a Grand Teton.'

'Yup, it happens.' The cop nodded. 'Tell you what. I won't write you up. Get it fixed right away.'

'For sure,' Green Man said. 'Next garage I see. And thanks. I appreciate it.' Now let me go, he prayed silently. Save your life and live another fifty years. Marry some girl in town, have kids, have grandkids, and die in bed at eighty. Just let me go.

But the young cop was still smiling. 'So I saw the Michigan plate. Never made it that far east.'

'Come on out and see the Great Lakes sometime,' Green Man told him.

'I might just. What brings you through Destry?'

'Just passing through.'

'Most people take the interstate.'

'I like to see a place when I drive through it.'

'Is that right?' the young cop said. 'Not much to see on Route 55. What exactly are you looking at around here?'

'I paint a little. I love the color of the hills.'

'Never noticed.'

'Yeah, well, I never pay much attention to the Great Lakes,' Green Man said with another chuckle, but this one caught in his throat and sounded dry and forced. Now, let me go. Please, God, don't push this any further.

But the young cop stepped forward and studied Green Man's face under the visor of his black cap. 'So where're you headed this morning?'

'I was just doing some fishing, and now I'm headed home.'

'All the way to Michigan?'

'Yeah, I got a long ride ahead of me.'

'Don't they have fish in the Great Lakes?'

'Some big ones and I've caught my share of them. But nothing beats a cutthroat trout.'

'I wouldn't know. I don't have the patience for fishing. Can I please see your license and registration?'

Green Man looked back at him. 'Sure. My registration is in my glove compartment. Mind if I reach down to get it?'

'Go ahead and get it out,' the young cop said. 'And then you'll be on your way home. We got an APB that we should check everyone we stop, on account of that dam. Can't be too careful.'

'No, you can't,' Green Man agreed as he reached down, and his right hand coiled around the pistol grip. He would either have to shoot the cop or himself. If he pressed the pistol to his own forehead, he would be firing at his own family, too. His kids would be damaged for years, and maybe irreparably. And despite all their precautions, Sharon – one of the only two women he had ever loved – would have a very hard time proving she wasn't complicit. He would get the easy way out, but she would take the fall. And everything he had tried to do for the world, everything he had set in motion, all the wonderful momentum that was building, would come grinding to a stop. So there was just one thing to do, even if it was abhorrent to him. His right index finger touched the trigger, and he started to raise the pistol.

But then came a burst of country music. It was the chorus to an inane song about love and loss. It took Green Man a half second to realize it was the young policeman's ring tone. He raised his cell to his ear. 'Yeah, Nancy, what's up?'

Green Man waited, holding his breath.

The young cop frowned. 'Tell Mabel not to try to get it down. Even if she reaches it, she'll just get scratched. Let her know I'm on my way and I'll be there in ten.'

The young cop put his cell away and grinned at Green Man. 'Damn cat goes up that same pecan tree once a week.'

'I'm a dog man,' Green Man said with an answering smile, his index finger resting gently on the trigger. 'Sounds like maybe you'd better get over there quick.'

'Yeah, I gotta hustle,' the young cop said, turning toward his car. 'Get that brake light fixed pronto.'

'Right away,' Green Man promised. 'Hey, good luck with the cat.'

6

Ellen woke to the news about the Boon Dam explosion, and she immediately tucked it away, carefully compartmentalizing it as she went about her Tuesday morning routine. She dropped Julie off at the Carlyle Academy, taught her morning seminar at Columbia on clean energy sources, met with two thesis students, and then changed in her office into sweats and set off on her morning jog to the Center. It was only when she was running on the steep and winding trails of Morningside Park that she allowed herself to be secretly elated.

It was a cool day, and there were few people on the sidewalks of Harlem. She took Malcolm X Boulevard all the way up and tried to do the three miles in a half hour, pumping her arms and lifting her knees to keep a fast pace. Jogging was part of her daily regimen, and Ellen knew that clinging to a routine would help her strike the difficult balance needed to keep her real feelings in check.

He had hit another big target – daringly, magnificently, brilliantly – and he'd gotten away with it. So far, what the TV anchors called an 'unparalleled national manhunt' had apparently not yielded any breakthrough clues. She knew the most dangerous time for Green Man had now passed, and every minute that ticked by made him yet safer.

Ellen could let herself seem excited because everyone in her little green activist world was buzzing, but she had to be excited in the same impersonal way they all were – their shared mysterious hero, their nameless, faceless, but beloved crusader, had struck another brave blow for the salvation of the species.

But as she ran, Ellen saw a face – a young, handsome, and determined face that swam to her out of the deep pool of suppressed memory. He had a shy but winning smile and was wearing a Yale baseball cap cocked to one side, a green T-shirt, and jeans. She heard his deep and strident voice giving an eloquent speech condemning federally sanctioned logging in national forests. She saw his brilliant and sexy black eyes looking back at her. She felt his strong arms around her, his soft, inquiring lips on her own. Ellen blinked away the sense memories and sped up.

No, he was long gone. Dead and buried. She had delivered the eulogy at his funeral and broken down in tears near the end. Ellen sprinted, her elbows pumping like pistons, driving away the ghost as she hurtled forward across 137th Street with such a fierce burst that a turning car nearly hit her and a man shouted out the window, 'Watch where you're fucking going!'

The Green Center was housed in a five-story brownstone that had been a speakeasy during Prohibition. When they had found it, it was a total wreck and scheduled for demolition, but with the help of their hedge-fund donor, they had renovated it from the studs up, and now it was glorious.

Wanda buzzed her in, and then Ellen was standing on the polished oak floor where it was toasty warm. A fire crackled in the large fireplace, and the smoky warmth was infused with the smell of sage incense and Yogi tea that someone was brewing in the snack room. There was an unapologetic hippy-dippy sensibility to the Center that gave it a relaxed and homey vibe, but on this Tuesday morning, the mood was anything but relaxed – Ellen was immediately surrounded by the excited chaos of an environmental hub on a red-letter day for Mother Earth.

Richard was pacing in the hallway, doing an interview with the mainstream press, shouting into his cell phone that of course he was sorry about the loss of life at the dam but what *really* mattered was what Green Man himself had cited – the moral imperative to act before it was too late. 'We are in a pitched battle to save our Earth, and the only way to win that battle entails the destruction of property and, yes, tragically, a few casualties. Don't you have kids of your own? You're damn right I'm making it personal. All he's trying to do is give your kids a chance to live out their eighty years on a sustainable planet, just like the one that your parents bequeathed to you.'

Josie – who ran their neighborhood outreach programs – had gathered several young employees around her desk, where an artist's imagined rendering of Green Man stared out at them from her computer screen. Greenpeace – realizing the importance of his face as a rallying point and no doubt also for fund-raising – had put this 'portrait' on its main page. They did not justify his actions, but they were showing the world a very human face. It made Green Man look powerful but also gentle, like a cross between Christ and a young Bob Dylan.

'Whatta you think?' Josie called out as Ellen walked by. 'They're raking in the big bucks. We need a sexy image, too.'

'That's not Green Man for me,' Ellen replied. '*She's* younger, black, and buff.'

'I think Green Man or Green Lady is sexier without

37

a face,' a tall researcher said. 'Leave it up to the imagination.'

'No way. His eyes are dreamy in that picture,' a young Latina intern with a nose ring commented. 'That's what I check out first. The soul is always in the eyes.'

'This isn't eHarmony,' Ellen told them all. 'We're going to gather in the conference room in five. Make sure everybody's there.'

She climbed the stairs to the second-floor offices and hurried down the long corridor. The old floorboards squeaked beneath her fast, thudding footsteps.

Louis was in his office, door wide open, reading something on his cell with his stockinged feet propped on his desk. His big toe poked up through one of the old socks. He waved as Ellen passed. He'd been an environmental activist for nearly five decades, and his scraggly white beard and kind eyes made him look like a cross between John Muir and Santa Claus. There were two treasured photos in his office – one of him in his twenties at the first Earth Day celebration in Philadelphia in 1970 near a bunch of icons, including Edmund Muskie, Ralph Nader, and Allen Ginsberg. In the second photo, Rachel Carson was presenting him with an autographed first edition of *Silent Spring*, which now sat in a hallowed spot on a shelf behind his desk.

'They haven't caught him yet?' Ellen asked, seeing his concentration on his cell phone. She didn't need to try to keep the worry out of her voice – no one at the Center wanted Green Man caught.

'Nope. They've shut down most of Idaho, but he's long gone.'

'And let me guess – our contributions are up?'

'Superheroes are great for fund-raising,' Louis told her gleefully. 'Folks are throwing money at us. There's a video of the dam collapsing on YouTube that's been viewed three million times, and I think each time someone views it, they send us five dollars. He's Green Man, we're the Green Center – maybe they think there's some connection. But hey, if it's green, we'll take it. We're gonna have a kick-ass budget.'

'We're all meeting downstairs in five. Whatcha reading?'

Louis held up the cell so that she could see photos of dams. 'The Sierra Club's got a great new piece up on the Snake River controversy. It starts with the Swan Falls Dam going up in 1901 and then describes the other fourteen going up, and the one that just came down. It explains how they damaged the salmon runs, and all the legal challenges. There's no way they could have cooked it up this morning – they must have had it in press and gotten lucky. Or maybe Green Man tipped them off where he was going to strike,' Louis suggested with a sly smile.

'I'm sure the FBI will be checking into that possibility,' Ellen told him, and went into her corner office. She quickly changed from her track shoes and sweats into comfortable jeans, a wool sweater, and loafers. Behind her locked office door, she checked the breaking news. Green Man's letter about the Boon Dam was the most-read thing on the Internet, and he was still free and clear. Ellen paused on her way out and steeled herself – she knew she had a fight ahead of her.

More than forty of the Center's staff were waiting for her in the main conference room, from the most junior eighteen-year-old intern, who was battling an acne attack, to their elegant octogenarian receptionist, Wanda Webster,

39

who walked in slowly, leaning heavily on her mahogany cane.

'Hey, everybody,' Ellen said. 'At ease.' It was a running joke – they were always completely at ease, sipping kombucha, slumped into window seats, splayed languidly on beanbag chairs while Wanda gently glided back and forth near the bay window on an old rocker. 'By now all of you have seen that Green Man struck again last night, blowing up a dam in Idaho. Apparently he's gotten away with it.'

There was applause and an enthusiastic chant of 'Go, Green Man, Go.' Ellen let it go on for several seconds and finally held up a hand for silence. 'Okay, that's what we're here to talk about. On a personal level, I don't entirely disagree with that reaction,' she admitted.

'But?' Richard called out, sensing where this was going.

'But,' Ellen said to him – and then she glanced from face to friendly face. She had known many of them for decades. 'While you have the right to your feelings as individuals, we've reached the point where we need to respond to what's happening as an organization – we can't remain silent any longer. After all, we share a name with him.' Ellen asked herself for the hundredth time, Out of all the catchy environmental nicknames in the world, why did the national press have to pick Green Man?

'Greenpeace is just as "green" as we are, and they've made him their poster boy,' Josie pointed out. 'And by the way, their contributions are up three hundred percent.'

'I've never compared us to other organizations,' Ellen answered. 'And we're not in this for the money. I founded the Center to go our own way and make our own choices, and that's how I've tried to steer us as your director. And my whole life has been a repudiation of violence.'

40

'What about the violence against the ozone layer?' Richard shouted. 'The murder of the coral reefs? The rape of the rain forests?'

There was a buzz of agreement in the large room. 'That is definitely a kind of violence –' Ellen began to answer.

'You're damn right it is!' Richard shouted over her. 'It's a war, and we're losing it. And I'm not just talking about rain forests and reefs, but fuck, what's this really about? Our future.' His voice rang with fury. 'I've only got thirty more years left, so I'll probably check out in time. But there are young people in this room who are going to have to deal in their lifetimes with an irreparably damaged and ultimately doomed planet, and I pity you. And still we elect presidents who deny climate change, and billionaire Secretaries of the Interior are appointed who support their obscene lifestyles by doing the will of rapacious corporations and gutting every protection we've fought so hard for. That bastard Ellmore deserved what he got.'

Ellen tried to rein him in. 'Richard . . .'

But the short man with the goatee had a full head of steam up, and people in the room were nodding. 'Ellen, we're not only losing the war, but it's almost too late. Finally someone stands up and says, "Enough. There's still time. Let's save it while we can." And he has the brains and the nerve to strike back and inspire a generation, and now we're going to condemn him for fighting for everything we believe in?'

Ellen let Richard's angry question and the clapping that followed his speech fade to silence. When she spoke, it was in a soft but very clear voice. 'I've always admired your passion, Richard, but I heard you out, and now it's your turn to listen to me. I grew up as a poor black girl in

41

Tennessee, the daughter of a single mom who cleaned rich white people's homes and had every reason to be bitter. She'd marched with Martin Luther King and cried the night he was killed, and she brought me up to believe in him, and we sat together and read everything he'd written the way some of my friends and their parents studied scripture.'

Ellen paused and remembered how exhausted her mom had looked trudging home after a fifteen-hour day. 'Twenty years after the Memphis march, my mother was still scrubbing the toilets of rich white people and we were skimping by on food stamps. When I was sixteen, I fell in love with a very different civil rights hero – one who the boulevard a hundred yards from here is named after. I sat up nights watching his old speeches online. He was sexy and passionate, and most important, he had been ready to fight back. His call to action struck me as the right path. If Martin Luther King had had a dream, then he must have been sleeping, and when I was sixteen, Malcolm X seemed wide awake and saying just what I needed to hear.'

Ellen paused and saw several of the young interns, from widely different backgrounds, watching her closely. 'Action now. Take the fight to them. So I went to Berkeley to be in Bobby Seale and Huey Newton territory, and I found my own cause, and I did some things in college I'm not proud of now. I was there when Earth First! knocked nails into trees so that if loggers tried to cut them down, their chainsaws would bounce off and cut off their arms. And I raised my fist and shook it with justified anger. And it sure felt good.'

Ellen focused for a second on the dignified face of Wanda Webster, who was rocking back and forth in front of the window. 'My mother died when I was in grad school, and it was only after she was gone that I slowly realized she had been right all along. I read Thoreau and Gandhi, and I slowly came to understand that nonviolent resistance is not only the most moral but also by far the most effective response – for both the civil rights movement in the sixties and for the environmental battles we're fighting now, literally today.'

Ellen locked eyes with Richard across the conference room. 'You're absolutely right, Richard – we are in a desperate war to save our planet. We've lost some major battles, but we have science on our side. We have the youth on our side. But most importantly, we own the moral high ground. And that's why we'll win, just the way Gandhi won and Martin Luther King won. But we can't give up that high ground. Violence is always wrong. Bombs and bullets are not the way to effect change. Killing innocent people is murder, and it's absolutely unjustifiable.'

Richard started to object. 'William Ellmore was hardly fucking innocent –'

But this time Ellen spoke over him. 'When Secretary Ellmore's yacht went down, his five-year-old granddaughter went down with it. That's child murder, plain and simple. We cannot endorse or condone someone who is doing these things. And it's immoral for us, as an organization, to profit from them by tacitly approving and remaining silent. We will no longer do that, as long as I'm the director here. I've consulted with the board about this. We're going to be one of the first environmental organizations to responsibly speak out against Green Man. If you disagree, go to the board and make your case – maybe they'll fire me.'

'So you want Green Man caught?' Richard demanded furiously.

'No, I don't want him caught. But I want him to stop,' Ellen said. 'That's my position, and that will be the position of our Center effective immediately. Green Man should cease and desist. He's struck six times, and there's no denying that he's accomplished a lot without harming the environment in any of his attacks. He's galvanized the Green movement at home and abroad. He's explained his justification eloquently in his letters. He's generated a national debate on the imperative to act, and he's inspired the youth to become active. He's helped good people raise lots of money for deserving causes. He's called attention to different significant threats to the global environment. If he stops now, he'll forever be a controversial hero who accomplished important goals. If he keeps going, he'll destroy everything that he's done. Because do you know what will happen, as sure as I'm standing here?'

And now she had them – and it had always been one of her gifts – because she was able to plug into something very real, and that was her own true fear that Green Man would be caught. 'If he keeps going, they'll find him. No matter how clever he is, no matter how careful he is, they'll track him down. And then they'll put him on trial, warts and all. It will be like a Roman triumph when the FBI leads him on a perp-walk in shackles. Do you want to see that? I don't want to see it.'

Wanda stopped rocking. Louis had been knitting, but his needles were still on his lap. They were all watching her, because there was deep passion in her voice that more than matched Richard's seething anger from a few minutes earlier. 'Do you want to know that Superman is

44

actually meek reporter Clark Kent? That Batman is really a rich and spoiled tycoon with a butler? That the Unabomber was just a bearded weirdo living in a cabin in the woods? And who is Green Man? Do you want him exposed as a weak and flawed human being – as weak and seriously flawed as you are and I am? If you really admire Green Man, join me and this organization in condemning his methods – not his goals – and urging him to stop now. Because the legend he has created is far more powerful than anything he can do with one or two more bombs. Let him be forever who he is right now, a legend, a mystery, a call to action, but not a man.'

She stopped talking then and studied their faces. There was no applause, but some of them looked convinced, or at least thoughtful. Richard and several of the younger staff who were under his wing looked pissed off. 'I know some of you have very strong feelings about this, so I'm going to give you a chance to talk it over without me present,' Ellen told them. 'Thank you all for hearing me out. I think you know how much I love this place and how I respect all of you.'

She walked back up to her office. She locked the door and checked the news. The national manhunt was continuing, which meant that Green Man was still free and clear. She looked up what was most trending on the Internet. His letter about the Boon Dam had been viewed and retweeted more than fifteen million times and had become a global sensation. Countries around the world, from France to China, were increasing security at their major dams.

Ellen felt such a powerful jolt of pride and fear that she had to press down on her desk with both palms to steady herself. She almost cried, but she was able to mask her powerful real emotions as she had so many times before. She remembered the moment two nights earlier when she had hurried up to a desolate mailbox in midtown, near the Port Authority, braving the cold, drizzle, and roaring winds, and dropped in the letter addressed to a news editor of the *New York Times*, her right hand shaking in the black glove that Green Man had told her to wear and then burn.

7

Tom followed a petite Asian morgue attendant in a white lab coat into the viewing area. She led him to a small, windowless office with two wooden chairs arranged by a desk. The only thing on the desk was a clipboard lying facedown.

She shut the door and said in a soft voice, 'I'm very sorry for your loss, Mr Smith. Let me tell you exactly what you're going to see. We do next-of-kin identity verifications almost exclusively by photograph these days. The photo of the decedent is on that clipboard. When you turn the clipboard over, you'll just see his face, and I have to warn you that since he died in an auto accident, there was significant trauma. But his features are identifiable, and you should be able to recognize your loved one. Do you have any questions?'

'No,' Tom said. There was a dull roaring in his ears, as if he were near the sea.

'Do you want me to stay here with you, or would you prefer to view the photo alone?'

'Give me a minute, if you don't mind.'

'I'll be right outside,' she said. She stepped out through the door and pulled it closed.

The walls were white and bare, and there was a single square-shaped fluorescent light on the ceiling. So it comes down to this, was all Tom could think. After a quarter century of trying to find a way to love or at least be close to his father, it came down to this windowless little cell of a room and this four-by-six photo. He reached down and turned over the clipboard.

His father's eyes were closed and the familiar features looked stiff and lifeless. A blue hospital sheet framed his gashed and battered face. Tom sat unmoving, not making a sound or shedding a tear. He felt nothing except a keen awareness of his own total lack of emotion that was in its own way exquisitely painful. He knew the police had been alerted to a car that had veered off the highway, through a side rail, and plunged down an embankment into a stand of trees. When they'd arrived, his father was dead. All signs pointed to a massive heart attack, and Brennan had mentioned on the ride to the hospital that Tom's father's last conscious act might have been steering his rental car away from other motorists and therefore adding a few more lives to the many he had saved in his long police and FBI career.

Tom found himself searching for a warm memory to savor and cling to in this moment, feeling that there should be one for him. There had been plenty of birthday parties, fishing trips, and sports lessons – particularly when he was young. And even when he was a teen and their relationship had grown increasingly fraught and even occasionally flashed into violence, his father had taught him how to tie a necktie, how to hit a fairway wood, and how to throw a right hook. But sitting on the hard wooden chair beneath a faintly humming fluorescent light, Tom drew a complete blank. All he could recall, over and over, was the end of their last talk ten hours earlier in the hotel bar, when his father had called him a little asshole and stalked away as Tom watched the news of the dam collapse.

There was a tapping at the door. 'Mr Smith. Can I come in?'

He turned the clipboard facedown again and said, 'Yeah, sure.'

She opened the door. 'I don't mean to rush you, but . . .'

'No, it's okay,' he said. 'And yes, it's my dad, Warren Smith.'

She sat down and presented him with a pen and several legal forms. Tom signed without really reading them, and he answered her questions mechanically, sometimes suggesting that she should run one or two matters by his mother in Florida. All indications pointed to a heart attack, but his mother should decide if an autopsy was necessary. His father would be buried in Boca, where he had purchased a gravesite, and Tom would make the arrangements to transport the body there. No, he didn't need to talk to a grief counselor or pray with a clergyman of any faith. Yes, he was sure he would be okay to get home.

Brennan was pacing in the hospital's generic waiting room when Tom emerged from the morgue. The big man was speaking excitedly into his cell phone, but he ended the call as soon as he saw Tom with a loud 'Don't let any so-called local experts near it. Pitch a big tent over it and guard it with your life. My flight leaves Dulles in four hours. Make sure there's a car waiting at Boise.' He hung up and told Tom, 'There's been a possible break in the case.'

It took Tom a second to refocus. 'You mean with Green Man?'

'A police dog picked up his scent on a rock shelf overlooking the dam and followed it for miles to an apparent campsite. There are tire tracks and the faint imprint of a tent. But I'm sorry, you don't want to hear this now.'

'I do want to hear it,' Tom said. 'Any witnesses or photos?'

49

'Nothing that definite yet. He camped out alone in a barren and isolated spot. But we don't need to talk about this now. I can tell from your face it was Warren, and I'm sorry. I've done my share of morgue IDs. They're always rough.'

'It was what it was,' Tom told him. 'My father knew he didn't have much time left. They really didn't find anything but a few tire tracks?'

Brennan looked hesitant to keep talking shop, but the new information was very much on his mind. 'Right now the most important thing is to preserve the site completely untouched till I get the right people out there. Well-meaning local experts will kill you in these situations. I've got my team on the way, and I'm heading out myself. And I guess you're on your way to Florida?'

'My flight to Fort Lauderdale leaves in three hours.' Tom hesitated, and then he said, 'Unless I can help you out in Idaho. I may be an elitist Stanford graduate, but I'd like you to know that I don't draw the line at menial tasks. I even get coffee.'

Brennan grinned. 'That's good to know, because I appreciate a hot cup of coffee.' He hesitated for a long second and then said, 'But go to Florida and bury your father.'

'We both know Warren would want me to join the hunt.'

'There's not much doubt about that. Do you have siblings?'

'An older sister. She had more problems with my father than I did.'

'Go home, say goodbye, and be there for your mom. Are you flying out of Dulles?'

'Yes, sir.'

'Then I can give you a ride to the airport,' Brennan offered. 'And we have time to grab a quick lunch. I loathe airplane food, and there happens to be a good local diner on the way.'

'Thanks, but I'm not feeling very hungry. And I can see how busy you are. I'll call a car and get myself to the airport.'

'If you want to be alone with your memories, I'll respect that,' Brennan told him. 'But I worked with your dad for years. The least I can do on a day like this is buy his son lunch. Come on, Tom. Never turn down a ride on a cold day.'

Improbably, fifteen minutes later, Tom found himself at a bustling local diner, nibbling a cheeseburger while Brennan enthusiastically devoured a meatball hoagie and told him not to worry about his father's rental car, which had been totally wrecked. 'Those car agency insurance investigators are more relentless assholes than anyone I can hire for the Bureau. They can keep at you night and day in situations like this, and it's the last thing you need. I've already had my people handle it internally.'

'You didn't need to do that, but thank you.'

Brennan's cell phone rang, and he pressed it to his ear. 'Earl, thank God you're there! Yeah, *seal it all off* by my order.' Brennan listened for a second, and his voice got louder. 'I don't care what the state police chief says or what jurisdiction they're claiming. Use my name, tell them we're a federal taskforce, and if anyone sets foot on that site, they'll be knowingly and willfully impeding a federal investigation, and the president of the United States will personally lock their asses up. I'll call you from the airport.' He lowered the phone and shook his head. 'Local experts.'

'You really think you're going to find something at that campsite?' Tom asked.

'With the people and equipment I'm bringing out, I like our chances.'

'He's too smart and too careful to leave a clue behind for you.'

'Goddamn it, you're as pessimistic as your father.'

'Not quite,' Tom said. 'But I try.'

Brennan took a last bite of the hoagie and pushed his plate to one side. 'Tom, we should be heading to Dulles in a minute. Listen, I wish I had something warm and fuzzy to tell you about your dad and what it was like to work with him off and on for almost three decades.'

'I wasn't expecting that, sir.' Tom hesitated and then continued softly: 'I knew Warren about as long as you worked with him, and I'm not coming up with much that's warm and fuzzy this morning, either.'

Brennan nodded his understanding. 'Your father was what he was. Old-school. Hardworking. Sharp instincts. Tough as hell to really get to know. If he'd been easier to get along with, he would have risen higher professionally. But Warren didn't have the best people skills. I guess we both know that sometimes he could be a real son of a bitch.'

'That he could, sir,' Tom agreed. 'But I do have one question for you. I'm afraid it might come out sounding a little ungrateful or even rude.'

'You're allowed one rude question today,' Brennan told him.

Tom hesitated and then asked, 'Why are you doing all this?'

'All what?'

'You and my father weren't comrades-in-arms or golf buddies or even friends. To be honest, I get the feeling you didn't really like him much. I'm not faulting you – I had my own issues with him. But why are you chauffeuring me around and buying me lunch on a day when you clearly have much more important things to do?'

The question annoyed Brennan. 'Why not just say thanks for the cheeseburger?'

'Thanks for the cheeseburger. But I want to understand.'

Brennan got up from the table and stomped away. Tom thought the big man might head out to his car and not come back, but he returned in thirty seconds with a fistful of mints and popped several into his mouth at once. 'Okay, here's the truth,' he said. 'I never talk about this, but that hard-nosed son of a bitch saved my life.'

'Warren did?' Tom asked. 'When?'

'We were on a stakeout, thirty years ago. Middle of the night. I fell asleep. It happens to everyone, but it never happened to me before or since. One of the guys we were after walked up from behind and spotted me. He had a gun out, and he would have shot me. Warren had my back and got the guy first.' Brennan slammed a fist down on the table so hard that the saltshaker jumped. 'What the hell was I supposed to do after that? He never told anyone I'd fallen asleep and endangered our whole operation, so it stayed between the two of us. And I was never close enough to him to find a way to thank him or repay him.'

'Maybe you didn't need to thank him,' Tom ventured. 'It sounds like he was just doing his job . . .'

Brennan scowled, clearly torn up about something. 'Ten years ago, just when Warren was getting ready to retire, a job came up that would have been a big promotion for him – the perfect cap to his career. He had more ability than the other candidates, and it was my call. I gave it to someone else. It involved managing people, and I just didn't think Warren could run a big team. But I felt bad about that. He saved my life, and then I fucked him.'

'We have something in common, then,' Tom said quietly. 'He gave me life, too, and I only disappointed him and never found a way to thank or repay him.'

Brennan waved to the waitress for the check. Then he fixed Tom with a steady gaze. 'Here's one thing I can tell you about your dad and then we'd better go catch our flights. You were right – Warren did call me early this morning to talk about you. We only chatted two or three minutes, but it was the most personal conversation I ever had with him.'

The waitress brought the check, and Brennan fished thirty dollars out of his wallet and dropped the cash on the table. 'He was proud enough of you to tell me your scholastic achievements. He asked me to give you a chance to help break this case. That was the last thing he said to me before he hung up, and it was also the only favor that he ever asked me for. What was the last thing he said to you?'

'He called me a little asshole.'

Brennan nodded slightly, looked sad, and he was silent for two or three seconds. 'Go home and bury him with as much love as you can muster,' he commanded Tom in a very low voice. 'And then you have a tough career decision to make. I don't directly supervise the data analysts, so I can't help you there. But your father had the best nose for a case I ever saw, and I can always use a smart field agent. If you want to come work for me, I can give you some autonomy, the chance to think outside the box, and the clout to follow up on at least some of your hunches. And I won't make you get me coffee too often.'

Tom looked back at him and thought it over quickly. 'Warren told you about my scholastic achievements, but did he tell you about the Golden Gloves?'

'No,' Brennan said, carefully sizing up Tom in a new way. 'I know he was a fighter. You boxed?'

'Did he tell you about the Olympic shooting team?'

Brennan raised his eyebrows. 'Really?'

'Not really,' Tom told him. 'He tried to teach me to box, but I refused to learn. I like my brains unscrambled. I barely know which side is the trigger and the muzzle. I was a big disappointment to Warren as a son, and I will be to you as a field agent. I am what I am, sir – a proud, smart nerd who's really good at crunching numbers.'

Brennan studied Tom for a few seconds more, shrugged, and stood up. 'The decision's up to you, but I don't have any problem with smart nerds, and my offer stands. The people close to me are good, but they tend to be a little too polite and respectful. Something tells me that won't be your problem. If you do come to work for me, your real job will be to be a pain in the ass, think out of the box, and keep asking me annoying questions that everyone else either hasn't thought of or is too afraid to ask me. I think you'll be good at that. In fact, you'll probably be such a big pain in the ass that I'll regret this. Now, go home to Boca and take care of your family business.'

8

There was no traffic on the main street of the small town in which Green Man lived, and every shop had long ago shut up for the night. He drove through the one stoplight, past the bank and the grocery, and turned onto a country road. The houses grew farther apart, and soon he was driving through a thick forest. Branches of old sugar maples reached out to one another above the winding roadway. He spotted his mailbox, clicked the remote, and the iron gate swung slowly open. Motion-sensing lights blinked on as he headed up the long driveway toward the house that emerged from the trees, silhouetted against the starry sky.

He had purchased the property for its proximity to town but at the same time for its privacy – his twelve acres were surrounded by protected state forest. Green Man had designed the house himself and had it built by a firm based in Detroit so the details weren't known locally. The house was large but not ostentatious by town standards – there was certainly nothing about the facade of the four-story white, center-hall colonial to make it seem remarkable.

The kids brought school friends home to romp around in the grassy backyard or splash around in the pool in summer, and Sharon often entertained on the back patio in nice weather. Savvy guests sometimes remarked on how energy efficient it was and that it was a 'smart house' – all the appliances were computer controlled and 'talked to one another.' But no guests were ever allowed in the upper two floors, and the kids had been brought up to stay out of the windowless shack known to the family as the 'hunting shed' and located deep in the trees.

Kim and Gus had gone to sleep several hours earlier, but Sharon was waiting up and heard him pull into the garage. By the time he'd climbed out of the van, she had hurried out through the connecting door and was running toward him. They embraced for several minutes without saying a word, and he could feel her trembling. He held her in his arms and gently stroked her hair, and she nestled her cheek against his as their bodies pressed together. 'I love you,' she finally whispered, and he felt the tears on her cheek. 'I missed you so much, Mitch. Welcome home.'

'I missed you, too, sweetheart,' he replied softly, his gruff voice quivering. He was just as emotional as she was, even if he masked it through the long force of habit of controlling every aspect of his behavior. He loved her deeply, and he had almost from the first moment he'd seen her in an art museum in Chicago. Every time he drove away on a mission, he thought it might be the last time he saw her and the kids, and that possibility was almost more than he could bear.

They walked into the house hand in hand, and Finn, their aging golden lab, began leaping and bounding around with a gleeful excitement that made him look almost like an exuberant puppy again. 'Someone else is glad you're home,' Sharon said with a smile.

Green Man knelt next to the faithful dog and scratched his ears, and the old lab nearly swooned.

Sharon led him toward the kitchen, which smelled faintly of roast chicken and wild rice. 'Something tells me you didn't stop for dinner.'

'Figured I might get lucky with leftovers.'

She sat with him while he ate, sipping red wine and watching him so closely that it felt almost like a first date. And it could have been a first date, because while they had much bigger things on their minds, they just made small talk – she filled him in about Kim's drawing class and Gus's travel soccer team and how the refrigerator's ice maker was too cold and kept freezing over and clogging up. Green Man didn't discuss his mission to Idaho or ask her about the latest FBI manhunt news that she had gleaned from the multiple sources she checked regularly – they never talked about anything serious below the third floor, even late at night when the kids were fast asleep.

Finn sat under the table, sometimes touching Green Man's feet, and every once in a while he found a way to covertly slide the dog a small piece of roast chicken. Sharon didn't like him feeding Finn at the table, but either he covered it skillfully or Sharon was willing to overlook his weaknesses on this night of homecoming.

They had the computer lock up the house, and Green Man checked with his usual meticulousness that the security and motion sensors had all switched on around the property. They climbed to the second floor together, and he opened Kim's door. The girl lay with her two big stuffed animals, Winnie the Pooh and Minnie Mouse, standing guard. Green Man bent and kissed his daughter lightly on the cheek, and the six-year-old stirred and smiled slightly. Straightening up, he saw a new drawing she had done that week that was now taped to the wall. While it was childlike, he was able to easily recognize the likeness as one of her best friends. Green Man had drawn and painted all his life, and he loved seeing that his daughter had inherited his keen eye.

59

Gus's room was five paces from Kim's, and Green Man stepped inside and saw his son sleeping diagonally with his feet dangling off one side of the bed and his head all the way on the other corner. The boy's face was tilted toward his nearby dresser, as if keeping watch on the dozen or so soccer trophies there. Sharon gently straightened Gus out on the bed and tucked his quilt over him.

Hand in hand, they climbed to the third-floor master bedroom. It was only there, after yet another layer of security had been activated, that they talked openly, albeit in soft voices. They debriefed each other for nearly half an hour – Green Man went first and recounted every moment of his mission while Sharon asked probing questions. She had been trained as a forensic anthropologist and worked in law enforcement for nearly ten years, including a two-year stint with the FBI's Chicago field office. She went over every step of his mission with him, and her questions reviewed his decisions and precautions in exhaustive detail.

When he got to his encounter with the policeman in Nebraska, she asked if he was sure the cop hadn't been wearing a body camera. 'Positive,' he told her. 'I checked for it in all the likely places. They're still not that common outside big cities. We got lucky.'

'We didn't get lucky with the taillight.'

'Can you believe that stupid bulb burned out, after so much careful planning? Okay, sweetheart, my turn.'

He began with their circle of friends. Had anyone asked anything even remotely inquiring or suspicious? The kids' friends and the family's acquaintances in town knew that he was a businessman who traveled frequently. They were all apparently satisfied – no one had asked any specific

60

questions about this trip or when he would return or what he was doing. He often took similar trips just to accustom everyone to his weeklong absences.

Green Man next made sure that Sharon had covered his tracks in case someone was smart enough to search for changes in his behavioral patterns. She had logged in from his email accounts several times a day. She had used his credit cards. She had made calls from his cell. And she had driven the family car on its regular routes at the normal times. Anyone searching for Green Man by trying to identify a data trail linking him to the journey to Idaho would come up empty. Anyone checking to see if he had been in rural Michigan would see evidence of his customary behavior.

When they were done with the debriefing, he asked Sharon the questions he dreaded most, knowing most of the answers already because he had heard them on the radio news while driving home. Twelve people had died so far because of his attack on the Boon Dam. Their photos and information were all over the Internet, and – knowing that he would insist on it – she had printed it all out for him, and it was in his bottom desk drawer. 'Look tomorrow morning,' she urged, 'or you'll never sleep tonight. And you seem so tired.'

'Fine,' he agreed, 'but what were those two families doing on houseboats? The season was over.'

'It was unseasonably warm, and an outfitter wanted to make a little extra money, so he stretched regulations,' she told him. There had been no way to foresee it.

He sat very still for nearly a minute and then whispered, 'How many kids?'

She put her arms around him and whispered, 'Five.'

61

'My God.'

She held him tighter and kissed him softly above his eye. 'You're doing something that has to be done.'

'And I would have shot that young cop.'

'But you didn't.'

'Shar, I had my finger on the trigger.'

'But you held off and saved his life.'

'Five kids.' He didn't add 'As innocent and dear as our own,' but they both knew he was thinking it.

'There's no other way,' she whispered, and her belief in the rightness of their actions was even more definite than his own. 'Go take a shower, Mitch. You'll feel better.' She kissed him again, this time on the lips. 'Frankly, my love, you stink.'

He took a shower that was almost scalding, six nozzles geysering hot water at him as steam filled the bathroom. He wiped the mirror in order to see himself to shave, and in the steamy glass that began to clear, a face slowly took on detail. Dark hair starting to lighten around the temples. Eyes that could appear hazel or gray-blue depending on the light. An aquiline nose that his father and grandfather had passed down to him. The strong chin that a Yale baseball coach had seized on to give him the nickname 'Chisel Chin,' which had stuck for four years in New Haven. It was a handsome face and had once been carefree, but there were lines of worry stamped on the forehead and pockets of regret softening the skin around his eyes.

Green Man entered the bedroom, and the lights were out. 'Come, my darling,' Sharon said softly.

He slid in next to her, and they kissed and touched each other and made love slowly and tenderly. Then it became more urgent, and he wasn't entirely surprised by his sudden hunger. People who have been in the proximity of death crave life. Sharon felt his urgent need and wrapped her arms around his back, and he was deep inside her, in a place that for a few blissful moments separated him from the burdens that he carried around every second of every day. They moaned together, and then they were silent in each other's arms.

Two minutes later she was asleep, and Green Man lay listening to her breathe. He loved the feel of this bed that he had built himself – Odysseus-like – from a great oak that had once grown beneath the very spot where they now lay together. He savored the smells of his wife, the same lavender shampoo that she had used in her brown hair since he had first met her, the French Peony perfume he had given her last Valentine's Day, the red wine that still faintly flavored her sleeping breaths.

But despite his great weariness, no sleep came to Green Man. He lay for two hours holding her and then gently disengaged and got quietly to his feet. He put on a bath-robe and slippers and crossed the hall to his library and turned on the light.

There were two desks – one for writing and a tilted drafting table for drawing. Nearly ten thousand books were arranged on shelves – many of them detailing dire environmental threats to specific areas of the world and gravely threatened species. Mountain gorillas and delta smelt, Amazon river dolphins and the South China pandas, all cried out to him desperately from the green shelves.

He heard their silent pleas, but he walked to his desk and opened the bottom drawer. He took out the pages that Sharon had printed from the Internet. Twelve faces looked back at him.

He sat alone in the library with them. The bright, innocent eyes of the children. Their names and personal information. All that they were and all that they could have been. From the books on the shelves, the weight of the threatened planet pressed in on him as he studied the faces of the children whose lives he had just ended, and he thought excruciatingly of Kim and Gus, who were sleeping safely one floor below and would wake up the next morning and welcome their father home from his business trip.

9

Brennan reached the campsite just after daybreak in a foul mood. The plane ride across the country had been bumpy, and he had only managed to sleep in brief stretches during the long night ride from Boise. A half hour earlier they had left the highway behind for a gravel path that soon degraded to a dirt track so rugged that in places it disappeared completely into the surrounding rocks and dirt. More than twenty vehicles, from state and local police cars to SUVs and two trailers, were parked on a flat near a bend of that rough dirt track, and Brennan's driver stopped there.

Earl was waiting for him beneath a wide-brimmed straw hat, looking sunburned and skeletal. 'Didn't expect you for another hour. Looks like you could use some coffee.'

Brennan gave the gaunt agent a handshake, searching his weathered face for signs of optimism and not seeing any. 'To hell with coffee. I could use some good news.'

'Wish I had some,' Earl told him as he led Brennan around two large boulders toward a hidden ravine. 'Green Man's not exactly a sloppy camper. We're not finding much.'

Five blue pop-ups had been set up side by side at the bottom of the ravine, curtains all the way down to keep out the wind and sun, so that they looked like private cabanas at an exclusive hotel beach. 'He couldn't have picked the spot any better,' Earl said with grudging admiration.

'No one could see his tent from the road, and those boulders screened his van.'

'So we're sure it's a van?'

'We can guess at the wheelbase but not much else,' Earl told him. 'Just a few faint grooves in hard dirt.'

'What about the tent? Did he pound in stakes?'

'Nope. I'm betting it was a collapsible frame. He didn't leave much behind for us. Want to go down?'

'Sure. In a minute.' Brennan paused at the lip of the ravine and looked around, trying to get the feel for the place as Green Man had first chosen it. Earl was right: for a remote campsite close to a dirt road for a quick getaway, it couldn't have been better hidden. 'Lonely spot, and it got cold at night,' Brennan finally muttered. 'Maybe he built a small fire. I sure would've. And once he got it going, it would have been tempting to cook something hot.'

'Not this guy,' Earl said knowingly. 'The cold didn't bother him, or the quiet. He cooked his dinners long before he got here. We've taken plenty of soil samples, and we're not getting a hint of ash. And he has excellent table manners, or he eats in his van. The dogs haven't found so much as a potato chip.'

'Where did the son of a bitch relieve himself after his home-cooked meals?'

'We've checked to a radius of half a mile, and there's no sign of urine or feces. Even if he shoveled it deep, the dogs would have found it by now.'

'So he carried everything in with him and drove it all away?'

Earl put his hands in his pockets, and the extra weight moved his trousers an inch down his slender waist. 'Every chicken bone. Every ounce of urine. Every turd.'

'Nobody's perfect,' Brennan said. 'Let's go down.'

They descended into the steep ravine, where a dozen members of the team were sipping coffee outside the blue pop-ups. Brennan greeted them by name and quickly corralled Tina, a top dog wrangler. She was in her late thirties, half Cherokee, with long black hair that matched her dark jeans. 'I heard you found this place?'

'It was Sheba, sir – she's maybe the best scent dog we've ever had. She first picked up the scent on the cliff above the dam, even though I'm betting he sprays his boots with Scent Killer. Green Man drove back here on a small motorcycle, and she was able to follow his scent for four and a half miles without his feet having ever touched the ground once. Which is kind of freaking remarkable, sir.'

'Give Sheba an extra lamb chop,' Brennan grunted. He walked over to the nearest pop-up and peeked in through the clear plastic window. Three crime techs in white Tyvek suits were walking in slow concentric circles, hunched over crablike in positions that couldn't have been good for their backs. They were wearing magnification headsets and using blue lights to cast side shadows.

Brennan spent the next six hours sipping lukewarm coffee and receiving negative reports. No hand- or footprints had been found on the cliff top where Sheba had first picked up the scent. The shards of the drone that had been recovered thus far at Boon were so tiny, fragmented, and blistered from the explosion that they would be useless. The letter to the *New York Times* had already been tested in a variety of ways at the main lab in Quantico and had not yielded any secrets yet. The scent dogs continued to sweep the area around the campsite in wider circles but found nothing. Inside the blue pop-ups, the crime techs pored over the thirty-by-thirty-foot patch of dirt literally grain of sand by grain of sand and saw no shadows.

Noon found Brennan sitting alone on a rock at the edge of the gravel-strewn bed of the ravine, looking up at the surrounding twelve-foot rock walls just as Green Man must have done after he pitched his tent. It was grim and grave-like even at midday – almost like being buried alive. What had it felt like to wait in such a rocky cleft through the afternoon and evening hours, alone, contemplating an act of murderous destruction? If Tom Smith was right and Green Man was empathic and had a conscience and truly regretted taking innocent lives, how had he spent those long, tense hours before the strike on the dam, communing with his gods? Had he experienced the almost sexual elation that most killers who stalk humans get as they prepare to move on their prey?

Or had it been very different? Had he felt regret and even guilt? Had he battled a constant temptation to give up and go home but been kept here by a sense of . . . what? Brennan forced himself deep into the character he was slowly creating in his own mind. It was a sense of duty that drove him. Not just a duty to act but a duty to those who couldn't act, to step forward for them and for the whole species. There was one phrase Green Man repeated in every letter: 'A moral imperative to act on behalf of the human race before it is too late.'

Earl touched Brennan gently on the shoulder, and one of the crime techs was standing there, too – the Scandinavian with the brilliant blue eyes – what was her name? Jensen. Her long blond hair was gone, wound up in a tight bun behind her head and contained safely by two layers of plastic caps. Without the softening touch of her hair, in

68

the white Tyvek with the headset still on, she looked androgynous and almost alien.

She was holding up a small plastic vial. Inside it, backlit by the noon sun, Brennan could see two tiny filaments that were intertwined and seemed almost to be dancing. 'I think they're glove fibers,' Jensen said. 'Maybe nylon, but we'll know as soon as we get them under the scope.'

10

On the evening before the funeral, Tom's mother drained two gin and tonics before swallowing an Ambien. Tom and his sister both saw her stumble on the stairs and cling to the banister, and Tom ran and supported her to the second-floor landing. 'Never mix alcohol and sleeping pills,' he admonished her, guiding her toward her bedroom.

'Just wanna sleep,' she said, her words slightly slurred.

Tom helped her into the bedroom, and she sat down heavily on the bed.

It was a depressing, low-ceilinged bedroom with a partial view of the fifth hole of one of Boca's less fashionable golf courses. The room held knickknacks from a forty-year unhappy marriage and was dominated by the same king-size bed the Smiths had transported back and forth across the country, from field office to field office. As a ten-year-old, Tom had practiced judo moves on this bed in Virginia, and he had been conceived on it when his father had started out as a state trooper in Texas. For more than four decades, two people who increasingly didn't like each other and eventually could barely stand each other had somehow found comfort in each other's arms on this bed. Tom's mother collapsed backward onto it, alone, and buried her head in a mound of pillows.

'Ma, you've got to get undressed,' Tom told her. 'I'll get Tracy.'

'Already here,' Tracy announced. She had followed them in. 'I'll put her to bed and stay with her awhile.'

'Go away,' their mother said, her voice muffled by the pillows. 'I'm goddamn fine.'

'You're not goddamn fine,' Tracy told her. 'Not by a long shot.'

Tom left the two of them and headed back downstairs. He put away the gin and spotted a bottle of his father's Jack Daniel's on the liquor shelf. He hesitated before pouring himself half a glass. His first sip made him gag, and he nearly dumped it all out in the sink – he had always hated the smell and taste. His father would not have liked him diluting it, but Tom dropped in three ice cubes and carried the clinking glass into his dad's study.

Warren had been a neat freak, and everything was in its proper place – fountain pens standing at attention in an FBI coffee cup. Who still used fountain pens? His father's prized golf clubs were in their bag by the window, the irons in club order, the driver and fairway woods with matching head covers. The books in the bookcase by the desk had been arranged alphabetically by author. His father's reading had been restricted to American military history, and there was a thick biography of Douglas MacArthur on the desk with a playing card for a bookmark. Tom opened to the ace of spades and saw that his dad had made it to the Inchon landing.

MacArthur had never been a favorite of Tom's, and after a paragraph about Red Beach, he closed the book and began his search. What he was looking for wasn't in any of the desk drawers, but in the bottom one Tom was surprised to discover a small album with photos exclusively of him when he was young. He turned the pages, watching himself grow up from a smiling infant, to a serious-faced Little Leaguer swinging a bat that was clearly too big, to a karate yellow belt trying to look menacing. Warren was not in any of the photos, but in a way, he was responsible for all of them – an invisible male presence that Tom had tried painfully hard from a young age to please.

Tom lingered for a few seconds on a photo of himself at age ten, shirtless, string-bean thin, and wearing boxing gloves, and then he closed the album and tucked it back in the bottom drawer. He took a cautious sip of whiskey and sat back in Warren's office chair with its lumbar support fastened on with Velcro. He let his eyes range around the study, and his gaze finally settled on the corner closet.

He walked over, opened it, and surveyed the contents. There were several old golf clubs his father no longer played with but apparently couldn't bear to throw away, a metal fishing-tackle box, a wooden tennis racket with a frayed grip, and a dozen folded sweaters from icy summers back east. Sure enough, the black leather case that Tom remembered from his childhood but hadn't glimpsed in more than a decade was perched on the top shelf. Tom reached up for it and carried it over to the table. He set it down carefully and swung open the two metal clasps.

The Colt pistol his father had carried throughout his career lay on a bed of black foam. Tom had seen the gun often but had never actually touched it before. He reached down and picked it up and wondered if this was the very same pistol his father had used to save Brennan's life thirty years earlier. Had he actually shot people dead with it? Tom slid his palm around the grip and slowly raised the pistol, pointing it at an antelope head on the wall. 'Put that stupid thing down,' an alarmed voice commanded from the door.

Tom hastily lowered the gun to its case as Tracy stepped into the room. 'How's Mom?' he asked quickly, a little embarrassed at having been caught.

'Out cold,' she said. 'And she's not gonna wake up any-time soon unless you start shooting hunting trophies. Let's get out of here.'

They slipped out the back door and stepped through a gate in the mesh fence onto the dark golf course. They made their way through dense rough onto the fifth fairway and trudged silently side by side through the low-trimmed grass, deep in their thoughts.

'So, is she like that often?' Tom finally asked.

'The pills or the booze?'

'Either or both?'

'If you were home a little more you'd know.'

Tom didn't want to fight. 'Yeah, I guess I have been away a lot. I didn't realize you were a frequent houseguest.'

'It's less than two hours from Key Largo,' Tracy said. 'I come for lunch or dinner and drive back.' She paused. 'She's been taking prescription sleeping pills for the last two years. I think she's hooked and can't sleep without them. The gin is more recent. Warren was hitting the bot-tle pretty hard toward the end, and people tend to get loaded together.'

'I think he knew it was coming,' Tom said.

'It didn't stop him from drinking,' she said, as they approached a green. They skirted a sand trap. 'And it sure didn't make him any nicer.'

'No, it didn't,' Tom agreed. 'But he's gone now, and I guess we should bury him with as much love as we can muster.' He realized he'd repeated Brennan's exact words, and they now sounded a little foolish. 'I just hope some people show up tomorrow. I think it will make it a little easier for Mom if there's a decent crowd. He had some golf buddies and poker cronies who will be coming, right?'

'Something tells me they're going to be on the links,' Tracy said, stepping onto the green.

'Trace, maybe we should stay on the fairway. These greens are hell to take care of.'

'Do I care?' Tracy asked, and angrily kicked a divot out of the green with the toe of her boot. 'If a dozen people show up tomorrow I'll be surprised.'

'You really don't think our dad's much of a draw.'

'*I* almost didn't come,' she told him bitterly. 'And I'm not planning to speak. Mom wants one of us to say some words, so you're up.'

'Fine. I'm sorry that you're so angry with him, even after he's gone. But I guess I knew you guys had issues.'

A small animal darted through the darkness ahead of them and disappeared into a clump of bushes. Tracy sucked in a deep breath of night air and exhaled very slowly, her arms now wrapped around her body. 'Did you know he put his hands on me?'

Tom was genuinely shocked. He stepped closer and said softly, 'I had no idea, Trace. I'm so sorry.'

'I was twelve. He was drunk. He ran his hands down my body. I bit him. He never did it again.'

'Maybe he was blind drunk.'

'Don't you dare make excuses for him.'

'I won't. But he used to beat me up right about then, and I could smell it on his breath. I tried to tell myself that maybe he didn't know what he was doing.'

'He knew what he was doing,' Tracy said. 'Tell you what: you muster some love for both of us tomorrow.' They walked off the green and headed for the sixth tee. For some strange reason, they were walking the course as if they were playing it. 'And then do me one more favor, bro,

75

before you disappear again,' she said, and she was looking at him with angry, warning eyes. 'Don't become him.'

'Why would you ever think that?'

'You were drinking his whiskey and holding his gun.'

'It's the night before his funeral and I was thinking about him is all.'

'You took his old job.'

'It's a completely different job.'

'Bullshit,' she said. 'It's the FBI.'

'The FBI does good work. They catch bad guys. That wasn't the problem.'

They reached the sixth tee, and Tracy stopped walking. It was a water hole, and the reflection of the moon gleamed in the round little lake. 'The children of abusers become abusers,' she said softly. 'The children of assholes become assholes. It's a well-known fact. You got far away, and I envied you that, and I also admired that you had the strength to break away from him. Don't fall into that trap now.'

'Is that what you brought me out here to tell me?' he asked her.

'Partly,' she said. 'I know what you're doing. With the FBI. Mom told me. Don't you dare catch him.'

'I have no idea what you're talking about,' Tom said, 'but maybe we should go back.'

'I talk to the dolphins about him,' Tracy said.

'You're still working at that place in Key Largo?' Tom asked, fearing she was going nutty on him and desperately trying to change the subject. 'I thought they . . . I thought it didn't work out.'

'I've been clean for almost a year. I went through a program. I get tested every week. They took me back on probation, and everything's going fine, and I just love it.'

'That's really great, Trace. You were always happy there.'

'I swim with them in the morning, in the bay. I know each of them, and they know me. And we have conversations. Don't look at me like I'm crazy.'

'I'm just listening.'

'I'm not saying they get every word. We understand each other on a different level. Come swim with us and maybe you'll see and you won't be so fucking skeptical.'

'Okay, I might take you up on that. Can we go back now? It's getting cold, and I have to figure out what to say about Dad tomorrow.'

'They understand the threat. You might not believe that, but they know there aren't as many fish in the sea and that the water temperature is getting warmer and that everything is changing in some slow, measured, horrible way that they can't understand. I think they also understand that we've almost ruined it – almost pushed it to a place where it will be too far and too late to pull back. And so when I swim with them, I tell them that there's finally someone doing something about it. Someone who's fighting for us. A man who can possibly save us. Unless you catch him.'

'You can stay out here, but I'm going home.' Tom turned toward the house, and she caught his arm. She was strong from working with her hands, and she held him. 'Don't do this. It's not who you are. I know you better than anyone alive.'

He pulled his arm free and looked back at her. 'He's a killer. He kills innocent people. And anyway, what makes you think I can catch him? I'm just a little cog in the wheel. Totally unimportant. I find patterns in data, or at least I search for them, but I haven't found any yet. I'm sort of beneath the bottom rung of the ladder.'

'Somebody called from the FBI office in Miami,' Tracy said. 'They're sending a car for you, to take you right from the funeral to the airport tomorrow.'

'What are you talking about? I'm going to stay with you and Mom for a few days. Who called?'

'They said to tell you Brennan wants you right away. Wasn't that someone Dad used to work with? They have your ticket and everything. Doesn't sound like the bottom rung of the ladder. It sounds like you're pretty important.'

'That's crazy,' Tom said. 'I don't know anything about it.'

'My little brother,' Tracy said with a smile that was both nostalgic and bitter. 'It was always the sibling rivalry from hell. Like I ever had a chance. Always the smartest in every class. Smarter than the teachers. You blew away every project. Got perfect scores on every test they threw at you. You were going to show him that in your own way you measured up.'

'Trace, I did it for me, not for him. He barely noticed. And I never competed with you –'

'Good, because he's dead. I'm a washed-out dolphin trainer on permanent probation. Mom's another pill-popping Boca widow. But you've got everything going for you, and I want you to make it, I really do, Tom. You've done everything right. Go out west, where you trained. Build a castle, start a family, and I'll come live in the guest-house on your vineyard. But don't you dare catch that man as a final attempt to measure up. Don't set that project for yourself, because we both know you'll find a way to do it. And he's really the only hope we have and deep down you know that as much as I do.'

11

Halfway through the briefing the attorney general's assistant hurried in and handed her a note. She looked angry to be disturbed, but when she glanced at the note, she immediately nodded and said, 'Tell them we're on our way.' Then she looked up at the half-dozen powerful men in her office and said, 'Gentlemen, we're being summoned, and that means now.'

Less than ten minutes later, Brennan and his boss, FBI director John Haviland, and the director of Homeland Security, Vance Murphy, and the rest of them were in two cars rolling through the White House gate. They were checked in by the Secret Service and without any wait were whisked inside. Brennan had been to the White House several times before, but he had never experienced anything like this. In what seemed like the blink of an eye, he found himself in the Oval Office, briefing at least ten high-level cabinet members and presidential advisors, not to mention the president of the United States, who sat behind the Resolute desk, sipping a ginger ale and shooting glances at a TV in the corner that was silently playing a college football game.

Brennan tried not to get too technical as he explained the relative rarity of nylon-and-copper-weave glove fibers and how they might have finally caught a break. By far the most likely possibility was a glove manufactured by a small, family-run company that was popular with deer hunters and was only sold in a dozen sporting goods stores in Minnesota, Wisconsin, and Michigan. 'So you're saying Green Man's a deer hunter from the bum-fuck Midwest?' the president cut in.

'We don't know that, sir. But yes, the glove was probably purchased in the Midwest, and we can be even a little more precise.'

'If he's so smart, why would he wear a glove that is only marketed to a narrow clientele in such a circumscribed area?' the attorney general asked. 'Why wouldn't he choose something generic and untraceable?'

'It's actually a wise choice. This particular type of glove is exceptionally sturdy –'

'Which means exactly what?' she followed up immediately, not even giving Brennan time to finish his sentence. 'Sturdy in what sense, in layman's terms, Jim?'

'It doesn't shed fibers. He apparently wears these gloves all the time when he's on a mission, and we haven't found any fibers up to now. The odds are he took a sudden swift and unplanned action, like swatting a mosquito, and we got lucky –'

'Or maybe he was jerking off because he was thinking about how he was fucking us,' the president said, and some of his male advisors dutifully grinned. Brennan had heard about his use of vulgar profanity during meetings, but still it was jarring to hear such things said in the Oval Office with portraits of Washington, Lincoln, and Jefferson looking down on them.

Brennan considered saying 'That's certainly a possibility, sir,' but he kept silent.

The president jabbed a finger at Brennan. 'So what good does this glove fiber stuff actually do for us?'

'Well, sir, if it was purchased in the Midwest, that gives

us – for the first time – some directionality in our search. If he came from there, if he was heading back there, we can start to project his route and what roads he might have taken in what we now believe was a van . . .'

'Assuming he doesn't live in San Francisco and he bought some gloves from the Midwest just to try to throw you off,' the director of Homeland Security contributed.

'I feel comfortable with that assumption,' Brennan said. 'Also, we were able to obtain a trace sample of DNA from one of the filaments. Sadly it was tiny and had degraded to the point where it won't tell us much, but our top experts are studying it, and at the very least it will be useful for verification purposes once the suspect is apprehended.'

'So when you catch Green Man you'll know you've caught him?' the president asked. 'I need better than that.' He leaned forward, propping his elbows on the desk, and looked at the attorney general. 'Meg, you've got your best people working on this?'

The question was clearly about Brennan, and they all knew it. 'Yes, Mr President,' she said without hesitation. 'We understand the gravity of this, and our very best and most experienced people are leaving no stones unturned.'

'Just to be clear, I don't give a flying fuck if the stones are turned or unturned,' the president told her. 'I want this guy nailed. But right now I want you guys to head over to the press secretary's office and help her craft a statement that she will deliver in half an hour to the national press with you standing behind her. It will be optimistic, and it will emphasize the innocent people who died in the most recent attack and in the other five attacks. She won't take questions, and you won't, either. And then I want you to catch this fucker before he strikes again. That's all.'

They all got up to leave, but the president pointed at Brennan and said, 'Hang around for a minute.'

Brennan glanced at the FBI director, but Haviland shrugged slightly and docilely followed the rest of them out of the office, and someone pulled the door closed.

'Take a load off,' the president suggested, and Brennan sat back down.

'You want something to drink?'

'No, sir. I'm fine.'

The president watched the football game for so long that Brennan couldn't help glancing at the screen himself. Duke scored on a long pass to put the game out of reach. 'Fucking arrogant Blue Devils,' the president grunted. 'You didn't go to Duke, did you?'

'No, sir, I went to Penn State.' On a shelf directly behind the president's head was the *Bronco Buster* statue by Remington. Brennan had a copy of it in his summer home in Tappahannock, but he knew that this was the original.

'Hell of a football program down there,' the president said. 'You didn't hear me say this, but Paterno got shafted. He built the place up from a cow town, and they reamed him.' The president pressed a button on his desk and said, 'Betty, bring me another ginger and make sure it's colder than the last one.' He looked back at Brennan and said, 'So you were hired by Hoover?' He somehow made it sound like a vacuum company.

'Yes, sir, in 1972. It was his last year, the year he died.'

'What did you make of him?'

'He was a complicated man, sir. I didn't have much direct contact with him.'

'He was a great American,' the president said. 'Because he got the job done. That's what it comes down to, isn't it?'

82

Brennan was usually good at figuring out if someone he was speaking with was intelligent, but with this president, it was absolutely impossible to tell. His confidence and bluster might mask a sly competence or a profound ignorance and gross stupidity. 'Yes, sir, that's what it comes down to.'

'Do you know who Chandler Evanston is?'

The name was vaguely familiar, but Brennan couldn't place it. 'No, sir.'

'He's the CEO of the parent company of the energy company that owns the pipeline in Oregon that Green Man blew up a year ago.'

'Yes, sir. Now I know who he is.'

'We had breakfast last week,' the president said. 'He mentioned that since his pipeline was destroyed, his company has been facing mounting obstacles, not just out west but in all the places they operate. And there are currently two bills in Congress that would make the kinds of pipelines they use a hell of a lot harder to get approved. Do you understand what I'm saying?'

Brennan hesitated. 'I'm not sure that I do, Mr President.'

'Green Man also hit the Mayfield Chemical plant, in Massachusetts. Among their products, as you probably know, are several that alarmists claim are severe ozone-depleters and are accelerating global warming. Of course, there's no evidence for any of this, but that's beside the point. Green Man's choice of a target created massive resistance by left-wing wackos who are calling for all kinds of regulations and inquiries into the kinds of products that Mayfield and half a dozen companies like it make and whether they should be allowed to manufacture such things. Are you with me now?'

83

'You're saying that when Green Man strikes a target, he not only destroys it but he also galvanizes resistance to that industry.'

The president smiled, which was a thing he did rarely, and it was menacing. 'When terrorism starts translating into popular resistance and even public policy, God help us, because we're down the toilet,' he said. 'Because for one thing, good, hardworking Americans are gonna lose their jobs, which is something I was elected to make sure doesn't happen. And for another thing, there are a lot of potential Green Men out there with socialist agendas. Capeesh?'

'We certainly are very aware of the potential for copy-cats,' Brennan said. 'That's one reason we're strictly limiting release of information about the specific techniques used in his attacks –'

'So you were hired by Hoover in another century,' the president interjected, 'but you still have your edge?'

'I want to catch Green Man very badly, sir. I'm doing all I can.'

'Then why haven't you caught him?'

'Because he's smart and very careful. But we're getting closer, and I will catch him.'

'And you're aware that there's a presidential election coming up in a little less than a year, and it will be hotly contested? You don't have a dog in this fight?'

Brennan paused. He had never been asked such a thing before. 'I'm not political in any way, sir, if that's what you're asking, and I certainly don't want Green Man to continue what he's doing and kill more innocent Americans to advance a political agenda. I've been a loyal public servant for five decades and –'

'You still have the fire in your belly?'

'Yes, sir. But if you think there's somebody better –'

'If I thought there was somebody better, then you wouldn't be sitting in my office making excuses right now.' The president held Brennan's gaze for ten full seconds and let his charisma do its work. Brennan felt it, whatever it was. It was undeniable and tangible, almost visceral. 'If you need anything,' the president finally said, 'you just ask for it. More money, more people . . .' He pressed the black button on his desk and roared, 'Betty, did you go to China for that goddamn ginger ale?'

12

The Endangered Species Club consisted of fourteen fresh-men, seven sophomores, one junior, and one senior, which reflected how interest in the environment had spiked at the Carlyle Academy over the past two years. Their presentation was given before a good crowd in the school's main auditorium in a handsome brick building on the Upper West Side. Julie, as the lone senior, went first, and Ellen felt a mixture of pride and dread as her daughter climbed onto the stage to talk about polar bears. Julie was a straight-A student, but she battled stage fright and hadn't slept for two nights worrying about this presentation.

She stood for a moment with her hands fumbling nervously at her sides, a tall girl with an afro, blinking out at the audience from behind her glasses. 'Come on, girl,' Ellen whispered. She herself had never had this problem – Ellen had spoken in front of thousands of people at lectures and rallies and college commencements, taught dozens of large and small Columbia classes, and was frequently a guest commentator on live TV. She didn't completely understand her daughter's fear, but she knew it was very real. 'You can do this, baby.'

'She'll do fine,' the woman on her right said kindly. Ellen realized that she had whispered too loudly. She thanked the woman with a smile and glanced around to see if anyone else had heard her. No one had, but looking around, Ellen was not surprised to see that she was the only black parent in the auditorium and that Julie was the only student of color. For all its talk of encouraging diversity, the progressive and highly selective Carlyle Academy remained rich and lily-white.

'I'd like to thank you all for coming here today,' Julie began tentatively, her thin voice quivering. 'We're the Endangered Species Club, and today you'll hear about species that are in real danger. Some of them you'll probably already know about because they're famous and cute. Others you might not have heard of because they're obscure and . . . frankly, some people find them ugly.' There were a few laughs from the audience, and Julie broke off for a second. 'But they all deserve a chance – polar bears and honeybees, tigers and monarch butterflies, and even the weirdest-looking tropical sea slugs that live in vanishing coral reefs. But before we start talking about those distant and exotic species, on behalf of my club members, I'd like to remind you about one other endangered species that's closer to home.'

Julie paused for a deep breath, and then she seemed to relax, or perhaps when she started talking again, her obvious nervousness started to work for the message she was trying to convey. 'People say that every generation grows up with a looming threat they have to deal with. For our great-grandparents, it was World War I and the Spanish flu. For our grandparents, it was World War II and fascism. For our parents, it was the Cold War and the arms race. But in all those cases, there was hope. They could cure the flu or defeat Hitler or limit missiles. We're different.'

Suddenly Julie had them, and Ellen was beyond thrilled, because she had this gift, and she could do this herself, but she had never seen her daughter capture a crowd and hold them in the palm of her hand, which was now outstretched, as if Julie was asking for something, or even demanding it. Her voice was still thin, but it was no longer quivering and had become evocative and powerful: 'We are the first generation to grow up without hope. In fact, we may be doomed.'

No one in the auditorium was fidgeting. They were all watching the tall, nervous black girl under the spotlights as she spoke softly: 'We all know it. A lot of us have decided not to have kids because we don't think it would be fair to them. And we especially know it in the Endangered Species Club because we see it happening to animals, fish, and insects, some of which have been around far longer than we have. We study how they're vanishing, and we can't help thinking that it will happen to us. Where the dodo went, where the Javan rhinoceros is going, we may be doomed to follow. How can we live in a world where we can't breathe the air or drink the water? So to the parents and grandparents in the audience who vote, thanks for coming today, but one thing we'd like to say to you is please give us what you had – some hope. And now I'd like to talk about the polar bears –'

She was interrupted by loud applause, and the woman sitting next to Ellen leaned over and said, 'Isn't she sensational! Your daughter should be in politics.'

'God help her,' Ellen responded, and then smiled proudly. 'But thank you. She's heard a few speeches at rallies, and I guess some of it must have sunk in.'

The rest of the day was magical. Julie's presentation on polar bears was a smash success, and the audience sighed at photos of forlorn cubs on drift ice that had broken off from

89

the packs where their parents hunted seals. The other club members did well also. Ellen already knew most of the information that was presented, but that didn't stop it from being powerful to hear fourteen- and fifteen-year-olds describing in vivid specifics the mounting global threats that were imperiling different species all over the planet, from the deepest oceans to the most remote islands to the polar ice caps, and how little time was left to turn things around.

After the presentation Ellen headed out for round two – to watch her daughter play soccer against Carlyle's arch foes. There is so little open land in Manhattan that the private schools played each other on Randall's Island in the East River, and on one of those fields Ellen watched Julie score three goals, including the game winner. There was nothing shy about the way her daughter took on defenders and flashed by them with bursts of speed.

Students were given the option of riding home on the team bus or with their parents, so after the post-game pep talk, Julie climbed into Ellen's red Prius and they headed home together. 'Baby, you were awesome!' Ellen told her as they headed up the ramp and turned onto the RFK Bridge. 'And your speech was a knockout.'

'I was so nervous I couldn't even see people's faces.'

'Whatever you were doing, just keep doing it,' Ellen said. 'And I swear you're gonna get a D-III soccer scholarship. There were definitely a few college scouts in the crowd. I've heard the quality they look for most is speed. I don't know where yours came from, because your mother runs like she's wearing concrete shoes . . .'

'Come on, you can jog pretty fast . . .'

'After a year I can keep up a steady pace, but you blaze, girl. Their fullback was terrified.'

90

'Then the speed must have come from my father,' Julie suggested softly.

It was something they never discussed. 'I guess that makes sense,' Ellen said, keeping her eyes on the highway that was crowded with rush-hour traffic.

Julie hesitated. 'Do you know if the donor was an athlete? I mean, don't they tell you things like that? Don't you get a profile or at least a name?'

'No, sweetheart, I don't know anything. They tell you a lot if you ask, but all I wanted to know was that he was tall, healthy, and very smart, like his daughter,' Ellen said, and then she blinked.

'MA, WATCH OUT!'

Ellen jerked the wheel, and they swerved wildly, missing a FedEx truck by two inches. She steered them into the slow lane and drove so cautiously that the car behind them honked.

'You okay, Mom?'

'Sure,' Ellen said, gripping the wheel a little too tightly. 'I'm fine. Sorry if I scared you.'

'I thought we were FedEx roadkill for sure.'

Ellen tried to laugh it off and managed an unconvincing chuckle. 'Give me some credit. I've driven you home from a million soccer games. Have I ever had an accident?'

'No, but there's a first time for everything, and that was really close. Do you need to pull over?'

'Honey, I'm fine. It was just a tough morning at work. I'm gonna put on some music.' Ellen switched on the radio and the news station she had been listening to on the ride out came on. The newscaster was announcing that they were going to replay the briefing earlier in the day, when the White House press secretary had given a statement to

91

reporters about recent progress in the hunt for Green Man.

Ellen quickly changed the station to some jazz, but Julie said, 'Hey, I wanted to hear that.'

'I listened to it driving out,' Ellen told her. 'There's really nothing new.'

Julie reached down and switched it back to the news station. The press secretary was beginning her statement: 'First, I want to reassure everyone that the law enforcement leaders behind me are doing their utmost to protect our country and catch this vile and cowardly terrorist who has taken the law into his own hands and already killed more than forty innocent Americans, including ten children.'

'And maybe saved the planet,' Julie said, talking over her.

'There's no excuse for killing forty-three people,' Ellen told her, reminded of the debate with Richard in the Green Center.

'How about saving six billion people? Isn't that a good excuse?'

'It *is* a good excuse, but when you let the end justify the means, it's a slippery slope . . . ,' Ellen started to explain, turning off the crowded FDR onto 116th Street.

But she was immediately shushed. 'Quiet. You're wrong, and I want to hear this.' Julie cranked up the volume.

'For the first time in this investigation,' the press secretary was saying, 'we now have solid and significant leads, thanks to our agents in the field and our expert forensics teams. I can't reveal the exact nature of those leads except to say that Green Man made several critical mistakes, and the investigation is now moving forward quickly on several different fronts to identify him and arrest him. The president has been fully briefed and expects more breakthroughs in this case shortly. Thank you; we will not be taking questions.'

Julie switched off the radio, looking worried. 'They wouldn't say they had solid leads if they didn't have them.'

'Relax, honey. They didn't say anything definite,' Ellen pointed out. 'A lot of the content in those scripted statements is political. I'm sure Green Man can take care of himself.'

'But they have so many people looking for him now. He's bound to slip up. Everyone makes little mistakes no matter how smart they are.' Julie looked at her mother till Ellen quickly glanced back at her. The teen looked angry and even accusing. 'But you want them to catch him, don't you?'

'No, I just want him to stop. That's a very different thing.'

Julie went on a rant, speaking faster and faster till her words blurred together: 'How can you say you liked my speech and also say that he should stop? The only reason there are fourteen freshmen in our club is because of him. The only reason we have any hope is because of him. Didn't you hear me say that we live with the knowledge that we may be doomed? He's fighting that, and you of all people should understand and care . . . Mom!'

Ellen had veered sharply off the road into the parking lot of a high school that was empty and dark.

'Why are we stopping here?'

Ellen tried to answer, but she couldn't stop the tears. She had held them back at the Green Center and in her classes, but now they came unbidden and unwanted, from some deep place, past all her defenses. They squeezed out through her eyelids and ran hot down her cheeks, and Ellen slouched forward to hide them from her daughter, leaning into the steering wheel and covering her face with her arms.

'Are you sick? Mom, are you crying? Please tell me what's going on?'

Ellen's body was shaking, and her tear-stained face was turned away from her daughter, toward the dark high school. 'Julie, I've never lied to you before, about anything important. And I never will again. I promise you that.'

She slowly turned back to look at her daughter, who nodded and reached out to her. 'Of course I believe you. I love you, Mom. But . . . what did you lie about?'

Ellen looked Julie in the eye and took two deep breaths. 'His name was James.'

'Who?'

'The sperm bank didn't give his last name for reasons of donor privacy.'

Julie was silent and frozen in her seat, repeating the new name softly to herself as if it held some magical power. 'What else do you know about James?'

'He had an IQ of 180, which is the biggest reason I chose him. He was an academic on the West Coast – tall, black, and healthy – and he didn't wear glasses or have any major health problems. He certainly could have been an athlete and a very fast runner, I just don't know. I didn't ask them any more questions.'

'Why? Didn't you want to know more about him?' Julie asked softly.

'No, honey, I wanted to know about you.'

'But I wasn't born yet.'

'But you were coming, and that's why I did it. I wanted to know about us and what we would be like together. I always thought it was about us, not him, and that I would be enough of a parent for you.' A pained gasp: 'Baby, I'm sorry I lied to you. I won't ever do it again.'

Julie leaned over and held her mother close and whispered, 'You are enough,' and 'I love you, Mom,' over and over again.

13

It was a war room. The manhunt for Green Man had swelled to totally unprecedented levels – more than four hundred agents nationwide – and this sprawling, high-tech space was its operational center. Tom had seen pictures of Churchill's cabinet war rooms, located beneath the Treasury building in Whitehall, that had tracked progress in all the theaters of war for twenty-four hours a day, and that's what this hangar at Quantico reminded him of.

The room was dominated by thirty or so senior agents and experts who seemed to never eat or sleep. They all knew one another and had worked on large and small cases together for years, and their mutual respect, professionalism, and shared resolve to crack this case made the hangar buzz with a nervous collaborative energy. Tom was one of a few new faces, but no one questioned his presence. He arrived from Florida and plunged in, fascinated by the older agents and practically inhaling their expertise and excitement. He worked with an almost feverish intensity for nearly a week, barely pausing to eat or grab a few hours of shuteye.

They were surrounded night and day by clusters of computers and giant wall screens on which flashed a constant bombardment of forensics and data. Agents from the field arrived to make reports, and experts on degraded DNA and domestic vans produced in the past ten years and fiber microscopy came and went. Many of the senior agents Tom worked with were specialists who culled the information from the far-flung agents in their respective divisions, distilled what was potentially useful, and synthesized it within the framework of the larger investigation.

Tom's role was much less clear – he floated from expert group to expert group and computer cluster to computer cluster, tracking the newest information, asking the probing and 'pain in the ass' questions he was becoming known for, occasionally summoned at odd hours to report directly to Brennan.

The taskforce leader maintained an almost Churchillian presence, brooding and pensive, popping into the hangar unexpectedly with sharp questions at all times of the day and night. He would arrive after briefings of higher-ups in Washington, in a rumpled suit and with his tie loose. Sometimes he would wander in in the middle of the night, once in a blue terrycloth bathrobe, too excited to sleep and eager to follow up a new idea that had just occurred to him. He had a small office that he often slept in at the very back of the hangar, complete with a desk and a cot, and it was there that Tom briefed him, usually with two or three other agents listening in.

The optimism generated by the so-called breakthroughs at Boon soon faded to a hopeful conviction that if the clues were re-examined by the right top experts in new ways, they would yield a eureka moment. That hope in turn gave way to a grudging recognition that this was still going to be a long slog and a frustration at the number of dead ends. No additional clues were found at the cliff or campsite. The DNA that had been recovered from the glove filaments turned out to be too degraded to be of help. The faint van tracks could not be used to further identify the vehicle. The family-manufactured deer hunting gloves from the Midwest remained the most likely source for the glove fibers, but the sporting goods stores that sold them did not have cameras. Even if Green Man had bought the gloves himself, if he'd paid in cash, there was no lasting record of him or the transaction.

Tom paid particular attention to the attempts to project what route Green Man might have chosen if he'd driven home from the Boon Dam to the Midwest. Six large and small highways emerged by consensus as the most likely routes, and every police department along those winding roadways had been contacted to see if anything suspicious had been noted or any tickets given out when Green Man would've been heading home. Thousands of cameras in gas stations and stores along the way had their film requisitioned and turned into metadata. Millions of images were compared by the latest facial-recognition software to images taken near the other targets that had been struck in the past two years, searching for a match.

On Tom's fifth night in the war room, he was unexpectedly summoned to Brennan's office and found the big man seated at his desk sipping hot oolong tea from a thermos and wading through a stack of reports that was at least five inches high. Several of his top aides were there with him, including Earl, his gaunt majordomo, and Grant, who people connected to the investigation often whispered was Brennan's most trusted advisor and heir apparent. The tall African-American agent was ferociously smart and super aggressive yet somehow also managed to be soft-spoken, methodical, and respectful. 'I want to know about roads, Smith,' Brennan said, and took a careful sip of the steaming tea. 'I want to know what my experts are saying, and I want to know why you think they're all wrong.'

Tom gave him the latest projections and filled him in on the most recent work that had been done to collect information along those six different routes. 'And now what do you think?' Brennan asked. 'And don't disappoint me and tell me my experts are right.'

'I'm sorry to be predictable, sir, but I don't think Green Man would have taken any of those six ways home.'

Brennan grinned. 'And why is that?'

'They just don't feel right to me.'

'And why don't they feel right? Because other people chose them and you always have to be contrary?'

'No, sir.' Tom hesitated. 'Because I wouldn't have taken them, sir, if it had been me driving home after blowing up Boon. I've studied all six in detail, and they're too big. Too fast. Sure, they're the most logical and obvious choices. But they're just . . . soulless. And they feel wrong to me.'

Brennan lowered his thermos of steaming tea and glanced at Earl. 'What do you think of this guy?'

The wizened field agent said, 'I like his sense of smell. He reminds me of his father.'

'I wouldn't go there,' Brennan cautioned. 'Okay, young Tom, why don't any of those highways feel right to you? None of them are big interstates. None of them have toll plazas or CCTV cameras. They'd get him home fairly quick. What's the problem?'

'They're too big for Green Man. And he never makes obvious choices. They say the top chess grandmasters don't actually look at more moves than average players, but they just intuitively look at the right twenty or thirty moves – the strategically sound yet tactically unexpected

100

moves that lesser players don't even consider. That's the way Green Man operates. He's logical but never obvious.'

'But if you were Green Man, wouldn't you want to go home to the Midwest quickly and directly?' Agent Grant asked in his polite way. 'Wouldn't you want to see Green Woman and Green Kids?' It was hard to tell if he was trying to understand Tom's thought processes or gently mocking him. Perhaps he was doing both.

'Green Man doesn't care about what's quickest because he knows that you expect him to care,' Tom said. 'An extra day wouldn't deter him if he thought that he could take a slower, smaller, more circuitous route and throw us off. I doubt he would try to speed through the Dakotas even though, if you draw a line across the map, that would get him back the quickest. I think he'd jog north or dip south.'

'What's this about "soul"?' Earl asked. 'How can a road be "soulless"?'

'I can't articulate that,' Tom admitted. 'But if you're Green Man, you're sure not feeling triumphant. You're listening to the news about what you've just done while you're driving home. You've just killed twelve people. Five were kids. That rips your guts out. There's a part of you that wants to take your time, gaze out at open countryside, and slowly come to terms with the horror of what's just happened.'

'But he totally destroyed his objective,' Grant objected. 'He'd be victorious and even euphoric – not miserable.'

Brennan waved for Grant to be silent. 'So what road would you take?' Brennan asked, and the small office got very quiet. 'I assume you've thought about that?'

'Well, I wouldn't go north,' Tom said, 'because I'd have to cross into Canada, and even though I'm sure he's got a

101

valid passport and all the necessary documents, there would be records made of that crossing. Green Man stays far away from borders and any action that generates hard data.'

'So then you'd go south?' Brennan asked.

'Yes, sir, if it was me, I'd meander south – maybe loop down into Nebraska.'

'And when you're wearing your Green Man hat and you've got the steering wheel of that van in your hands, what specific road appeals to you?'

'Route 55, sir. Through Nebraska and dipping down into northern Kansas.'

'We looked at it,' Grant cut in quickly. 'It's not even a highway. It's a two-lane road that in places becomes just one-lane and would take him five or six hundred miles out of his way. And it has stoplights, which our profilers say he'd avoid –'

'The towns with stoplights are spaced far apart –' Tom said.

'In a lot of places it's got speed limits of forty miles an hour or even less.'

'And it's got beautiful wide-open vistas that flow into each other,' Tom said. 'If I'd just done something that I thought was necessary but was tormenting me, I'd drive slowly and carefully home and try to find some peace and tranquility by the banks of the Missouri River or in the Prairie Lakes region or looking out on the timeless Glacial Hills of Kansas.'

'We've checked with the police departments along Route 55 and also collected images,' Grant said, glancing at his laptop. 'Nothing.'

'It's been less than a week since Green Man drove home

along one of those roads,' Tom pointed out. 'Before any more time passes, let me drive Route 55 myself. If he was there, somebody may have seen him, or a security camera we don't know about filmed him, or maybe he stopped for coffee one night because he was tired and he just wanted to see a smile and hear some human conversation. Give me a few days and let me beat the bushes before everyone there forgets.'

Brennan hesitated. 'Nothing ties him to that road. And our people have already checked it out and they came up empty. Seems like a damn long shot. Earl?'

The gaunt agent studied Tom. 'Tell you the truth, we're not having much luck with all our computers and forensics and recognition software. Maybe you should give this kid a long leash. As we both know, there's something to be said for driving the roads and beating the bushes.'

Brennan reluctantly nodded. 'Sounds like you wouldn't mind riding shotgun?'

'Now that you mention it, I haven't been sleeping too well in this beehive for the last week. Not that I'm complaining. But I wouldn't mind a few days on the road, asking questions to folks who just might have seen him drive by in his van.'

'Then get out of here,' Brennan snapped, almost as if it made him angry. 'I'll give you both three days. Beat the bushes and follow your noses. I'll have every police station and sheriff station along the way ready to talk to you. Even if they didn't see anything themselves, they might suggest some nosy neighbor you can talk to or some camera we don't know about. If you don't find anything useful in three days, we need you back here.'

14

It was one of Green Man's dark days. He felt the shadow lengthening over him almost the moment he woke up. He was able to push it away long enough to eat breakfast with Gus and Kim and go over their homework. It was starting to get very bad when he drove them to school, but he somehow kept up his side of the fun family banter and promised to try to come to Gus's soccer game that afternoon, even though he knew that by then he would probably be flat on his back. He finally pulled up near the crossing guard as the kids got out, spotted friends, and headed up the walk toward their brick elementary school. Green Man watched them tromp happily away, and then – behind the tinted windows of his car – he put his head in his hands and nearly screamed.

A few blocks from the school, the first wave of anxiety broke over him so hard and fast that instead of heading back to Sharon and their home, Green Man fled out of town. He kept pills in the car and swallowed five of them – well beyond the recommended dosage. But the powerful drugs barely cut the crippling dread, and he could feel a second wave coming fast, looming, rising up – a much larger and more threatening wave that would crash down any moment. He craved music or any kind of distraction, but he didn't dare turn on the car's radio because every station – even the country music stations – played constant updates about the hunt for him. Fear of being caught was a key trigger of this attack. He had been listening for more than a week to hear how he had made mistakes when he struck the Boon Dam and the FBI now had clues and solid leads and was closing in on him.

That feeling of being hunted and closed in on was with him as he drove, constricting his breath and blood flow like the tightening coils of a python. He lived with the anxiety, but he was usually able to keep it at a manageable level. Once triggered, it flared wildly into panic – a fear that he had made some tiny mistake and the hundreds of law enforcement experts who were chasing him had found it and were using it against him, figuring out where he was, finding out the identities of his family members, coming for him in their black sedans, with their guns and handcuffs and decades in isolation wards, coming to the elementary school for his children, coming to his home for Sharon, coming, coming, coming to use that one tiny mistake to destroy everything that he loved and had worked so hard to build . . .

'Mistake' was the anxiety trigger. He was careful and meticulous, but it was impossible to avoid mistakes, and he'd spent the past week agonizing about what he might have done wrong. He had definitely made mistakes coming home from the Boon Dam attack – they were small ones, but when the policeman had unexpectedly pulled him over, he had said things he shouldn't have said and done things he shouldn't have done, and the patrolman might have seen things that Green Man should never have let him see. His hands were trembling so that it was too dangerous to keep driving. Green Man pulled onto the gravel shoulder a mile from the river, got out of his car, and ran into the forest. There was something freeing about running among the trees, but after a half mile, the second wave crashed down on him, so that he found himself staggering and weaving between the pines.

His heart was pounding, and he was hyperventilating. He stopped running, clung to a tree, and tried to control the panic by visualizing something specific and calming. He focused on the memory of Gus and Kim walking toward their school that morning, and he used his photographic memory and artist's eye to sketch in the details – how they had been smiling and Kim had begun skipping along in her red sneakers with her braids bouncing and her silver barrettes flashing in the sun . . .

But it did no good. The vivid image of his smiling children ricocheted Green Man to the ten kids who had become a sort of second, secret family to him. He knew each of them by name, knew their ages and faces, and today Andy Shetley was with him – no matter how deep he plunged into this dense pine forest, he couldn't hide from the boy. Andy, who would have been eleven next week, who played soccer just like Gus, but who had drowned on a houseboat he should have never been on, three hundred miles from his home.

Andy Shetley was calling out to him now, softly, by name, *Paul, Paul,* a name no one had used for more than a decade, a name that he had buried six feet under, he was Mitch now, *Paul, Paul,* telling him that he had made a mistake and that they were closing in on him and he would be caught soon, and he deserved to be caught, that he wasn't a hero at all but a monster, and then they were all shouting at him, Sam Terry in his tiger-striped pajamas, and five-year-old Anne Ellmore from the deck of her grandfather's luxurious yacht as the freezing Atlantic closed over her . . .

107

Green Man reached the river and saw the crab-apple tree. It was old and gnarled and sat above a mossy bank with branches dipping low over the water. He didn't know why he came here, but this was where he always waited out his worst attacks. He staggered toward it, and he could smell the fruit – the tree had blossomed in mid-summer and now it was dropping crab apples the size of ping-pong balls onto the grassy bank where they were rotting in the sun. *Paul, Paul,* and now it wasn't just the children but someone deeper, from much further back, a woman who loved him dearly, and he had done something beyond horrible to her, left her with a gaping hole in her heart.

She must be seventy now and have white hair, but he saw her in her fifties, as she had looked when he last saw her standing behind the screen door of the small house in the New Jersey beach city where he had grown up, and he had buried the memory deep, but she had found him by this grassy riverbank, Paul, Paul, why did you leave me with such pain and longing, you monster? He sat down beneath the crab-apple tree and stopped fighting them because they were all too strong.

There was no point in running from the people he had victimized. He understood that the guilt he felt over them was deeply linked to his own fear. He had caused great pain and suffering, and rather than deny that, he sat very still under the tree and practiced the meditation of acceptance, inviting the children into his mind and apologizing to them one by one. Green Man admitted to himself that the manhunt was indeed taking place and that he was being chased night and day by hundreds of police and FBI agents and might be caught at any moment. To deny it just made the panic worse, feeding it like a fire, so he forced himself to look at the truth squarely and to accept the reality of what it might mean for the people he loved most.

The third wave rose up, and he desperately reminded himself of the reasons why he had decided to put those people he dearly loved at risk. Green Man had a deep understanding of the gravest threats to the global environment. He had studied them for decades, and taken together, they had convinced him that humanity was in terrible peril and he must fight back, whatever the costs. He repeated those reasons to himself, knowing how valid they were, and he ranged them with his acceptance of the manhunt and the dangers to himself and his family, and he sat with it all and half shut his eyes and tried to control his breathing for as long as he could stand.

But when the third wave broke over him, it was absolutely shattering, and there was nothing he could do. Somewhere in town, on a grassy soccer field, Gus was playing midfield, but the afternoon found Green Man on his side among the rotting apples, curled into a fetal position, moaning in agony and wishing he were dead and that it could all just be over.

15

It wasn't till they left the Tetons behind that Earl let Tom ask the questions. In every police station, ranger station, and sheriff's office along the first thousand miles of their route, the old field agent insisted on doing all the talking while Tom sat there smiling like a dummy. Earl stuck very much to his script, literally – he had written out ten questions in black pen on a white pad from the crummy Holiday Inn where they had spent the first night. They knew exactly when Green Man had blown up the dam, so assuming he'd jumped into his van and headed east, staying just under the speed limit and not pausing to sleep, they could predict almost to the minute when he would have passed through each town and campground.

'My young colleague and I want to thank you for taking the time to meet with us,' Earl would begin. 'We know how busy you are, and we appreciate it. This could not have a higher priority. We're looking for one man, age and appearance unknown, driving a van with a thirteen-foot wheelbase.' And then would come the ten rote and generic questions, always asked in the same order with exactly the same words in the same slow cadence, about whether any tickets had been issued or anything out of the ordinary witnessed by any of the officers on duty.

'You're not giving them enough,' Tom told him as they wound through the mountains. 'You're not taking enough creative chances to make this valuable.'

'It's not about taking chances,' Earl told him. 'It's about being accurate. What we can ask is limited by what we know. Look, son, I've done these for forty years, probably more than five hundred times. Listen up and learn.'

'The reason you won't catch Green Man is because you've done this for forty years and a hundred times, and if you think those ten questions of yours will unlock this, you can forget about it, because they won't,' Tom fired back. 'And please stop calling me your young colleague.'

'You *are* my young colleague, and slow down on the curves. There's a thousand-foot drop.'

'This was my idea,' Tom reminded him, speeding up slightly. 'You were just supposed to ride shotgun. Those were Brennan's exact words. He knows what I'm like, and if he sent us on this mission, it was so that I can do what I do.'

Earl lit a cigarette and took a puff. 'Keep your eyes on the road. And just what is it that you do?'

'I'm really good at being a pain in the ass. Don't smoke in the car.'

'It's an SUV, and yes, you are good at that. *Slow the hell down.*'

Tom took a curve so fast they almost brushed the guard-rail that rimmed the cliff. 'If you don't like me taking the turns this way then roll down your window. If you want to experience the joys of lung cancer, that's your choice but not mine.'

Earl gave in and rolled down the window two inches. He tilted his straw hat to screen out the sunlight and thought it over for a minute. 'Okay, hotshot. Now that I've shown you what it should sound like, I'm going to give you a chance to ask the questions. But stick to the script.'

At the next small police station, Tom addressed a chief

and two deputies, starting off haltingly. 'My colleague and I want to thank you for taking the time to meet with us. We know how busy you are. This could not have a higher priority.'

Earl nodded encouragingly, as if to say, 'Stick to the script and you'll do fine.' Tom broke off and asked him, 'Earl, could I have the list of questions?'

Earl passed him the paper from the Holiday Inn pad with his ten questions written out in small, neat handwriting. Tom asked the policemen, 'Can I borrow a match?' One of them handed him a book of matches, and Tom lit the paper on fire and dropped it in an ashtray. While it burned, he looked over at Earl, and when the ten questions were reduced to cinders, Tom said to the surprised policemen, 'So, to continue, we're looking for one man, thirty to fifty years old, who would have been unshaven and looked exhausted. He'd driven through the night, so, careful as he is, he might have had trouble staying in his lane or missed a speed trap. That's why you might have stopped him. He was driving a van with tinted windows and wearing a hat or cap tilted over his eyes. We think his Michigan, Wisconsin, or possibly Ohio license plate would have all numbers and no letters –'

Earl exploded. 'What the hell are you talking about?'

But the policemen were listening carefully, and Tom kept going: 'He wouldn't have wanted to stop and talk, but if he was pulled over for anything, he would have been polite and even conversational to a point, and he'd follow all commands perfectly. His goal would have been to get away with a warning and not have the policeman at the scene give him a ticket, run his plates, or generate any data from the stop.'

After they left, Earl furiously demanded an explanation.

113

'What the hell was that nonsense you were spouting? We have no idea about any of that. Green Man could be twenty or he could be eighty.'

'Thirty to fifty is not just my guess; it's part of the FBI's profile,' Tom told him.

'It's just their guess,' Earl said. 'We don't know it, so we shouldn't ask –'

Tom cut him off. 'It feels right to me. He doesn't stay in hotels or even use public bathrooms, so there's no mirror or hot water available, and even if there was, I don't see why he'd take the trouble to shave . . .'

'All he needs to shave is his car mirror,' Earl pointed out. 'Most men shave in the morning as part of their routine. I have for the last forty years or so.'

'Yeah, but why would Green Man shave on a mission? He wants to alter his appearance and hide his face as much as possible. Why would he do anything to clean it up and make himself more recognizable? And why risk drawing blood or leaving any hair follicles or suds? No, he'd let his hair and beard grow out during his trip.'

'And that's why you think he'd wear a hat and drive a van with tinted windows?'

'Green Man likes privacy. He's especially careful about hiding his face.'

'What's that nonsense about the numbers on his license plate?'

'Numbers are much harder for people to recall than letters, which people remember in patterns. If I was Green Man, I'd get a vanity plate with a random sequence of seven numbers and then doctor the first few numbers before setting out, just in case some hidden camera snapped a picture of my van. But that carries a risk – if any police along the way ran the plate, it wouldn't come up, so he'd have to drive slowly and carefully and be ready just in case that ever happened.'

'Be ready for what?'

'For whatever he'd have to do to stop a cop from running his plate. Why are you laughing?'

'Brennan was right.'

'About what?'

'He said you have a real good sense of smell but you don't know it and maybe because of your father you hesitate to use it, so you have to be provoked into it. He told me to keep you on a really tight leash and stick to the facts till it pissed you off enough to blow a gasket, put your Green Man hat on, and take over.'

'He really said that about me?'

'Yeah, he gave me those ten questions and told me to keep repeating them till I drove you crazy. He has a very high opinion of your ability to be a pain in the ass,' Earl said, taking the window down five inches and lighting another cigarette. 'Not to swell your ego, but we wouldn't be here if he didn't think you had a chance to crack this. Except he thinks you might be soft.'

'What does that mean?'

'Compromised. A greenie.'

Tom considered that. 'He thinks I might be sympathetic to some of Green Man's environmental motives?'

'Are you?'

'I admit I'm fond of the planet I live on,' Tom said. 'Aren't you?'

Earl puffed white smoke out the window from both nostrils. 'It's done okay for itself for six billion years. I don't know if we can kill it that easy.'

'This from the man who smokes a pack a day and is destroying his own lungs?'

'That's different.'

'How? You're killing yourself. If we keep fucking with the earth, we're all killing ourselves. You're being a short-term idiot. We're being suicidal fools long-term.'

Earl looked over at Tom and said in a flat voice, 'My wife of thirty-one years, Susie, died last Christmas in a very painful way, and that's when I started smoking like this. I don't really care fuck-all about living long without her.'

Tom slowed for a sharp turn. 'I'm sorry,' he said. 'As long as you keep the window down, it's none of my business.'

'Nope, it's not,' Earl said. 'But you did good back there. You're gonna be asking all the questions from now on. I'll just ride shotgun and try to find us some good burger places along the way. Fair enough?'

'Fair enough,' Tom said, and hesitated. 'But there is one thing I'd like you to teach me.'

'What's that?' Earl asked, a little surprised.

'Could you teach me how to shoot?'

'A gun?'

'I have my father's Colt with me.'

16

Gus juked right and then cut the ball back left, and the defender bit hard on the fake, lost his balance, and fell on his ass. Suddenly alone in midfield, Gus didn't hesitate. He ran right up the gut of the opposing team till their sweeper had to step up and take him on. That left the center of their defense wide-open, and one of Gus's wings cut swiftly in from the side of the penalty box. Gus led him with a well-measured pass that the winger smashed into the upper corner of the net for the winning goal.

The parents' section erupted, and Green Man was on his feet, punching the air and shouting, 'WAY TO GO, GUS!'

Sharon tried to pull him down. 'Mitch. Chill.'

'Did you see that move? He faked that kid out of his shorts. GREAT PASS!'

'You don't want to be one of *those* parents.'

Gus had separated from the congratulatory scrum of teammates and was searching the stands for him. Green Man raised his right hand, and Gus spotted him and proudly raised his own palm, an imaginary father-son high-five across fifty yards of soccer field.

After the game, Gus's team headed off to celebrate at a local ice-cream and video arcade. Kim was sleeping over with her best friend.

The big white colonial house was empty when Green Man and Sharon drove home. He had been waiting for a moment when they were totally alone. In the garage, he used a razor blade scraper to carefully remove a small, square decal from the black van's rear bumper. He cleaned it with alcohol to remove any trace of the adhesive, and then scrubbed the entire bumper with a dry wash of river clay so the surface looked equally weathered. Sharon inspected it carefully and nodded her approval.

They armed the security system, double-locked the second-floor door, and climbed to the third-floor library. They knew they were all alone. 'So,' she said, 'have you decided?'

'I have,' he told her. 'It's the last one, so it's got to be big and also deeply symbolic. There's nothing bigger in America now than oil. Probably there never has been.' He led her over to a map of the United States that hung on a wall and pointed with a finger. 'West Texas,' he said softly. 'The Hanson Oil Field in the Permian Basin.'

Sharon looked at the map and then at him and nodded. 'It's the right choice,' she said. 'They're making obscene amounts of money, and they're doing so much damage with their fracking and the chemicals they use and the methane leaks – and they don't care at all. Do you know how you're going to do it yet?'

'I have some ideas,' he said. 'It's tricky because I can't take the chance of lighting the oil tanks on fire. If they went up, I'd be doing exactly what I'm trying to prevent. And security's real tight. They have money to spend on keeping people out, and they're spending it. On the other hand, the field I'm looking at has a giant perimeter, and there's a river that cuts through the heart of it. Security never pays enough attention to rivers. I think I can bring it off.'

'I know you can,' Sharon told him. She added softly, 'And after you're done, it will be time for us to go.'

'Yes,' he agreed. 'If we can wait that long.'

She reached down for his hand, and they stood together, looking at the map and the big square stretching from near Lubbock, west into New Mexico, and all the way south to the Rio Grande, where the massive shale field held billions of gallons of oil and natural gas that some of the most brilliant engineers in the world had finally figured out how to unlock and blast free and suck out of the earth.

'I know it's been terribly difficult,' Sharon said softly. 'But they don't have anything solid on you.'

'We can't know that.'

'If they did, they wouldn't say they did. It's just a bluff, just psychological warfare.'

'Whatever it is, it's effective,' he told her. 'Sleeping is so hard now. I can feel them closing in. I worry about Gus and Kim all the time. And if anything happened to you, I wouldn't want to keep living.'

She kissed him gently on the side of the cheek. 'You wouldn't be the man I love if you didn't fear for us or feel guilt over the casualties.'

He tightened his grip on her hand and led her two steps to the window, where they stood arm in arm, looking out over the treetops that were soft in the afternoon light, and they were silent for several minutes. 'Shar, maybe I should stop at six.'

She looked up into his eyes. 'You're so close,' she whispered. 'It was always seven, with the seventh being the biggest. You should see it through. Finish what you started. We'll make it, and we'll go.'

'But if I slip up, even in some tiny way . . .'

119

'You won't,' she promised. 'There's no one else in the whole world strong enough and smart enough to do it. Hundreds of years from now people will recognize that you turned things when they absolutely needed to be turned and saved the world for generations to come. Someone had to do it, and you were the one. And I know as well as you do how mad that sounds, but we both also know it's absolutely true.'

'I believe it is true,' Green Man admitted in a low and solemn voice. 'But maybe you and the kids should go to the summer house ahead of me.' That was how they always referred to it.

'We always said we'd go together. The break works best and cleanest if we leave together – same hour, same minute, same second. That's what you always said, and you made a break work once before.'

'Sure, but it could also work if you went on ahead. I could make the strike in Texas and join you there. I'd worry less.'

'We should stick to our original plan,' Sharon said firmly. 'It's worked so far, and it will take us the rest of the way, to a safe and beautiful place with no more worries . . .'

The security monitor beeped as a blue SUV pulled up to the gate. It was Coach Ross, bringing Gus home from the arcade. Green Man pushed the button to open the front gate and then turned to Sharon and nodded very slightly. 'All right,' he said. 'I'll hit number seven in Texas and see this through just as we always planned. Now we'd better head downstairs. There's a young man about to walk through the door who, I believe, may need medical attention because he has eaten at least three pounds of chocolate ice cream.'

17

'Aim at that dead tree,' Earl told him, 'and don't close one eye like they do in the stupid movies.'

'It's an ash.'

'What?'

'That dead tree is a green ash.'

'Maybe it *was* a green ash. Now it's just firewood. Feet apart the distance of your shoulders. Weight evenly balanced. That's not bad at all. You've done this before?'

'Long ago,' Tom admitted, feeling the grip of his father's pistol and, very oddly, touching the best and worst of his father at once. He felt his father's coolness and confidence, and also his cold-blooded ruthlessness and taste for violence. As his finger stroked the trigger, he remembered his father taking him to firing ranges when he was as young as seven. 'Green ash are beautiful trees. They were all over Nebraska. But the emerald ash borer has got their number.'

'The emerald ash borer can crawl up my ass,' Earl said, and flicked away a cigarette. 'You really are a greenie. Fire when ready and expect the kick. Aim for that big branch about three feet up.'

Tom adjusted his aim slightly. 'You wouldn't want an ash borer to do that, because the females lay eggs, and the larvae feed voraciously,' Tom told him, and fired. The big branch splintered, and the dead tree shook.

'Well, looky here,' Earl said, impressed. 'Warren would have liked that one.'

It was the first time that Earl had mentioned Tom's father's first name out loud.

'It wouldn't have been good enough for him,' Tom said quietly.

'The hell it wouldn't. It was bang on target.'

'He would have found something wrong with it or my stance or he would say that my hair is too long and I look like a girl.'

'I've been meaning to talk to you about that hair,' Earl said. 'We're getting looks from some of the police.'

'Fuck you,' Tom said, and fired again, and the top half of the dead tree shuddered and then cracked and toppled over.

'Hey, you killed the dead tree,' Earl said. 'Is there anything else you want me to teach you about shooting, or can we go find the nearest barber?'

They got back in the SUV and drove along the long, flat roadway. Endless fields of corn and sorghum stretched away on either side of them, and in the far distance the low mountains were molten bronze as the sun rose over them. A sign announced the town of Destry five miles ahead. 'Talk about the middle of nowhere,' Earl said, and spat out the window.

'It's on our list,' Tom told him. 'The Destry Police Department.'

'What the hell is there to steal around here?' Earl asked. And then, carefully: 'I'm guessing your dad taught you to shoot like that?'

'Thanks for the refresher course.'

'I'm not sure you needed it.'

Seconds ticked by. Tom swerved to avoid some roadkill. 'Did you know that my father saved Jim Brennan's life?'

122

'No, I never heard that.'

'Many years ago. He shot a man who was going to kill Brennan.'

Earl fished out a package of beef jerky and tore it open. 'Your father had a way of being in the right place at the right time. You like the teriyaki?'

'It's too salty, but it's good. Do you think my dad used this Colt I'm carrying around to shoot the guy?'

'Probably,' Earl said. 'We get fond of our guns, and we keep them. Here, don't try to swallow this in one go or I'll have to Heimlich you.'

He handed Tom a piece of jerky, and Tom popped it into his mouth and chewed for several seconds and then said softly, 'You don't have to answer this.'

'Go ahead.'

'Have you ever killed anyone?'

Earl gazed out over the small town that was swimming toward them across the fields. It was red rooftops and stunted trees and a water tower with the name 'Destry' in big letters. He nodded.

'What does it feel like?'

'Not good,' Earl said. 'If it feels good, there's something wrong with you. But you do what you need to do, and it sounds like your dad needed to do it.'

'I'm not sure I could,' Tom told him.

'When the moment comes, anyone can do it.'

'I don't think I'd think I have the right, if that makes any sense.'

'Sometimes you think too much for your own good,' Earl told him, and then grinned and pointed. 'Look, there's a barber right across from the police station.'

A half hour later, with a buzz cut so short that it looked

like there was a black bowl inverted on his scalp, Tom faced the two members of the Destry Police Department. The chief was older than Earl and had stained teeth that he kept running his tongue over, as if to try to lick them clean. And there was a short female officer who went by Andrea and insisted on getting the men fresh coffee, which she proudly made from whole Starbucks beans. A sack of beans and the grinder were on a little table next to the coffee maker.

The chief and Andrea listened politely and shook their heads in unison at Tom's questions. 'I'm really sorry we can't help you guys, but I haven't seen anybody like that in the last week. Andrea?'

'Really wish I could help but nope,' she said. 'Would you guys like one more cup of joe for the road?'

'No thanks,' Earl said, getting up, apparently eager to say goodbye to Destry. 'We'll be on our way.'

Tom had noticed some platoon photos on a desk by a window. They looked like they could be from Iraq, but neither the chief nor Andrea seemed likely to have served recently. 'Is there someone else on the force we should talk to?' he asked. 'What about the guy who sits over by that window?'

'Oh, that's Dwight,' the chief said. 'He hasn't said anything about stopping a van.'

'Dwight just started here a month ago, and he's always out on the road,' Andrea added.

'Is that where he is now?' Tom asked. 'On the road?'

'No,' the chief said. 'He's helping Mabel Parker cut down her pecan tree.'

Tom and Earl traded glances. 'Maybe we should just get going,' Earl suggested. 'We've got a long drive ahead of us.'

'Why does she want to cut down her pecan tree?' Tom asked.

'Her cat climbs up that tree all the time and she can't get it down,' the chief said. 'So it was either the cat or the tree, and the tree's coming down this morning.'

'Where will she get pecans?' Earl asked, poker-faced.

'Oh, she can buy them at the produce stands,' Andrea said.

'Or at the grocery over in Fairmont,' the chief added. 'They sell nuts.'

'Can you give me Mabel's address?' Tom requested. 'I'd like to ask Dwight a few questions on our way out of town.'

The young policeman sipped a Sprite near the pecan tree, which stood untouched. 'She couldn't bring herself to cut it down, after all these years,' he explained, and gave Tom a glance and a knowing smile. 'Looks like you stopped at Felix's.'

'Who's Felix?' Tom asked.

'The barber. He's savage, but he's quick. You have to give him that.'

'He is quick,' Tom agreed, noticing that Dwight had exactly the same buzz cut. 'I wanted to ask you if you happened to stop a van, exactly one week ago, about an hour later than it is now. The only passenger would have been the man driving it, thirty to fifty years old, wearing a cap or a hat, who would have followed all your commands promptly. We think the license plate would have been from Ohio, Michigan, or Wisconsin, and the digits would probably have been all numbers –'

'Michigan,' the young cop said, cutting Tom off.

'I beg your pardon?'

'Sorry to interrupt, but the guy in the van had a Michigan license plate,' Dwight said. 'He had come to do some fishing out west, and he was headed home with a busted brake light.'

18

'Don't embroider,' Earl cautioned. 'You might want to help us by telling us things that you think could be true, but you don't know for sure. Actually, that will set us back. Just tell us exactly what you can remember.'

'You understand that we need to record this?' Tom asked, readying the recorder.

'Sure, and I'll do whatever I can to help,' Dwight said, glancing from Earl to the digital recorder a little nervously. 'You really think it was Green Man?'

'We don't know yet,' Tom told him. 'All we know is that the timing works.'

'Chief Griffin and Andrea aren't gonna be happy about being kicked out of their own police station,' Dwight noted.

'We need to talk to you alone, and this is the best place,' Earl told him. 'They'll understand. The questions that we're going to ask you and your responses are highly privileged information. You can't talk about them with anyone – your girlfriend, or some local reporter you've known for years, or even Chief Griffin. If you're asked, don't be polite, just directly refuse.'

'Yes, sir. There were things I was warned I couldn't talk about in Iraq, and I didn't say one word about them.'

'How many tours did you do?' Earl asked.

'Two, sir. Saw a little of Afghanistan, also. Almost three years, total.'

'That's a long time in a hard place. You served your country well.'

'Thank you, sir. I can't say I liked all of it, but I did my best,' Dwight said. 'Is it okay if I sit down for this?'

'Why don't we all sit down,' Tom suggested, switching on the recorder and setting it down on the table between them. They sat on identical black swivel chairs. 'Want some coffee before we jump in?' Tom asked. 'A Coke?'

'No, sir,' Dwight said. 'Let's get to it. I'm kicking myself that I didn't run his plate. I could have caught him. I was about to run it.'

'Let's start at the beginning,' Earl suggested, taking the lead in asking questions with his slow, measured cadence. 'You were out on solo patrol that morning?'

'Yes, sir,' Dwight said. 'I'd been on the roads since about six A.M. Still got a bad habit of waking at the crack of dawn from my time in the service. Drives my girlfriend crazy. I'd given a few tickets. Helped change a flat. Stopped at the Dunkin' for a coconut glazed. I was a mile out of town on Route 55 . . .'

'Is that east of Destry or west?' Earl asked.

'East, sir, so the van would've already driven through town when I saw it. I can take you there. It's the last Destry traffic light, even though it's technically outside of town limits.'

'We'll head out there after we talk,' Earl said. 'And you saw a black van?'

'It was doing everything it should, and I wouldn't have given it a second look except when it came to that stoplight, it braked, and the right brake light was out.'

'Where were you watching from?'

'There's a hedge on the side of the road. I was parked

behind the hedge. Some people don't stop for that light when they think no one's around. They just blow through it. Others speed up to fifty and even sixty to beat the yellow. So I was sitting behind the hedge, sipping my coffee, eating my glazed, and waiting.'

'The van drove by you, reached the light, and braked,' Earl recounted, 'and you saw that its brake light was out, so you turned onto Route 55 and pulled him over?'

'No, sir. I waited for the light to change and let him get going. Then I pulled out and followed, keeping about a hundred feet back, and I crept up on him.'

'Why didn't you pull him over right away?' Tom cut in curiously.

The young cop turned to Tom and seemed to relax. Earl's seniority was clearly intimidating, but Dwight and Tom were almost the same age and had the same buzz cut. 'I like to follow them for a hundred yards. Let them see me, and I check out how they react. Do they speed up or slow way down? If they've got anything to hide, you can usually tell it by what they do when they first spot you.'

Tom nodded. 'Good, I like it that you were judging his state of mind. Anything you can tell us about that, even hunches, might be useful.'

'But don't embroider,' Earl warned again.

Dwight looked from one of them to the other, clearly puzzled about how he could talk about his hunches without embroidering.

'So the driver of this black van didn't react to your subterfuge?' Tom followed up, and saw Dwight blink at the word. 'He didn't react to the little test you were giving him? He stayed calm and didn't speed up or slow down?'

'Nope. Steady as they come.'

'That sounds about right,' Tom noted. 'Do you think he saw you following him?'

'That hedge is a blind spot, but once I pulled out he probably saw me. I kept back a hundred feet, and then I closed the gap and hit my flasher.'

'Did you also turn on your siren?'

'Yes, sir. Gave him the sound-and-light show. He pulled over right away.'

'Did you call the stop in to Dispatch then?' Earl asked, but Tom cut in again.

'Before you get to that, I'd like to focus on how cooperative the driver was. Did you need to give him a verbal command? Or did he just know what to do?'

'He knew,' Dwight said. 'Some folks, you gotta flash 'em and then order them to the side two or three times. This guy couldn't have been more cooperative.'

Tom nodded and sat back, trying to hide his mounting excitement. He popped the tab on a Coke and took a sip. He had the strong sense that he was brushing Green Man for the first time, and he was surprised to find that his hand was shaking slightly. He closed his fingers around the cold can of soda.

Earl's poker face never twitched, and his voice remained slow and steady. 'So did you call the stop in to Dispatch?'

'Not right then,' Dwight said. 'I had just been chatting with Molly in Dispatch over in Fairmont, and I knew she was taking a bathroom break. I figured I'd get his license and registration and come back and run them in a minute.'

'But you'd already decided you were going to run them?'

'Yes, sir. We'd been told because of what happened over in Idaho we should run everybody we stopped. I'd given

130

three tickets that morning, and I'd run all their tags. You can check.'

'We believe you,' Tom said. 'You're doing great. Keep going.'

'I parked twenty yards behind and got out. Walked up to the driver window.'

'So when you walked up, from the left rear, you saw the van up close?' Earl suggested.

'Clear in the morning light, sir.'

'Describe it for us. Be as specific as you can.'

Dwight spoke carefully. 'Black cargo van, thirteen to fifteen feet long, maybe seven to ten years old. It had seen a lot of road, but it was well taken care of. The chrome strip with the model number wasn't there, but I didn't think anything of it. A lot of time those strips peel off and people don't replace them.'

'Could you tell the make and model just from looking?' Earl asked.

Dwight shook his head, just a bit frustrated. 'A lot of those vans from ten years ago look kinda the same. If I had to guess, I'd say a Ford Transit or maybe a GMC Savana, but you told me not to embroider, and I can't say for sure.'

'Good, you're being careful to stick to the facts, and I appreciate that,' Earl told him. 'Were there any markings or bumper stickers or dents or deep dings?'

The young cop hesitated, closed his eyes, and tilted his head back slightly. 'There was something small, on the far right side of the back bumper.'

'Like a little bumper sticker?' Earl asked. Tom waited, curious but dubious.

Dwight kept his eyes closed, replaying the scene in his

131

mind. 'Yeah, it was a little bumper sticker or decal and maybe there were one or two words and some kind of picture or logo on it. I didn't get a good look from the angle I walked up, and I can't remember more. But I can tell you the van had a Michigan plate. I always check out where they're from. I remember the slogan was "Pure Michigan."'

'Do you remember any of the numbers or letters from the plate?'

'Definitely they were numbers. A seven to start. I figured I'd be running it in a minute so I didn't look close, and it was a week ago. They blur together.'

'That's understandable,' Earl said.

'And if it makes you feel any better,' Tom added, 'if it was Green Man, he almost certainly doctored the first few numbers or letters so even if you could remember them, it probably wouldn't help us.'

Earl gave Tom a cautioning glance and then continued with his slow questions. 'So you walked up to the driver's side?'

'Yes, sir. He already had his window half down.'

'Were the windows clear or tinted?'

'Tinted gray. Side windows can't be reflective, but they can be tinted to keep out the UV. This one was tinted pretty dark. But like I said, it was already half down, and I could see the driver looking down at me.'

'How close were you when you first saw him?'

'I stayed back maybe two feet, like they teach at the academy. If you get too close or lean in and they open the door fast, you can get a door in your nuts.'

Earl was ready with his next question, but then he paused and reluctantly nodded for Tom to take over. They had reached the moment when Dwight might have been face-to-face with Green Man, and they had agreed before-hand that this would be Tom's territory. Tom tried a sip of Coke to calm down and realized that somehow he had already drained the whole can. 'Is it normal for drivers to already have their windows down when you walk up, or do you think he was being extra careful and polite?'

'Sometimes they're already down and sometimes not,' Dwight answered. 'But this guy was definitely being cooperative.'

'What can you tell us about the driver?' Tom asked, and he couldn't keep the excitement out of his voice. 'You looked up at him. What can you remember seeing in your mind's eye? Anything, no matter how small, might help us.'

'I couldn't see his eyes because he was wearing a black cap with the visor tilted low. I could see the bottom half of his face, and I remember thinking that he hadn't shaved for a while. Which made sense, because he told me he'd been camping and fishing.'

'Was there any writing or design on his cap?' Tom asked.

'No, sir. It was just a black driving cap.'

'How old did he look?'

'Forty to fifty, sir. If I had to guess, I'd say closer to forty.' Dwight shot a nervous look at Earl. 'But you don't want me to guess.'

'Anything you can tell us is helpful,' Tom said. 'Could you see the driver's eyes?'

'I stepped forward a little, and I think maybe they were black, but they were in the shadow of the visor, and I'm not super positive. They could've been brown.'

'But definitely not blue?'

'No, I don't think so.'

133

'And his hair under the cap?'

'Couldn't really see it.'

'The stubble on his chin?'

'Black.'

'Streaked with a little white if he was forties to fifties?'

'No, sir. It was all black. Maybe a week's growth.'

'Could you see his hands on the steering wheel?'

'Not that I remember.'

'So you don't know if he had a wedding ring?'

'No, sir.'

'Or if he was wearing gloves?'

'No, but I wouldn't think so. It was a nice, sunny morning.'

Tom nodded, imagining Green Man with the deer hunting gloves still on, driving through Destry and then realizing some local cop was pulling him over and the situation was critical. 'Tell us as much of the conversation as you can remember.'

'I always start by asking them if they know why I pulled them over. He said he didn't. I told him about the brake light, and he made a joke about how he had hit a bump in Wyoming that might have knocked a wire loose and it might have been a Teton.'

'So he said he came from Wyoming and he could actually make jokes with you?' Tom marveled. 'He was that relaxed?'

'Yes, sir, he seemed totally calm. I asked him what he was doing on Route 55 because most people take the interstate. He said he was an artist and he liked the color of the light on the hills. I'd never heard anything like that before, but it kind of made sense.'

'Did it sound to you like he had that answer ready,' Tom

asked, 'or did he come up with it naturally the way people do in conversation?'

'I'm not sure,' Dwight responded. 'But from the way he said it, I believed he was an artist. And he also knew about fish. I remember I asked him why he didn't just fish in the Great Lakes and what pulled him so far west, and he said he had caught his share of fish in the Great Lakes but he came west for cutthroat trout.'

'But he didn't tell you where he'd been fishing or camping?'

'No specific place, sir. And then I told him I would let him go with just a warning and he should get the light fixed right away.'

'How did he react to that?'

'He thanked me. He seemed real grateful.'

'I'll bet,' Tom said quietly.

'But then I told him that I had to run his license and registration anyway, on account of what had happened in Idaho. He didn't argue, the way some people do. He told me he'd have to reach into the glove compartment with his right hand and get the papers. I said go ahead, and then he'd be on his way. He started to reach down and that damn phone call came.' Dwight glanced at the pecan tree as if he'd decided to chop it down after all. 'Mabel's cat, Greta, was up in this stupid tree and wouldn't come down.'

'So you had to go help her right away?' Tom suggested.

'I didn't want Mabel to get scratched,' Dwight told them. 'She's more than seventy and doesn't see real good. So I let the driver go with a warning, and he said he'd get the light fixed at the next gas station. He wished me good luck with the cat.' Dwight suddenly thumped the table with his palm hard enough to make the Coke can jump.

'Guys, I'm sorry. If I'd run his tag, I would've caught him right there.'

'No,' Tom said, 'he never would have given you his license and registration.'

'He was reaching down for them.'

'If it was really Green Man, he was reaching down for a gun, and that phone call saved your life,' Tom said quietly.

Dwight looked back at him and swallowed. 'You really think he would've shot me?'

'He wouldn't have had a choice.'

'But we don't know that it was Green Man,' Earl pointed out, taking over again. 'Listen, you've been extremely helpful, but there will be more questions coming. So my young colleague and I would like to bring you back to Washington with us.'

Dwight hesitated, surprised. He had clearly not contemplated such a thing. 'Well, I sure wanna help, but I don't know if I can get away from my work here and I guess the plane ticket's pretty high . . .'

'We'll take care of all that stuff,' Earl assured him. 'It won't cost you a dime, and you'll be where you're most needed. I'm sure Chief Griffin won't mind sparing you for a few days when I explain things. Now we'd like to see the traffic light where you pulled him over, and then you should stop at home and pack up whatever you need to travel, because there are some folks in DC who would like to speak with you as soon as possible.'

19

Using his researcher's pass, Green Man had wandered through the stacks of the largest library collection in the world to fish out two dozen volumes and periodicals by hand. He was dressed in frayed corduroys and an old maroon sweater, and he could have passed for a rumpled college professor researching a book that would shed light on an esoteric subject and secure him tenure at some middling college.

When it came to keeping records, libraries were dinosaurs. Many of them used computerized systems and had digitalized their collections, but they preserved their old card catalogs and let visiting scholars browse in the stacks. It was possible to come to a library and access a great amount of material oneself, read it, and put it back on the shelves with no permanent data record that it had ever been looked at.

He now sat in the splendid main reading room of the Library of Congress with books and medical journals on fracking piled in front of him on a small reading desk. Studying intently around him – beneath the towering dome and glittering marble columns – were scholars from all over the world, leafing through obscure volumes and tapping away on laptops as they took notes. Green Man opened the first book and felt like an eager grad student sitting down to start researching his final thesis. This would be his last strike, and he was aware that he was starting to research and write his parting message to the world, so he wanted to get it exactly right.

He had followed this same process on his previous six strikes, and he knew his reading would grow progressively narrower as he began to laser in on a specific target and create a method for destroying it. He already knew a great deal about fracking, so today's reading was mostly background research. But he still took it extremely seriously because it was linked to the solemn act of passing judgment, and the stakes in this attack couldn't possibly be higher.

If he decided to move forward with this seventh strike, he would be taking on an industry that was among the richest and most powerful in the world and was also quintessentially American. He would be calling its newest and most profitable techniques into question and challenging its cutting-edge security, which was already on high alert and fully integrated with the national manhunt for him. He also knew he could not strike without killing innocent workers who had labored long and hard in the sweltering Texas oil fields in order to feed their families.

Before starting, Green Man clasped his hands in silent prayer and looked up from his books to the coffered dome nearly two hundred feet above. Decorating it was a century-old mural of the Evolution of Civilization, which showed twelve winged figures illustrating the civilizations thought to have contributed the most to world progress. The twelve started with ancient Egypt and ended with America, the cocky new kid on the block. America was depicted as an engineer, seated next to an electric dynamo, to emphasize how the incipient power's contributions to engineering and technology at the turn of the twentieth century had transformed the world.

And that was where Green Man started his background research, in America's brash and vibrant 1870s and 1880s, when the country had been bursting with keen and eager – not to mention greedy – engineers and great tinkerers who had created a series of dazzling inventions that seemed like miracles. There had been Bell and his phone, Glidden and his barbed wire, and Edison and his lightbulb and phonograph.

But there was one challenge that was in every way even deeper – pools of oil that were liquid gold and had collected for millions of years far beneath the earth's surface. The first wells had been drilled in northern Pennsylvania in the 1880s. The drill holes went straight down and tapped into small pools, and the profits were modest. The men who drilled them knew there was much more oil and gas in the rock layers around those vertical holes, but how could it be unlocked?

Edward Roberts, a Civil War veteran who had seen the effects of Confederate rounds going off in narrow canals at the Battle of Fredericksburg, came up with the idea of sending explosives into the depths of the earth to fracture the rock layers and free nearby oil so it could be sucked to the surface. He got the first patent for an exploding torpedo that could be dropped deep into the earth, and fracking was born.

Generations of engineers had improved Roberts's methods, seeking the right combinations of explosives to shake more oil free. In 1949, the company Halliburton had hit on the idea of abandoning explosives and instead pumping liquids at high pressure deep into the earth to crack the rock and liberate the buried treasures of oil and gas. This new 'hydraulic' fracking process was used with some success, but its very small profits made it too expensive.

By the 1970s and 1980s, there was a feeling that the once-great American oil and gas industry had peaked, and more and more oil was imported from overseas. Then things had taken a wild turn. In the 1990s, the American oil and gas industry had roared back to life with two innovations that allowed America's vast shale formations to be tapped.

First, horizontal drilling allowed engineers to drill straight down and then 'turn' the well parallel to the surface so that it could run through great shale deposits. Second, the fluids used in hydraulic fracking became more sophisticated as it was found that the right mixture of water, sand, and highly toxic chemicals could unlock shale formations. Oil production once again boomed across America, and the Permian Basin on the border of Texas and New Mexico became the second most productive oil field in the world, behind only the Ghawar field in Saudi Arabia. But America's sudden return to being a world leader in oil production had come at a wildly destructive price to the environment, and this was what he had come to judge.

The more Green Man read, the more troubled he became about this deal with the devil that had generated billions of dollars for a resurgent industry but done untold damage to the rock layers, the water supply, and the atmosphere. He read about the increasing number of earthquakes near fracking fields in Kansas and Oklahoma, in places that had previously been nearly earthquake free. He studied the statistical links between fracking and a variety of severe health problems, from birth defects in Pennsylvania to elevated rates of breast cancer in Texas. For every study there was a counter study, for every argument against fracking, the industry put forward its own statistics or proposed 'new safety practices' that would 'solve' the problems.

The scientists and lobbyists who spun these counter-arguments were handsomely paid. The ones Green Man hated the most were the handful who had once been environmentalists but had sold their souls and were now well-paid apologists for the booming oil and gas industry. He felt there was a special circle of hell for those turncoats.

As day turned to dusk and visiting scholars around him departed, Green Man homed in on the two threats he feared the most, because they would be nearly impossible to reverse: danger to the water table and danger to the atmosphere. He knew what a precious resource water would soon become – in the next few decades, millions of people would die and wars would be fought as reserves dwindled.

More than a hundred new wells were being fracked in the United States every day, and the hydraulic fracking process required between one and five million gallons of water for each well. What were the long-term effects of drilling through and beneath water tables and fracking beneath lakes and aquifers, towns and cities, and even the pristine Arctic Sea? No matter what safeguards were installed, could engineers really control the toxic brew needed to bust apart rocks when that liquid leached away deep beneath the earth or bubbled up to the surface as flowback?

It was that flowback – that ever-changing cocktail of destructive chemicals used in hydraulic fracking – that

Green Man began to consider as not just a part of the problem but as a potential weapon. In most of his attacks – as at the Boon Dam – he had used intrinsic weaknesses in the target itself to bring about great destruction. Flowback was stored near oil fields in tanks and ponds. It was often flammable and combustible as volatile compounds accumulated. It was a bomb waiting to be used.

Last, and most worrying, he considered the damage fracking was doing to the atmosphere and its potential to make climate change irreversible. Vast quantities of methane – a powerful greenhouse gas thirty times more dangerous to the atmosphere than carbon dioxide – were spewed into the atmosphere by the fracking process.

But even if that could be cut down, there was a danger that was greater and more insidious. Ironically, oil and natural gas were so-called 'cleaner' fossil fuels because they were less harmful to the atmosphere than coal. The industry touted them as 'bridge fuels' that would forge a necessary link from 'dirty fuels' like coal to 'clean fuels' like solar and wind. But Green Man felt this was a very dangerous premise – a tempting half measure that might doom the earth. It was a bridge to nowhere – climate change was too dire; there were only a few years left to make a radical change and cease using all carbon-burning fuels or the world would be out of time. The world had to see the grave danger, and fracking had to be stopped right now.

Green Man finished his reading and felt both the weight of having made a great decision but also the certainty that it had to be done. It would be a fitting final strike, the right way for him to go out, warning the world one last time of a serious threat. He left some of the books on active reserve for the next day and put the rest of them away so there was no record of what he had read. When he left the great library, a light rain was turning into a strong shower, and without an umbrella he let it wash over him. Thunder rolled, and lightning flashed above the capital.

The Library of Congress had an unmatched collection, but Green Man always came to this city before an attack for another reason. The men and women who ran the country were here. Though it terrified him to be so close to the people who were chasing him, it also energized him to walk near enough to the White House to see the columned portico of the northern facade, with its American flag flying on top. A president he abhorred slept here soundly while Green Man lay awake night after night, worrying about being caught but also about the fate of the world.

He ate dinner alone and returned to his hotel. He called Sharon and spoke to the kids, took a hot bath and a pill, but he knew he wouldn't sleep well, so close to his enemies. When the feelings of dread came over him, he lay back in his bed and tried to take refuge in something hopeful. There was a fantasy he sometimes indulged in, that was for him the environmental equivalent of John Lennon's song 'Imagine.'

Lying awake hour after hour in his dark hotel room, Green Man imagined an Earth a hundred years in the future, when humanity had successfully navigated past the current crisis. As dangers had mounted and the point of no return had been reached, people worldwide had realized the gravity of the threat and forced their governments and key industries to change their behavior. In his fantasy, a sudden groundswell of furious popular activism had, at the last second, saved the planet.

Greenhouse gases had been drastically cut back, and global warming was halted. Human population was controlled and drinking water rationed and protected. The overfishing and bottom trawling that had devastated the oceans were ended, and the fish stocks and coral reefs had rebounded. Pods of whales swam through plastic-free oceans, and polar bears hunted seals on great sheets of sea ice.

Green Man pictured smogless cities and pristine countryside with bountiful crops as free from genetic tampering as the fields of ancient Greece. Parents passed on to their children an appreciation for this beautiful world they had saved but also a sense of how fragile it was and how close they had come to destroying it. It was a future world run by responsible human caretakers who treasured their planet and had – at the last second – found the wisdom to protect and restore it.

But for this to happen, humanity would have to come to its senses very, very soon. People had to be shown that they could act to change things, even if it required tremendous personal sacrifices and risks. The wise but cautious masses needed someone to personify this risk-taking – someone who took on the greatest challenges, acted decisively no matter what the arguments were for moderation, and pointed the way forward to bold individual activism.

Was it crazy, or was it in fact the only way forward? Had he been chosen for this, or was he mad? Green Man had asked himself these questions thousands of times, and he had no sure answers, but he felt the truth in his heart. A city of policy makers slept around him, but Green Man got out of bed before dawn and walked the dark streets of the capital, seething with a sense of purpose and destiny.

20

There was no day or night in the war room. Dwight rubbed his eyes and tried to concentrate. He had never seen anything like this vast hangar filled with screens and high-tech gadgets and the best experts and investigators in the country. He was awed to be there with them and more than a little frightened to realize that somehow, improbably, he was the center of their attention.

A small crowd watched him from a distance. The two agents who had met him in Destry, Tom and Earl, seemed to always be there, Tom smiling encouragingly and Earl watching with his weathered poker face. They were joined by an ever-changing group – a tall, young African American, a short Asian woman, and a giant older man who lumbered over and introduced himself simply as Jim Brennan, handed him a business card, and said, 'Thanks for helping us out. If you need anything here, from strong coffee to six hours of bad sleep on a hard cot, call Jim Brennan, night or day.'

Dwight began by working with a young female police sketch artist, except that she didn't really sketch at all. She skillfully manipulated images on her computer screen to get a closer and closer approximation of the face he'd seen when he'd peered up through the window of the van. He had not seen the eyes or forehead, but he'd seen the neck, and the jaw covered in stubble, and the chiseled cheekbones. In response to her questions, he was able to describe the mouth that had spoken back to him, the thickness of the lips, the even teeth, and the slant of the aquiline nose that disappeared into the shadow of the cap visor. Slowly, incrementally, the image on her screen began to match the lower half of the face he had seen a week ago.

Then had come an automotive expert with a faint European accent who sat him down in front of a giant screen and showed him images of different black vans for hour after hour. The images were presented in exactly the way he had seen the van in Destry, first from the rear as he had followed it in his police cruiser and then closer up and unfolding toward the front as he had walked up from behind. The expert had pointed out slight design differences from model to model. After viewing the images and considering those differences, Dwight had been able to eliminate twelve van models and put five in a ranked pool of 'possibles' and 'more likelys.'

Now, they had actually driven the van he considered most likely – a decade-old black GMC Savana – into the hangar. A tall agent with a strong resemblance to the motorist sat in the driver seat, wearing a black cap pulled down low over his eyes. Dwight, feeling self-conscious, sat on a stool so that he was looking up at the man through the half-open tinted window. They both had computer tablets on which the lines that he could remember from the traffic stop were typed out, with 'Dwight' and the 'Motorist' speaking by turn, as if it were dialogue in a scripted play.

They were sweeping over this script again and again, and Dwight was surprised to find that, using this play-acting technique, he started to recall more words and phrases than he thought possible. A bookish-looking female agent who could have been a high school drama coach guided them with prompts and questions and constantly revised the master script on her tablet as Dwight filled in gaps and tweaked words. An older man stood next to her and occasionally stepped forward to ask Dwight the nuances of exactly how a particular word had been pronounced, repeating it two or three different ways and nodding at Dwight's responses.

'So you told him there's not much to see on Route 55, and then you asked him what exactly he was looking at, and he said he was an artist?'

'Yes, ma'am.'

'And he liked the color of the hills?'

'That's right, ma'am.'

'Try saying it.'

Dwight looked up through the van's window and wet his lips. He tried to sound casual. 'Not much to see on Route 55. What exactly are you looking at around here?'

The agent playing the motorist glanced at his tablet and replied, 'I'm an artist. I like the color of the hills.'

Dwight thought for a second and then told the female agent, 'I don't think it was "artist." I think the word he used was "painter."'

'How sure are you of that?'

'Definitely "painter."'

She typed 'painter' on her master script, and it instantly replaced 'artist' on Dwight's tablet and on the version on a large screen that the dozen agents were watching twenty feet away.

Brennan leaned close to Tom. 'So Green Man's a painter? Or maybe he's just a liar with a talent for being very specific.'

'He was asked an unexpected question. The best liars

147

work from the truth,' Tom said. 'He mentioned the color of the hills, and I've been on that road, and I sort of believe the whole thing. We're looking for an engineer who paints.'

'Green Man da Vinci?' Grant suggested in his gently mocking tone.

'Right idea, but he may not paint *that* well,' Tom said, ignoring the ambitious agent's skepticism. They all watched Dwight squint down at his tablet and rub his eyes. 'You should let him take a break and get some sleep,' Tom told Brennan. 'If he woke up in Destry at the crack of dawn, he's been awake for nearly forty hours straight.'

'It's not like he's going to sleep for eight hours and wake up with a better memory,' Grant pointed out. 'A week has passed. Any delay, any significant time break, will just make the memories fade more. If there *are* real memories.'

Brennan hesitated and studied the obviously exhausted young policeman. 'After they get through the script reading, we'll break for five hours. Before he goes to sleep, we should mention to our young policeman the possibility of hypnosis.' Brennan paused and looked from face to face, and cautioned them: 'The idea of hypnosis scares people, and he's got to do this willingly, so let me be the one to tell him about it.'

'I have nothing against hypnosis except that the results yielded from it can be controversial and they can also waste a lot of our time with false leads,' Grant said carefully. 'Does it make sense to keep pushing down this road and trying to confirm what's really little more than a hunch, given the resources we've already expended here without finding one confirmable and actionable clue?'

Brennan glanced at Earl, and the two men did not need to speak. 'We'll try the hypnosis in five hours,' Brennan said.

21

High in his tenth-floor corner office, Brennan tucked his big hands into the pockets of his gray slacks and finished briefing the attorney general. She had just gotten off the phone with the president, who apparently wasn't in a friendly mood.

FBI director Haviland was also on the line and listened to Brennan explain about their possible break in the case, but the attorney general didn't seem impressed. 'So this cop from Nebraska may or may not have stopped Green Man a week ago? The president has read some of the reports and has his doubts, and so do I.'

'The timing works perfectly, and everything from the van to his appearance checks out,' Brennan told her. 'My best people agree that it was probably him.'

'Let's say they're right. What has this cop told you about Green Man that pushes your investigation forward in any significant way?'

'We're concentrating on Michigan now,' Haviland interjected, and Brennan wished the director, who had no real investigatory background, would keep silent.

'You were before,' she pointed out correctly.

'There were three or four states equally in the mix,' Brennan explained. 'Now one has emerged as the clear favorite. And the cop has been helpful in narrowing down the make and model of the van. We already have agents going door to door, with our profile and a sketch of the face, checking out vans that fit the description and their owners. If necessary, we'll look at every van in Michigan.'

'How many is that?'

'Nearly twenty thousand,' Brennan admitted.

'And what if he stole it or it's registered in a different state?' she probed.

'The license plate was from Michigan. And we have the first digit of that plate.'

'Which may have been doctored. And the bumper sticker or decal that your cop says he may have seen was so small that he can't remember any words or images, so how does any of that help us?'

'Baby steps, but they add up,' Brennan said. 'We can only do what we can do.'

'And I can only do what I can do,' the attorney general replied, and it was clearly a threat. There was a pause that was longer than just for an intake of breath: 'The president is considering turning this over to Carnes at Homeland Security.'

Brennan stood very still, controlling his anger.

'Meg, I really don't think that's wise or warranted,' Haviland said.

'This is a domestic law enforcement case,' Brennan added quickly. 'All the targets were domestic, and many decades of precedent dictate that –'

'It has serious national and potentially international security implications that the president feels could move it into the DHS ballpark,' the attorney general interrupted. 'Truth be told, he doesn't give a damn about jurisdiction or process. He's just frustrated. Livid. Steaming. And he's not known as a patient man.'

'Neither am I,' Haviland said, 'and neither is Jim

150

Brennan. We get the urgency over here. We're doing everything right. We'll break it.'

'I've been betting on you,' she said, notably using the past tense. 'Let me know if there's anything you need.'

'Will do,' Haviland promised. 'Jim, anything else?'

Brennan hesitated, hating to ask. 'Did he say when he might bring Carnes in?'

She had built a career out of smarts and directness – which was often mischaracterized by her misogynistic opponents or the press as bitchiness – but Brennan had never found her to be anything less than fair. She gave them the bad news in a hard, flat voice. 'You have less than a month, and then you're out.'

'Okay,' Brennan said. 'Thanks for letting us know where we are.'

She wasn't done with them yet. Frustration was clear in her voice, as if she had picked up the impatience of her boss in the White House along with some of his colorful phrases. 'Where we are now is that Green Man is still out there, and he's presumably planning a new attack. If he's caught, it could swing a national election one way, and if he succeeds, it'll swing it the other way. He's become a nutty folk hero and rallying point, and the numbers are that close. And the man who has the most to win or lose is the man who appointed me, and he wants results now.'

'Jim and I understand the realities of that,' Haviland said. 'We're going to get back to work now and get some results. I'll personally call you night or day the minute we have a whisper of something good.'

'Wake me up with good news,' the attorney general said, and then she instructed Haviland to stay on the line and Brennan's phone went dead.

151

Brennan lowered his phone to his desk and glanced out the window as lightning forked over the Capitol dome. The White House was just visible from a side corner of the window. He stood very still, watching the rain slash the large window. Politics always played a role in this city, but from long experience Brennan knew that when political calculations began to interfere with a law enforcement investigation, it was a slippery slope to hell.

There was a knock on his door. 'Yeah?'

Tom entered. 'He's in a trance.'

Brennan turned from the window and apparently didn't do a good enough job of hiding the tension he felt, because the sharp young agent asked, 'Are you okay, sir?'

Brennan covered it with a question. 'Do you believe that cop saw Green Man?'

'Absolutely,' Tom said. 'Anyone who wouldn't believe that, at this point, would be . . . an idiot.'

Brennan nodded. 'The guy living in the White House has doubts.'

'Proves my point.'

The big man grinned. 'You did a good job finding that cop in Nebraska. Earl was impressed the way you sniffed him out, and nothing impresses Earl these days.'

Tom hesitated and then said, 'Earl smokes a little too much.'

'Yeah, I know. I was at his wedding. His wife was special, and they had a real thing going, for a long time.' Brennan studied the young agent. 'You've been working out since you came back from Florida? Lifting weights?'

'And swimming a lot. Just trying to deal with the stress and the crazy hours. I do better when I put myself on a routine, even if I have to work out in the middle of the night. I did a lot of late-night swims in college.'

'So you're not just a total nerd after all. That haircut?'

'Small-town butcher in the wrong profession.'

'And the pressed khakis?'

'Turns out if you look the part around here, it makes it easier to deal with people.'

'Don't take this the wrong way,' Brennan told him, 'but you really are starting to remind me of your father.'

Tom looked back at him. 'We'd better go observe the session, sir.'

They left Brennan's corner office and walked into the hallway, which was completely empty at this time of night. 'So you believe that Green Man lives in Michigan?' Brennan asked in a low voice.

'Yes, sir, I do. But the dialect specialist doesn't think he was raised in the Midwest. His pronunciation of a few key words suggests he grew up in New England.'

'What do you think about the bumper sticker?'

'Not a chance. Green Man doesn't tip his hand.'

'You think he's perfect, but he's not. Everyone slips up, everyone has blind spots. You do everything that's difficult right but one obvious thing wrong. It happens.'

'A bumper sticker, sir? Not Green Man.'

'I've got a couple on my car from long ago that I never notice,' Brennan said.

They reached a door, and Tom opened it and then followed the big man into an antechamber. There were double doors to a suite, but Brennan opened a side door and they stepped into a soundproofed viewing room that faced a much larger room through one-way glass. Brennan nodded to agents Grant and Lee.

In the larger room, the young cop from Nebraska reclined in an armchair. His hands were on the armrests. Dr Singh, a short man with graying hair, dressed in an elegant dark suit, sat just to his right and spoke to him in a resonant voice. 'You're walking up to his van. You can smell boxwood and sand. What do you hear?'

The answer was several seconds in coming. Dwight's speech was halting, as if he was filtering the questions and someone had hit a delay switch on his answers. 'Katydids . . . in the bushes.'

'What can you feel?'

'The sun . . . and the breeze on my face.'

'Can you hear your own footsteps?'

'Yes.'

'What kind of surface are you walking on?'

'Gravel.'

'Now you're getting close to the black van. Is there an outside mirror?'

'Yes.'

'Can you see the driver watching you through it?'

'No.'

The psychiatrist moved always from the general to the specific, careful never to impose himself or suggest answers. 'Look at the outside mirror. What shape is it?'

'Round.'

'Can you see his eyes in that round mirror?'

'No.'

'So you can't tell the color of his eyes?'

Silence.

'But you do see the back of the black van more clearly as you walk up?'

'Yes.'

154

'You're approaching that van from the left rear side. You're very close. You see the license plate. What color is it?'

'White and blue.'

'The letters are blue and the background is white?'

A pause. 'I don't see any letters.'

'The numbers are blue and the background is white. And you've told us the first number is a seven?'

'Yes.'

'What number is next to the seven?'

'I don't know.'

'We're filming this like a movie,' Dr Singh said smoothly, without the slightest change of tone. 'We're slowing down the speed of the images coming through our camera. Now we're freezing frame on the blue numbers of that license plate. We're starting to film the numbers through a tele-photo lens. The images are becoming larger and clearer. What number is next to the seven?'

The young cop sat very still, staring into space. 'It's curved.'

'Keep looking at that curved number. When I say the number out loud, please raise your right index finger. Is it a zero? One? Two? Three? Four? Five? Six?'

Dwight's index finger elevated slightly off the chair's arm.

Despite the fact that the viewing room was completely soundproofed, they had all gone silent. 'Jesus, he's really good,' Grant whispered.

'Vivaan is the best,' Brennan agreed softly.

In the examination room, Dr Singh neither praised nor chastised, neither accepted nor discounted. He went on in his sonorous voice, asking simple questions in a cadence that was both lulling and metronomical. 'What number is next to the six?'

155

'I can't tell.'

'We are looking through our telephoto lens. The first number is seven. The second number is six. Raise your index finger when I say the third number.' Dr Singh spoke the numbers from zero to nine, but Dwight's finger never twitched.

'Is it a straight number or a curved number?'

Silence.

'We are panning to the right, across the van's rear bumper, with our camera, to the far right side. There's a small sticker there. We are freezing frame on that sticker or decal. We are looking at it through our telephoto lens. The sticker is becoming bigger and clearer. Can you see the bumper sticker?'

'Yes.'

'What shape is the bumper sticker?'

'Square.'

'What color is it?'

Silence.

'Is it a dark color or a light color?'

'Light. And it's faded.'

'On that faded, light-colored, square bumper sticker, there is an image. We are looking at that image through our telephoto lens. The image is getting clearer.'

The young cop's fingers tightened around the armrests.

'Can you see the image on the bumper sticker?'

A whisper. 'Yes.'

'Describe what you see.'

'A . . . face.'

'What kind of a face is it? Describe the face.'

Dwight's lips twitched, but he did not make a sound.

'We are taking another step forward. The face on the

bumper sticker is looking back at you. What kind of face is looking back at you?'

Dwight had started trembling. He finally gasped out one syllable. 'Teeth.'

'The face that is looking back at you has teeth?'

'Yes.'

'Describe those teeth. What sort of teeth are they? Why did you notice them?'

The young cop's trembling grew more pronounced. He was sweating, even though the office was well air-conditioned.

'The sun is shining on you,' Dr Singh said reassuringly. 'You are walking across gravel. You can hear your footsteps crunching. You can smell the boxwood on the side of the road. You can feel the morning breeze on your neck and arms.'

Dwight seemed to relax slightly.

'You can see a face with teeth on the faded square bumper sticker. We are looking through our telephoto lens. That image is becoming clearer. Describe the face that you see. Why did you notice the teeth? What is so noticeable about them?'

The long silence was painful.

'Can you see other features on that face besides teeth?'

Nothing.

'Raise your hand and point to the bumper sticker.'

Dwight's right hand left the armrest and swam up through space and stopped.

'Point to the face on the bumper sticker with your index finger.'

Four of Dwight's fingers retracted.

'You are pointing with your index finger right at the

face. What kind of a face are you pointing at? Who or what is looking back at you with its teeth showing?'

Seconds ticked away. Dwight's index finger quivered slightly, jabbing at the air and also at the fabric of memory. He said very softly, 'Badger.'

'It's the face of a badger, with a muzzle and prominent, sharp teeth showing?'

'Yes.'

Inside the observation room Grant was already running a search on his laptop, and Agent Lee was dialing a number on her cell.

Tom glanced dubiously at Brennan and shook his head. 'I just don't believe it. No way in hell Green Man would ever leave a bumper sticker on his van and go on a mission. Especially a sticker with a picture that would tell us so much . . .'

'It doesn't tell us as much as you think,' Grant said in a low voice, glancing at his computer's screen. 'There are more than two thousand schools and sports clubs in Michigan that have a badger as their mascot.'

22

They discussed the toxic chemicals in flowback as they climbed through the deserted North Woods beneath the darkening sky. It was the least romantic subject of conversation in the world, but every minute of their time together was emotionally poignant. They had been lovers – and then friends and secret allies – for almost thirty years, and they knew they would never see each other again.

Even on the most tourist-filled weekends, this hilly forty-acre woodland sanctuary on the northwest corner of Central Park was fairly empty save for the occasional bird watcher, but on this cold weekday afternoon, with a downpour imminent, Green Man and Ellen had the Adirondack-like scenery all to themselves. It was hard to believe that they were in the middle of Manhattan and not three hundred miles to the north, except that they would occasionally mount a hill and the gray facades of tall buildings would appear, specter-like, over the treetops.

Green Man had spent two days as a visiting researcher in Columbia's Science and Engineering Library. He had fished out the journals he'd needed by himself and returned them to the shelves, so there was no data record of what he'd read. He was now certain that the liquid called flowback was the best way to strike the oil field. What better or more symbolic way to attack the fracking industry than with a flammable, combustible, and sometimes even radioactive liquid bomb of their own making? The fracking liquid was shot into the earth at high pressure by a diesel engine with the express purpose of blowing apart rock, and after accomplishing that, it bubbled back up to the surface as a convenient agent of further destruction.

Ellen stumbled, and he took her arm and felt an electric charge. It was always like this when he touched her. He had been married to Sharon for thirteen years and had kept his marriage vows and never been with another woman, but he and Ellen shared a history that neither of them could forget. He had met her in Berkeley when he was twenty-four and she was nineteen, and they had been wildly attracted to each other on every level. They had shared long arguments about the best way to affect different kinds of environmental change, they'd explored the forests of Northern California together with a tent and a double sleeping bag, and a year after they met, he'd bought a small boat and they'd sailed up and down the coast and made passionate love in every rocky inlet they anchored in for the night. He let go of her arm and quickly asked a question about volatile hydrocarbons to cover what they were both pretending they hadn't just felt.

Ellen's degree was in chemistry, and while she was now a world expert in greenhouse gases and the threat to the ozone layer, she easily discussed volatile hydrocarbons and the other toxins used in the fracking process that bubbled back up in flowback. Flowback liquid was always comprised of water, sand, and salt, but there were dozens of other flammable and combustible chemicals used in fracturing shale. After the liquid came back up, it had to be disposed of, so it was either injected deep underground or stored in metal tanks or in pits at the drilling site. The metallic tanks were vented, but volatile gases collected in them, and at the giant Hanson Oil Field that Green Man was starting to zero in on, there were thirty tanks a hundred feet from the Kildeer River, which flowed in under the security fence. That river would be his way in, and the bomb would already be waiting for him.

'If you ignite a flowback tank, in addition to the explosion, volatile hydrocarbons will be released in a gaseous state,' Ellen told him as he let go of her arm. They had climbed a hill and now stood at the top, looking at the red oaks and the buildings of Central Park West that loomed above them, and the gray sky that was darkening quickly to black overhead. 'The gas will be toxic and carcinogenic. But given the distance to the nearest towns, I don't think it'll pose a major health threat.'

'Except to the oil field workers themselves,' he said softly.

'Many of whom have safety equipment, including their own breathing systems,' she pointed out.

'But some don't. Or they won't hear the alarms in time.' He went quiet as he thought of them, and the pain was so evident in his face that she raised a hand and touched his cheek where the circles under his eyes showed nights of sleeplessness. 'I suppose it's unavoidable,' he finally said, pulling back. 'What about if a few of the oil tanks go up? There was an explosion like that in . . . ?'

'San Juan County, New Mexico, in 2016,' she told him. 'Thirty-six tanks caught fire. All the tanks were extinguished in a few days, and there were no deaths.'

'Thirty-six tanks went up and there were no deaths? That's hopeful. But I'm sure there was significant damage to the atmosphere?'

'Some environmental damage will be unavoidable if you

161

hit an oil field,' she told him. 'There will be less damage if you hit the flowback tanks than the oil tanks. And you'll be calling attention to something really harmful to the ozone layer that a lot of people don't yet recognize as a serious threat. And it's good that we're on high ground, because otherwise we might both drown in about five minutes.'

Green Man felt the breeze quicken as the foul weather system blew east from New Jersey and thunder rumbled over the Hudson River. 'I can't get away from this damn storm,' he muttered. 'It followed me here from DC.'

'I hope it's the only thing that followed you here from DC,' Ellen said, making a bad joke, and they looked at each other and smiled nervously. They both knew that it was almost time to say goodbye forever. She lived north of the park, and Green Man's hotel was on the west side, so the coming storm was hastening the moment when they would have to split up for the very last time.

They made a dash for the park exit on 110th Street, but the wind began gusting and the rain came down. Within seconds the first drops turned to a downpour. Ellen had come straight from a morning of teaching at Columbia and hadn't brought an umbrella, and Green Man had picked up a small and flimsy one for ten dollars from a corner vendor that morning. They huddled together beneath it as they ran, but by the time they neared the park exit the worthless umbrella had blown inside out twice, and the two of them were drenched from head to foot.

They stopped fifty feet from the park exit, beneath the partial shelter of a wide-branched maple. They were alone in the storm. He put his hands on her shoulders and spoke very tenderly. 'This is it, my dear. Go home and get dry,' he urged her.

Her hands on his chest became fists clutching his shirt, and she shook her head. 'This is not how I want to say goodbye to you, Paul.'

It was a name from another life, absolutely forbidden to mention now, but in the intensity of the moment, he let it pass. 'El, it really doesn't matter how –'

'To me it does.'

'Long goodbyes are no better than shorter ones.'

The raindrops were running down her beautiful and slightly desperate face, intermingling with her tears. 'Come back with me.'

'What? Where?'

'I live three blocks from here. I have a big, beautiful, dry, and completely empty apartment. Come back with me so I can make us some hot tea.'

'That's crazy.'

'I'll dry your clothes. I'll even throw in a high-functioning umbrella for the road.'

He held her tighter as lightning forked near them. Sirens blared as a procession of fire trucks sped around Frederick Douglass Circle. 'Crazy, crazy, crazy. Look, maybe I do want to go back with you and say goodbye properly. But we can't risk being seen together. We've been so careful for so long . . .'

'Who's going to see us? Nobody's around in this storm.'

'Your daughter . . .'

'She's got soccer practice for three hours after school.'

'Canceled due to flooded fields.'

'It's never canceled. They practice in the gym till six.'

'Your doorman.'

'Don't have one.'

'Cameras in the lobby and probably the elevator.'

'Not in my Harlem walk-up,' she told him. 'I don't know

what kind of posh joints you've been hanging out in. And if there are one or two cameras along the way, which I very much doubt, we're under an umbrella, so we'll be invisible.'

'We're not exactly under it,' he pointed out, squinting some rain from one eye, 'and let me say for the record that it's a worthless, porous, piece-of-shit umbrella that wasn't worth the ten dollars I shouldn't have paid for it.'

Ellen sensed that she was winning and laughed. 'We're under it enough. Stop arguing and just come.'

They were looking into each other's eyes. 'Why?' he whispered. 'Even if there's nobody on the street and your building doesn't have cameras, it's nuts.'

'This is the last time we'll be together and . . .' She shivered, and he held her tighter. 'It's important to me, Paul, or I wouldn't ask.'

'And I want to come . . . but it's too risky . . . I'm thinking of *you*, Ellen.'

'Sometimes you think too much these days. Just come.' She looked up at him and said softly, 'The first time you kissed me you didn't think so much; you just grabbed me.'

They were so close beneath the dripping shell of the umbrella that he could feel her heart beating. 'I was twenty-four, young, and foolish. Not to mention a little horny. El, I'm sorry, but it's really not safe . . .'

But she put her right arm around him, grabbed his belt, and guided him a step, and then dragged him another one. 'When it's time to go I'll let you go and never look for you or reach out to you again. But now it's time for you to come, so stop fighting me.' She dragged him a third step, and very reluctantly he let her lead him on. Scrunched together beneath the tiny umbrella, they hurried out of the park and up the street toward her apartment.

164

23

'Do you think it was the hypnosis, baby? Did they mess with your mind?'

'No, I'm just real tired from the travel,' Dwight told her. 'They barely let me sleep for three whole nights.'

'Poor baby.' Jenna came over to him and kissed him on the lips and straddled him.

He held her up by the hips. She was wearing short-shorts, and the muscles in her long legs were taut.

'Did you see the president?' she purred in her sexy voice.

'No, I told you, I didn't see anyone.'

'Did you see the Washington Monument? You know what it's supposed to look like?'

'No, I didn't do any sightseeing. I saw the inside of the FBI building.'

'Did you miss me?'

'Jenna, honey, please.'

She lowered herself onto his lap. 'Is that a yeaahhhh?'

'Sweetie, I'm really sorry.'

Jenna looked a little shocked. 'Wow. You really must be tired.'

'I could crash right now, but then I wouldn't sleep tonight.'

'So take a little nap.'

'I'm gonna watch some golf.'

'How will that help?'

'It's like taking a nap without sleeping. Could you get me a beer?'

'Oh, so now I'm the beer girl?'

'I picked up a sixer in Fairmont. It should be cold by now. Beer girl, please.'

'Call me that again and I'll smack you.'

'Don't bother with a glass, beer girl.'

She smacked him and got off him. 'Okay, couch potato. Sit there and veg. I'll get you your damn beer.'

Dwight sat back in his leather chair and watched a golfer with a big gut prepare to drive. He took a practice swing and then stood over the tee. He pushed the driver back high on his backswing and then pulled it through, and his torso turned and opened up as 1-wood met ball with a *crack*. The ball disappeared skyward, and the TV screen showed the path of the drive with a thick white-line graphic.

Jenna brought the beer. 'Here you go, Mr Excitement. And I brought you some corn chips in case they didn't feed you. Anything else before I head out?'

But Dwight didn't answer. He was sitting forward, staring fixedly at the TV screen, watching a tall golfer in a blue shirt drive. Again driver struck ball, and again a thick white-line graphic split the screen to show the arced path of the drive.

'Did you even hear me? Do you want me to pick up something for dinner?'

The golf action cut to the tournament's leaderboard, but Dwight was still hunched forward on his chair, staring at the TV, unblinking.

'Baby, are you okay?'

'It had a white line on it,' he said softly.

'What had a white line on it?'

He swung his eyes to her. 'So it couldn't have been a badger.'

'What couldn't have been a badger? Was there an animal on the golf course? I bet it was a skunk . . .'

But he was out of his chair and running for his laptop. He turned it on and started searching, and Jenna walked up next to him. 'Can you tell me what's going on? You're kind of creeping me out. Seriously, Dwight, I'm a little worried –'

'There!' he said. On the screen was a photo of what looked like a large and ferocious weasel, with a broad white stripe down its back.

'Oh, a honey badger. I know all about those,' she said. 'They were on some TV show I watched about the bravest animals. It said they kill poisonous snakes, and they eat honey from beehives even if they get stung a million times, and they'll fight a lion. So they're either really brave or really stupid. What's going on? What are you looking for?'

Dwight had his wallet in his hands and quickly found the business card. He dialed it on his cell phone. 'Hi, I'm calling for Mr Brennan. Sure, this is Dwight Hall. H-A-L-L. Just tell him it's Patrolman Dwight Hall from Nebraska. He'll know what it's regarding. Even if he's in a meeting I think he's gonna want to hear this right now . . .'

Jenna looked at the title and FBI insignia on the card and whistled. 'Wow, you know some important people.'

'Mr Brennan,' Dwight said. 'It's Patrolman Dwight Hall from Nebraska. No, sir, there were no problems. The flight was just fine. But I remembered something. I'm really sorry, but it wasn't a badger. Well, it kind of was and it wasn't, sir. It had sharp teeth, but it also had a thick white stripe down its back. Regular badgers don't have those. So I looked it up. It was a honey badger.'

Dwight glanced at the laptop screen. 'I'm looking at a picture of one right now, sir, and yes, I'm absolutely one hundred percent sure.'

24

She gave him a yellow cotton bathrobe to wear while his clothes dried. She had put on a soft flannel one of her own, and her long, wet hair was wrapped in a yellow towel. Green Man had never been in her apartment before, and Ellen showed him around with pride. She had bought it just before the Harlem real estate market had surged, using most of her savings and the money that her mother had left her. The living room had exposed brick and high ceilings and felt like a downtown loft. The kitchen was small but functional, with stainless steel pots hanging from a rack next to a window that looked down on an elementary school. A short hall led to the two bright bedrooms.

Ellen's was first, and he saw that above her bed hung a landscape he had painted more than twenty-five years earlier of the Middle Fork River in Kings Canyon, where they had camped together. She led him on to the last room and hesitated.

'Teens are private about their space,' he told her, misreading her hesitation. 'If this isn't comfortable, you really don't have to –'

'I want you to see this part of my life,' she said decisively, opened the door, and walked inside.

He followed her into the small bedroom, which was dominated by a four-poster bed and a wall of overflowing bookshelves. 'Looks like a bookworm raised a bookworm,' he said, taking in the nearest titles of an eclectic

169

collection that was stacked double deep on the shelves and included everything from romance novels to hard science.

'She started reading at four and never stopped.' Ellen's eyes moved from the wall of books to the four-poster bed, which was covered with an elegant quilt.

'Julie sewed that herself.'

'And I bet I know who taught her how.'

She led him to the dresser, on top of which were framed photos of a pretty black girl growing up from a chubby six-year-old jumping double Dutch in a playground to a tall and willowy eighteen-year-old young woman ready to take on the world.

'She's beautiful,' Green Man said, his eyes moving from photo to photo. And then, softly, with real emotion: 'She reminds me so much of her mother.'

Ellen stood next to him, pointing to different photos. 'That's Julie taking the penalty kick that won the league championship last year. She's gonna play D-1 for sure. Here she's picking up the eleventh-grade science award. To go with her math and French awards.'

'Her friends must hate her,' Green Man joked, but there were several photos of Julie with smiling groups of friends that proved otherwise. 'El, you're trembling. Are you okay?'

'Just still thawing out from that freezing rain,' she lied, guiding him over to a desk piled high with thick textbooks. 'And just in case you don't believe me, here are the awards.' Framed testimonials hung on the wall above the desk, from the Carlyle Academy's French, science, and math awards to a plaque from the Global Leaders for Tomorrow and a Gold Key citation from Scholastic's national short story contest.

'She's gonna have to get a bigger wall soon,' he said. 'Ellen, you've done so well, and you should be so proud.'

'When you're gone, she's going to be all I have . . .' Ellen's voice quivered, and she suddenly fell silent, with her arms wrapping around herself as if to contain some powerful emotion that she was afraid of.

Green Man sensed her pain and suggested softly, 'I think we both could use some of that hot tea.'

They walked back to the kitchen, where the kettle was steaming and preparing to whistle. Ellen poured one mug of hot ginger tea for him, and one for herself, and they sat side by side on the couch and sipped. 'This is good, but I should go soon,' he said.

'Your clothes will be dry in ten minutes. Finish your tea.'

He took another sip. 'Julie's sensational. You've shown me plenty of photos of her over the years but . . . I really felt her presence in her room, and it's such a strong and original presence. She's gonna do great things.'

'Yeah, I think so, too,' Ellen told him, lowering her mug to the coffee table and slowly turning to look at him. She took a breath and said softly, 'She's a big fan of Green Man. She gave a speech the other day that was just incredible . . .'

'Don't start crying again, or I'm leaving for sure,' he threatened in a gently teasing but also slightly worried voice, as he saw her eyes begin to glisten and well up.

'I'm not crying.'

'Then what are these?' He reached up to wipe away her tears and blinked away one of his own. And then they were kissing passionately.

It had been more than fifteen years, but he remembered

the heat of her cool breath and the soft hardness of her lips. For a few seconds he couldn't stop himself. Then he pulled away. 'I'm sorry,' he gasped.

'No, I'm sorry.' She was smiling through her tears. 'Or maybe I'm not sorry, but I know we shouldn't have.'

He stood up awkwardly, his voice husky and catching in his throat. 'Yeah, listen, I have to go.'

'So you're planning to walk out of here in a bathrobe? Good way to avoid being noticed.'

'My clothes must be almost dry.'

'I don't send old friends away in "almost dry" clothes.' Ellen dragged him back down by one arm. 'Just a few more minutes. I promise no more smooching, and I'll find a way to stop crying. But I don't want you fleeing awkwardly out the door in wet clothes as my last memory of you, either. Let's just sit together in a friendly and dignified fashion and talk about what comes next. Your summer place is all ready?'

He hesitated and then sat back on the couch. 'Yes, El, it's all set.'

'Do your kids know about the trip?'

'No, we haven't told them anything. We thought it was better to surprise them.'

'I'm sure you're right. It'll be tough for them, but they'll manage.'

They both sipped tea and lowered their mugs at the same instant. 'No more tears, but I'm going to miss you,' she said softly. 'The top theoretical physicists say there are an infinite number of universes out there – one in which every different eventuality that could possibly happen has actually happened. So in that multiverse there has to be one dimension where we somehow ended up together.'

172

'I wouldn't listen to theoretical physicists,' he told her. 'They're insane.'

'Can I just say I wish I lived in that dimension?' she asked.

'Sure, it's probably a nice dimension,' he admitted, and put his arm gently around her. She leaned against him in her flannel bathrobe and closed her eyes, and he slowly closed his own. He meant to open them in a few minutes and slip away, but it was a soft couch in a warm apartment, and he could smell her wet hair and the ginger tea. They were old and dear friends and very comfortable with each other. Green Man hadn't had a night with more than three hours' sleep in a week, and he didn't even feel himself drifting off.

He dreamed of his boat from years ago, rocking under a gentle swell from an evening breeze. They were anchored in a small bay, beneath a rocky cliff on top of which tall trees poked the purple sky. He was sketching the cliff and the trees, and Ellen was reading to him from one of her poetry courses. It was 'Lines Composed a Few Miles Above Tintern Abbey' and Wordsworth's poetic musings were more music than words as rendered by her soft voice. Then they were down in the dark cabin, their lips and bodies gently touching, and the boat had stopped rocking and lay silent and becalmed, and suddenly there was a crack of sound that might have been thunder . . .

But it wasn't thunder at all, it was the front door of Ellen's apartment slamming shut. Green Man opened his eyes and heard a voice say, 'Mom? There was a leak in the gym so they canceled practice, which is a good thing because I have a calc test from hell . . .'

Julie had walked into the living room, her dripping coat

173

in her hands, and Green Man bolted to his feet just as she spotted him and Ellen, both in bathrobes. 'Well, isn't this a surprise. Please excuse me for intruding . . .'

'Julie, it isn't what you think . . . ,' Ellen said.

Julie stepped sideways, giving Green Man the cold shoulder and facing her mother. 'I think it's pretty clear what it is. If you want to bring your boyfriends or hookups or whatever home and dress them in my bathrobe, could you please at least bring them to your bedroom so I don't have to walk in on you, and just maybe you should consider following your own rules . . . ,' and she was heading for the door again.

'Julie, really, *come back here.*' Ellen followed her toward the door and caught her by the arm.

'*And you dare to give Ron and me shit?*' the teen demanded, and pulled loose. She opened the door and ran out, and the door slammed behind her.

'Go after her,' Green Man said.

'She'll be okay. She's just upset because I walked in on her and a boy a few weeks ago and I threw him out and grounded her, and we made rules –'

'No, Ellen, she was really upset, and justifiably so. I shouldn't have let her see me, especially like this, in her bathrobe, a complete stranger, and she kind of has a right to be mad because we –'

They were both on their feet. '*Don't you tell me about raising my daughter,*' Ellen snapped, and the tears had started again, which was a very strange thing. She usually wasn't a crier, but in the past few weeks she had become more and more emotional, and now she was practically heaving with deep, conflicting feelings that caused her to hold on to the side of the sofa and fight for each breath.

'Hey, try to calm down,' he urged, genuinely worried. 'I didn't mean to upset you. Just take a few regular breaths and don't try to talk.'

But while Ellen was struggling to breathe, somehow fast, short sentences seemed to fly out of her mouth between gasps. 'No. It's not you. It's her. She's been all over me lately. And it hurts so much.' Ellen stood away from the sofa to face him and said, 'She's so angry with me.'

'Why? I can tell you've been a great mother.'

'It's not enough anymore. She's mad that she doesn't know much about her father. I told her his name and a few other details. But she wants more, and it hurts . . . like I'm not enough for her . . . like she feels incomplete, and she blames me for it, so much that part of her now is starting to hate me . . .'

He saw her deep pain and wanted to help. 'Of course you're enough. Believe me, she knows how lucky she is. But it's understandable that she's curious. She's at an age where she's struggling with identity. So don't take it as criticism. Just tell her all you know about the donor. The truth is always best.'

'Is it really?' Ellen asked furiously, and turned away from him. The towel wrapping her hair had come loose and fallen onto the wooden floor, and her long, wet hair shook wildly when she whipped back around to face him and said, too loudly, 'I don't know more about him than I already told her. I didn't want to know any more details about somebody who wasn't going to be in my life.'

He glanced at the door, knowing it was long past the time when he should leave, and said logically, 'Well, if you call the clinic where it was done, they'll probably send you some profile stats, because they legally have to keep that

175

kind of info for years, and it's hard to blame Julie for being curious – I'd be, and you'd be – and, Ellen, look, I'm really sorry to leave you like this, but I've got to go now.'

His calm and reasonable words seemed to infuriate her even more. She lost all control and struck him, a blow to his chest with her right fist, hard enough to knock him back a step.

He grabbed her, partly out of surprise, and her eyes were flashing at him in a way he'd never seen before in all the years they'd known each other. 'What the hell?' he asked. 'What is it? Ellen? Tell me! What? WHAT?'

'There was no sperm donor,' she said, looking into his eyes.

Green Man held her at arm's length and looked back at her and read the truth in her face, and he realized why she'd insisted that he come back to her apartment and what had been so terribly important that she'd needed to show it to him since they would never meet again. His hands fell to his sides in stunned shock as he gave a little moan and slumped back against the wall.

25

The envelope had arrived in the early afternoon. It had come into the FBI's main mailroom, a large manila envelope with a hand-typed address label. It had taken more than three hours for someone to open it and for it to be passed up the chain till a supervisor realized what it purported to be and that it just might be authentic.

Meanwhile, Brennan and his team had been busy with honey badgers. There were more than two thousand schools in Michigan that had the badger as their mascot, but only three had had the humor and creativity to select the much more exotic Internet celebrity animal, the fearless honey badger. One was an elementary school up north near Traverse City, the second was a Catholic school in a port town on Lake Huron, and the third was a public-school system in the city of Lansing.

Hannah Lee's people made the connection that one of the sporting goods stores that sold the deer hunting gloves with the rare copper-and-nylon weave was also in Lansing, and in a briefing with his top aides, Brennan decided that – for the near future – the van-by-van search would focus on Lansing and radiate out from there.

Lansing was the state capital and had the government buildings and courthouses. Its population was more than 120,000, and it had a range of industries, from government service to healthcare to automobile manufacturing. Several different environmental organizations had branches in

Lansing, since the state legislators were there, and there were also lobbyists from the automobile and fossil fuel industries. It wasn't by any means a radical hotbed, but it was a place a person concerned about the environment might choose to live near.

There were depressed sections of Lansing but also million-dollar homes, and lots of hunters and fishermen lived there and in the surrounding towns. Ingham and Eaton Counties had a high percentage of registered gun owners, and more than five thousand vans were owned by residents of Lansing or people who lived in a thirty-mile radius. The sports teams of East Lansing Junior and Senior High Schools were affectionately known as the Honey Badgers, and the cars of many team supporters sported bumper stickers with colorful, snarling, toothy images of the ferocious school mascot similar to the one Dwight had recalled.

Most of the senior FBI agents in the briefing room were intrigued enough to agree that the Lansing area should be a top priority of the search. A few, like Tom, doubted that Green Man would have made such a foolish slip-up and argued that it was either a false memory or – if the patrolman had really seen the bumper sticker – Green Man was trying to throw them off his trail. But the deer hunting gloves that were sold in Lansing couldn't be easily dismissed as just a coincidence, and there were strong arguments voiced on both sides.

In the middle of that contentious briefing, an out-of-breath agent had literally burst into the room with the news that an envelope had been received several hours earlier that contained a thirty-page hand-typed manifesto apparently written by Green Man. It was addressed to

178

'Taskforce Commander Jim Brennan,' and it contained the ten-digit numerical sequence by which Green Man always identified himself – which was a closely guarded detail never released to the media or the general public. The envelope had been mailed two days earlier from Manhattan, and the return street address turned out to be the Central Park Zoo.

A day that had already been intense suddenly became chaotic. A top forensic photographer shot the thirty pages of typescript from different angles, and the original copy and the packing materials were rushed to the labs at Quantico. Word quickly came back that the preliminary analysis showed almost conclusively that the typeface used in the manifesto matched the one used in Green Man's earlier letters and that two partial fingerprints had been found on the title page.

As Brennan feared, the fingerprints turned out to belong to two mail clerks. All the mailroom workers who had had any contact with the document were printed, with the results sent to Quantico. Brennan sequestered the mail workers in a downstairs room till he found the time to go down and personally warn them in the strongest possible terms that any leak about the contents of the manifesto or even news of its existence would be prosecuted as a federal offense.

Access to the manifesto was tightly restricted to only the top twenty members of the taskforce, all of whom soon sat in a silent briefing room on the tenth floor of FBI headquarters, reading hard copies of it side by side around a large conference table and taking notes. The tension in the room was intense – they had hunted this man for months, and now he was speaking directly to them and challenging them.

Brennan wrestled with the option of keeping the news of the manifesto from his boss until it could be vetted, but he knew Haviland would want to know about this possible break immediately. Sure enough, the director's excitement was palpable, and Brennan had to implore him not to share the news with the attorney general yet. 'If she finds out, it's going straight to the White House, and we don't know what we have yet or how it will help us.'

'But you're sure it's from him?'

'It has his code. It's in his distinctive writing voice. And it's real smart.'

'Smart how?'

'In both style and content. Yes, we definitely think it's him.'

'And you've also got that image of the honey badger from the van tied in with the store in Lansing that sells hunting gloves? You're following that up aggressively?'

'I've got fifty agents in Lansing and the surrounding towns, but we don't have anything solid there yet.'

'Jim, I've gotta brief the attorney general on all this. This is good news, and she'll absolutely want to know. And Carnes from Homeland Security is also following this closely and wants to help . . .'

'I'll bet he's following it closely,' Brennan said, and couldn't keep the anger out of his voice. 'But for the time being, this is my investigation and not his, so as long as I'm still running it, you've got to let me decide when to share information and who to share it with.'

'Okay, sure, Carnes can wait till you're ready. But the AG said very specifically she wanted to hear about any possible new leads . . .'

'And she will very soon,' Brennan promised. He knew

he couldn't keep it under wraps for long, but he was fighting for every half hour. 'I just want to be on firm ground so I don't embarrass myself or you.'

'Sure, I get that. How long do you need?'

'We'll know much more very soon. I'll call you in an hour or less.'

'Make sure it's less. And well done, Jim. I can feel you getting close.'

Brennan returned to the conference room looking so uncharacteristically exhausted and harried that several senior agents sitting around the big table who had known him for a long time stopped reading and stared at him, concerned. He told them that he had succeeded in buying them a little more time but that every minute counted. 'We have only two considerations now,' the big man told them urgently. 'Is this Green Man speaking to us, or is it a clever copycat? And if it is him, which seems increasingly likely, what in these thirty pages can we use to catch him fast?'

26

In the tense briefing room, surrounded by older and more senior agents, Tom read the thirty pages very carefully. The more he read, the more his initial skepticism gave way to utter confusion. This manifesto puzzled him even more than the honey-badger bumper sticker had, because he was certain Green Man would never tip his hand this way. Releasing a long and personal manifesto was exactly the way the Unabomber had been caught, and Green Man knew that. It didn't make sense that he would send his enemy a thirty-page screed chock-full of personal refer- ences and observations – every one of which might potentially break this case.

But Tom was confounded because the farther he read, the more he also became convinced that this was indisput- ably the work of Green Man and that on some deep level, the release of this manifesto right now did actually make a great deal of sense. Simply put, it was an eloquent call to action. Green Man sensed that the net was closing around him, and he was reaching out to his global audience and especially his young fans in a way he never had before. He called on them to organize, rally, and spread his message to the world. For the first time, he made his cause overtly political, challenging the president by name and describ- ing his policies with scorn. And he encouraged his followers worldwide to take bold and direct actions of their own.

They would not be terrorists, he assured them, and he was not one, either. He described himself as an environmental activist pushed by necessity to extremism – an Earth Defender, to use his own catchy phrase. He claimed to be taking up the honorable mantle from American heroes like John Muir and Aldo Leopold. He mentioned Edward Abbey and his writings, which had sparked the formation of Earth First! and the Earth Liberation Front in the 1980s and 1990s. Tom made notes on his laptop about several obscure activist organizers whom Green Man mentioned by name. It seemed likely that Green Man had known some of them personally, and by placing himself among them in the Bay Area and New Mexico in a specific time period, Green Man was providing the exact type of material needed for a metadata search that could unmask him.

Green Man seemed concerned by how he would be judged from a moral standpoint. He used his manifesto to place his actions in the honorable tradition of civil disobedience that he traced from Thoreau to Gandhi and Martin Luther King. He was doing what had to be done to right a wrong – and it happened to be the greatest and most dangerous wrong in the history of the planet – so he claimed that his actions were not only moral but were in fact mandated of him and every other right-thinking person. He explained to his followers, almost apologetically, that the fact that what he had done was more violent and destructive than Gandhi or King was not at all his preference – it had been forced on him by the scale and immediacy of the threat. The ringing focus of the body of the manifesto was about that threat – that the earth was at a dire crossroads, and the moment when its destruction would be irreversible was breathtakingly imminent.

Green Man reached back to his six earlier attacks and the letters he'd written to the public about how those targets posed grave dangers to the environment. He now sewed them all together with the most current science to create a frightening tapestry of a nearly doomed planet, its atmosphere trapping heat, its temperature rising, its oceans acidifying and emptying, its biodiversity dying off at an unprecedented rate, with all the harm driven by a species that had named itself 'homo sapiens,' or 'wise man,' but was seemingly hell-bent on its own annihilation. Soon, soon it would be too late, he warned his young fans, and they would pay the terrible price.

Tom found his loyalties divided in an almost painful way. Part of him followed Brennan's urgent injunction, and he read looking for any clues in the science or the references to specific people and places that might lend themselves to a metadata search that would ID Green Man. He parsed every sentence for obscure facts that could be sourced, or names or dates that might be cross-referenced to reveal where Green Man had met a specific person or when he had traveled to a remote location. For example, the manifesto described the destruction of two Caribbean coral reefs in such vivid detail that it seemed likely Green Man had swum over them, and a vanishing glacier in the Andes as if he had climbed up and seen it with his own eyes.

But even while Tom was making notes that might help catch Green Man, he couldn't stop himself from agreeing with the manifesto's central argument that time was running out on humanity and extreme remedies needed to be taken. He glanced up at the faces of Brennan, Grant, Lee, and Earl. They were committed law enforcement agents but not dumb people. How could they not be affected by this powerfully argued warning that all the rules had to be broken?

The agents sitting around him, with their strict, almost blind adherence to duty, reminded Tom of his father. When Tom had joined the taskforce, his dad had told him that he would never catch Green Man because he was a green sympathizer himself. After Warren had died, perhaps as a reaction to that last paternal snipe, Tom had tried to push all thoughts of Green Man's agenda from his mind and dedicated himself to simply catching him. His father's presence had always made him more determined and competitive but also shortsighted, pushing him to step into a boxing ring or try out for a football team without any thought about if he really wanted that or if it was the wisest thing for him to do. Now, hearing Green Man's voice speaking to him very directly, Tom couldn't help wondering if he and the agents around him were blindly and foolishly trying to stop the earth's last best hope.

He remembered his wacky sister on the golf course in Boca imploring him not to catch this man who might yet save the planet. Tracy had grown up with Tom and knew him better than anyone, and she had told him that he had to be true to himself. And the truth was that he had been an environmentalist since he was in grade school, and he cared deeply. He had never joined Earth First! or the Earth Liberation Front or any radical organization that promoted violence, but he had belonged to the Sierra Club, Greenpeace, and several activist environmental clubs at Stanford and Caltech.

While Tom hadn't traveled to the Caribbean reefs that Green Man described, he knew of them. He had been to

Australia and seen the bleaching of the Great Barrier Reef firsthand – and he understood that the world's dying coral reefs are environmental canaries in a coal mine, giving the critical warning for ecosystems nearing destruction. He had never been to the Andes, but in the summer after he'd graduated, with two college buddies, Tom had climbed Mount Kilimanjaro and stood at the top, not exultant but ashen faced, looking at the dwindling Furtwängler Glacier that once crowned the summit and would soon be no more.

'Time's up,' Brennan snapped. 'We've got to start making connections and finding smart and specific ways to use this. Any and all suggestions are welcome.' They had had long investigative careers with very different areas of expertise, and Tom was impressed by the analysis they shined – like a spotlight – on these thirty pages. Hannah Lee had picked up almost all the same data points that Tom had noted – she was thorough and razor sharp. For the first time Tom saw in person that Brennan had been right about just how good she was.

Tom sat listening and occasionally making suggestions while in deep inner turmoil, wanting to help them catch Green Man yet unsure if he should really be caught, doubting the manifesto yet more and more convinced of its authenticity. He had a doc on his laptop with photos of all of Green Man's victims in the order they had been killed. He clicked to it quickly from the manifesto, and as he glanced at the dozens of young and old faces, his resolve hardened. The arguments and expert suggestions flew wildly around the conference table, and if things weren't confusing enough, suddenly Brennan had to break off and take a phone call from Carnes at Homeland Security, who demanded to know if the rumors were true and a manifesto from Green Man had been received, and if so, why the hell Brennan hadn't shared it with any of his sister agencies?

Brennan didn't bother to leave the room to answer. In front of his top aides he replied tersely that yes, a document had been received, but it was being validated and under active investigation and would be shared promptly – if it was found authentic – with everyone who could help. Earl and Grant grinned as Brennan told the aggressive DHS officer in barely muted subtext to back the hell off.

They returned to analyzing the manifesto, but less than ten minutes later, the attorney general herself called, demanding an update and an explanation of why she had been kept in the dark. As politely as he could, Brennan began explaining to her the necessity of restricting access till the document was validated and initially vetted, but she interrupted to inform him that the manifesto had either already been leaked or simultaneously sent out by Green Man to the media, because it was now popping up all over the Internet. In fact, the president himself had just read the first five pages in the Oval Office, and he didn't appreciate being referred to as a belligerent, bumbling egomaniac with the brains of a cabbage, and he wanted to know what the fuck Brennan was doing about it.

27

He sat on a bench a hundred feet from the swirl of bodies and loud chants, and he watched the youth rally with a mix of pride and bemusement. They had clearly read his manifesto and taken it to heart. Their signs read 'Proud Earth Defender' and 'The Cabbage Head Must Roll,' and the angry speech booming out over Columbus Circle via a sound system was about how it was their planet and their generation's destiny and they must take matters into their own hands. It wasn't a direct incitement to violence, and the policemen watching the rally on foot and horseback did nothing to stop it or arrest anyone. But it was damn close – a clarion call to action – and Green Man had little doubt who was to blame for their passion, because he spotted several placards with his own supposed image on them, downloaded from the creatively imagined portrait of him on the Internet.

The young man speaking ended with a chant of 'Save the Earth,' shook a fist, and stepped away from the podium. Green Man watched as a tall, young black woman walked to the mic and said, 'Hi, everybody, I'm Julie, and I want to talk to you about the great die-off.' The speeches before had been loud and strident but short on facts. Julie spoke softly and stressed the science. She explained how, of the roughly eight million species living on Earth, more than a million were directly threatened by human behavior and were dying off at an accelerating rate. In detailing the chief causes for this die-off, she displayed an impressive command of biology, chemistry, oceanography, and atmospheric science. She wasn't showing off but building a case, and rather than cheer her on, the audience fell silent and drank it in.

Green Man watched, mesmerized, remembering Ellen speaking at rallies in Berkeley and San Francisco in the 1990s. Julie's voice and manner were eerily similar to her mother's – the understated yet infectious passion, the intellectual depth and easy command of hard science that lifted and transformed a political diatribe into an almost indisputable logical argument, and the charm and charisma that held a fractious crowd captive.

She ended by getting personal, telling the audience, 'Look, I'm not a terrorist. I'm just a high school student, getting ready for midterms. I don't want to hurt anyone or destroy anything. The most destructive I usually get is a hard foul in a soccer game. I hate public speaking, and giving speeches like this scares me almost as much as the AP Physics test I have to take next week.' There was appreciative laughter from the audience that this charming speaker who had built such a strong and scary scientific argument was now revealing her own normal teenage angst.

But then Julie finished her speech by switching to the manifesto, and she quoted Green Man's lines as if she had written them: 'But there are causes bigger than ourselves. There are struggles that require us to give up our own identities to take on something larger. We are under attack, and we must defend ourselves. Our lives are under attack. Our future on this earth is under attack. Our unborn children and the generations to come are under attack. And when you are attacked, you can't just remain passive. You must take action. The time when that action could be limited to peaceful protests and small acts of conservation is past. The

Bengal tiger, for all its deadly strength, will soon be gone. The Sumatran elephant, for all its great size, will be a memory. We're next, and we need to fight back as hard as we can!'

Green Man heard his own lines coming from his daughter's lips, and it moved him and exhilarated him in a way he could not have anticipated. The painful days of depression, the endless nights of insomnia, the constant dread of being caught, and the guilt over bringing danger to those he loved all seemed for a moment worthwhile and absolutely necessary. Flushed with this sudden elation and sense of vindication, he knew what he had to do. He had come just to listen and to see her once before he left forever, but that wasn't good enough now. She was right: it was time to act rashly, boldly, impulsively, and Green Man stood up off the bench.

Julie concluded her speech not by shaking her fist but rather with a bow of respect to the crowd, and the applause for her was the loudest of the day. She did several interviews with youth journalists and chatted with other rally leaders, and when the protest broke up, she walked to the bus stop on Sixty-Eighth Street and jumped on an uptown Broadway bus heading home.

Green Man broke into an effortless fast jog and ran with the bus. The early-evening traffic was heavy, and the bus didn't make the light on Sixty-Ninth Street and jerked to a stop. Green Man sped on by, passed it by half a block, waited at the next stop at Seventieth Street, and got on.

Julie was seated at the back, all by herself. She had taken a calculus textbook out of her backpack and was reading with deep concentration. Green Man walked over and sat next to her. He could tell she was aware that a man had sat down next to her while there were empty seats all around, but

191

instead of looking at him or confronting him, she turned her body completely away. She was at an age where she was starting to get hit on all the time, and she chose to ignore him.

The doors closed, and the bus started uptown. 'Hi, Julie,' he said in as quiet and calm a voice as he could manage under the circumstances. The truth was that he had no idea what he was doing on this bus and no notion at all of what he was about to say. All he knew, after hearing her speak, was that he had to see her and talk to her once.

Julie glanced up, surprised to hear her name from someone she didn't recognize, and then she stared at him: 'I know you. You're my mom's boyfriend. What are you doing here?'

'I'm not your mom's boyfriend.'

'Boyfriend, hookup, nooner, whatever. I saw you guys together, and it was pretty obvious what was going on. What are you doing on this bus?'

'I can understand why you think that, but you're wrong. We're just very old and dear friends, and we got caught in a cold rain, which is why we were wearing bathrobes. I'm sorry about that. I know the way it looked must have been upsetting. But we're really just close friends, which actually explains what I'm doing on this bus. I'm here because I want to talk to you about your mom.'

'Well, I don't want to talk to you about that,' she said. 'Go away.'

'I will,' he assured her. 'Very soon. And I won't try to talk to you at all if you don't want or force you to hear anything you might not want to hear. I promise. But I'd ask you to listen for a minute or two. I heard your speech at that rally, and it was tremendously powerful and impressive. I know this sounds a little strange since we just met,

192

but you reminded me of your mom and . . . I couldn't be more proud of you . . .' His voice broke, and he fell silent.

Julie put the calculus book on her lap and glanced quickly around the bus. They were alone in the back, but there were a dozen people in the middle section, including three teens from the rally, and the front was packed, so it clearly felt safe to her as a place to talk to a possibly insane stranger who somehow knew her mother. 'Well, that may be intended as a compliment, but it sounds like you were stalking me. And if you really are an old and dear friend of my mom's, don't you think I would have met you before?'

'Nope,' Green Man told her. 'Oddly enough, no.'

'Why not?'

'I can't explain that. And we only have a minute to talk now. I promise everything I tell you will be true. Your mother is the best person I've ever known. And she loves you very much. You mean everything to her.'

Julie's face softened despite herself.

'And I get that you're at an age where you have questions and she can't give you the specific answers you want, so you blame her. Please don't do that. It's not her fault. I know this isn't what you want to hear, but you should just thank her and feel grateful that you won the mom sweepstakes, because you really did and –'

'*Don't tell me what I should do or feel.* Whoever you are, you're making me really uncomfortable. I want you to get off this bus now, or I'm going to let the driver know that you're bothering me, and there's a police car right on that corner up ahead.'

'I'm going to get off at Ninety-First Street,' he told her, 'and you'll never see me again.' He almost pleaded, in a soft voice: 'So just give me ten more blocks and I'll be gone for good. Okay?'

Julie hesitated. 'Ten blocks, and they're short. If you have something to say to me, you'd better say it fast.'

'You remind me so much of your mother,' Green Man told her, speaking more quickly. 'That's exactly what she would have said. I met her when she was just one year older than you are now, and I saw her speak at rallies, so it was kind of eerie watching you today because you are her spitting image. And as much as she's accomplished, I think you're going to accomplish even more.'

The deep emotion in his voice made Julie turn fully around in her seat to study him. 'Who *are* you?'

He met her gaze. 'Julie, your mom would like to answer all your questions, but she can't. And what I really wanted to tell you is that you shouldn't keep asking her things. You're making her feel incomplete and like she hasn't been a good mother, and she's going through a more difficult time right now than you can possibly know, so she needs your unconditional love and support. I know I don't have the right to ask this, but please just be there for her.'

'If you care about her so much, why don't *you* be there for her?'

'Because I can't.'

'Why not?'

'Because I'm going away.'

'There's email, right? And telephone calls?'

'No, there's no email and no telephone calls. I'll never speak to her or you again after today. I'll be dead and buried to her. But I'll feel better knowing that you're there for her, and not angry . . . And, Julie, my ten blocks are up. This is my stop.'

194

Green Man wanted to say much more, but a nanny and the two young brats she was supposedly watching were heading up the aisle into the back. The nanny was on her cell, speaking in fast Haitian Creole, and the two brats were swatting each other with plastic swords. The space in the back of the bus was no longer private, and the bus was already slowing for the stop on Ninety-First and Riverside.

Green Man stood and whispered, 'Goodbye, Julie, and may God bless you,' and then he dodged a brat's plastic sword, walked to the door, and stepped off onto the curb. He stood still, facing out at Riverside Park and the river. He listened to the bus pull away behind him and exhaled. Then a voice said, 'Hey, you, wait a minute.'

He turned and saw Julie standing there as the bus drove away up Riverside Drive. She was a tall and obviously very nervous teenager in jeans and a denim jacket, and she stood awkwardly, with her long arms dangling down to her sides. 'You can't just say those things to me and leave like that.'

'You're right,' he acknowledged. 'I didn't plan to talk to you, but I couldn't stop myself. It was selfish and self-indulgent. I'm sorry. I shouldn't have.'

'But you did,' she said. 'So why don't you have the courage to tell me what you really came to say?' She stepped a little closer. 'Before you die or go off to the ends of the earth or erase yourself from the picture or whatever weird thing you have in mind.' Her voice got a little softer as she asked, 'Are you dying?'

'No,' he told her. 'That wasn't meant to be taken literally.'

'I didn't think so. Because you look healthy. But I volunteered in a hospice, and the way you talked reminded me of

195

how people there sometimes spoke about dying. So where are you going that you can't write or email anyone?'

'To my summer house.'

'And where is that?'

'I can't tell you.'

She put her hands in the pockets of her jacket. 'Are you always this annoying? It's hard to believe my mother would put up with it.'

He didn't remember either of them starting to walk, but they were both moving along the sidewalk beneath the trees. It was a cool but beautiful late-fall evening, and parents who had come home from long workdays were taking their kids to the park for a precious half hour in the playground before it got too dark.

They reached the Soldiers' and Sailors' Monument, and Green Man sat on a marble bench. Julie hesitated and sat down a few inches from him. 'I don't mean to be annoying,' he said.

'But you are.'

'And I also don't think we should really be talking.'

'But you followed me to a rally, and you followed me onto a bus, and now we're here. Nothing that you say makes any sense. Why can't you just talk normally?'

'I wish I could.'

'So you are capable of that?'

'Yes.'

'Are you married?'

The question was unexpected. He nodded.

'Do you have kids?'

'Yes.'

'Do you talk straight to your family?'

'I try my best.'

'Do you tell the truth to my mom? She must trust you if you're really such an old friend and she brought you to our apartment.'

'Yes, I've always told the truth to your mother.'

'Then try telling it to me. On the bus, when you told me not to ask my mom any more questions, what kind of questions were you talking about?'

'The ones you've been asking her lately.'

Julie looked at him. 'You mean about how when she neared thirty she got fed up with men disappointing her so she went to a clinic in LA to get pregnant?'

He nodded.

'By some donor named James, who I don't know hardly anything about?'

'Those kinds of questions.'

Her voice trembled. 'Do you know more about him than I do?'

'All I know is how much Ellen loves you and that you should leave it there, and not press her –'

'Quiet,' Julie said. 'When my mom first told me about James, she was crying and she got really emotional. She said it was because she had lied and told me she didn't know anything about him.' She was silent for a moment, studying Green Man carefully. 'But was the lie she was crying about really the one she was about to tell me?' Julie was staring at Green Man very closely now, studying his face and the lines of his cheekbones and forehead. When she spoke, it was barely a whisper, but it somehow seemed very loud. 'Are you fast?'

'What?'

She was sitting perfectly still, frozen, as if she didn't dare move so much as a finger or it might snap off. 'Are you a fast runner?'

'I wouldn't say that . . .'

'I saw you running alongside the bus, before you got on. You were really moving. You passed us.'

Green Man found it almost painful to look back at her, but he also couldn't look away. 'I guess I can run okay for a man my age. Julie, I need to go . . .'

Her lower lip quivered, but when she spoke, her voice was steady: 'When you were young, I bet you were super fast.'

'Maybe.'

And then, so softly it almost wasn't asked at all: 'Are you my father?'

There was a long and silent moment, and then Green Man said gently and very carefully, 'Your mother told me what she told you. That she got pregnant from an anonymous donor at a clinic in Los Angeles, and she's never lied to me . . .'

'That's not an answer.'

'It's the only one I can give you.'

'So if you *were* my father, you wouldn't tell me the truth even now?'

He couldn't say anything.

She exhaled a long breath and stood up, hands on her hips, looking down at him, and her voice swelled with anger. 'Because if you *are* my father, giving me some sort of lame goodbye speech before you disappear forever, I want you to know that I hate you. I really do. I hate you for not being there and for your silence, which was really a lie, and for missing out on my childhood and then showing up suddenly like I should just accept it and listen to your advice and platitudes, and for all your weakness and the fucking cowardice . . .'

198

He stood also and surprised her by putting his hands on her shoulders. 'And what if there was a good reason your father couldn't tell you the truth?'

'That's total bullshit. What good reason could there possibly be for a lie like that? It's just another excuse –'

'But what if it's not? What if the truth was something you couldn't possibly handle? What if it was unfair to ask you to handle it?'

'You don't know me,' Julie told him fiercely. 'I can handle anything. You're just a coward, and I don't want to hear any more of this . . .'

He knew he couldn't explain, and it would be beyond crazy to even try. Anything further he revealed would only endanger her and himself, and he had been so incredibly careful for many years. So he was absolutely shocked to hear himself ask, 'What if the truth would put the weight of the world on your shoulders?'

The scale of the question took her by surprise. She was thinking wildly – furious but also excited and baffled. 'What do you mean? Who are you?'

He looked deep into her eyes, and for a long moment they were both silent as the stiffening evening wind from the river gusted around them, and then he whispered the words that she had ended her speech with a few minutes earlier: 'There are causes bigger than ourselves. There are struggles that require us to give up our own identities to take on something larger.'

She didn't understand at first, but then her eyes narrowed as she recognized the words from the manifesto and a glimmering of comprehension and terror flooded her face, and she broke away from him, and turned and ran into Riverside Park.

28

'It was developed to debunk Shakespeare?' Brennan said doubtfully, and took a big gulp of Guinness. This was the first time he had been away from the taskforce's war room or FBI headquarters in almost a week, and while he was clearly exhausted, he also looked determined to try to enjoy this hour in an Irish pub in Georgetown. The Clancy Brothers' 'Wild Colonial Boy' blared from the sound system, and in a corner four men were throwing darts.

'Well, not exactly to debunk him,' Tom explained, and to be polite he took a small sip of his own beer. 'But it's pretty conclusively shown that he didn't solely write all of the plays that have been attributed to him. And it's not limited to Shakespeare. Stylometrics has been used on lots of other texts, from the Old Testament to the Book of Mormon. But I happen to know about it because I studied with a brilliant and slightly nutty Shakespeare professor at Stanford who also has a background in statistics and computer modeling, and he was at the forefront of what's going on with style analysis and artificial intelligence.'

'Only at Stanford,' Brennan muttered, shaking his head. 'Why don't they just let old Shakespeare alone?' The taskforce commander had a linen napkin tucked over his white shirt and a heaping plate of corned beef and cabbage in front of him. With the clear joy of a big man who liked to eat, he dug in, and Tom took a forkful of his lamb stew. 'So, does it actually work?' Brennan asked as he chewed.

He swallowed, washed down the meat with some stout, and demanded, 'And why do you think this can help us catch Green Man? Because I'd put my money on a thousand law enforcement officers going door to door in Michigan looking for black vans and honey badger bumper stickers.'

'That might work, too,' Tom admitted, 'but stylometrics could be a lot faster and cost a lot less. The techniques have been developed for more than a century, and in the last twenty years they've taken a giant leap forward. The basic idea is simple – you can use statistics to analyze texts stylistically and tell who wrote them. For example, Shakespeare scholars like my Professor Shaw at Stanford want to know which of his plays he wrote by himself and which he collaborated on. If it was a collaboration, they're eager to identify which of the speeches Shakespeare wrote himself and which other Jacobean playwrights like Thomas Middleton might have contributed.'

'And can they really tell that?' Brennan asked doubtfully. 'Break five-hundred-year-old plays down speech by speech and figure out who wrote which lines?'

'With almost freakish accuracy,' Tom said. 'It's a kind of literary forensics that combines computer modeling and artificial intelligence. The number of syntactical, philological, and lexicological elements they take into account increases year by year, so it keeps getting more sophisticated and accurate. My professor was working with an artificial intelligence expert at Oxford named Leung, who's world class.'

Brennan looked back, and it was unclear if the big man was having difficulty trying to swallow a large bite of corned beef or understand the word 'lexicological.' 'Okay,' he finally said, 'but when you're talking about Shakespeare and who was it . . . ?'

'Middleton.'

'Those are two well-known playwrights, and I get it that an expert might be able to use their bodies of work to compare their styles and word choices in a statistical way to figure out who wrote what lines. But we don't know who Green Man is, so what would we be comparing his manifesto to?'

'That's what I'm trying to tell you. You don't need to know that any longer,' Tom explained. 'We've reached the point where experts can use stylometrics to create a statistical stylistic profile of a writer – just like a creative fingerprint. And once they have it, they can do what they do with fingerprints – run it by millions of other documents on the Internet till they get a match with a real person. And that real person will be Green Man.'

Brennan lowered his fork. 'Just like that.'

'Well, in theory. There are some variables, like how much Green Man has written in his life that's out there. Considering his education level, I'm betting it's a lot, and it wouldn't surprise me if he's published professionally, which would make this even easier. I've given the names of the world experts on stylometrics to Hannah Lee, and she's already following up.'

'Yeah, she's very gung ho on this,' Brennan acknowledged. 'But she wanted to know what I want to know – why don't you do it yourself?'

'Hannah's great. You were right about that. She's as good or better than I am.'

'Nice of you to say. But this was your idea. You're bringing us an interesting approach, not to mention one of your old professors in the mix. Why not lead the charge and see where it goes?'

Tom pushed some lamb around with a fork. 'I'm not sure I believe in it.'

'This statistical approach to style?'

'No, the manifesto.'

'I had plenty of my own doubts,' Brennan admitted. 'But we're comfortable now that it's Green Man's work.'

'Yeah, but in some way that I don't understand, it's also not him,' Tom said.

'What does that mean?'

'I'm not sure.'

'You think he's fucking with us?'

'He'd never show his hand this way. It goes against everything I understand about him. It must be some kind of smoke screen or misdirection.'

'We know enough about him now so that if he's misdirecting us, we'll pick it up almost immediately. We know where he struck, when he struck, and in each case exactly how he struck. And whatever else he's trying to do with the manifesto, he's also certainly showing us his hand. You can't write thirty pages and not reveal very specific and significant things about yourself.'

'No doubt that's true. I don't pretend to understand why he's doing it. But he's been ahead of us every step of the way.'

The bar was well air-conditioned, but the big man had started to perspire. He drew the back of a hand across his glistening forehead. 'You tend to give him too much credit, Tom. Nobody bats a thousand. He wasn't one step ahead of us when we found the fibers from the glove. And I don't think he was counting on the Nebraska cop pulling him over for a broken brake light.'

'Those were minor mistakes. Unpredictable accidents.'

'He didn't make any minor mistakes in his first five attacks. I've been doing this a long time, and believe me, he's feeling the pressure. I haven't slept well in weeks. I carry this case around with me. And whatever pressure I'm feeling, he's feeling it times ten. He wouldn't be human if he didn't start making mistakes.'

'I'm sure that's true, but I don't believe he'd leave a bumper sticker on his van, and I don't trust the manifesto. I wish I had an answer to why he sent it.'

Brennan dabbed sweat off his cheek with a corner of the napkin, and it slipped off and slid down his chest onto the table. 'Suppose his real motive is political? The president is a shrewd political animal – what if everything he fears about the coming election is exactly correct? It's gonna be close, and the environment will be a crucial issue – a watershed moment in American history. Each time Green Man has struck, he's given the polls a solid nudge. By politicizing his cause in his manifesto and taking on the president directly, he may have done more to change the course of American history than blowing up five more dams.'

'That political motive at least makes sense,' Tom conceded. He didn't add that he had a lot of sympathy for Green Man's politicizing his cause. There were many good reasons for wanting to change the direction of the country's environmental policies, and very quickly. But sitting across from this taskforce commander he admired, who was wholly committed to catching Green Man, reminded

Tom that if they didn't catch the terrorist quickly, he would strike again, and more innocent people would surely die. 'But there's something about the manifesto that I still just don't buy. If you and Hannah Lee want to pursue it, I've given you my best shot. But since there's significant time pressure, I think I can be more helpful going off in another direction that I do believe in. And there is significant time pressure, right?'

Brennan nodded, grimaced slightly, and massaged his neck.

'You okay?'

'Just a stiff neck. I've been reading too much. Yeah, there's a loudly ticking clock.'

Tom hesitated and then asked more softly, 'If you don't mind my asking, how long do you think we have?'

Washington DC was a small town, and Brennan glanced to either side. No one was within earshot. 'Two weeks. Three at the outside . . . and then it'll be gone.'

'That's insane. How could they possibly take this case away from you?'

The older man's face perceptibly hardened. 'No one's gonna take this away from me because we'll crack it in time. And I trust your instincts. They were spot on about going to Nebraska . . .'

'I got a little lucky there.'

'I don't believe in luck,' Brennan told him. 'Your father followed his instincts, and I always gave him a long leash. So where do you want to go this time?'

'It's not so much a place as a different way of looking for him.' Tom met Brennan's sharp gaze. 'I'm not convinced that Green Man's manifesto will lead us anywhere useful, but I'm absolutely sure his attacks will.'

206

'So it's something about the Boon Dam?'

'And the other five, all taken together. He might have had some help along the way, but I think they were mostly his work. I sense one mind behind the attacks, planning, preparing, and executing them. He's a craftsman, and they all show different sides of his tradecraft. What he's good at. What he knows how to do. And the way he prefers to do it.'

'You're talking about his skill set?'

'That's right. I want to look closely at exactly what techniques he used in each attack. What would he have had to know to sink the yacht or blow up the factory or knock down the dam? Which different areas of science and particularly engineering would he need to be comfortable with? He clearly has a range of interdisciplinary knowledge that's so broad it's rare. I think I can create a profile of what he knows on a professional level that will reflect what he's done and how he trained – and once we have that profile, it should be straightforward to search for matches.'

'You're gonna need to work with someone,' Brennan said.

'The best would be a mechanical or structural engineer who works across disciplines. I've already reached out to some people at Caltech for suggestions . . .'

'There's a super sharp mechanical engineer at Carnegie Mellon who's already helped us. After the second attack we didn't know yet exactly what we were dealing with, but in a limited way we started to explore the kind of approach you're now taking, and someone at Defense recommended her for her wide knowledge. She'd just won some massive award. A Dingus. A Dickman?'

207

'She won a Draper? Are you talking about Dr Ronningen?'

'Yeah, I met her briefly and was extremely impressed and . . .' Brennan frowned, broke off, and took a few breaths as he rubbed his chest.

'What is it?' Tom asked, alarmed.

'Nothing. I get this sometimes. It's just indigestion from that corned beef . . .'

'Bullshit.' Tom already had his cell out.

'What are you doing?'

'Calling for an ambulance.'

'Don't be an idiot. I need to get back to work. A doctor will just tell me to lose thirty pounds and give up beer and –'

'Sit back and take deep breaths and shut up,' Tom told him. 'I lost my father to a heart attack, and I'm not planning on losing you.' And then, into his cell phone, 'I'm at Flanagan's Pub in Georgetown. I need an ambulance right away. Someone's having a heart attack except he's too stupid to know it.'

29

Green Man could have flown to Lubbock, and Midland would have been even closer, but those were small airports, and the closer he flew to the oil fields, the more his travel record might come up in a search of possible targets. Flying at all was a risk that he had previously avoided. When he was scouting his six earlier targets, he had driven to them on back roads in his van. It was safer, and it left less of a carbon footprint – few things were as harmful as air travel. But time was pressing on him now – his manifesto was out, the president had furiously vowed in a televised press conference to catch him, and he could feel the FBI manhunt closing in.

The Dallas/Fort Worth International Airport was more than six hours' drive from the oil fields, so landing there at least gave him some separation. It was also the fourth busiest airport in America, and the greater the volume of travelers passing through and the more destinations it served, the harder it would be to run a search for him. He rented a dark blue Jeep Grand Cherokee, cranked up some kick-ass bluegrass on the radio, and drove off into the Texas sunshine to do some shopping.

At a sprawling army surplus store, he bought light assault boots, Apache binoculars, a boonie hat, handless night-vision goggles, and a canvas duffel. His eyes ran over a rack of guns, but he settled on a KA-BAR knife that he could purchase in cash without any ID. 'Planning an invasion?'

asked the good-natured checkout clerk whose tentlike Semper Fi T-shirt didn't begin to hide his potbelly.

'Just stocking up,' Green Man said. 'They don't have stores like this in Vermont.'

'That's why you should move to Texas,' the affable clerk told him.

At a secondhand clothing store in a tough neighborhood of northeast Dallas, Green Man picked up some heavy-duty cotton work dungarees and several black T-shirts. He tried them on in the store's tiny dressing room, and when he glanced in the mirror, he looked less like a traveling businessman and more like a roughneck who might be heading out to the oil fields looking for work.

His hotel in Dallas was less than a mile from Dealey Plaza, and after checking in, Green Man strolled through the early evening to the famous intersection of Elm and Houston. The Sixth Floor Museum was still open, but he had seen its exhibits several years earlier, and they had been almost physically painful for him to view. Instead, he found an empty bench near the famous grassy knoll and sat down as the shadows lengthened. He imagined Kennedy's motorcade turning at the Book Depository and driving up Elm Street toward the bench where he now sat. The route had been published in the Dallas newspapers to assure a good crowd, and Lee Harvey Oswald was in his sniper's nest on the sixth floor of the depository, with a clear shot of the intersection below.

JFK was a hero of Green Man's — he admired what Kennedy had done with the space program and the Peace Corps, and he liked to believe that that was a moment when America had been headed in the right direction. If Kennedy had not been shot, would he and his brother have embraced the civil rights movement and pulled America out of Vietnam? And with all their smarts and openness to science and new ideas, would they have heeded the warning first sounded by Charles David Keeling in the early 1960s from his Mauna Loa observatory that carbon dioxide levels were rising dangerously according to the Keeling Curve, and humans were responsible?

It was a moment in time when a prescient leader might have studied the research, peered into the future, and glimpsed a looming danger. A highly credible scientist had sounded a specific alarm based on hard facts, and had it been taken seriously, there would have been decades in which to act sensibly and the world wouldn't be in the precarious plight it was now. But Oswald had fired three shots, killing the president, and the chance had been lost. If one man had pulled a trigger and changed history for the worse, sinking America into gloom and causing the world to miss a clear chance, could not another man change history for the better, save America from its worst demons, and give the world a last-minute reprieve?

Green Man sat on the bench, surrounded by the signs and pergolas of the plaza that had been painstakingly restored to look exactly the way it had on November 22, 1963. It was a place redolent with an almost tangible sense of how fragile fate and destiny were and how one individual with the boldness to act and the ingenuity to do it in a way no one could foresee or prevent could change the course of human history. Green Man drank it in the way a vampire feeds on blood and left feeling almost heady with the certainty that he really could do this enormous thing.

He walked back to his hotel in darkness, took two pills, and tried to sleep, but he only drifted for a few hours and

211

woke up with a nervous, buzzing energy. It was always like this when he was about to scout a target – his eagerness grew steadily through the early-morning hours till he couldn't wait in the small and silent room any longer. He checked out of the hotel at sunrise and headed west on I-20, and it felt odd and exposed to be driving a rented Jeep without tinted windows on a major interstate, but it was also a little thrilling.

West Texas was flat and brown, depressing to him even at sunrise. He tried to concentrate on his mission – in a few weeks he would be driving back in this same direction in his van with enough explosives to turn a massive oil field into a hell on earth. What would he need to set it on fire, and what would be the best way to slip in and get out? The only thing he already knew for sure was the time of day when he would strike. After studying worrying new numbers from satellites about the spike in greenhouse gases in the atmosphere and the rapid melting of the Antarctic ice sheet, the radical environmental group in Sweden had turned their Östersund doomsday clock forward dramatically, signifying that the earth was approaching its final midnight. Taking his cue one last time from the doomsday clock, Green Man would hit the oil field at the stroke of midnight.

He stopped in Midland and ate lunch in a Mexican dive in the shadow of a towering office building. This was Bush family territory – the quintessential boom-and-bust oil city. The downtown area had a few tall buildings that had been built in the boom of the early 1980s, before the ensuing bust had halted construction. The half-dozen aging tall office buildings seemed to mock the ambitions of this self-styled Tall City that had once dreamed of being another Dallas or Houston.

From Midland it was a short hop to Odessa and then

two hours to the Permian Basin city of Pecos. Oil pump-jacks began popping up in strange places – nodding donkeys, as they were called locally – moving back and forth over the roofs of houses, bobbing next to highways, pumping oil in school playgrounds, desecrating church-yards, and breaking the monotony of farm fields. The small towns along the way looked to be poor and strug-gling, but beneath them was liquid gold.

Twenty minutes west of Pecos, Green Man arrived in Baines, a formerly obscure speck on the map that now found itself at the epicenter of the world's biggest hydraulic shale boom. Baines was also the closest town to the mas-sive Hanson Oil Field that Green Man had come to figure out how to destroy. He parked and walked the dusty streets, the wide brim of his boonie hat keeping the blaz-ing sun off while he took in the vibe of what felt like an uneasy pairing of a sleepy West Texas hamlet with an end-less, roaring, cash-infused frat party.

There were quiet back streets of neatly kept low-income homes, a tiny school, a Family Dollar store, and a small Baptist church with a sign that warned: 'If You Park in This Church Parking Lot You're Gonna Get Baptized.' But the traffic through town was heavy and increasing steadily, and they weren't small cars with people coming to get baptized. They were pickups and company buses as roughnecks and roustabouts got off ten-, twelve-, and fourteen-hour shifts at the oil fields and flooded into Baines looking for hot barbecue and cold beers.

Restaurants and bars on the main drag advertised Texas brisket and Bud, and three gentlemen's clubs hinted at a lot more. A trailer on Main Street offered haircuts for thirty dollars, far above what a town like this would

213

normally support. An upscale tattoo parlor a few doors down was doing a brisk business. Everyone Green Man saw on the streets was male except for a few young women in bright outfits and short skirts, standing on corners or heading into bars in groups of two or three. His throat was dry, and he wanted very much to go into one of those air-conditioned bars and order a burger and a beer, but security was tight in boomtowns, they might have cameras at the door, and old habits died hard.

So Green Man stayed in the shadows and watched the workers, taking in details of what they wore and how they talked and acted. He was close enough to hear the thud of their work boots and to see their dark sunburns. If he set an oil field on fire with flowback, harmful gases would be released that some of these men would inhale. They might asphyxiate on the spot or suffer terrible health problems for years to come. They were tough men, but they weren't evil and didn't mean to destroy the environment. They were just taking the best jobs they could find, and Green Man bore them no malice. He felt the weight of what he would soon do to them, and before turning back to his Jeep, he prayed to God that once again his end goal justified the damage he did to innocents along the way.

He had seen oil fields before, but nothing like the Hanson spread that soon rose out of the arid landscape like a metallic Oz. It was a gleaming city of enormous storage tanks and serpentine pipelines and thousands of drilling rigs with diesel engines driving toxic fracking liquid deep beneath the earth to bust up shale. Workers dotted the rigs, trucks drove back and forth carrying supplies in and oil out, and security was tight. The wire fence that surrounded the field was thirty feet high, and atop it gleamed coils of razor wire. Green Man glimpsed a sentry tower and didn't even slow down in his Jeep as he drove around the perimeter.

He followed the road that skirted the field and headed north to the spot where the Kildeer River flowed in under the fence. He was gratified to see that there were no special precautions or guard stations there. He turned off onto a dirt road that ran alongside the river and drove a mile upstream, out of visual sight of the oil field, and parked on the black, gravelly bank.

Green Man kicked off his shoes and waded into the river. It was thirty feet wide and surprisingly cold. He dove beneath the surface, enjoying the jolt of cold, and kept his eyes open. It wasn't deep, but in its central channel he was more than four feet beneath the surface, which would certainly suffice. Even in daylight, it would be difficult to spot a diver dressed in a black rubber suit that matched the basalt of the riverbed. At midnight, he would be invisible.

He climbed out of the river, and within ten minutes the Texas afternoon sun had dried him off. He had spotted a butte several miles away from the Hanson field. Green Man headed for it, bouncing on dirt roads and cutting across flat stretches of gravel and sand, keeping more than a mile from the perimeter fence. A stand of oak trees stood at the bottom of the butte, and he left his Jeep among them and climbed to the flat mesa-like top, looking down on the Hanson field. From this vantage point, he could see the layout clearly, and the glittering Kildeer that flowed under the fence at the north end, bisected the field, and flowed out the south side.

He fished the Apache binoculars out of his pocket and raised them. Sector by sector he examined the field that he had already memorized from published maps. His magnified view moved slowly over the bulbous oil and gas storage tanks connected by webs of piping, the seemingly endless rows of tall fracking rigs with work crews swarming over them, the flat storage buildings for sand and chemicals, to the metal flowback tanks that stood off by themselves, near the river. They were forty feet tall, cylindrical, and painted a lime-green color, and they were clustered side by side. Each tank was connected to a vent so that gas broken off from the fluid could be combusted by a flare.

He would swim in from the north end and stay submerged in the river for a half mile to the flowback tanks. It would be best to go in on a moonless night, but the oil field would still be lit up with machine lights and flares. When he climbed out, the night shadows of the flowback tanks would shield him. They were heavy metal, but their vents – designed to dispose of harmful gases – made them vulnerable, and their proximity to one another was a fatal flaw. If one tank blew, the one next to it would also blow. If five blew, all fifty would blow. If fifty blew, the Hanson field would be destroyed – hopefully without the oil and gas tanks far away on the opposite side catching fire and further poisoning the atmosphere.

Green Man ate a ham sandwich in his Jeep, and as evening fell, the thousand gas flares in the field below – visible but not particularly dramatic in bright daylight – began to dance against the gathering darkness. He had seen what he needed to see and he could have left, but he still lingered at the butte. It was a calculated risk – every minute he stayed risked exposure – but he very much wanted to see the field in pitch darkness, the way it would look when he came back to destroy it.

216

30

'How's your boss doing?' Dr Ronningen asked. She was thirty, stunning, and formidable – nearly six feet tall and an improbably beautiful and forceful combination of Norwegian and Israeli. 'I liked old Brennan very much,' she said. 'He's a real original. I was sorry to hear he was ailing.'

'It was just an arrhythmia, and they gave him a pacemaker,' Tom explained. 'It was scary when it happened, but he should be fine. He has to watch his diet and he can't overwork, both of which are probably pure hell for him.'

'Yeah, I bet he really hates that,' she said, grinning as she scrolled through the six summaries of Green Man's attacks. She was able to keep up steady small talk while reading at great speed. Tom noticed that she didn't take notes, but perhaps she didn't need to. She had a rock star reputation – a Rhodes scholar who had published widely, lectured internationally, won several major engineering awards, and was a full professor at thirty.

'I think he misses working twenty-hour days more than the Guinness,' Tom told her, 'but that's a tough call. I just hope he follows some of the doctors' orders.'

'I wouldn't count on that,' she said as she finished skimming the summary of the destruction of the Boon Dam. 'These breakdowns of the specific skills he used in each attack are thorough and will be very useful. Who prepared them?'

'That would be me,' Tom admitted. He had spent a lot of time in academia and had never seen an office this big, especially for such a young professor. It was more lab than office – a dozen engineers could work here without crowding one another.

'Well done,' she said. 'But why do we need to look at the letters he sent after each attack and his manifesto?'

'In each letter he details some specifics about the methods he used. And in his manifesto his evaluations of the different threats to the earth and how they link together reveal a lot about the organic way he thinks about different branches of science. And also I think it's important that we hear his voice.'

'You do, do you? It seems to me like a waste of time.' She decided not to argue. 'Fine, it's not that much more reading. I'm ready to jump in, and I warn you, I don't believe in sleep or even taking long meal breaks. Especially because I understand we're facing a time element.'

'Yeah, we need to full-court press this. I'm fine with all-nighters, so I can stay with you as long as we need.'

'We'll see about that,' she said almost competitively. 'Javad should be here at any minute. Let's start with the attack on Boon and work our way backward, because the engineering needed to build the drone and take down the dam was especially distinctive. And the homemade torpedo he used to sink the yacht was also pretty special and will tell us a lot.'

'Who is Javad, and what does he do?' Tom asked.

'Computer modeling. He'll convert my engineering assessments into a data profile that can be searched –'

'I can do the computer modeling myself,' Tom told her.

'I'm sure you can.' Her polite but slightly dismissive smile was one she gave grad students who weren't quite up to snuff. 'No offense, but Javad is very good at this.'

'None taken, but so am I.'

She studied him. 'What exactly do you do for the FBI?'

'Whatever they want these days. But my degree is in computer engineering, if that's what you're asking.'

'And where did you train?'

'Caltech.'

'Who with?'

'Dr Boyer and Dr Iwasaki were my two main faculty mentors.'

Her brilliant black eyes widened slightly. 'You studied with Kenji?'

'I never called him that.'

She pulled out a cell phone. It was three hours earlier in Los Angeles. She rapidly searched through her contacts, hit a contact number, and pressed it to her ear. He heard her say, 'Kenji, Lise. No, I'm afraid Ernst and I won't make it to Spoleto for the opera festival. Listen, I'm here with one of your former students. He says he works for the FBI now. No, really. His name is Tom Smith, and he says that . . . ,' and she walked away holding the phone to her ear.

Tom watched her circle the lab. She was in constant motion and always multitasking, checking this reading and adjusting that dial while she talked. She returned to Tom and said, 'Thanks, Kenji. Yes, I'll tell him.' She hung up. 'You apparently made a strong impression. He says hello and that I won't be needing Javad.'

'That's good to hear.'

'It's especially good for Javad, because he has a new baby, and sleep is precious for him. Let me give him the good news.'

A Middle Eastern man carrying a computer case had hurried into the lab, and she walked over quickly to intercept him and spoke to him for a few seconds. He nodded and immediately headed back out, and she returned to Tom and sat down next to him. 'So your name really is Tom Smith? I thought that was some kind of bad FBI cover.'

'No, I was born with that.'

She cocked her head to study Tom quizzically, and her long black hair, which hung down almost to her hips, swished to one side. 'Just so I know who and what I'm dealing with, why the FBI, with your level of training?'

He gave her his stock answer. 'I went into the family business.'

'And what exactly is your family business?'

'Catching bad guys,' he told her with a sheepish grin.

The smile she gave him back was no longer dismissive but warm and even slightly playful, and it lit up her face. 'Good,' she said. 'Then let's see if we can catch one. It's pretty clear we're looking for a highly trained mechanical engineer with significant interdisciplinary skills and an unusually wide range of professional experience. I'd bet he did at least graduate-level study in a world-class program and then probably worked in several affiliated fields, which should make him fairly identifiable . . .'

'Yeah, that's exactly my premise,' Tom agreed excitedly, beginning to take notes on his computer. 'As you suggest, let's start with Boon. The targeting had a very small margin of error. The way he got it right, do you think he'd need to have worked professionally as a structural engineer?'

'Not necessarily,' she said, 'but the way he used hydrostatic pressure shows a deep understanding of structural analysis and especially in calculating stresses and displacements. I'll get back to that, and we'll drill down into the math he'd need. If he built the drone himself – and it was capable of carrying that heavy a payload – it's tempting to say he has a background in aeronautics, but I think avionics is an even better bet, because training in avionic engineering might also help to explain that homemade torpedo . . .'

31

Just before midnight, Green Man left the Jeep in the shelter of the oaks and walked down to the perimeter fence. He wore night-vision goggles to negotiate the rocky terrain near the butte and then took them off and was guided by the glare of the oil field in front of him. The approach to the fence was initially dark and quiet, but when he got close, the bright lights from the rigs illuminated his steps, and he heard the steady background growl of diesel engines and the endless hissing of gas-burning flares.

It was midnight – the hour when he would strike. Hanson Oil Field – lit up and roaring – looked like something out of a science-fiction horror film. The pace and scale of the operation was shocking, frightening, and unearthly. The ground trembled with the pulse and drone of the machines, and an acrid sulfur smell hung in the air. It was a violent rape of the biosphere – its surface, its bedrock and water table, and, most worryingly, its atmosphere – and it went on unceasingly.

He reached the fence and stood outside the mesh, beneath the razor wire. Fracking had come a long way from the Civil War veteran who first sent explosives down into holes. As an environmentalist, Green Man was horrified at the damage being inflicted, but the trained mechanical engineer in him was fascinated by the giant machines working in perfect tandem to suck oil and gas out of the deep shale. Now that he could see hydraulic fracking close up, and smell it and taste it, he knew that he had chosen the right final target. What they were doing was deeply harmful to an already possibly doomed planet, and it was only going to get worse.

More than a hundred new wells were being drilled across America every day, and virtually all of them were for hydraulic fracking. The company engineers and chemists were busy experimenting with new drilling methods and more potent brews of toxic chemicals to find even more powerful ways of splitting deep rock shelves apart. A constant ramping up in the number of drilling rigs meant ever more methane, leaking up into an atmosphere that was already choked with greenhouse gases as the earth warmed beneath. It had to be stopped soon, and the world had to be warned. He would take this final great risk, and then he would vanish.

He imagined himself in three weeks in the cold and dark river, and then climbing out on the bank with the hulking flowback tanks all around him. He pictured that fateful moment when he would set several time fuses and the destruction of the field would be inevitable. The clustered flowback tanks would go up one after the other like a great firecracker ribbon. The giant fireball above him would turn night into day as he swam away in the Kildeer, racing to make it out alive.

The yellow and crimson flares flickering nearby were mesmerizing, and as Green Man watched them, his mind drifted from his own mission to Sharon, and to Gus and Kim, and to what their future might hold if he made it back alive. It would be traumatic to leave everything they had known. When he had made his own first break, it had been a time of great sorrow. There were people who loved him whom he could never contact again, and allowing them to think that he had died had been a betrayal. But it had been necessary, and Green Man knew the upcoming break was also necessary. He and Sharon had planned it for years, and now they were ready.

If they succeeded, he relished the idea of his family spending time together in a new and beautiful place. Eventually the kids would come to understand what their father had done and the need for such life-changing personal sacrifice. That thought led Green Man to recall Julie and the conversation they had had on Riverside Drive and the way she had looked at him as she realized who he might be. It had been mad to tell her, and yet he didn't regret it, and the memory of that dramatic encounter was so distracting that he didn't hear the footsteps till a flashlight beam clicked on and pinioned him. 'Hey, you – what are you doing there?'

'Just minding my own business,' Green Man said, holding his hand up in front of his face as if the beam was bothering his eyes.

'And what exactly is your business here?' It was a man inside the fence, walking the perimeter alone. Peering back up the flashlight beam, Green Man could see that he was dark-skinned and in his sixties, short and powerfully built. He was wearing a security guard uniform, with a gun on his belt.

'I'm looking for work, and I thought you guys might be hiring. And would you mind not pointing that at my eyes.' Green Man knew he looked the part of a roughneck – his clothes and boots were right, and why shouldn't he be here checking out an oil field where he might apply for a job?

'We're not hiring anyone in the middle of the night,' the

guard told him a little skeptically, 'and you're on company land.' He stepped closer and directed the beam at Green Man's face. There was something peculiar about the intense way the man kept staring at him. Green Man kept his arms up, as if shielding his eyes from the light. 'I know you,' the guard said with deep certainty. 'I've seen your face before.'

If Green Man had had a gun, he would have shot him. But the combat knife wasn't much help when they were on opposite sides of the fence. 'I doubt that,' Green Man said. 'I'm not from around here.'

'Neither am I,' the guard said. 'And I never forget a face. Who are you? What's your name? Don't move.'

Green Man abruptly turned his back and began to walk quickly away. The beam of light stabbed at him and followed him through the darkness, and so did the guard's warning voice: 'Stop. *Stop right there.* Don't make me shoot you.'

Green Man doubted the guard would shoot him in the back, when he hadn't broken any law. Still, as he hurried away, he could almost feel a gun being raised and pointed at him. It would be a leg shot, and something told him the guard wouldn't miss. If he ran, that would prompt the shot for sure. So he resisted the urge to flee. Instead, he walked steadily away from the fence, never looking back.

'I'm telling you to stop,' the guard shouted out again. 'Goddamn it, STOP!' Then Green Man heard the security guard calling for help on his radio, and that told him the man had decided not to shoot. When Green Man was two hundred yards from the fence, he allowed himself to break into a jog. Soon he was all-out sprinting.

By the time he reached the Jeep, he was sweating and

gasping for breath. Below him he saw several security vehicles speeding toward the section of fence where he had been standing, and powerful searchlights already sweeping the nearby flats. He switched on the Jeep and drove in the opposite direction with the lights off, using the night-vision goggles to navigate, bumping over unseen rocks, heading away from the Hanson field as swiftly as he dared.

32

Sharon was surprised to hear the husky voice of Sergeant Dolan at the gate intercom, apologizing for dropping by unexpectedly and asking if she could spare him twenty minutes. Fear flashed and then quickly subsided, and she said, 'Sure, Ted,' and buzzed the gate open. She wished that Mitch was home to help deal with whatever was coming, and at the same time she was glad he was in Texas. Ted was a family friend and a bit of a simpleton, and he'd always had a thing for her that he did a bad job of hiding. She was sure she could manage him. As the police cruiser came up the driveway Sharon stepped outside the kitchen door and waved.

He climbed out of his car and said quickly, 'Don't worry, Sharon, it's nothing about the kids or school or anything like that.'

'Oh, thank God,' she said. 'I mean, I didn't think, but still . . .'

'It's the times we live in.' He walked closer, large and ungainly, in his late twenties but with something of the gruff and awkward loner teenager still clinging to him. 'First thing everyone thinks when they see us drive up is that there's something wrong at school. Is Mitch home?'

She'd been gardening and was wearing tan shorts and a black scoop-necked tank top, and she could feel that he didn't know where to look when he looked at her. 'He's away on a business trip. He'll be back in two days. Can it wait till then?'

'It'd be better to talk now, if you can spare me a few

minutes. Sorry to come without calling. I was close and near the end of my shift, so I thought I'd swing by. The FBI wants us to get back to them quick, so why not just take care of this?'

'The FBI?' she repeated. 'It sounds like maybe you'd better come in.'

She led him into the kitchen, and the screen door swung shut behind him. 'Would you like something to drink?'

'No thank you.'

'I have a pitcher of iced tea in the fridge.'

He took his hands out of his pockets but didn't know what to do with them. He stuck them behind his back and then pulled them out, and she saw that he now held a pad, a black pen, and some sort of printout. 'That sounds good, if it's not too much trouble.'

'It's no trouble at all,' she said, and turned her back on him to get the pitcher out of the fridge. While she was turned away, so that he couldn't see her face, she asked in a steady voice, 'So what is this about the FBI?'

'Just some crazy stuff,' he told her. 'They want us to talk to everyone in town who owns a black van. This is my third time today I'm explaining this, and it still doesn't make much sense, but they want answers right away.'

She poured the tea and carried it over to him. 'And what does the FBI have against black vans?'

He reached for the glass, and their fingers brushed. He jerked away quickly, so that a little iced tea sloshed out onto the tile floor. 'Sorry.'

'It's no problem,' she told him. 'Enjoy.' She knelt and wiped up the spill with a paper towel, while he sipped and tried not to look at her bending over.

'Thank you, Sharon. That really hits the spot.' He

230

opened his pad. 'The thing is, Green Man apparently drives a black van.'

She let that register for a second, as if it was surprising news. 'Green Man as in the terrorist who blew up that dam and killed those poor children?'

'That's the nutcase I'm talking about. They want us to check out all the vans in town and ask the owners a few questions.'

She balled up the paper towel and tossed it in the trash. 'Okay then, sit down and fire away.'

They sat at the kitchen table, where she had fed Gus and Kim breakfast two hours before, and he said apologetically, 'Forgive me, I didn't come up with these.'

'It's important that the FBI get the answers they need. Go ahead and ask me anything.'

He tapped the top of the printout with the point of his pen. 'Have you or your husband ever been arrested?'

She allowed a smile and chuckled. 'Not that I remember.'

'Of course you haven't. I mean, I know you and Mitch real well. I feel kinda silly doing this.'

'Just keep on and we'll get through it.'

'Have either of you ever belonged to a radical environmental group?'

She thought about it. 'When I was in college I used to get calendars from the Sierra Club with different animals for different months.'

'Yeah, those are cute. I remember my mom had one with penguins. Do you have any registered guns?'

'Mitch hunts.'

'Deer?'

'He never has much luck.'

'Does he wear gloves when he hunts?'

'I'm not sure. I guess he probably does when he's field dressing game. Not that there's a lot to dress. Sometimes he gets a few birds.'

'Sorry to ask, but could you show me his hunting stuff later?'

'I'll show you whatever you need to see.'

'Thanks. Almost done. How many cars do you guys have, total?'

'Three. Mitch has his Jeep. I have my Accord. And we have the van.'

'That's an eight-year-old Ford Transit, right? If you don't mind my asking, why is it registered to you?'

'Because I drive it mostly. It sounds like you've been checking up on us.'

'They sent us details about all the vans. What do you use it for?'

'Antiquing. For the bigger pieces.'

Ted looked up from his pad and glanced around the kitchen at the vases, plates, and paintings. 'It's really beautiful stuff.'

'Thanks. They're not worth much, but it's fun to collect, and every once in a while I find something good. Do you want to see his hunting stuff now?'

'Just a few more questions. Do either of you drive the van out of state?'

She hesitated as if she needed to think about it. 'Maybe once in a while. I go to a few big antique shows in Ohio, and Gus's soccer team played in a tournament in South Bend. Mitch drove five of the boys, and they had a ball.'

'I'll bet. But you don't drive it across country?'

'Never.'

'Did you repaint it or do any bodywork on it or take any stickers off it in the last six months?'

'No, it mostly just sits in the garage, and sometimes the kids use it for their hide-and-seek.'

'I bet Gus does more hiding than seeking.'

Sharon laughed. 'He's getting less lazy.'

'They grow up fast. Pretty soon he's going to be chasing girls.' Again, Ted didn't seem to know where to look, and then for a long and uncomfortable moment their eyes met.

'I think there might be one he likes,' Sharon said, 'but he would never tell me.'

He closed his pad and stood up. 'I'll need to take a look at it, if you don't mind.'

'The van?'

'Yeah, they want us to take some pictures.'

'Do you want to see the hunting stuff first? It's in the basement.'

'Sure.' He started following her and then stopped. 'Hey, I know that spot. It's the Mosley River, maybe ten miles out of town. I caught a bass right there.'

They stood before the landscape. 'Mitch likes the shape of that apple tree.'

'No kidding, he painted it? I didn't know he was an artist.'

She instantly regretted saying it, but there was no way to take it back. 'I wouldn't call Mitch an artist. He just fools around with it.'

'I think it's really good. How long has he been painting?'

'Oh, it's just kind of an off-and-on hobby he's done since high school,' she said. 'Come, let me show you his hunting stuff.'

233

The basement was cool and dark. She flicked on a light and led the way down the narrow steps. The main room held a ping-pong table and some old toys.

'I bet the kids are great since they have their own table,' Ted said.

'It's kind of hard to tell. A lot of the time when they play each other there's more yelling than playing.' She led him through a door that opened to a smaller room, and over to the gun safe. For two nervous seconds she blanked on the combination and then it came to her. She twisted the dial three times, and the door opened.

He peered inside at the gun rack and studied the rifle and shotgun and neatly stacked ammo. She was standing next to him, and while he pretended to examine the guns, she sensed that he was keenly aware that their bodies were almost touching. His uniform shirt was rolled up to show his pumped-up biceps, and she could smell his perspiration.

For a wild instant Sharon wondered if she should seduce him. It was something she knew that she could do. They were all alone in the semi-dark basement. It would throw him wildly off-balance, and he would probably forget all about the checklist for the FBI. Mitch would forgive her and tell her she had done the right thing. After all, Mitch had killed innocent people to accomplish his goals. He wouldn't hold a meaningless onetime physical act against her. Or she could do it and just not tell Mitch, and it would be a justifiable secret.

She resolutely moved a few inches closer to him. Her hair brushed his shoulder, and he glanced at her and then back at the guns. But she just couldn't bring herself to do it. Something deep inside her recoiled from the idea of touching him, of being that intimate with him, and she stepped back and the moment passed.

'Fine,' he said, breathing just a little heavily, standing away from the gun safe and letting her close and lock it. 'Where's his hunting gear?'

Sharon led him over to a nearby closet. She opened the door and turned on the light for him and this time stood several steps away. He studied the orange hat and the two hunting jackets. His eyes ran over side shelves holding thermals, camouflage pants, and socks and boots, and they lingered on several packages of gloves. Each held a dozen pairs of wrist-length heavy-duty latex sportsman's gloves for field dressing game. 'Those are the only gloves he takes hunting?'

'They're the only ones I've ever seen. Do you want to see the van now?'

'Sure,' he said, and he made a quick note on the pad and then glanced awkwardly down at his pants as if to make sure his fly was fully zipped. 'Let's go.'

She led him back up the stairs and down a short hallway to the door to the garage. Mitch's gray Jeep and her silver Accord Hybrid were parked side by side. 'So wherever Mitch is traveling now, I guess he didn't need his car?'

'He's in New York for business.'

'Must be nice. I've never been.'

'He'd better remember to bring back something for the kids.'

'And for you. You deserve something nice.'

She looked back at him, and this time his gaze was fixed – he was looking right at her breasts. She looked back at him steadily, and when she spoke, her voice was calm and flat: 'You said you needed some pictures of the van?'

Ted exhaled, nodded, and walked over to it. The black van was parked on the far side of the garage. He circled it and said, 'You guys keep it clean.'

'You should see it when Mitch comes back from hunting.'

'Looks like there's something in the back.'

'Just some antique chests I haven't unloaded yet. Do you need to see the inside?'

'No, just some photos.' He took out his cell and snapped a picture of the front, and then walked behind the van and crouched. She could see him studying the right side of the bumper, but there was no indication that any sticker or decal had been removed from it. He straightened up, took a picture, and said, 'All done.'

She didn't want him back in the house, so she opened the garage door and walked him out onto the driveway to his cruiser. 'I hope you saw everything you needed.'

'Yeah, now I gotta go type it up. Sorry for the bother. Thanks.'

But he didn't leave. They stood for a long moment, awkwardly, and then she said, 'I'd better get some snacks ready for the kids. They always come home starving.'

'Yeah, I can understand that. I'm always hungry as a bear myself.' He very awkwardly stuck out a big hand. 'Thanks, Sharon.'

She hesitated and shook his hand. It was large and sweaty, and for a moment he closed his fingers around her palm and she felt trapped. She tugged it free, and he let her go and quickly opened the door of his cruiser. 'Tell Mitch I said hello.'

'I sure will. Good luck finding the right black van.'

He got into his car and drove off down the driveway,

and Sharon watched till his cruiser disappeared behind a curtain of trees. She walked back into the house and began shaking. She poured herself a shot of brandy and slugged it down and stood completely still and silent, looking at the painting of the Mosley River and the beautiful crab-apple tree that stood tranquilly on its bank.

33

'Roger Barris,' Brennan said, still in his blue terrycloth bathrobe, rubbing his eyes and studying the report in front of him with both fascination and obvious doubt. 'He lives here?'

'He's got a house in Arlington and an office a block from Dupont Circle. He's been a lobbyist for the oil and gas industry and also for some mining companies for more than a decade,' Grant said, unable to hide his excitement.

'Does that really make sense?' Brennan wanted to know.

'It could make a lot of sense,' Earl pointed out.

'The best cover is deep cover,' Grant agreed enthusiastically. 'He's advocated for all kinds of deregulation, easing restrictions on federal lands and offshore; he's called climate change a "threat multiplier" and a "liberal hoax" –'

'But the really interesting thing is that he has another side, or at least he radically changed his colors,' Hannah Lee cut in. 'We're still filling in background reports, but Barris started off as green as they come. He was in San Francisco for twelve years, right when we think Green Man was there in the 1980s and 1990s. He was tied in with Earth First! and the Earth Liberation Front, and he was friendly with some of those early organizers mentioned in the manifesto. His first two published articles defended tree spiking and the spotted owl. But then he underwent a slow conversion, and now he's swung all the way the other way.'

'People don't change that much unless they have a good

reason to,' Earl observed, sipping coffee from a giant take-out cup.

'Lobbyists are well-paid,' Brennan pointed out. 'Money is always a good reason.'

'True enough,' Earl admitted. 'Anyway, Jim, it was too interesting not to wake you up.'

'You could have at least brought me some of that damn coffee,' Brennan snarled. He looked at Hannah Lee. 'So he popped up on the stylometrics search?'

'Professor Shaw first pinged us at two A.M. He's spent the rest of the night verifying stylistic indicators, while we've been gathering background info.'

A tall man with a goatee had been standing in a corner of the room, but now he stepped forward. Shaw didn't look like he had stayed up all night. He had showered, trimmed his beard, and was wearing a beige linen jacket that matched his stylish titanium eyeglass frames. In the past few days he had worked mostly with Hannah and her team, but the distinguished professor clearly wasn't intimidated by this assemblage of high-powered FBI agents in the taskforce commander's living room at seven in the morning. 'It was fortuitous that he's so widely published,' he explained. 'That allowed us to compare a broad range of factors, which gives us an extremely high level of assurance. Barris has written on many of the same subjects that Green Man addresses, and the stylistic and contentual parallels are telling.'

'But if he's really Green Man, wouldn't he have taken steps to distance himself from his published writing?' Brennan asked. 'Try to muddy his trail?'

'He did muddy it,' Shaw said. 'First of all, when he advocates for development as a lobbyist, he's on exactly the

240

opposite side as when he writes from Green Man's point of view. That's an extremely slippery dodge tactic – it foundationally reverses his arguments and frequently shifts his points of emphasis.'

'So you think he's intentionally trying to throw us off?' Earl asked.

'There's no question. Stylistically, when Green Man touches on the same subjects that Barris wrote about, even ten or twenty years previously, he varies his sentence structures and even the lengths and rhythms of his sentences. Green Man leans toward shorter and punchier declarative sentences. Barris, as a lobbyist, is much more analytical and sometimes long-winded. A number of times Green Man's word choice and syntax, usually clean and straightforward, becomes muddled and cumbersome, as if he's intentionally reaching for new words or turns of phrases.'

'But you can see through that?' Brennan asked.

'Those are known subterfuges,' Professor Shaw said, and then raised a finger as if making an important point to a room of students. 'People can't change the way they think, and that is reflected in the seminal choices they make in formulating and expressing the architectonics of their thought arguments . . .'

Hannah Lee's phone pinged. 'Okay, get this. Barris's primary residence is in Arlington, but he has a second house in East Lansing, Michigan.'

The mood in the living room was becoming more excited by the minute. Brennan had stopped rubbing his eyes, and someone had given him a steaming mug of hot coffee. 'So he could be a Honey Badger fan? Do we know if he was free and could have traveled on any of the six strike dates?'

Their phones were all ringing as reports flooded in

241

from teams in the field. 'It seems likely that Barris was free for at least two of the dates. We don't know about the rest yet, but we're checking,' Grant said. 'He has three main oil industry clients and largely sets his own schedule, so he travels quite a bit . . .'

'His undergrad degree is in engineering from Michigan State,' Hannah Lee reported, studying her phone. 'He's married with four kids. Two of his grown sons live in Lansing and don't have steady employment. He helps support them.'

'So he could be running the show, but with help from them, which is something we've always considered,' Brennan muttered.

'One of his sons has a cargo van,' a square-shouldered agent chimed in.

'What do we know about it, Dale?'

'Nine-year-old GMC Savana. Registered as silver, but it could easily be repainted.'

Brennan lowered his coffee to a table. 'Okay, I want warrants for Barris's phone calls, Internet, and let's find a fast way to search his house and property.'

'We've already started the paperwork for those warrants,' Agent Slaughter, the chief lawyer on the taskforce, announced in his southern drawl.

'Proceed quickly and quietly,' Brennan said. 'I don't want a word of this to get out yet. Not one whisper.'

'The quickest way would be to go directly through the attorney general to the FISA courts,' Slaughter counseled. 'That cuts out several steps but since it's not technically an international case it could be tricky . . .'

'Also, it cuts in the attorney general, and potentially everyone she's connected to,' Grant pointed out.

'She's gotta be part of this sooner or later,' Brennan said. 'It's a balancing act. We need to be fast yet deliberate.' He folded his arms over his large stomach and slowly turned away, gazing out of his window at the hammock in his backyard, deep in thought. They watched him mull it over for five seconds.

Hannah Lee glanced down at a text, and when she broke the silence, there was suddenly real worry in her voice. 'Uh, Jim.'

'What is it?'

'Roger Barris is on his way to the airport.'

Brennan turned back from the window. 'Dulles?'

'No, he's in New York. He's headed to JFK in an UberLUX.'

'Do we know where he's flying?'

'Senegal.' She studied her phone. 'Dakar.'

'There's lots of oil drilling in Dakar,' Hannah Lee said. 'He's gone there several times before to consult.'

'Is it a nonstop?' Brennan asked. 'Can we stop it or turn it around if we need to?'

'Air Maroc. Eight hours. No stops, and we have no authority over it once its wheels leave the tarmac.'

'I'd have to check this,' Agent Slaughter said, 'but I'm pretty sure Senegal is on the "no lift" list?'

'What is "no lift"?' Grant asked.

The answer came back in the slow southern drawl: 'That's the list of countries we can't extradite from.'

34

The Royal Air Maroc jetliner waited on the tarmac as passengers filed on. Most of them had already threaded their way down the rows and found seats in economy and business when a portly, vigorous man with a salt-and-pepper beard left the first-class executive lounge and – limping slightly – wheeled his carry-on across to the jetway, his soft Italian leather computer bag slung over his right shoulder. He flew constantly at the behest of his well-heeled oil company clients, and luxury travel had become a pleasant annoyance to him.

Even after all these years and millions of miles, the truth was that Roger Barris didn't like flying. Every time he got on an aircraft, he still wondered fleetingly if it might crash. He was an engineer turned journalist, and he had studied enough physics to understand the theory behind flight – how engines move the plane forward, which pushes air over the wings and down, generating lift. But he had made a very profitable career casting doubt on scientific realities that didn't make sense to most people, and there was something counterintuitive, something that bothered even him, about a three-hundred-ton plane being able to climb into the skies.

Since there was no way around it, he had learned to control his fears and enjoy being pampered. He was greeted by the first-class cabin supervisor, who personally escorted him to his spacious, leather, fully reclining seat and took his suit bag to hang up in a closet. A pretty flight attendant hurried over with the menu, and Barris ordered a steak with a nice Bordeaux for the evening meal and watched her ass and legs as she turned and walked away. Not bad, not bad at all.

He kicked off his shoes and flexed his toes and glanced at the passenger sitting nearest to him in first class. It was an older man with a sour countenance sipping what looked like milk and reading *Le Monde*. Jesus, what a dour face! He was clearly one of those supercilious French businessmen or diplomats who spoke every language perfectly and yet had utter disdain for anything not French. Despite the fact that they were first-class neighbors and clearly both successful and important, he didn't give Barris so much as a glance. Barris turned away toward the window and took out his own reading for the flight – the specs for a new oil field. It could potentially get Senegal back on the list of profitable oil producers, but it was unfortunately right smack in one of Senegal's few pristine wildlife reserves and also bordered by two potentially hostile neighbors.

There was some minor activity outside the plane. They had started to remove the jetway and were now reconnecting it. Perhaps an important passenger needed to make a connection, so they were extending him or her a service. Barris hoped it was that and not one of those mind-bogglingly stupid technical snafus that delayed flights for hours. He had once been held at Heathrow for four hours while inept mechanics tried to fix a seat in economy that wouldn't come fully upright. In economy, no less! Barris felt that people who flew economy deserved everything they got.

He reached into the carry-on bag under his seat and

fished out his cashmere slippers and slid them on. He was just getting over a gout attack, and it was painful to walk in shoes, but these extra-large and sublimely feathery slippers barely irritated his sensitive big toe. It was the beer – he would have to cut down on the beer. But how could one go to West Africa and not drink a few cold beers?

They had finished reattaching the jetway, and he was pleased to see that the first-class cabin supervisor had drawn the curtain, sealing them off from the hoi polloi behind them and whatever nonsense was about to occur in the bowels of the plane. He heard a knock from the jetway side, the door was opened, and whispers were exchanged. Barris put his slippered feet up on the cushioned footrest and glanced down at a promising chart from the Mauritania–Senegal–Guinea-Bissau basin.

'Mr Barris?' A woman in a black pantsuit was looking down at him, and he could tell that she wasn't part of the flight crew. She was smiling, but it was a serious smile, and there were two men in blue jackets standing on either side of her who weren't even attempting to smile.

'Yes, what is it?'

'There's no reason for alarm, Mr Barris, but I'd like to ask you to please come with me.'

He looked back at her and then glanced at the French diplomat with the sour face, who was being led away from his seat by a member of the flight crew.

'Why would I be alarmed? What's going on? Is my family okay?'

'Yes, everyone's fine. Please come with me.'

'You mean off the plane?' Barris asked incredulously.

'Yes, please accompany me off this aircraft immediately.'

'But there's not another plane to Senegal today that will

247

get me there in time for my meeting. And it's a crucial meeting. Look, what's this about?'

'We'll talk about it after we deboard, and I'll explain everything. Right now I need you to do as I ask: stand up and please accompany us off this plane right away.'

'But what about my luggage?' His voice got a little louder. 'I have every right to be on this plane. I don't even know who you are . . .'

She held out a badge. He saw that she was a special agent of the FBI.

'I haven't done anything wrong.'

'I didn't say that you did. All that I asked is that you stand up and accompany us off this aircraft.' She gestured up the aisle, to the open door to the jetway. 'Come. Please don't make this any more difficult than it is.'

'Don't make what difficult?' Barris looked at the two men on either side of her. They both looked to be in their thirties and more than fit. 'Are you threatening me? Who are these gorillas? Listen, I'm an American citizen traveling on a first-class full-fare ticket with a valid passport so you have no right . . .'

The captain and assistant captain stepped out of their cockpit. 'Captain,' Barris called loudly, 'come over here. You have the authority on this aircraft . . .'

But the captain and assistant captain walked right by him toward the back of the plane and disappeared through the drawn curtain. Following them with his eyes, he saw that the entire first-class cabin had been quickly and quietly emptied, and he was now alone with these three FBI agents. 'Am I under arrest?'

'No, you're not under arrest. But I need you to come with us right now. I promise you your luggage will be looked after. At this very minute it's being taken off the plane.'

Barris processed that and didn't like the sound of it. 'I'll tell you what I'm going to do. I'm going to call my lawyer,' and he leaned down toward his computer bag to get his cell phone, which was in the uppermost zipped pocket.

Then things happened very fast. The woman said, 'Keep your hands where I can see them and *stop moving*.' Just as he touched the zipper on his bag, one of the young men darted forward, grabbed his right arm, and yanked him back. In a second he was flipped over on his stomach and they were putting some sort of binding on his wrists while he screamed that he was an American citizen and how dare they treat him this way and they would be very, very sorry.

35

Tom checked his phone to make sure he had the right address. This was Millionaires' Row in Shadyside, and it was difficult to believe that a young academic lived in one of these Victorian mansions, even if she consulted internationally and was married to a potential Nobel laureate. He rang the bell, half expecting a maid in livery to open the door, but when it was finally pulled open, Lise stood there in red pajama bottoms and a white T-shirt, rubbing her red eyes as if she'd just woken up.

'Sorry if you were napping, but you said to come by with the first results.'

'I wasn't napping, and you don't have to remind me what I said,' she told him curtly, and led him into the elegantly decorated house. They walked through a double living room, and it was like touring a museum – the furniture, paintings, rugs, grand piano, and chandeliers were expensive, old, and European.

'This is beautiful,' he said.

'Do you think so?' she asked, and again he heard a distinct prickliness.

He waited a few seconds and asked politely, 'Is your husband home? I studied some of his work in grad school, and I'd be honored to meet him if it's appropriate . . .'

'He's not home,' she said. 'He's in fucking Mainz.'

Tom wasn't certain exactly where Mainz was, but he took what sounded like a third hint to shut up, and he

251

stayed silent as she led him to a back study that looked out on a well-tended garden. The roses were still in bloom, there was a stream with water lilies, and it appeared more like a Monet painting than a real view. 'I don't know how you get any work done here,' Tom said, watching the stream meander by.

'I was getting plenty of work done till you dropped by. But since you're here, I take it our profile didn't get any hits?'

'Why do you say that?'

'Because if it had, you'd be on your triumphant way to Washington,' she said. 'I know how you guys operate. You need help, and when it works, you disappear.'

'I said I'd come with the results, and I'm here,' Tom told her. 'You couldn't have been more helpful working through the night, and I really appreciate it. We got four hits on our profile.' He hesitated. 'But are you really sure this is a good time?'

'A good time for what?' Her black eyes blazed. Was she angry with him? Flirting? They were alone in a mansion, and she was in pajama bottoms and a skimpy top. Her long raven hair was uncombed and spilled wildly over her shoulders and T-shirt as if in challenge to the curated order of the garden beneath the window.

'Look, I'm here to share the preliminary results and because I value your opinion going forward. But I don't want to disturb you, Dr Ronningen.'

'Lise, for Christ sakes, I'm not that much older than you. Sit down and stop apologizing. You want coffee? Booze? My husband is a fan of sherry in the afternoon, and he keeps more bottles than most restaurants. I've already had a glass.'

'Nothing for me. I don't drink much. But thanks.'

'Aren't you fun,' she said. 'Okay, I take it the four hits weren't promising?'

'I had hoped for more and better,' Tom admitted, 'but I still believe in our profile. This search was just a first try.' He powered up his computer. 'It was very limited in scope – the top ten engineering grad programs going back thirty years. Brennan said I was making a mistake limiting it to the best schools. He thinks I'm an elitist.'

'You're a sober, self-effacing elitist, which is the worst kind of snob,' Lise said, and poured herself a generous glass of sherry. He noted that after pouring, she deftly concealed the half-empty bottle beneath a chair. He wondered how many glasses she'd had and if her eyes were red from crying rather than from lack of sleep. 'Give me that,' she said, grabbed his laptop, and she studied the names and the biographical information he'd quickly pulled together. 'I thought you said four names. There are only three.'

'We had four hits. But one of them, Paul Sayers, is long dead, which means we only have three possibilities.'

She was speed-reading and ignoring him. 'This Miura guy is a stud. He crosses all kinds of disciplines, and his educational background exceeds our profile.'

'Yeah, he'd be terrific. Too bad Miura lives in Japan.'

'Maybe he travels to America when he feels like blowing something up.'

'He consults all over Asia – especially in China – but he hasn't been to America in five years. Which rules him out and leaves us only two. One is a female academic –'

'Oh, let's just discount all female academics,' Lise said angrily. 'Surely the brilliant and dynamic Green Man can't possibly be a passive and weak female professor.'

'Actually, I always considered that a real possibility,' Tom told her. 'Until we found a cop in Nebraska who we think pulled Green Man over –'

'But you're not one hundred percent sure the guy that cop pulled over was Green Man, right? So how can you completely rule out Professor Fiona Harvey? She was a rock star at Cornell engineering. Strong professional credentials, and she's published tons.'

'Because she lacks the freedom to do what Green Man does. For the last decade Dr Harvey's taught at Auburn, and she rarely leaves Alabama.'

'How do you know? She wouldn't need to fly across the Pacific like Miura. Dr Harvey could covertly get in her car – or van – and drive wherever she wants.'

'True, but she's battling stage four cancer. She's spent a lot of the past two years in a hospital in Birmingham, right when Green Man was striking.'

'Which leaves us with only one,' Lise admitted grudgingly. 'Alec Petrov.'

'Alec's got it all,' Tom said. 'A brilliant mechanical engineer from Rice who dazzled his professors and jumped right into a stellar career. But he's *too* high-flying – the managing partner of an electric car company that went public and is valued at more than a billion dollars. If there's one thing I can tell you that Green Man is definitely not, it's high profile. Alec is on every business news show that will have him. He's been busy launching his company twenty-four seven. There's no way he's also been running around blowing up factories and sinking yachts.'

Lise reluctantly shrugged. She clearly didn't like to admit defeat in anything. 'I did my job. The profile's damn good. You did the computer modeling, and you decided the parameters of the search, so it's your problem.'

'Absolutely,' Tom agreed, standing up. 'I'm gonna search much wider. And look, I know I'm not supposed to apologize, but whatever's going on here, I'm sorry to have barged in at the wrong time, and I hope it works out. I should go now. I may have to fly back to DC on very short notice, but I'll text you if I get any other hits.'

He tried to take his laptop back, but Lise didn't let the computer go. 'What makes you think something's wrong here?'

'Nothing,' Tom said, avoiding her eyes. 'I just really need to go now.'

'What's the big emergency in DC?'

'I can't tell you.'

'I have a higher security clearance than you do. Ask Brennan.'

'I know you do.'

'Then come on, FBI Agent Smith. Tell me the truth.'

He met her gaze. 'I think something's wrong here because that's at least your second glass of sherry and it looks like you've been crying. You're pissed off about something, and I'm sure you have good reason to be, but it's nothing that I did.'

Lise took a sip of sherry and gave him an appraising smile, as if she wasn't quite sure what to make of him but she was starting to like him. 'I meant tell me the truth about what's going on in DC.'

'I know you did.'

She poured a second glass of sherry and held it out to Tom, and he hesitated and then took it. 'I warn you, I'm not a strong drinker. My father considered it a sign of weakness. One of many that he saw in me.'

'Spare me your family tsuris. Let's hear about DC.'

He tasted the sherry and found it warm and cloying. 'They've got someone in custody.'

'Who they think is Green Man?'

'There's some circumstantial evidence.'

'Which you don't buy?'

'I'm not sure.'

'You don't buy it. How strong is the circumstantial evidence?'

Tom hesitated for several seconds. 'This is not public knowledge.'

'My security clearance is fully invoked, and my lips are sealed.' And she ran her tongue over her full lips.

'They searched his house, in Michigan. In a small pond in the back of his property they found traces of the explosive used to blow up the chemical factory near Boston.'

'Sounds like they got the right guy,' she said.

Tom couldn't keep his voice from swelling louder with doubt and anger: *'Green Man would never be stupid enough to walk out his back door and dump explosives in a pond in his own backyard.'* He got himself under control, took a bigger sip of the sherry, and met her eyes. 'Okay, your turn. Why were you crying?'

'Because I got a call from my husband,' Lise told him. 'Ernst has accepted a distinguished guest professorship at a university in Paris for next semester.'

'Paris is a nice place to visit.'

'Yes, it's a lovely and romantic city,' she agreed, and her eyes suddenly glistened. 'But I don't think I'd be welcome. You see, his mistress lives in Paris.'

256

Tom handed her a tissue from a box and said, softly and almost shyly, 'I thought your husband was supposed to be smart. He must be dumb as well as blind.'

She gave him a smile as she dabbed at her eyes. 'It's a very sad story. There was a young woman who everyone said was the smartest around and she won all the prizes – her brilliance was unquestioned. Her father was a cold, austere, older, philandering scientist in Norway who gave her no love when she was young, so what did she do? She married a cold, austere, older, philandering mathematician from Germany who also gives her no love. Have you ever heard anything so stupid?'

Tom's head was swimming with the sherry. 'Matter of fact, I have,' he told her. 'A young man who was a bit of an environmentalist grew up with a father he hated, who mocked everything about him. The father was an FBI agent and toted around a gun and a badge. He pretended to be a moral paragon, but he was really abusive and narrow-minded and beat the shit out of his kid. When the boy grew up, he broke away and he could have done anything. But he ended up an FBI agent, toting around a gun and a badge, and he's helping to hunt down someone who may be the last hope of saving the planet.'

She studied him with interest. 'Do you know why you're doing it?'

'Something has a hold on me that I can't shake. You?'

She raised a glass. 'Pure masochism. Fuck it. Here's to getting bombed in the afternoon.' They clinked glasses and drank. 'You're unexpectedly complex for a Tom Smith,' she said. 'Tell me something about yourself that I wouldn't guess.'

'I almost became a pianist. My dad was against it. But I was really good.'

'Prove it.' She led him out of the study to the living room, and he found himself sitting at the grand piano. It was a Blüthner, hand-crafted in Germany.

He hadn't practiced in months, so he played something he loved and knew well, a Chopin piano concerto. He got caught up in the emotion of the music, and when he finished, he saw that Lise was sitting very still and that a tear was sliding down her cheek. 'I'm sorry,' he said.

'Don't be.' She wiped the tear away with a thumb and covered the display of emotion by changing subjects quickly. 'Why do you think he had that explosive in his pond if he's not Green Man? Do you think he's being set up?'

'That wouldn't make sense. We know too much about Green Man. The truth will come out, and he'll be cleared. I don't trust it, but I don't pretend to understand it.' He turned on the piano bench to look at her. 'Your turn. Tell me something about you that's fun and embarrassing.'

Lise hesitated and then shrugged and said, 'One night at Oxford I took some pills and ended up dancing naked in a fountain and this snarky blog voted me the sexiest Rhodes scholar since Kris Kristofferson and also labeled me a total nutcase.'

Tom laughed and said, 'Nutcase or not, that's pretty good company.'

'I guess,' she said, chuckling despite herself. Then she asked him, 'Why do you think Green Man may be the last hope of the planet?'

'You read his letters and manifesto. You're a scientist, so you recognize hard facts. The last seven years have been the hottest on record. The ice sheets are melting, the oceans are rising, and there are freak weather events all over the globe. Species are dying off, and there's precious

258

little time to turn things around, but that's what he's trying to do. He's focused world attention on the most critical problems –'

Lise emphatically shook her head and cut in: 'Every terrorist thinks he has to do what he does, that God has assigned him that mission.'

Tom replied by asking the question that he'd carried around with him – one that had tortured him for months. 'You're absolutely right, and I couldn't agree more. Every terrorist thinks his cause justifies his actions. No one has the right to take the law into his own hands, and especially to spill innocent blood. Anyone who does that must be stopped.' He paused and then asked softly, 'But, Lise, what if in this single very unique case, Green Man happens to be one hundred percent right?'

There was a deep seriousness in her face when she answered. 'I served two years mandatory military service in Israel. I've been to bombsites, from attacks on opposite sides of the same issues. I've used tweezers to pick up the blown-apart little pieces of women and children. Nothing justifies fanatical extremism. Nothing. Never.' She broke off and studied Tom as if she couldn't quite make him out. 'I can't believe they picked you of all people to hunt this guy down.'

'Yeah, well, I don't seem to be doing a very good job of it. Do you have anything else to drink?' Tom asked her. 'Preferably not so damn sweet.'

'How about some chilled red wine? And I can show you the rest of the house.'

She carried the red wine and two glasses as she led the way up to the second floor and opened a door to an enormous bedroom. 'Ernst's bedroom.'

259

'You guys sleep separately?'

'He likes privacy. I think he brings his students here. The lucky ones.' The bitterness in her voice was palpable. She led him a short distance down the hall. 'Here's where I hang out.'

He peered into a smaller bedroom and saw the canopy bed and gorgeous view. 'It's lovely.'

She was standing next to him, so closely that their hips and shoulders brushed. 'Why don't you come in and we can drink the wine?'

'I'd like to,' Tom said, 'but . . .'

'You have a girlfriend?'

'No, but you have a husband. And I've never been with someone who's married. I'm not sure I believe in that.'

Lise stepped in front of him and leaned so close that he could feel her breath on his cheeks. 'I thought your family business was punishing bad guys?'

'It is.'

'My husband is a real bad guy,' Lise said softly, looking into his eyes. 'I want you to punish him.' Somehow her hands had gone to his belt and with one deft flick of her fingers had undone the clasp. 'You see, I really am a good engineer.' She looked both vulnerable and ferocious. 'Now, not a word more.' She kissed him on the lips and drew him into the bedroom, and step by step Tom followed her in.

36

'How sure are you that the stuff you found in the pond is the same stuff Green Man used when he torched that chemical company?' the president asked as Marine One descended toward the White House.

'C4 is a powerful plastic explosive, sir, composed of several component parts, so even small traces are very distinguishable,' Brennan told him. 'There are the explosives themselves, a plasticizer, a binder, and a chemical marker, and the composition of those ingredients can vary considerably. For example, the C4 that our military uses has a ninety-one percent explosive component that's RDX and a five-point-three percent dioctyl sebacate binder –'

'Jim, this isn't a chemistry class,' the attorney general cut in. 'The president just wants the big picture.'

Brennan nodded and said simply, 'The traces of C4 that we found in Barris's pond match the potent but slightly unusual formula that was used in Massachusetts. It was home brewed, sir, so it's like a fingerprint or even a retina scan – extremely distinctive.'

'Home brewed, eh? How good was the match?' the president asked.

'Perfect, sir.'

'Can't do much better than perfect,' the president noted, and smiled smugly. He turned quickly to an assistant: 'I don't want the First Lady too close when we come down.

She always does that. The rotor wash messes up her hair for the photos.'

'Yes, Mr President,' the assistant said, and whispered urgently into a mouthpiece. The White House helipad was now visible below, with a growing crowd waiting.

'DOD's top people have done their own analysis of the C4, Mr President,' the attorney general chimed in. 'They concur. It's definitely the same stuff.'

'But the bastard still claims he's innocent?' the president asked.

'Vociferously. And he's retained top counsel, who are limiting our ability to question him.'

'So he's lawyered up,' the president said. 'Meg, needless to say, I want our very best people on this.'

'They are, sir. I handpicked them myself.'

'Good, I want them to stick a spike up his ass. You know that King of England who got spiked in the ass?'

There was silence except for the loud drone of the helicopter. A scholarly looking aide named Harburg said hesitantly, 'Edward II, sir.' And he cautiously added, 'It was actually a red-hot poker . . .'

'Love it,' the president said. 'The fucking Brits. They pretend to be so hoity-toity and then they shove a hot poker up their king's keister.'

Brennan hesitated, but they were less than two hundred feet above the emerald lawn, and he knew he only had seconds. 'Mr President, I'd like to emphasize that we're still in the information-gathering stage and no charges have yet been filed –'

'Jesus Christ, Brennan,' the president erupted at him, looking very serious and even a little angry. 'You know what you just did?'

'Not exactly, sir.'

The chief executive broke into a broad grin. 'You just knocked this one out of the fucking ballpark.'

'Thank you, sir, but what I'm trying to emphasize is the necessity to still be cautious —'

'So when you knock one out of the fucking park, you let yourself enjoy it. Right? Do you think when Reggie Jackson clubbed those three home runs against the Dodgers he was walking around the dugout second-guessing himself?'

'No, sir,' Brennan said. 'I bet he was pretty happy, but the salient point here for us now is prudence —'

'I was at that game, by the way. Front-row boffo box seats. Fucking Mr October bangs three out. Stan, damn it, she's way too close. Her hair is gonna be a tumbleweed.'

'The First Lady has been strongly advised to stay back, sir —'

'Tell the Secret Service it's unsafe for her to be that close. NOW!'

'Yes, sir.'

An aide held a mirror, and the president carefully checked his own appearance as the chopper came down. He smiled almost flirtatiously at his own reflection.

Then they were on the ground and the First Lady was hurrying forward across the lush lawn. The president stepped out of the cabin and kissed her on the lips, while photographers snapped pictures.

Brennan eased his bulk carefully out of the copter and watched the circus. Several aides were standing on either side of the president, trying to get his attention to inform him of different pressing matters, but the First Lady was speaking over them all and complaining about how the

White House chef's oysters had given her diarrhea, while a small cluster of reporters – held back by security – shouted questions from thirty feet away.

Brennan had never liked or trusted helicopters, and with the rotor blades still turning above his head, he walked a short distance away. Suddenly an arm snaked around his back and the president was leading him forward. 'Come on, Jim, let's have some fun.'

Brennan looked around wildly for the attorney general, but she was nowhere to be seen. Before he knew what was happening, they were standing in front of the pack of reporters and the president was saying, 'Listen up. This here is Jim Brennan, an American law enforcement icon who was hired for the FBI by J. Edgar Hoover himself shortly after the Civil War. And this old heroic son of a bitch just broke the Green Man case!'

Photographers snapped pictures furiously while reporters called out questions: 'Is it the lobbyist who was taken off the plane at JFK?' 'Is Roger Barris Green Man?' 'Are you charging him with multiple homicides?' 'His lawyer said his detainment is the biggest legal travesty since O.J. was found innocent. Do you have a comment?'

'It would be premature to say anything yet . . . ,' Brennan started to tell them, but the president's arm tightened slightly around his back and guided him forward.

'O.J. was one hell of a running back,' the president noted, 'and a jury of his peers found him innocent.'

'Mr President, does "broke the case" mean that you're charging Barris with being Green Man?' a reporter shouted.

'What do you think "broke the case" means?' the president asked, horrifying Brennan. But even with his five decades of experience, he couldn't quite figure out how to politely correct the president on live camera on the South Lawn.

Meanwhile, volleys of questions were flying at them: 'Did Roger Barris confess?' 'When they searched his house in Lansing, did they find hard evidence?' 'Are other people being charged as accomplices?' 'Does this look like a death penalty case?'

'You'll be given all the answers at the appropriate time,' the president assured them with a big smile. 'The important thing for you to get out there now is that Americans can finally sleep safely. All credit to Jim Brennan – this big, modest warhorse of an FBI agent who's as much of an authentic American hero as . . . Secretariat. Flash them a thumbs-up, Jim.' Brennan found himself arm in arm with the president, flashing the photographers a thumbs-up.

37

Tom woke in darkness. He was hungover and sore in strange places – the sexiest Rhodes scholar since Kris Kristofferson had scratched his back and bitten his neck. He lay happy and drifting, listening to Lise breathing next to him. He thought of the women he'd dated in college and grad school. Few had challenged or really understood him. It was his own fault – some of them had been nice, but truth be told, he had pursued the kinds of girls his father would have liked.

Well, his father damn sure would have hated Lise. She would have bitten his head off. The thought of them meeting made Tom smile, and he felt a little guilty. Warren Smith was dead, and it was time to forgive and forget. Yet the dead and buried can unquestionably have a strong power over the living.

That thought led Tom to something, but he couldn't quite grasp it. Then he did. A name. Sayers. He slipped out of bed, left the bedroom, and quietly descended the stairs. His laptop was on the table in the back study. He turned it on and started to research the fourth name on the list – the name he had discounted because Paul Sayers had been dead for nearly twenty years.

Tom called up information and read more and more intently, suspicion giving way to fascinated shock. Undergrad at Yale. Mechanical engineering at MIT. After graduating, Sayers had worked at impressive jobs that required interdisciplinary skills. He'd ended up in the Bay Area, where he'd become involved with several nascent radical environmental groups. And he'd started a company that designed airplane guidance systems and had sold it for more than twenty million dollars.

Paul Sayers had pumped some of his new fortune into radical environmental activism. He was linked to several destructive attacks, and the FBI had begun hunting him. Sayers had evaded the FBI in a very original and convincing way. He'd died. A radical group he was associated with had struck a natural gas company, there was a massive explosion, and his badly burned corpse was found in the wreckage. There had been a big public funeral with several notable environmental activist speakers and a celebrity folk singer . . .

'Are all FBI agents trained to skulk away from bed like that?' Lise had come down the stairs and found him, and she was smiling, but her smile vanished when she saw his face. 'What's wrong? Is it the news from DC?'

'Do you believe in ghosts?' Tom asked her, glancing up from his laptop screen, where he had just called up an obituary photo of a young-looking Paul Sayers.

'Not normally,' she said.

'Neither do I,' Tom told her. 'Until now. But I think this guy is haunting us,' and he nodded toward his screen, where the news photo stared back at them. And then Tom blinked and said, 'Wait a minute. What news from DC?'

'I don't think you're going to like this,' Lise told him, and she showed him what she had just been watching on her cell as she'd come down the stairs. She was streaming a live CNN panel on which they were discussing the breaking news from Washington. Roger Barris had incontrovertibly

268

been able to establish his innocence, and he had been released. On two of the attack dates he had rock-solid alibis and had been thousands of miles from the targets. His family members also couldn't possibly have done it. He was back in DC with his big-ticket lawyer, who was now threatening to sue the government for one hundred million dollars for defamation of character.

Meanwhile the president had reacted swiftly, transferring jurisdiction and leadership of the Green Man investigation from the FBI to the Department of Homeland Security. Assistant Director Harris Carnes of DHS was now in charge.

The news show played a clip of the press secretary announcing the shake-up and denying that Barris's exoneration had anything to do with it. 'This realignment simply reflects jurisdictional realities that the president has recognized for a while. The investigation is now where it should have always been. Green Man is a terrorist and poses a direct threat to the security of the entire world.'

'But didn't the president say just hours ago that Jim Brennan had broken the case and was a law enforcement icon?' a newscaster asked her.

'The president retains the highest respect for Jim Brennan,' the press secretary said, 'and wishes him well in his retirement. And there are other factors, including health issues, that make this prudent and necessary. But the important thing is that the Green Man investigation will be ramped up under the auspices of DHS, and positive new results will be announced shortly. No more questions.'

Tom felt paralyzed for a moment – he literally couldn't move or even breathe.

'I'm sorry,' Lise said gently, touching his shoulder. 'I liked Brennan.'

'That's it,' Tom finally gasped. 'That's what Green Man was trying to do.'

'Get Brennan fired? He couldn't have known it would work out this way.'

'Not exactly, but he knew the president. He knew the incredible pressure Brennan was under to get results. With his manifesto, he increased that pressure and made it personal. He knew we were getting close, so he created the perfect red herring and let it play out. Jesus, I should have seen this coming.'

'I don't think anyone could have seen this coming,' Lise told him. And then: 'If you're right, what does it do to you? From what you've told me, you were kind of Brennan's pet project . . .'

'I'm just a lowly computer analyst he jumped about ten rungs up the ladder,' Tom said. 'I'll go back to being what I was, if I have any role in the new investigation at all.' He glanced down at the photo on his laptop screen and said, 'And I think I know who Green Man really is, or at least was, but now I have nobody to tell.'

'If you have solid evidence, I'm sure they'll listen to you,' Lise consoled him, and then added warningly, 'but you'd better make damn sure that you're right.'

Tom nodded at the good advice and studied the biographical information on Paul Sayers that he had pulled up. In one of the news articles, there was a photo of a young and dynamic-looking African American woman who was identified as Sayers's girlfriend and who had delivered his eulogy.

38

Green Man and Sharon walked down a leafy path toward the hunting shed. They had just turned off the news. It had worked out better than he could have hoped. Brennan was gone, and Carnes was an aggressive fool who would sweep in with a new broom. He was bringing in his own leadership team, and all that the FBI had found out would now be cast out or at least regarded with suspicion.

One shelf of Green Man's library contained the writings of Roger Barris going all the way back to when he had been an environmentalist. Green Man had known him slightly back in the day and had always disliked and distrusted him. When Barris had changed his colors and become a pro-development lobbyist, Green Man had followed his profitable new career with growing fury but had also seen an opening.

He had studied stylometrics and found the pseudoscience relatively easy to subvert. Barris's fatuous musings and faulty analysis contained many distinctive phrases that Green Man could co-opt for his own purposes, rewording them and weaving altered versions into his own letters and manifesto. It had been hard work, and he'd disliked the echo of Barris's voice in his own writings, but it had paid off.

A month earlier, he had driven four hours to Lansing and covertly poured three gallons of solution into Barris's backyard pond. Heading home, he'd passed a young girl at a lemonade stand outside her Lansing home. In addition to lemonade, she was selling Honey Badgers T-shirts and bumper stickers for loyal fans. Green Man had bought a glass of cold lemonade and a decal and stuck it on his back bumper, just in case his van was ever photographed while on a mission.

'Even with the shake-up in DC, I still think you and the kids should go to the summer house ahead of schedule,' Green Man said. He had checked all security monitors on his property and knew they were alone, but they still spoke softly.

'No, we should go together, as we always planned. If we make the break separately, we raise all risk factors. The cleanest break is one break.'

'Then let's go right now,' he told her. 'Tomorrow or the day after. I can set it up with one phone call.' Eagerness rang in his voice. 'We've already achieved so much. We have a moment of daylight now, when Carnes takes over and everything is up in the air. Let's use it to just disappear. We're both starting to make mistakes. I can feel them getting closer. Let's just go now.'

The hunting shed swam into view through the thick tree cover. It was a hundred-year-old stone shed with no windows and a heavy iron door with a massive padlock. Since they had bought the property, only the two of them had ever been inside.

'I want what you want, Mitch,' Sharon told him, 'but we've come this far, and we have to finish.' Her steely resolve was improbable – she was loving and supportive but beyond obdurate. 'One more attack, one more loud message to the world, and then we're gone. You've bought us the extra time we need, so let's use it. We can move up

272

the timeline. Texas is all set. It's the most important strike of all. The president has taken you on personally. So if you carry this attack off, it'll have tremendous symbolic and political impact.'

'And if I don't carry it off?'

'You've done it six times before. Brilliantly. No one else could have.'

'Texas is different. I'm worried.'

'The hard work has been done.'

He slowed as they neared the shed and swatted away a gnat. 'Shar, I'm positive that security guard recognized me.'

'How could he possibly?'

'I don't know. But he did. And the police came to this house.'

She looked just a bit uncomfortable. 'As they did to twenty other houses in this town and ten thousand in Michigan.'

'But they came here.'

'One goofball cop came. Saw nothing useful. And he left.'

They reached the shed, and Green Man took a key from a string around his neck and unlocked the padlock. The heavy door creaked open. Sharon stepped inside and flicked on the overhead light, and he followed her in. It was cool and windowless, and the space somehow seemed bigger inside than it looked from the outside. Green Man pushed the door closed and drew the heavy inside bolt, and they stood side by side looking at the workbenches.

The diver propulsion vehicle he had been building for weeks was finished. It was little more than an underwater scooter, modeled on the ones that Navy SEALs used to deliver swimmers and equipment to targets. He had built it from parts, and it consisted of a watertight casing with handles and equipment mounts, a battery-powered motor, and a hard-plastic propeller. His DPV was exactly the black color of the Kildeer River's basalt bottom. The engine was strong enough to drive the eight-inch propeller and carry him and a hundred pounds of demolition equipment down the river at nearly three hundred feet per minute.

The time fuses and other incendiary equipment he would take with him lay spread out on the workbenches in various states of readiness. He would need a few more days of tinkering to get it all mission-ready, but Sharon was right. He could move up the timeline if necessary and head to Texas in less than a week. The thought excited and terrified Green Man. In less than a week, he could strike the Hanson Oil Field, triumph brilliantly, and vanish forever. Or in less than a week he might screw things up and die or be caught and never see his wife and kids again.

As if reading his mind, Sharon took his hand and said, 'Mitch, I know.'

He lifted his gaze from the workbenches to her sympathetic hazel eyes. 'I'm so tired. I haven't had a good night's sleep in months.'

'We'll both sleep well soon.'

'That security guard in Texas said he recognized me, and I really think he did.'

'How is that possible?' Sharon asked. 'You have a great memory, and you said you never saw him before.'

'I do have a very good memory, but it's not perfect. There are people who are called super-recognizers. They literally never forget a face. Scotland Yard uses them to crack big cases.'

'You think that's what the guy was?'

'I've never been looked at the way he was looking at me.

It was like a camera in his eyes. Many super-recognizers gravitate to law enforcement or private security. They work for the police. They work for casinos and identify card counters.'

'So even if he was a super-recognizer, where could he have seen you? You've never been to Texas before.'

'I've been thinking about that. He might not know Mitch, but he might have known Paul. The FBI circulated posters of Paul Sayers when they were hunting him. That security guard wasn't a young man. If he was in private security back then, he could've seen the wanted poster . . .'

'And remembered a face for twenty years? A face that's aged and been surgically altered?'

'I know it's a stretch, but they literally never forget a face.'

'So, even if it's true, what of it?' Sharon asked. 'He recognized someone who no longer exists.'

'I just don't like the feel of it,' Green Man said. 'I never should have walked down to the oil field. I should have left after checking out the river. I wanted to see the field at the exact time when I would strike, but there was no specific need to do it. It was a mistake.'

'And I shouldn't have told Ted Dolan that you painted that landscape,' Sharon admitted. 'That was a mistake, too. You told the trooper in Nebraska that you were an artist. So that information could be on the profile the FBI is sending out to local law enforcement.'

'The real mistake was for me to tell that Nebraska trooper something true about myself,' Green Man said. 'But the point is that we're both making little errors and they mount up. Someone smart is going to catch on and follow one up.'

275

'Not Jim Brennan,' Sharon said.

'No, not Brennan. But someone.' He took her in his arms. 'I love you very much, Sharon. And the kids.'

'And you're the strongest and bravest man in the world, and you're doing this for them. And for our grandchildren.'

'If I don't make it –'

'Don't even say that. You will.'

'Tell them that I'll be there with them in spirit –'

'No, I won't listen.' Her eyes were almost fanatical as she looked up at him. 'You will strike in Texas. You will complete this vital last mission. And then you will come home and we'll make the break together. Yes? Say it.'

He gently stroked the side of her cheek and whispered in her ear, 'Yes, I'll do it.'

39

The president led a short man with a pencil mustache out of the Oval Office. He spoke in short, simple, optimistic sentences. 'We're gonna get this done. And fast. I'm bringing in a great team. A kick-ass team, Mr President.'

'That's what we need. Spare no expense.'

'I know the FBI tried to silo this and keep things from the press. I think we can use the press.'

'Harris, that's exactly what they're there for.'

'But I may have to skirt a rule or two, or step on some toes, sir.'

'Stomp away. Results are what I care about right now. I want this guy nailed.'

'Understood, Mr President. Thank you for your trust. I won't disappoint you.'

They shook hands, and Harris Carnes headed out while the president returned to the Oval Office and clicked on a sports channel to watch a basketball game. It wasn't on yet, and they were showing curling, of all things. He grimaced and clicked the TV off, and for a moment he simply didn't know what to do. He glanced down at some reports on his desk. He hated reading, but he picked up a report and flipped through a few pages, and then buzzed his secretary and said, 'Send Harburg in.'

The scholarly aide entered his office seconds later and saw him holding the report. 'Mr President, thank you for reading –'

'I just met with Harris Carnes,' the president said. 'I want him to have everything he needs.'

'Yes, sir. Jim Brennan has been trying to contact you to see if –'

'Send him a fruit basket,' the president said. 'Have you met Carnes?'

'Not yet, sir.'

'I like him. He's a street fighter. That's what we need to catch Green Man.'

'Yes, sir.'

The president nodded down at the report. 'Now what's this about India?'

'Well, Mr President, as you know, they've been experiencing a heat wave –'

'It's a hot country. Hot curry. Hot climate. I'm not much of a fan.'

'Yes, sir. But it's been going on for five months, and temperatures reached a hundred and forty degrees last week.'

'Jesus Christ. Can people live in that kind of heat?'

'Not easily, sir. Among the worst stories were thirty children who died in a train compartment.'

'Terrible. Draft a letter of condolence to the prime minister. I'll sign it. But how does this affect us?'

'Well, Mr President, it seems like maybe the monsoon rains won't come to cool things off this year. If that happens, the long-term effect on the crops necessary to feed billions of people will be devastating. I spent two years in India, and there's never been heat like this before. And it's gone on so long –' He broke off, terrified.

The president was staring at him, sympathetic but slightly exasperated. 'I don't know why smart people have

278

such a hard time with this. That's the thing about a one-time weather event. It hasn't happened before. Like Noah's flood.'

'Yes, sir.' The young aide hesitated and then said softly, 'That's a good example, sir, of what is seen as an apocalyptic event that destroyed all life on earth.'

'It didn't destroy all life on earth,' the president said. 'We're here.'

'I meant symbolically, sir. I don't think we should take that biblical story literally, but it speaks to the importance of –'

'Listen, we're monitoring the situation in India, and we'll take care of it, and everything will be fine. What you need to do is leave the worrying to me. The monsoon rains have always come, and they'll come this year. Right?'

'I hope so.'

'Of course they will. Try not to look so worried. Do something fun this weekend. Do you like football? I'll get you tickets. And take this report back. I've read it.'

'Thank you for your consideration, sir.'

'Shut the door on your way out.'

The aide left, and the president was alone. He walked to the window and looked out at the immaculate grounds. A sprinkler was pumping. For a moment he thought of 140-degree heat and thirty kids slowly dying in a metal train car. He was not a stupid man, and on some deep level he knew that the earth was warming in a way that would soon be unstoppable. But the thing was . . .

The president stepped closer to the window and turned slightly so he could see the lush White House lawn and his own reflection in the polished glass window. The thing was that he was going to die. All men died, and

279

somehow – and it was almost inconceivable to him – he was also going to die. Given his age, it would happen in the next twenty years. And when he died, he would cease to exist. He would be gone. And when that happened, nothing really mattered, the world would be gone, because he wouldn't be here.

40

Ellen was marking papers and Julie was doing her calculus homework when the buzzer sounded. They glanced at each other to see who was busier, and Julie finally gave up, put down her calculator, and walked to the intercom. 'Yes?'

'This is Agent Tom Smith of the FBI,' a voice said. 'Is Ellen Douglas there?'

Julie looked at her mom, who stood up from her stack of papers and walked quickly to the intercom. 'This is Ellen.'

'Dr Douglas, I'm downstairs.'

'I figured that out.'

'I was wondering if I could speak with you in person.'

'About what?' Ellen asked.

'I would prefer to talk about it privately, in your apartment.'

'About what?' Ellen repeated.

'A case I'm working on that I can't discuss in public.'

Julie looked worried. Ellen gave her a reassuring smile and then said into the intercom, 'Well, it appears you already know my apartment number?'

'Yes, I do. Thank you. See you in a minute.'

Ellen pressed the button to buzz open the downstairs door and turned to her daughter. 'It'll be okay, sweetheart.'

'Mom, it's the FBI.'

'I've talked to them before about different things. Trust me. This is nothing.'

'Bullshit it's nothing.'

'They probably just want a reference on someone they're thinking of hiring.'

'Sure, and that's why they're dropping by our apartment so late without calling first.'

'Maybe it would be better if you left us alone to talk.'

'No way.'

'Really, sweetheart.'

'Really, no,' Julie said back to her, softly but firmly, refusing to leave. She folded her arms, and mother and daughter stared at each other in silence.

'Okay, I admit it may not be nothing,' Ellen finally said. 'But I promise you I can take care of this. I've talked to my share of law enforcement people over the years. It'll be easier if I do it alone.'

'Why is that?'

'Trust me.'

'Maybe it's about me. I've been going to all those climate rallies. People get excited and say things they probably shouldn't say in public. Maybe I can help. Or is there something you don't want me to hear?'

'This isn't about you,' Ellen said.

'How do you know?'

'And there's nothing I don't want you to hear. But I need to do this alone.'

There was a knock at the front door.

'Julie, I'm asking you not to make this more difficult than it already is. Please, sweetheart.' Ellen waited and then repeated, this time with a clear note of desperation, 'Please, dear,' and she went to open the door.

Julie, left alone in the living room, hesitated. Then she switched on her cell phone and slipped it into a decorative Berber pottery bowl on a shelf and left the room.

Ellen opened the door and saw a tall, gangly young man in khakis and a light blue button-down shirt and a very short haircut standing a little nervously. 'Hi,' he said, 'I'm Agent Tom Smith. I'm sorry for dropping by so late –'

'And for not calling first.'

'Yes, but it's urgent. Can you give me fifteen minutes?'

Ellen led him into the living room and was pleased to see that Julie had vanished. She gestured him toward the sofa, and the FBI agent sat down. Ellen sat opposite him on an armchair and studied him. 'Is "Tom Smith" your real name?'

'Yes, ma'am. I mean, Dr Douglas.'

'You can call me Ellen. How old are you?'

'Twenty-six, ma'am. I mean, Ellen.'

'Can I please see some credentials?'

He fumbled with his wallet and showed her a badge. She studied it and handed it back. 'What's your rank and specific job title?'

'I'm a field agent. Right now I'm working for a major taskforce. The one pursuing Green Man. I'm a special assistant to the commander.'

She didn't flinch at the mention of Green Man. 'And your commander's name?'

'Jim Brennan. But the reason I came tonight is –'

'Don't you think I listen to the news?' Ellen asked, cutting him off. 'That investigation has been shut down and moved to another agency. Your commander is out of the picture. Which presumably means that you are, too.'

Tom looked back at her and nodded. 'Unfortunately,

you're right about Commander Brennan. But I still work for the FBI, and I'm still very much on this case. If you don't want to talk to me, I can go to the people who are now running this investigation and you can talk to them. I guarantee you're much better off with me, but that's your choice.'

Ellen sensed that he was telling the truth. He was shy, and he seemed honest, and he was also young and clearly nervous. She felt that she could manage him, and she didn't want to dig in and seem defensive and make this bigger than it already was. 'Let's get this over with,' she said. 'What do you want?'

'You hold a chemical engineering degree from Berkeley, and you're a professor at Columbia and the director of the Green Center, an environmental nonprofit. Do I have that right?'

'Yes, that's all correct,' Ellen said. 'I assume you don't want to question me about Columbia, so you're here to talk to me about the Green Center?'

'No, actually I'm not. I'd like to ask you some questions about the time when you were a student at Berkeley.'

Ellen tried to hide her dismay with a soft chuckle. 'That was decades ago.'

'You arrived in California when you were eighteen. You were a chemistry major. A straight-A student. You graduated from Berkeley summa cum laude.'

'I assume the FBI doesn't have any problems with my high college grades?' Ellen asked.

'No, Dr Douglas. I mean, Ellen. But I also graduated summa, so I know what that takes. You must be very good at chemistry.'

'Look, you can call me whatever you want. But you said

fifteen minutes. We're already down to ten. Why don't you get to the point.'

'Sure,' Tom said. 'Shortly after you arrived at Berkeley, you became active in several radical environmental groups.'

'It wasn't illegal to join them.'

'And through one of those groups you met a man who was slightly older and had just graduated from MIT and moved out west. You became friends.'

Ellen looked back at him.

'You were his girlfriend for almost five years. Can you tell me his name?'

'You must know it,' Ellen said. 'You've done your homework.'

'Tell it to me anyway. His full name, please.'

Ellen hesitated a long beat and then spoke his name out loud to a stranger for the first time in nearly twenty years: 'His name was Paul William Sayers, but he disliked the William and never used it.'

In her bedroom, at her desk, Julie had accessed her cell phone through an app and was listening to the conversation. Within seconds she had pulled up information on Paul Sayers, including his obituary photo in the *San Francisco Chronicle*. She gasped as she recognized the man she had spoken with in Riverside Park, who had quoted Green Man's manifesto to her. She felt light-headed and gripped the edge of the desk. When she zoned back in, the FBI agent was asking fast questions, and her mom was giving short answers.

'Did you and Paul Sayers belong to the same radical environmental groups?'

'Some of them.'

'Did you go to meetings and rallies and speeches together?'

'We did everything together.'

'So when those groups staged protests or activist missions, you went to those together?'

'You'll have to be specific.'

'Tree spiking in Northern California?'

'Paul and I never spiked trees.'

'He was wanted by the FBI for setting fire to the Gunderson Logging Company's plant in Humboldt County. Were you part of that?'

'No. And I know nothing about it.'

'But Paul led and financed that attack?'

'The FBI said he did.'

'I thought you two did everything together?'

'Mr Smith, you have less than five minutes left. I'm doing my best to answer your questions. Don't play games with me and ask me about things you already know.'

'What I already know is that the FBI never caught your boyfriend because he died in another attack four months later that I assume you also weren't part of?'

'Correct. And this is getting rather painful for me, so . . .'

'It must have been painful for him, too. His group blew up a gas facility, there was a large explosion, and his badly burned body was found in the wreckage. Yes?'

'Yes.'

'If it was so badly burned, how was his body identified?'

'You'll have to consult the legal records of that case. My memory is that the coroner identified it.'

'A coroner who a year later left his job and spent his last five years in Europe, living rather well.'

'I know nothing about that. Paul died. We buried him.'

'You delivered the eulogy at his funeral.'

'I did.'

'It was published in a local paper. I was able to find a copy of it. It was moving. Your last line was that while Paul was dead, his spirit would live on forever.'

Julie heard her mother sob, and she stood up and took a step toward her bedroom door. Then she stopped herself. She was confused and not thinking clearly, but she knew she had to do something beyond just comforting her mother.

In the living room, the young FBI agent looked genuinely concerned. 'Ellen, I'm sorry if my questions upset you. Can I get you a tissue?'

'Just get out.'

'I will very soon, and I promise I won't come back. We're almost done. I know this could sound contemptuous and scornful, but it's not – it's actually just completely practical. I need to ask you if you were just taking poetic license with that eulogy or if you think Paul's spirit really lived on forever?'

Ellen looked back at him and realized that he was much smarter than he appeared and that he used his youth and nervousness to mask his cleverness. 'What do you want from me? Why don't you just say it?'

'Did Paul Sayers really die in that explosion?'

'Yes, my boyfriend died. We buried him.'

'You're aware that you can get into serious trouble if you lie to the FBI?'

'I'm aware that you asked me for fifteen minutes and you've gone over – in a lot of ways.'

'Paul Sayers's mother – Willa Sayers – is still alive, living in the same house in Cape May, New Jersey, where Paul grew up. Have you spoken with her?'

'Not in twenty years.'

'So you don't know if she also believes her son is dead?'

'I have no idea what she believes. She did come to the funeral.'

'I'll be talking to her soon, and it'll be interesting to compare her memories to yours. It must have been a very sad day for both of you.'

Ellen stood and took a step toward the front door. 'I'm tired, and your questions have brought back painful memories. I'd like you to go now.'

'I'm genuinely sorry,' Tom said, also standing up. 'By the way, I've seen your website for the Green Center. It's inspiring. You do great work.'

'Thank you. The door is this way, just in case you don't remember.'

He nodded and then said softly, looking directly into her eyes, 'So you don't think Paul Sayers is still alive and that he's Green Man?'

'What? That's ridiculous.'

'Is it? He's got the perfect background.'

'Except that he's dead.'

'Yes, except that he's dead. But if he was Green Man, and blowing things up, he might need a very smart chemist to help him from time to time.'

'Paul is long dead. Green Man uses violence, which I abhor. He kills children. I would never help him. Since you've been reading our website, you presumably know we've taken the position that he must stop. That what he's doing is morally wrong and indefensible.'

'Yes, I saw that,' Tom told her. 'And I know that you strongly advocated for that position. It's very principled of you. Good night, Ellen. Thank you for your time and help. I'll let myself out.' He walked to the door and pulled it closed behind him.

Ellen followed him and drew the chain, and just as she drew it, she heard the back service door of the apartment also close. She ran quickly down the hallway and saw that Julie was gone from her room and that her computer was on. The app was still connected, and it took Ellen all of five seconds to realize that Julie had listened to her conversation with the FBI agent.

She was tempted to run out in search of Julie, but she knew that her daughter had sped down the stairs and was already out of the building. There was no way to catch her. And Ellen had something else to do that was extremely time-critical.

She carefully wrote out a warning message about Tom Smith and the questions he had posed. She used special software to encrypt it, and she sent it over the dark web to an email address she had never used before and would never use again.

41

Julie hurried after the young FBI agent and caught him fifty feet before the corner. The usual crowd was hanging out at a bodega up ahead. She had only to shout and they would come running, but she made an instant decision that she preferred to confront him alone. Julie was usually a clear thinker, but her mind was whirling. 'Hey, Tom Smith.'

He turned, puzzled, but figured it out quickly: 'You must be Ellen's daughter.'

'You asshole. You made my mother cry.'

'I didn't mean to,' Tom told her, sounding sincere. 'You're Julie, right? Listen, sometimes I have to do things I don't want because I'm trying to catch a murderer.'

'Green Man.'

He looked back at her. 'So you were listening to our conversation?'

'Aren't you smart,' Julie said 'But then you graduated summa cum laude, right? Where from?'

'Stanford.'

'I would think they'd have better job placement.'

'You seem pretty sharp yourself,' Tom told her. She was surprised by how young and unsure of himself he was – he reminded her of a genius math nerd from her high school. 'Do you know a man named Paul Sayers?' he asked. 'He probably goes by a different name now. He was an old friend of your mom's.'

'Sure,' Julie said. 'I call him Uncle Green Man. He stops by for brunch and we discuss what he should blow up next.'

'That's not as funny as you think,' the FBI agent said. 'Have you really met him?'

'You wouldn't believe me anyway.'

'Probably not,' Tom admitted, 'But here's something you should believe. There's a way that you can help your mother.'

'Why would you care about helping her?'

'I admire your mom, and the more I know about this situation, the more I can protect her. And you.' He was looking at her sympathetically. 'We're not as different as you think.'

'Then try telling me the truth. How did you find my mother?' Julie demanded.

'I can't tell you all the details. But I don't condemn any of the choices she's made. I can tell you're also a very good person, and I'd like to help the two of you get out of this mess.'

She stepped forward to face him. 'Why should I trust you if you can't even admit the truth to yourself? I can tell that you're really smart. You must know that what you're doing is wrong, deep down. You're trying to catch some- one who can't be caught and stop something that can't be stopped, or none of us will have a chance. If you went to Stanford, you understand the science as well as I do, and I can see in your eyes that on some level you know I'm right.'

'On some level you are right,' Tom admitted, 'but this isn't always an easy world. Now let's talk about how we can both help your mom before it's too late . . .'

His gentleness and sincerity confused Julie, and for a dizzying moment, she was tempted to trust him. She recoiled from the thought, but she had taken in too many things too fast, and she stumbled back, suddenly light-headed.

'Was Paul Sayers in New York recently?' he asked her softly. 'Do you know the last time your mother saw him? Julie, are you okay?'

She looked back into his eyes and whispered, 'Damn you to hell.' And then the pavement under her feet seemed to reel, and she sagged and almost fell.

He stepped forward and held her up. 'Do you need a doctor?'

'TOLD YOU IT WAS JULIE!' a loud voice shouted from the direction of the bodega.

'Get out of here,' she said to Tom, trying weakly to pull free.

'Not till you're sure you're okay.'

'Let her go, motherfucker,' a man commanded from the corner. Tom glanced toward the lights and saw shadows hurrying toward him. He released Julie, and she was able to stand.

Deep and angry voices boomed: 'Jules?' 'You okay?' 'He messing with you?'

They were big and street tough, with chains and ripped abs and first beards, and she didn't hang out with them, but she had grown up with them, and she was one of them.

'No, he's not messing with me. He's getting out of here.'

But they had circled Tom. 'Somebody's begging for an ass whupping.'

She warned them, 'He's FBI.'

'Oh shit, then he's gonna bust all of our asses,' Terrell, the leader, said, and there was laughter as the circle closed tighter.

Tom took out his father's Colt and raised it. His hand visibly shook.

'What are you waving that around for, you piece of shit?'

'Let him go,' Julie said to Terrell, and then she crumbled to the pavement.

Terrell reluctantly nodded that they should let him go, and while they clustered around Julie and tried to revive her, Tom hurried up the block, and soon he was running for the nearest subway station.

42

The Garden State Parkway was wide-open in the weekday morning, and Tom took the express lane and cruised past shore points, never dipping under eighty. He was in a rented Dodge Charger, sipping an enormous cup of coffee from a rest stop and listening to Bruce Springsteen on a local radio station when his cell phone rang. With reluctance he switched Bruce off and took the call from Grant.

'Tom, where the hell are you?'

'On the Garden State Parkway, thirty miles north of Atlantic City.'

'Planning on some early-morning gambling?'

'No, I'm on my way back to DC. I'll take the ferry from Cape May to Delaware and get back this evening. How's Brennan?'

'Not so good,' Grant said. 'He's tried everything to turn this around – reached out to every friend he ever had and called in every favor he was ever owed – but I'm afraid that ship has sailed.'

'Meaning what?' Tom asked.

'It's over. Let's just say it wasn't the most graceful transition to retirement, but I think he's finally accepted that it's a done deal.'

'That's fucking unbelievable,' Tom said with real anger. 'I tried to call him a few times, but he's not taking my calls.'

'He's not taking anyone's calls right now,' Grant said.

'He's in self-imposed seclusion. But he knows the way this town works, and he'll get over it.'

'I doubt that. And Earl?'

'Also took retirement. I heard he was on some tropical island. Hopefully at a hotel that allows smoking in the rooms.'

'So I guess that puts all of us outside the investigation.'

There was a noticeable hesitation, and then Grant said, 'Not exactly.'

'What does that mean?' Tom asked, suddenly on his guard.

'Of course no one feels worse about Brennan than I do. He was like a father to me. But they've asked me –'

'Who asked you?'

'The attorney general asked me to be a bridge to the continuing investigation at DHS, making sure they have what we had and they know what we knew.'

'Someone has to do it,' Tom said.

'This investigation has to go forward, and Green Man has to be caught.'

'Sure, you had no choice,' Tom agreed, thinking that even Grant, for all his ambition, couldn't feel very good about himself.

'And Carnes is moving forward very aggressively, with the full cooperation of the administration.'

'I'm sure he is.'

'I also have to help clean up the loose ends of what the FBI was doing. And it's come to my attention that nobody knows exactly what the hell you're up to.'

Tom spoke carefully. 'I came up with an idea, a hunch, and Brennan let me pursue it.'

'What was the hunch?'

'That I might be able to profile Green Man based on his engineering skill set.'

'You were doing this alone?'

'No, I was working with a professor at Carnegie Mellon.'

'Any luck?'

Tom glanced down at the pad on the seat next to him, on which he had jotted down notes. An address in Cape May for Willa Sayers was written at the top in blue pen. 'One or two possibly interesting things. I'll brief you as soon as I'm back.'

'Tomorrow morning.' It was not a request but an order.

'Sure. Are you in the war room, or did they close that down? Are you in the Hoover building?'

'I'm over at DHS,' Grant said.

'I see.'

Grant didn't like Tom's tone, and his own voice hardened noticeably. 'Be in my office at nine A.M. I want it clear that you are no longer considered operational on this investigation. Whatever you've found out in the past week – or think you may have found out – write it up tonight and send it to me. Brief me in person tomorrow and then you'll check in with Hannah Lee, who will reassign you to another case. Clear?'

'Crystal,' Tom said.

'So why the hell are you taking the roundabout scenic route?'

'It helps me think clearly.'

'Like Green Man driving through Nebraska,' Grant suggested in his mocking tone.

'Same concept, I guess. And I've heard the ferry to Lewes is worth the ticket.'

'Well, just ferry your ass back to DC tonight and be in my office tomorrow morning bright and early,' Grant commanded, and rang off.

Green Man sped southward, trying to deal with mixed feelings of nostalgia and dread. His loaded gun was in his right jacket pocket, and this time he was ready to use it. He had gotten Ellen's encrypted message a little before nine P.M., and had spent a half hour furtively learning all he could about Tom Smith online. After a brief conversation with Sharon, he had set out in his Jeep and driven through the night. Despite the wide-open roads and his anxiety about this meddlesome FBI agent, he'd forced himself to stay close to the speed limit and made it from Michigan to south Jersey in ten hours. As he drove into the beach city where he had grown up, he fought unsuccessfully against a rising tide of decades-old guilt.

When Green Man had made his break, he'd reluctantly said goodbye to this entire part of his life. His mother was an unstable and emotionally volatile woman who could neither keep secrets nor be trusted to follow a set of protocols, even if her son's life depended on it. If she'd known that he was alive, she would not have been able to keep it to herself or let him have the separation he needed to make the break work. She would have endangered everything about his new life.

Luckily she had two other children and a growing brood of grandchildren who lived close. Green Man had provided for her in his will, and with terrible reluctance he'd let her believe that he was dead. For twenty years she had carried the grief of having lost her son, and not a week had gone by that he hadn't thought of her and felt guilty at having let her believe that he was dead. He knew there had been no choice, but as he drove by the stately Victorian bed and breakfasts, he hated himself for telling such a lie and causing such pain to the woman who had given him life.

He skirted Lake Lily and saw the famous lighthouse in the distance. He had spent many days in his teenage years at the three-mile strip of town beaches, breaking all the rules as a rebellious adolescent and then enforcing them as a town lifeguard. He had learned to surf and scuba dive and had bought a sea kayak and fished from it much farther from shore than was safe. He recalled gleaming dawns, a mile from shore, watching the sunrise as he rode swells and chased schools of bluefish.

Green Man cruised past the wetlands and turned north into narrow side streets. His part of Cape May was less than a mile from the fashionable B&Bs that beckoned to rich weekenders, but it was a completely different world. He drove past his elementary school, and as the houses got smaller and the yards knitted closer together, he slowed and tried to contain the memories, few of them good. When he was in fifth grade, his father – whom he had been very close to – had died of a massive stroke. He'd died in a wicker chair on the back porch, and Green Man had found him slumped over the next morning and tried in vain to wake him.

He had never been that close to his mother and two siblings, who had stayed in south Jersey. He had been the one to get out, and from New Haven to Boston to San Francisco, he had never looked back. Now he was turning onto his old street, and damn this FBI agent for bringing him back to this sad block that hadn't changed in twenty

299

years. Green Man's guilt about his past was also forward-looking – one of the horrible things about making his break had been leaving family and dear friends behind, and he knew that if Sharon, Gus, and Kim made a similar break in a few weeks, they would suffer the same way. A break from the past was exactly what it sounded like – even if it was successful, it left a life smashed and forever in pieces.

Tom found Topsail Street and parked in front of a white clapboard house. It was a block of modest two-story houses with neat yards, many of them festooned with small garden plots. Far up the street, two boys punted a football back and forth and laughed when it bounced off a parked car. Tom watched them for a moment, imagining Green Man marching past these flower beds on his way to school and sitting up in a bedroom of this run-down white house, studying high school chemistry on his long path to trying to save the world. It was exactly the kind of house Tom had lived in in about six different states, and he couldn't shake the feeling that he was hunting himself as he trudged up the front walk to the screen door.

Grant's words rang in his memory. He was off the Green Man investigation and no longer operational. So he had no real authority to be doing what he was doing, and he knew he had to be very careful. If he alarmed this woman enough so that she called the FBI, he could be reprimanded or fired or probably even worse. But at the same time, he was almost certain that Green Man had grown up in this house, and Tom had been on the trail so long that he had to see it for himself. He cautioned himself to go easy and rang the buzzer.

He had called her from the road, and she was expecting him and came quickly. Willa Sayers was thin and even starting to look a bit frail, a white-haired woman in her seventies with a nervous, birdlike tick of moving her head from side to side. 'Come in. I called my daughter, Robin, because she's really smart about these things and I thought maybe she might be able to help answer your questions, but she has to work this morning. She said you can call her if you need to.'

The house was low-ceilinged and dreary, badly in need of a paint job and some new furniture. The matching sofa and love seat looked like they had been purchased thirty years ago, and a large cinnamon-colored tabby curled up on a footstool eyed Tom suspiciously. 'I'm sorry, what question did your daughter want to help me with?' he asked, sitting down on the edge of the love seat.

'This is about taxes, isn't it?'

'No,' Tom said with a smile. 'I'm sorry for the confusion, but you can relax, I'm not from the IRS, and I have nothing to do with taxes. I hate paying them myself.'

She was sitting facing him, and he could see her visibly relax. She was not good at hiding her feelings, and her thoughts were immediately reflected in her facial expressions and nervous gestures. 'Well, that's a relief. But why are you here?'

'I'm from the FBI, but please don't worry. You're not in any trouble, and no one you know is, either. I'm just following up on some old cases, and one of them touches you slightly. If you could give me some answers, I'd really appreciate it.'

'So these are cold cases?' she asked. 'I think I heard that term on TV.'

301

'Yes, ma'am. That's exactly right. Very cold cases. In fact, the one I need to ask you about is almost twenty years old.'

Willa Sayers did the math, wet her lips with her tongue, and leaned slightly forward. 'So you're here to ask me about Paul?'

'Yes, ma'am. I wanted to ask you a few questions about Paul William Sayers. I understand he never liked the William much,' he said with a smile.

'That was his name, and he liked it fine.'

'What was Paul like as a child? Was he happy here in Cape May?'

'Of course he was happy. At least when he looked up from his books. He read all the time. But you didn't come here to ask me about any of that. Forgive my directness, but what do you want?'

'Okay,' Tom said, 'maybe it's best if we jump in. I hope this isn't painful for you, and I promise to be brief. I'm here to review what happened at the Gunderson Logging plant. As you know, the FBI, at the time, felt that Paul –'

'My son had nothing to do with that fire.' Her tone had become shrill and was unequivocal.

'How do you know?'

'Because Paul was a good boy and he had a heart of gold. Some people died in that fire, and Paul wouldn't hurt a fly.'

'So you think the FBI was wrong?'

'Yes, you were wrong.' She clasped her hands together.

'Actually I was only three years old,' Tom told her with a grin, and she gave him a nervous smile back. 'So I had nothing to do with what they thought back then. I'm just trying to clarify the old records. From those records, I

302

know Paul was involved with some environmental groups that did things like that. And he had a girlfriend, Ellen, who was also involved in a bit of radical behavior. Did you ever meet her?'

'Paul brought her out here once. And I met her at the funeral.' As Willa spoke the word 'funeral,' her clasped hands trembled.

Tom followed up softly: 'Paul's funeral in Oakland?'

She choked back words and just nodded.

'Have you spoken to Ellen Douglas since then? She lives nearby in New York.'

'Why would I speak to her?' She was incredulous at the suggestion.

'To remember your son with somebody else who loved him,' Tom suggested.

'I don't need anyone's help to remember my son,' Willa told him indignantly, and fell into a stony silence. As if sensing her agitation, the cat jumped off the footstool and, with a contemptuous look at Tom, padded away.

Tom looked down at his notes to give her a few seconds to recover. He was coming to the most difficult questions, and he reminded himself not to push too hard. 'So if you don't think Paul would have started the fire at the lumber plant, why do you think he participated in the attack at the gas company a few months later?'

'I don't know,' she admitted. 'Good people get dragged into trouble. Since my son died in that attack, I guess he wasn't very good at attacking things. Was he?'

'I see your point,' Tom said. His eyes were still on his pad, but he slowly lifted them to her face and studied her carefully as he asked, 'So you're sure that Paul died in that fire?'

Her confusion and anger were evident as she snapped, 'What kind of a question is that? I just told you I went to his funeral.'

'Yes, ma'am. But . . . his body was badly burned. You never had any doubts about the identification by the coroner or anything like that?'

'You will please have some respect for the dead,' she hissed, 'or I'll ask you to leave.' A charged silence followed, and while Tom had serious doubts about whether Ellen had been telling him the full truth in her Harlem apartment, he completely trusted the outrage of this high-strung and still-grieving mother in Cape May. Somewhere to the back of the house wind chimes tinkled faintly.

'I'm sorry if I upset you,' Tom said. 'I hate this part of my job. I'll be leaving very soon, and I appreciate your time. Could I ask you about the money you inherited? Paul left you a million dollars. Yet you never moved . . .'

"Why would I move? This house is where I raised my children. It's where my husband died. And it's where I will die.'

'Sure,' Tom said, 'but you don't seem to have spent any of that million dollars . . .'

'Most of the money has been divided into college funds for my grandchildren. Paul liked education, and I think he would have been pleased with that use of the fruits of his hard work.'

'I think he would have,' Tom agreed. 'Mrs Sayers, this is a strange question, but when I was growing up in small towns there were a few faraway places I used to fantasize about traveling to and even living in one day. Was there a place like that for Paul, when he was a boy, that he talked about one day moving to that would give him a whole new life?'

304

'Paul was happy here in Cape May,' she answered resentfully. 'He didn't need to dream about other places.'

'Has there ever been a time when a member of your family was in trouble or maybe there was a money problem, and somehow it disappeared or got taken care of in a way that you didn't quite understand, and it seemed like a miracle? Like someone was watching over you?'

'Someone is watching over us,' she told him with certainty. 'We're a churchgoing family, and we pray, but we don't need miracles. We can take care of our own. And I'm sorry, but I've had enough of this.'

'Okay, here's my very last question. Besides Ellen in New York, was there anyone Paul was very close with, who you think might shed light on some of what we've talked about?' She looked back at him and didn't answer, so he tried again. 'Someone who, if Paul had lived, he would have remained lifelong friends with? A boyhood friend or maybe a college roommate who I should talk to next?'

Her head twitched anxiously from side to side, but she remained silent, as if she had run out of answers to his endless foolish questions.

Tom stood up. 'Thank you very much, Mrs Sayers. You've been incredibly patient and helpful. Oh, just one more thing – I believe your son was a bit of an artist growing up. Do you still have anything that Paul drew?'

She glanced over at a nearby wall where a framed pencil sketch of a seascape hung near a window. Tom stepped over to it and studied the wave rising toward a rocky shore, above which three gulls circled. It was skillful and minimalist. A few pencil strokes captured the torque and energy of the cresting breaker, and the gulls with their wings

305

extended were single squiggly lines yet unmistakably sea-birds hanging above pounding surf. 'It's really very good,' Tom said.

'My son was gifted, and it was a great shame he died so young,' she said with finality, as if twisting closed the clasp on a treasured locket. It clearly signaled an end to a conversation that had upset her. She was standing to see Tom out, her palms smoothing down her blue housedress. 'Where are you off to now?'

He took the hint and headed for the front door. 'DC,' he told her. 'I'm taking the afternoon ferry.'

'There's one in forty minutes,' Willa Sayers told him, opening the door for him. 'If you hurry you can catch it. Mind the rain.' The screen door swung shut behind him.

43

Drizzle was stiffening into hard rain when Tom drove his rented car onto the ferry, bought a ticket, and parked in a numbered space on the first level. Anticipating a rough ride, workers were chaining the cars together. Tom headed up to the second and third levels, where there was passenger seating. The outside deck spaces were drenched and deserted, so Tom walked into the covered section and found a seat by a window. He sat by himself looking out at the Atlantic as rain pelted the glass. Just before the ferry departed, there was an announcement that the ride would be rough and anyone who wanted to leave could still get off. Those who stayed on board were advised to remain seated.

The ferry pulled away from the Cape May dock and chugged off on its seventeen-mile crossing to Lewes, Delaware. The boat was only half full, and the passenger section was calm till they left the shelter of the shore and the first waves hit. The ferry was soon rocking wildly as it plowed forward, and a little boy began screaming while a teenaged girl in the row ahead of Tom puked into a bag.

Tom tried to ignore the rising din in the pitching boat and focus on what he would do in DC. He couldn't directly disobey Grant, so he would have to type up some sort of report that described his theory about Paul Sayers surviving the gas company explosion and Tom's subsequent meetings with Ellen Douglas and Willa Sayers. But he didn't trust Carnes to follow up correctly, so he decided to write a report that – while accurate – underplayed the evidence that Paul Sayers had become Green Man. He could easily make it seem like a far-fetched theory that still lacked hard evidence.

Tom felt someone's eyes on him. Alarmed, he turned and quickly scanned the large seating area. He had always had a keen sense for when he was being watched, but no one seemed to be staring at him. Then he spotted a middle-aged female ferry worker in boots and a wet rain jacket who was passing out free bottles of water. She had walked by his row, but when she saw him looking around she stomped over in her boots and grinned: 'I thought maybe you were sleeping.'

'Not in this,' Tom said, as the ferry rode a wave and juddered down into a trough.

She tossed him a bottle. 'Don't worry, I've seen us cross in worse.'

'Does it delay the trip much?'

'It slows us a bit, but we'll be fine,' she promised. 'Want a second bottle?'

'One will do. Thanks.'

The girls in front of him had gotten their sick friend onto her feet and were leading her toward a bathroom.

Tom glanced back out the window. The ferry's ads claimed that dolphins could often be seen during the crossing, but visibility was low on this stormy afternoon, and there was nothing to see except angry sky and tumultuous ocean. He returned to his thoughts about the investigation. He would turn in a report to Grant and DHS that was factually accurate but that soft-pedaled the secret he'd uncovered. Then he would seek out Brennan, whom he trusted and who had first gotten him into this. Brennan would know what to do with his discovery, or at least whom to take it to. Tom still held a faint hope that what he'd found might be a big enough break in the case to vindicate Brennan and allow the old commander to take an active role in the final phase of the Green Man investigation.

Sitting in the wildly pitching ferry, Tom knew that he had unearthed a nugget of pure gold. He wasn't sure how quickly the secret would lead authorities to Green Man, but he understood its intrinsic value. No one else knew it, and Tom had to be wise and careful in figuring out what to do with it. There were chain of command considerations and there was also considerable time pressure – he couldn't dare keep the discovery to himself for too long. But one thing was certain – he knew he was right. Green Man was Paul Sayers, and Paul Sayers was alive and living somewhere in Michigan. Ellen had skillfully tried to parry his questions, and Willa hadn't known the truth about her son, which was a testament to Green Man's iron will and sense of purpose. But the two conversations had convinced Tom that he was absolutely right and also given him a much fuller picture of the man he was chasing.

Green Man had grown up as Paul Sayers in that unassuming white house in Cape May, a brilliant boy who'd never quite fitted in. He'd left it behind, the way Tom had escaped his own stifling childhood, and had become a successful engineer on the West Coast. He'd fallen in love with Ellen and moved into radical environmentalism till the FBI had closed in on him. He'd faked his death with an explosion, paid off a coroner to misidentify a burned corpse, and vanished. With his wealth, brilliance, and meticulousness, he'd probably had all the documents for a new and very different identity prepared and waiting like a fresh set of clothes. He'd skipped his own funeral, climbed into his new skin, and started fresh – at least until the same radical call to action that had nearly doomed him in San Francisco had been too strong to resist in Michigan two decades later . . .

'Excuse me, mister.' It was a nervous scrawny kid, maybe fourteen years old. 'You're in seventy-two, right?'

Tom blinked and tried to focus. He glanced down at his seat, but there was no number. 'What?'

'You're driving the Dodge Charger parked in space seventy-two, aren't you? There's a problem with your car. You'd better come.'

Tom stood. 'What's the matter with it?'

'Make sure to bring your ticket,' the kid said, and headed for a nearby exit.

Tom followed him. Soon he was trailing the kid down dimly lit concrete stairs toward the parking deck. They emerged onto a dark landing at the stern of the ferry, and Tom glimpsed the outlines of dozens of parked cars and trucks. The vehicles were chained together, and when the ferry listed, their chains rattled. 'So what's wrong with my car?' Tom turned to ask, but the kid was no longer next to him. 'Hey, where is my car? Where'd you go?' Tom's questions were swallowed by the howling wind and the drone of the ship's engines. The kid was nowhere to be seen. Tom spun back toward the stairway, and a powerful blow hit him in the side of the face and nearly knocked him cold.

He landed hard and almost blanked. He was vaguely aware of being dragged over a rough surface. Hands searched his pockets. His wallet was taken, and something was being tugged away from inside his shirt – his father's Colt from its shoulder holster. That realization got Tom going again. His hands moved to his chest and tried to hold on to the gun, but

310

it was ripped free by the strong man who was now kneeling above him, aiming his own gun at his head.

Tom's vision cleared. The man had a thick black beard and mustache and was wearing a dark cap tilted low over his forehead. Tom opened his mouth to scream, but the man rammed the pistol barrel in hard enough to chip teeth. 'No one can hear you. But if you make a sound or struggle in any way, I'll blow your brains out.'

Tom looked into the man's gray eyes and nodded. The Colt was withdrawn so that he could breathe and answer back. 'You know who I am,' the man said. It was not a question. 'I was afraid that someone would be dumb enough to be smart enough to find me, and unfortunately that person is you.'

'The FBI knows I'm taking this ferry,' Tom gasped. 'If you kill me, they'll come looking. That kid'll come forward and talk . . .'

'That kid will take the two hundred bucks I paid him to get you and keep his mouth shut and stay out of trouble. But even if he does come forward, he knows nothing.'

'He knows the way you look.'

'This is not the way I look.'

'They'll find my car on board.'

'I have your parking ticket. I'll drive your car off the ferry in Delaware. No one will miss you, and by the time they do, you could be anywhere. And I'll be long gone. You must realize that we're both almost out of time.'

'What do you want?' Tom asked.

'Your life is over,' the man said simply. 'All you can do now is tell me the truth and save yourself pain. I would prefer to kill you with one shot. You will feel nothing. But that depends on your telling me the truth.'

Tom looked up at him, still trying to clear his head. 'Everything I've learned about you tells me that you kill for a cause but you don't execute in cold blood. And I don't think you could deliberately make someone suffer.'

Tom saw a flicker of annoyance in the man's grim eyes. Was it anger at Tom for challenging him? Or was he aware of his own humanity and worried that they both knew it? 'You're smart, and in order to find me, you must have learned a great deal about me. So you should know that I will do whatever I need to for my cause. Unfortunately for both of us, pain is the only leverage I have over you now.'

Tom believed him and glanced at the Colt. The barrel was pointed right at the center of Tom's forehead, and the hand holding the gun was rock steady.

'Stand up,' Green Man ordered, getting off him.

Tom got to his knees and then climbed to his feet. The cold rain was helping to clear his mind. He understood why Green Man wanted him to stand. It would look much less suspicious if anyone happened to see them. They might be two friends having a private conversation. But Tom saw that they were in a totally deserted corner of the rain-swept parking deck, and he doubted anyone would spot them. If Green Man fired, the roar of the engines and the crashing of waves against the ferry would mask the sound of the shot.

'How did you find out about Paul Sayers?'

'I profiled Green Man's engineering skills and ran a search for graduates from top schools. Four names came up. The most qualified one happened to be dead.'

'Who helped you create that profile and run the search?'

'Nobody. I went to Stanford and Caltech, and I know how to do things like that.'

'When you found out about Paul Sayers, who did you tell?'

'I didn't talk to anyone yet. My boss, Brennan, is off the case.'

'You're lying. I warned you not to do that. You've made a very important discovery. You would have told someone. Who?'

Tom started to repeat: 'I didn't tell anyone —'

The gun tilted down and fired, and Tom gasped in pain. It was a leg shot — his left knee. He staggered and almost went down.

'Tell me the truth,' the man said.

'I talked to an FBI agent named Grant,' Tom gasped, in agony. 'This morning. He called me . . .'

'You're still lying. The FBI is no longer running the investigation.'

'Grant's helping Homeland Security take over the case,' Tom said quickly. 'I don't trust him, so I didn't tell him about Paul Sayers. I was going to find Brennan when I got back to DC and let him advise me. I swear, I'm telling you the truth.'

'I believe you,' Green Man said. 'Last question. Did you find out where I live now or anything about my family?'

'All I know is that you're in Michigan and you've started over.' Then Tom said very quickly and desperately, 'And you may want to kill me, but you can't just execute me. It goes against who you are. I've been learning all about you, and I understand you. I'm the one who found that cop in Nebraska who stopped you, and you didn't kill him, even though you could have and should have. I've read all your letters and your manifesto, and I know you struggle with guilt, and I believe in your cause —'

'Then you know what's at stake and that I have no choice now,' Green Man said, cutting him off. 'Close your eyes.'

Tom kept his eyes wide-open, maintaining the link between them. 'There's something I need to tell you first.'

'What is that?'

'Your mother is still in great pain. Poor woman, mourning you for twenty years.'

Tom saw a reaction in the gray eyes, and he followed up quickly: 'Ellen still loves you, and she lied to me to protect you. She'd do anything for you, wouldn't she?'

Green Man tried to keep his face an opaque mask, but the decades of self-doubt were now evident. 'Enough.'

The ferry was riding up a large wave, and Tom knew he had to buy himself just a few more seconds. 'She still loves you even though you wrecked her life, and her daughter's life, too. You've destroyed the people you love just as you've killed innocent victims in each of your attacks, and you have to live with that. And I know what it's doing to you. If you kill me in cold blood, you'll just be making it worse.'

Green Man clearly wanted to shoot, but still he hesitated.

They were looking directly into each other's eyes. Tom asked softly, 'How can you save the world if you can't save yourself?'

'I have no choice,' Green Man replied, and his finger tightened on the trigger.

The ferry slammed down into a trough and listed wildly, and using that sudden disorienting instant, Tom ducked away into a crouch and in one smooth motion dove as far as he could off the back of the deck. When he was in the air, he heard the gun go off and felt a sting in his side and then he was foundering in the churning and freezing Atlantic.

44

Tom dove deep in case Green Man tried another shot and stayed down as long as he could. The cold Atlantic revived him, and by the time he shot back up to the surface and sucked in a breath, he could think clearly. The ferry was more than fifty feet away. He could just make out a lone figure standing at the stern. Tom ducked back into a wave and didn't know if Green Man had spotted him in the churning sea, but no more shots rang out, and soon the boat was out of range.

He knew his situation was beyond desperate and whatever tiny chance he had of surviving this hinged on his very first decision. They had left Cape May less than twenty minutes ago. The ferry trip was seventeen miles, which meant the New Jersey shore must still be much closer than Delaware – perhaps just five miles away. It was very tempting to follow the ferry, which he could still see and even hear clearly, but instead Tom turned and struck out swimming in the exact opposite direction, into a wild and open sea without any landmarks.

His left knee throbbed, and there was a searing pain in his right rib area, but he somehow found the awkward rhythm of an unsteady crawl. He had been a strong high school swimmer and had almost made the team at Stanford. He routinely swam two or three miles and trained for longer distances. The waves were the problem. Tom had swum in choppy seas but never in anything this rough. He knew he had to swim over waves that were rising and dive under them if they were breaking, but it was hard to do that and keep moving forward. Sometimes several waves broke in fast succession or a freak one sideswiped him from an oblique angle.

Then there was the fear of sharks. He had been shot twice and was bleeding from both wounds. Tom had always been fascinated by sharks – the perfect hunting machines of the deep. He remembered reading that a shark could pick up a blood trail from a quarter mile away. He felt terribly vulnerable thrashing his way across the surface, unable to see what might be lurking just below. Sharks struck from beneath, stalking their prey and then darting up to clamp razor-sharp teeth around a limb. It might happen at any second, and there was no way to defend himself.

He tried to push the fear from his mind and concentrate on keeping a steady stroke. Long-distance swimming was all about mechanics. He dove under a cresting wave, arms forward to protect his neck. It was agony to try to kick with his left leg, but his right was fine, and both arms could stroke and pull water. He urged himself onward with the knowledge that he had just talked to Green Man face-to-face and was the only person who knew the truth and could possibly stop him. If Tom drowned, the vital secret would die with him. Green Man would strike again and again, and more innocent people, including children, would die just the way he had been shot and left to die now.

He held on to that thought, clinging desperately to it like a life preserver. Green Man had shot him at point-blank range to cause pain and would have executed him in another few seconds. Altruistic motives or not, he was a torturer, a murderer. If Tom made it to shore – no, *when* he made it to shore – he would tell Green Man's secret to the

316

world and make them listen. They would catch Green Man quickly and Tom would have done his job, all that Brennan or even Warren Smith could have ever asked of him.

He could feel himself tiring. The battle with endless cold whitecaps was sapping his energy. A wave slammed Tom from the side, and while he was recovering, another busted him head-on, and he swallowed seawater. He retched and lost the rhythm of his crawl. He would die here. Sharks or no sharks, he would tire and give in and sink to an unknown watery grave. Drowning was supposed to be a terrible, painful death. No one knew how long the brain continued to function as the lungs filled with water. Tom felt rising panic and struggled to keep thinking clearly.

But the panic had him. There wasn't a setting sun or a starry sky to steer by. He could be heading farther from land with every stroke. Wasn't that a great last joke? Tom Smith, who had always been so smart, was trying to swim from New Jersey to England! Specters from his past were watching now, laughing at him. His sister brayed: 'You should never have tried to catch Green Man. But you thought you were so smart. You betrayed yourself, so no wonder you're all turned around.'

His mother's sad voice reminded him: 'You were the one I was closest to, Tom. I gave you your love of reading and the piano, and you were my only comfort and joy. But you left me all alone with a brute I abhorred.'

Then there was the menacing presence of that brute, who now mocked his every stroke. 'You're swimming the wrong way, fool,' Warren Smith said, laughing.

'I'm doing the best I can.'

'You'll never make it. You'll never be a man.'

Tom was twelve years old, and he could smell the

alcohol on his father's breath as his dad slammed him into a wall so hard that Tom's teeth shook. 'Fight back.'

But he didn't fight back. He just curled up inside himself and took it silently.

'Goddamn it, be a man and fight back.' His father's hand came again, and this blow felt like it had shattered his face, and Tom whimpered as blood poured from his nose, but he still didn't punch back, he just silently took it . . .

But now he was fighting back, stroking and pulling water and kicking with every bit of rage he had. He must have been swimming for an hour or even two, and his last reserves of strength and stamina were gone. Still he battled on, but finally, almost mercifully, it was time to give in and let the ocean swallow him, because there was no point, no point at all. Green Man had bested him, and Warren Smith was right that he wasn't strong enough, and the world would take whatever sad course it would take with him gone. If there was a God in his sunny white heaven, far from this cold ocean, Tom was ready to meet him and ask some tough questions.

He stopped stroking and accepted the inevitable as a whitecap slugged him full in the face. Let it end here. He was ready for heaven. He swallowed a bitter mouthful of seawater and choked as he felt himself turning off, on some deep level, switching off, starting to sink. But even as he gave up and was ready to die, there was something else, something distant but there, yes, unmistakably there.

Tom had been sinking, but an angry wave had grabbed hold of him and dragged him back up. Rising with it, he'd glimpsed the tip of a finger upraised as if to say fuck-you to life itself. But no, it wasn't a finger, it was a distant white conical lighthouse, sharp against the dark storm clouds.

45

Heaven had white walls and bright lights, and there was an angel in a bonnet who smiled at Tom and softly called him by his name. He looked up at her and felt her hand gently gripping his as he sank back into blissful sleep. When he returned to heaven, it was more crowded because there were police in the room, and one of them was asking him questions that he couldn't find a voice to answer, and who had stolen his voice, and what were police doing in heaven? The bright lights hurt his eyes, so Tom sank away from them. The third time he woke it was dark outside and the police were still there, but so were several men in khakis and jackets, and then Grant strode into his hospital room and said, 'Tom, Jesus, who the hell shot you, and everyone who doesn't need to be here, I want you out now.'

Tom was still very weak, but he was able to gasp out a little about what had happened on the ferry. Grant at first had trouble believing that Tom had escaped from Green Man and survived a long swim with two bullet wounds. But then he seemed to accept it and even admire it, and he asked Tom a bunch of excited questions. A doctor intervened: 'That's enough. He needs some rest now.'

When Tom woke again he was much stronger. Morning light filtered in through a curtained window. He was given hot soup, a doctor examined him, and then he was lifted into a chair that was wheeled swiftly down a hallway into a larger and more secure room where a camera crew was waiting to record his answers. Grant was there, but he wasn't the one asking questions. A short and aggressive man with a pencil mustache introduced himself as Harris Carnes and did nearly all the talking.

They had already spoken with Lise, so they knew what Tom had found out and how he'd uncovered the secret of Paul Sayers. Carnes was far more interested in Tom's encounter with Green Man than he was in Tom's meetings with Ellen Douglas and Willa Sayers. He kept probing Tom's account of what had happened on the ferry from different angles, as if he didn't quite believe the whole thing and might eventually find a way to get Tom to agree that he'd made it up.

'So he paid some random kid to get you? That doesn't sound like the master planner we've been chasing.'

'All I know is that it worked. The kid brought me down to the parking deck and took off.'

'And just when the kid vanished, Green Man punched you?'

'He was behind me. I don't know if it was a punch. I didn't see it coming.'

'After that, you never attempted to fight back?'

'He had my gun pointed at my head.'

'Did he admit to you that he was Green Man?'

'He never used those exact words, but it was clear from our conversation and that he knew I had uncovered his past identity.'

'You two had a nice little chat while he held the gun on you?' When Carnes was doubtful or displeased, he had a habit of stroking his thin mustache inward with his thumb and index finger, so that he seemed to be trying to erase the lower half of his face. 'He acknowledged that you were right about Paul Sayers?'

'Yes. He spoke his own real name before I did.'

'And he also spoke your name? He knew things about you?'

'He knew that I worked for the FBI. I could tell that he'd read up on me, probably online.'

'That must have been very flattering to you. That Green Man would take the time to consider you his adversary.'

Tom shrugged.

'Did he mention Jim Brennan?'

'He knew who Brennan was and what had happened with the investigation.'

'And did he mention my name?' Carnes asked.

'No.'

Carnes pinched his upper lip in a way that looked painful and almost made his mustache vanish between his fingers. 'And he had this chummy conversation with you while holding you at gunpoint on a crowded ferry, but no one saw it?'

'We were on a deserted parking deck.'

'He didn't happen to mention anything about his next strike?'

'No. He wasn't there to try to explain himself or talk about his future plans. He wanted information from me. Specifically, he wanted to know who I had told about his Paul Sayers past identity and whether I knew where he now lived or anything about his family.'

'Not his old family in Cape May but his new family, presumably in Michigan?'

'Right. He started over.'

'Why would he even mention this new family to you? He's gone to great lengths to conceal everything about himself.'

321

'I guess he felt comfortable doing it because he was about to kill me.'

'But you got away? If he really wanted to kill you, why didn't he just shoot you?'

'He did shoot me. Twice. But I dove into the ocean.'

'And then you swam five miles to shore while he drove your car off the ferry at Lewes and disappeared? We haven't been able to find it.'

'He said you wouldn't.'

'We also haven't been able to find the kid he sent to get you. Or any witnesses to your conversation with him on the deck. In fact, we have no corroborating evidence that anything you say actually happened.'

Tom looked back at him. 'Do you think I shot myself and dove off the ferry?'

Carnes's tone became almost derisive. 'So this man who's destroyed six targets, most of them heavily guarded, caused billions of dollars of damage, and killed more than forty people had a gun pointed at your head and yet one-on-one you escaped?'

'He could have killed me if he'd wanted to.'

'You'd uncovered his past identity, and he knew you could use that to track him down. Why wouldn't he want to kill you?'

'He couldn't execute me in cold blood.'

'Green Man has moral scruples? You two bonded and he showed mercy? He didn't have trouble blowing up a dam and killing twelve people.'

'They're two very different things.'

Carnes snorted and then moved on to the fact that Tom had set up the meetings with Ellen Douglas and Willa Sayers *after* he had discovered Green Man's past identity.

'So you'd discovered the secret of who Green Man was but you didn't report it to anyone? Instead you decided to follow up all by yourself?'

'Yes, I had a theory, but it seemed a little far-fetched.'

'So far-fetched that you didn't make even one phone call or send one email to let a superior know the rather enormous thing you had found out?'

'I wanted to be sure that I was right.'

'You were sure enough to travel from Pittsburgh to Manhattan and from Manhattan to Cape May.'

Grant tried to intercede. 'He did just take two bullets and swim five miles in heavy seas to bring us some vital information . . .'

Carnes gave Grant a furious look that silenced him and then demanded: 'Did it not occur to you that if you asked questions of people who might still be in touch with Green Man, one of them might notify him and he might try to stop you?'

'I didn't think he could possibly react so quickly. Ellen Douglas must have contacted him, or maybe it was her daughter.'

'Or it could have been his mother.'

'No, I don't think Willa knows that her son is still alive.'

'You don't know what she really knows,' Carnes snapped out disdainfully. 'You don't know what any of them really know. They're all denying that they contacted him and we haven't found any connection yet. If one of them did reach out to him through some secret prearranged channel, we'll suss it out. The point, Tom Smith, is that you put him on his guard. Once you found out about his past identity, we had a clear chance to catch him, and your bumbling cost

323

us that chance. As soon as you found out what you did in Pittsburgh, it was your duty to report it.'

'I was going to,' Tom said.

Carnes leaned forward, furious. 'After you talked to Ellen Douglas, when you were driving to Cape May, did you not have a phone call with Agent Grant?'

Tom glanced at Grant and nodded.

'And did he not ask you specifically what you had found out? Wasn't that a direct request for information from a superior? Did he not also inform you explicitly during that phone call that you were no longer operational on this investigation? So when you had the meeting with Willa Sayers, you in fact had no authority?'

Anger finally came to Tom's rescue. He sat up in the chair and glared back at Carnes. 'Look, if I hadn't found out what I did, you wouldn't know squat about Paul Sayers. I broke this case and I was right. And you can keep tearing into me if you want, but what should be important now is catching Green Man and how you use the information I've brought you. And I'm the only one who's met him, so you should let me help instead of attacking me.'

Tom's outburst quieted the room. Grant whispered to Carnes, 'Tom has had an uncanny feel for this guy right from when he first came on board.'

Carnes scowled and asked reluctantly, 'Okay. Let's hear it. What would you do?'

'Now that we know who Paul Sayers was, it should be relatively easy to figure out who he became,' Tom said. 'We know exactly when Paul Sayers went missing, which will tell us when Green Man started his new life. He must've found a way to keep some of his fortune, so there will be a money trail leading from San Francisco to the

Midwest. You're looking for a millionaire, twenty-eight or twenty-nine years old, with a distinctive engineering skill set who suddenly appeared in Michigan. He would've moved to a small town and bought a house on a large lot –'

'Why do you think that?' Carnes asked.

'Because that's what feels right to me. He had just shed a skin. He craved privacy. But there are some things he couldn't change. If you get some family DNA from his mother or siblings in southern Jersey, you can search genetic databases and health records in Michigan. It's the same way the CIA caught Bin Laden – using his family's DNA to zero in on him in his hiding place.'

'They could do that in Pakistan. I can't search public health records in Michigan.'

'He's a major terrorist, and I'm sure the president is willing to let you bend a few rules to catch him. Jim Brennan wouldn't have done it, but I think you might.'

Carnes looked back at Tom, and his eager eyes gleamed. 'What else?'

'I don't think you'll have to start from scratch. The FBI was doing a lot of local legwork, so I'll bet somebody somewhere has already talked to this guy. You should go back to the reports from local Michigan law enforcement about well-off families in small towns who own black vans.'

'All twenty thousand of them?'

'Now we have a much better idea of what Green Man looks like, right down to his gray eyes. We know when he first appeared in his town, and how well off he is, that he has a young family, that he's been traveling a lot lately, and even that he's an artist with a talent for nature paintings. It should be enough to find him quickly.'

'And I will find him,' Carnes promised. 'The only thing

we need from you now is to answer any follow-up questions my investigators come up with, and to stay the hell away from this case while I catch Green Man and figure out what to do with you.' He waved for the camera crew to stop filming and leave.

The room emptied till only Carnes and Grant were left. The little man stood and walked closer to Tom. 'What do you want from this? I mean you, personally?'

'Nothing,' Tom told him.

'Credit? You were shot twice. Do you want to be a hero?'

'Not at all.'

'What are you holding back?'

'Nothing.'

'Why can't we corroborate anything you've told us?'

'He's very good at cleaning up after himself. But I've told you the truth.'

Carnes stepped yet closer and bent so low over Tom's chair that spittle from his mouth wet Tom's cheek as he whispered, 'It's my investigation, and I'm catching Green Man. Jim Brennan is out of this, and so are you.'

'He left me to die. Let me be part of stopping him.'

'Since you have problems understanding orders, I want you to listen to this carefully. You will not talk to the press. You will not reveal to anyone any details of what you have learned. You will not contact anyone who is in any way involved in this investigation or who was previously involved. You will now completely separate yourself from the Green Man investigation and take some time off to recover from your wounds, while we figure out whether to let you go back to being a computer analyst or to throw you in prison for impersonating an operational FBI agent and for gross dereliction of duty.'

46

'So you were the one who questioned this guy and filed the report?' Carnes asked, glancing out the second-floor window of the small-town police station at the nearly deserted main street of Glenwood, Michigan. A sunny Friday afternoon was giving way to a cool evening, and the town center was emptying fast.

'Yes, sir,' Ted Dolan said nervously, his big hands tucked into his pockets. 'Well, actually Mitch wasn't home, so I questioned his wife, Sharon.'

'But you do know him?'

'Yes, sir, Mitch is a big police booster. And I know both his kids. I taught Gus, his son, junior lifesaving. And his wife is involved in a lot of causes and town projects, so I also know her. Sharon.'

Carnes heard something in Dolan's voice and lowered the report. 'What's she like?'

'She's . . . a fine woman, sir.'

Carnes gave the awkward, small-town police sergeant a conspiratorial smile. 'Out of ten?'

Dolan looked back at him. There were only men in the room. 'Nine, sir.'

'No wonder you questioned her instead of her husband,' Carnes said. There was laughter, and Dolan relaxed noticeably.

'When you were in the house, did you see anything that might be used in any way to resist a rapid police entrance?'

'Only the hunting stuff I told you about, in the basement.'

'The painting you saw hanging on the wall was good?'

'Really good, sir. I didn't know Mitch was an artist. Sharon said it was just a hobby he fooled around with.'

Carnes brought his cell phone over and showed Dolan the pencil sketch of the seascape that hung in Willa Sayers's house in Cape May. 'Similar to this?'

Dolan studied it intently for a few seconds. 'I'm no expert, but I'd say very similar.'

Carnes's cell buzzed. He stepped over to a window, read a text, and typed a few quick words back. Then he turned to the men in the room. 'The perimeter has been secured, and the SWAT team is ready to go in. I want to emphasize to everyone that there may be two kids in the house. We are not like Green Man — we are not child killers. The children may have been trained to fight back. We will only engage with them if forced, and all efforts will be made not to injure them in any way. Sergeant Dolan and Chief Parry, since you know the layout of the property, I'd like you both to come in with us. As advisors and observers, but not to fight in any way.'

'Yes, sir,' Chief Parry said. 'It'll be an honor to be part of this, sir.'

'For me, too,' Sergeant Dolan said. 'You bet. Thank you.'

Carnes was looking past them. He had spotted an elegant, wide-brimmed leather hat hanging on a peg above the chief's desk. 'What is that?'

'That's my Lord Saybrook safari hat,' Chief Parry said. 'I brought it back from South Africa a couple of years ago. Paid more than two hundred dollars for it. Would you like to try it on?' He took the hat down and passed it to Carnes, who put it on and looked at his reflection in the window.

The SWAT team was dressed in black boots and coveralls, with dark gloves and form-fitting shrapnel-resistant skull-caps. Since they were dealing with a bomber, their bulletproof Kevlar body armor had been reinforced with heavy inserts that were also designed for shrapnel. They had set up at the back of the property, where it was dark and quiet. The six-foot fence that ran completely around the ten acres brushed a northern red oak, and three team members had silently trimmed the great tree's low-hanging branches.

Hwang, the sinewy, panther-like SWAT commander, gave his report to Carnes quickly and succinctly as his men listened, ready to fill in information if necessary: 'We've detected several different kinds of sensors all over the per-imeter. This rear section of the property seems to have the least, and we're out of all visual sight lines from the house. A trip wire runs on top of the fence. We jumped it on both sides and then cut the center. No one in the house will know that. They'll see a constant signal, but we've breached their system on both sides of a seven-foot section of fence, and we're ready to go over the center whenever you say.'

'I say now,' Carnes told the men. 'Let's do it.'

Hwang turned to his men and gave an order with a silent hand gesture. He was first to the fence and seemed to glide to the top. He leapt to a branch of the red oak and dropped soundlessly to the ground. His men followed him one by one, and then Carnes, Grant, Dolan, and Chief Parry clambered over noticeably more slowly and awk-wardly. A two-man camera crew came over last and

329

carefully lowered their equipment to the leafy ground inside the fence.

The SWAT guys didn't seem particularly happy about the small crowd joining them on this operation, and they didn't wait around. As soon as they were inside the fence, they spread out and sprinted for the house. As planned, they approached it from three directions, and in less than a minute they were demolishing the front door with a piston-driven battering ram.

They threw in a flash-bang concussion grenade and came in after it at high speed, fanning out through the large house, expertly covering one another as they moved from room to room and to the danger spots – up the stairs to the second and third floors and down to the basement. They carried short-barreled, fully automatic assault weapons for maximum maneuverability, and when they covered one another and spun into open spaces, it looked like a sequence of well-practiced dance moves.

Carnes, wearing the safari hat and cradling a semiautomatic, and Grant, with Chief Parry and Sergeant Dolan, followed the SWAT team into the house. The camera crew walked with them and filmed everything that Carnes did. He was soon standing in the third-floor library, where he had found a laptop that he was slowly powering up. While he waited for it to turn on, he received a series of negative reports. 'There don't seem to be any family members in the house, sir.'

'They may be hiding. Check for tunnels. Remember, they've been preparing for something like this for a long time. I want every computer secured and –'

'Sir, we haven't found any computers yet,' Hwang said.

'You will. There's one right here, and we'll find more.

Green Man has lived here for more than twelve years. Trust me, this house contains a treasure trove of crucial information, and we need to find it and secure it –'

Suddenly the house lights all blinked off and then on again as a deep male voice spoke to them from everywhere and nowhere. 'You have two minutes to vacate this house before it is destroyed.'

They looked around. There were no visible speakers. Perhaps the voice was coming through the vents.

'That sounded like Mitch,' Sergeant Dolan said nervously.

'Yeah, definitely Mitch,' Chief Parry noted, edging a step closer to a door.

'It's his recorded voice,' the SWAT team's tech guy said. 'This was set up. We triggered it somehow when we came in.'

'We should get out of here,' the guy holding the camera said.

'No one goes anywhere,' Carnes told them all in a strong, confident voice. 'Think about it. If Green Man really had this place rigged with explosives and wanted to kill us, would he be dumb enough to give us a warning? No, he'd take us all down.'

'One minute and forty-five seconds,' the voice said.

'Continue the search,' Carnes said. 'This is just a bluff –'

'This guy has destroyed six major targets,' Grant cut in. 'He doesn't like to kill innocent people, but he's shown a willingness to do so. He's never been known to bluff. He just blows things up. I'm out of here.'

'You're a coward,' Carnes told him. 'And you're disobeying my direct order.'

Grant looked back at the little man in the safari hat. 'If you stay in this house, I don't think you'll be around to

331

prosecute me.' Then he left quickly, and they could hear his boots thudding down the wooden stairs.

'One minute and thirty seconds,' the deep voice said. 'Vacate the house now.'

The two camera crew guys fled out the door. 'Hey, you two, get back here!' Carnes shouted after them, but they had taken the stairs so fast that one of them could be heard tumbling down.

Sergeant Dolan glanced down at a dark stain spreading at his crotch and realized that he had pissed himself. Without a word he lumbered for the stairs, and Captain Parry followed him.

'One minute and fifteen seconds,' the voice said.

'This study is where he planned his attacks,' Carnes said to the SWAT team members, his voice coming out unnaturally high-pitched. 'Let's start here. What he's been reading will tell us what he's been thinking . . .'

The SWAT team members looked at their commander, who turned to Carnes. 'I'm taking my men out.'

'Captain, you are under my command,' Carnes snapped, 'and I'm giving you a direct order to search this study and secure vital evidence.'

Hwang gave a hand gesture to his men, who immediately left the study. He followed them out.

Carnes stood, suddenly alone. Something flashing on the desk caught his attention. He glanced down and saw that the laptop had finally powered up. On its screen was a beautiful screen saver photograph of the earth, taken from space on one of the NASA missions. The earth looked like a precious jewel, its seas and landmasses gleaming. And then the image slowly morphed into something else that was round. It was an antique stopwatch, the hand moving, ticking down so that every tick was audible and seemed a little louder than the previous one . . .

Keep the camera trained on the house,' Grant ordered the cameraman, but it was no good. They were in a ditch fifty yards from the front door, and the man's hands were shaking so badly he couldn't hold his camera. He dropped it and ducked low to the ground, trembling.

Grant picked up the camera and saw that it was turned on and operational. He hit the record button and pointed it toward the house. He peered through the viewfinder and saw the remains of the front door that the SWAT team had busted inward.

Then a shape appeared, hightailing it out. It was Carnes, minus the safari hat. He came hurtling out the door, short legs churning, and he vaulted down the four front steps in one desperate leap. As soon as his feet hit the ground, he was sprinting. He headed for a stone fountain on the front lawn, and dove behind it, and disappeared from Grant's viewfinder.

A heartbeat later there was an earth-shaking BOOM and an explosion so violent that Grant nearly dropped the camera himself. The three-story colonial house seemed to rise up on its foundation, as if the basement had suddenly sprouted another floor beneath it. But the new floor wasn't a floor at all – it was a fireball of explosive energy that consumed wood and hurled rock outward as the structure fell back down and imploded, collapsing in on itself in a plume of fire and a cloud of smoke and dust.

47

Sharon drove northward, in her silver Accord, with old Finn curled up and napping happily between Gus and Kim on the back seat. At first the kids were full of questions about this unexpected trip. 'How come you can't tell us where we're going?' Gus asked.

'Because your father and I thought this should be a surprise,' she told them, staying just at the upper edge of the speed limit. She had let them each bring one bag, and she had now been driving for more than three hours, on small roads that Mitch had chosen for them. She had never appreciated how hard it must have been for him to drive to and from missions – how the pressure not to make any slight mistake turned the simple act of driving a car into a tense ordeal.

'What about school?' Gus wanted to know. 'My report on the Puritans is due on Tuesday.'

'Don't worry about it.'

'Mrs Lowell is gonna be mad.'

'And I'm supposed to go to Emma's birthday party,' Kim said.

'Everything will work out,' Sharon promised. 'You kids should get some sleep.'

'How come Dad's not with us?' Gus asked.

'He has something to finish for business and then he's going to join us,' Sharon replied, gripping the wheel a little more tightly.

'When?' Kim asked.

'Soon.'

'How soon?'

'Do you want to hear some music? You guys can choose the station.'

Soon they were both fast asleep, and Sharon drove alone through the darkness. She wanted to switch on a news station and find out if anything had happened with their house, but she resisted the impulse and just turned the music down and concentrated on the driving.

She pulled off the mountain road on a winding driveway and bumped along slowly for two hundred feet till she spotted the dark silhouette of an old barn. She stopped near the barn and flashed her lights twice and waited.

A vehicle slowly approached them out of the darkness. It was a large red pickup truck. The truck stopped, and an older man climbed out. He was thin, with silvery hair, but despite the fact that he was well into his seventies, he walked with a light step as he approached the Accord. Sharon jumped out of her car and hurried to him and hugged him, and she was surprised to feel herself trembling in his arms.

The man must have felt it, because he whispered, 'You've done great. Everything is set,' and then he gently released her and peered into the Accord. He saw the two sleeping kids and their dog and smiled. 'Hey, Gus and Kim. Time to wake up.'

The kids woke, disoriented, and looked up at this older man in confusion.

'This is your uncle Arthur,' their mom told them. 'He's a very old friend of your father.'

'We're gonna have some fun now,' Arthur told them.

'I've got a boat less than two miles away. We're all going on a boat trip together.'

'Cool,' Gus said, now fully awake.

'I don't want to go on a boat trip at night,' Kim said nervously.

'There's nothing to be afraid of,' Arthur told them, 'but I need you guys to help me. I hear you each brought a bag. Grab 'em and stow 'em in the back of my big red truck over there and climb into the back seat. And there's plenty of room for your four-legged friend there.'

'What about our car?' Kim asked.

'For this part of the trip we're gonna ride in Arthur's truck,' Sharon said. 'But we need to go quickly.'

'The back seat of the truck is gonna be the kids-and-dog section,' Arthur said, glancing at his watch. 'You can do whatever you want back there. Let's move it, guys. I'm gonna park your car in my barn, to keep it safe, and then we'll drive down to the coast in my truck and take our boat trip.'

An hour later they were on the deck of the large, nondescript fishing boat setting off into a dark sea. Both children were scared, but Arthur knew exactly what he was doing. 'The cabin is down those stairs, and there's a warm bed all made up and waiting for you,' he told Kim. 'Your dog is already asleep down there, and there just might be a chocolate chip cookie sitting on your pillow.'

'I'll take you down,' Sharon said. 'Those cookies sound good.'

'I'm staying on the deck,' Gus announced.

Sharon and Kim headed down the stairs, and Arthur and Gus were alone on the deck on the dark sea.

'How did you meet my father?' Gus asked him.

337

'We worked together a long time ago.'

'On a job?'

'Kind of a job,' Arthur said. Then he added, softly, 'Your father is a hero of mine.'

Gus looked up at him, intrigued but a little suspicious. 'Why do you say that?'

The older man kept his eyes on the dark ocean. 'Do you want to steer?'

'I don't know how.'

'We'll do it together. We're heading straight across this bay. I'll show you.'

Gus walked over to him, and the older man arranged his hands on the wheel. 'That's it,' Arthur said. 'Steady as she goes. You're a natural.'

They steered together. It was a calm, almost windless night. The sliver of moon was a golden scythe slicing through dark clouds. Gus finally asked, in a very scared voice, 'Uncle Arthur?'

'Yeah?'

'You're not really my uncle?'

'No.'

'What's happening?'

'Don't worry,' Arthur said. 'It's necessary and for the best. And it'll be a real adventure.'

Gus's hands shook on the large steering wheel, and the older man put his own hands on top of them, to steady them.

'Can you at least tell me where we're going?' Gus asked softly. 'My mom wouldn't say.'

Arthur hesitated and finally replied, 'Canada.'

48

The lagoon was surrounded by mangroves. The last families had swum with the dolphins, purchased their pricey photos, and departed, and the facility was technically closed. 'Are you sure this is okay?' Tom asked, buckling on a life vest.

'The other trainers bring in guests every once in a while,' Tracy told him. 'It's one of the perks of working here. I've never brought in anyone before, so they're totally cool with it. How's the knee?'

'Healing up fast. The doctor said I got lucky.'

'Yeah, super lucky, you only got shot twice,' she said sarcastically, and searched his face. 'Why can't you tell me what happened?'

'I'm not supposed to talk about it. But the good news is I get some paid vacation time, so I can swim with the dolphins.'

'No,' Tracy told him, 'the good news is you're gonna get a new job. This time, try being yourself and not someone we both hated and it might work out better.'

For a moment, standing on the dock looking across the lagoon at the sinking sun, Tom recalled the previous evening in Boca. He had stood alone at his father's grave. The inscription on the granite stone – chosen by his mother – was simply Warren Smith's name, the dates of his birth and death, and 'He served his country.' There was nothing about being a loving husband or a good father. Tom was not religious, but he'd said a prayer and wished his father

339

goodbye, and just before he'd left, he'd touched the stone and – feeling foolish – whispered, 'Rest in peace, Dad. I also did my best to serve. I couldn't quite catch him, but I came damn close.'

Tom looked out over the lagoon as he finished buckling the life vest and pulled the strap taut. 'I already have two job interviews set up for next week,' he told Tracy. 'And you'll be glad to hear neither of them involve law enforcement.'

'Silicon Valley, baby!' she said enthusiastically. 'Take the money. I'm planning to retire to your guesthouse. Okay, ready to have your world rocked?'

'Rock away,' Tom said, checking that the leggings of his wetsuit covered his knee bandage. 'I have to warn you, I'm not planning to set any swimming records today.'

'You won't have to,' Tracy told him. 'Lou and Ginny are going to take you for a ride.' She stepped off the dock into the lagoon, and Tom followed her. It was medium cold and three feet deep, and they waded out together till they were up to their shoulders.

'Where exactly are Lou and Ginny?' Tom asked.

'They hang out on the other side of the lagoon, but they'll know I just stepped into the water and they're coming.' A moment later two gray shapes darted toward Tom and leapt fifteen feet out of the water above him. He found himself grinning and clapping as the two dolphins splashed back down. In another second they were next to him, their beak-like rostrums nuzzling him.

'Younger brother, meet Lou and Ginny, Atlantic bottlenose dolphins and my dear friends. You may kiss them back if you so choose.'

Tom lightly kissed the dolphins back, and they both made a series of high-pitched squeaks that sounded like

340

two rusty doors slowly being opened. 'They're saying hello and thanking you for not catching Green Man,' Tracy told him. 'The earth has a chance now. Especially the seas that they love so much.'

The two dolphins looked back at him with wise, sparkling dark eyes and smiling faces, as if they all shared a secret. 'You really think they're worried about climate change?' Tom asked. 'Maybe they just want some fish for dinner.'

'They know a lot more about what's happening than you think,' Tracy said. 'Lou was born at this facility, and even the water in this lagoon has had problems with plastic debris and algae blooms. Ginny is a rescue dolphin. She's been out in the world and seen lots of bad stuff, and she worries for sure.'

As if on cue, Ginny flipped upside down, exposing her lighter-colored belly to him. 'She wants you to pet her.' Tom tentatively stroked the dolphin's skin. It was smooth and gently curved, like an eggplant with a heartbeat. For the first time, he understood his sister's dolphin mania. There was definitely an unexpectedly strong connection, much more intimate than petting a cat or stroking a dog. This was a very smart mammal, and touching her, Tom sensed somehow that Ginny was capable not only of love but of a kind of mysterious wisdom. 'What happened to her?'

'Ginny was hit by a propeller. It penetrated to the bone. When we got her, she was in real bad shape and almost died. But as you can see, she's made a complete recovery. They like you, Tom. Not as much as me, but they say you're okay. They want to take you for a ride.'

'Do I hold on to their dorsal fins?'

'Nope. Just float on your back, and relax.'

Tom turned over and floated on his back, hands at his sides. He tried to relax and clear his mind, but he couldn't stop thinking about flying out to San Fran next week for one particular job interview that an old friend of his from Stanford had set up.

A small startup had quickly become a large startup and gone public six months ago. Now it was rolling in cash, and the potential salary they had mentioned was more than four times what the FBI paid him. He could get a nice apartment and a car, and it would be challenging and fun to work with such a bright and gung ho crowd. Tracy was right. It was time to give up the Green Man chase and move to something that was for him and not for his father.

Tom felt gentle pressure on the soles of his feet, and suddenly he was flying. The dolphins were pushing him through the lagoon at such speed that Tom actually started rising up and was soon half out of the water. He screamed in surprise, fear, and pleasure. Incredibly, they could steer him, so the ride seemed to go on for thirty seconds, and when they finally stopped and he sank back into the lagoon, he was exhilarated and laughing out loud.

'That,' he told Tracy, 'was one of the coolest things I've ever done.'

She beamed. 'See, I told you it would rock your world,' she said, and then suddenly her demeanor totally changed and she warned, 'Don't do it, Tom.'

'Don't do what?'

She half shouted, 'This is private property. Get the hell out of here,' and she was looking not at Tom but behind him, where a tall, athletic black man in khakis and a blue jacket had walked down to the dock.

It was Agent Grant, and he ignored Tracy and said, 'Tom, sorry to intrude, but something's happened that doesn't make any sense.'

342

49

They talked at the bar of the Fish House, a local hangout with eccentric decor and fresh seafood. 'After your adventure on the Cape May ferry, Carnes did what you suggested and concentrated on finding out who Paul Sayers had become,' Grant told Tom. 'They soon found out that he was now Mitch Farley of Glenwood, Michigan.'

'I saw what happened when they went into the Farley house,' Tom said. 'Not exactly a notable success.'

'It was a total disaster,' Grant agreed with a rueful nod, 'and I was there to experience it firsthand. Not only was Carnes spectacularly incompetent, but everything in the house that was of any possible use to us was destroyed.'

'Have they picked up the trail of the wife and kids yet?'

'Not that I know of. At least for now, they got away clean.'

'Amazing,' Tom said. 'He switched identities twenty years ago and he's trying to do it again, and not just for himself but for the people he loves. And he's had lots of time to plan it. Is that why you're here? To get my take on where they've gone?'

'Nope,' Grant said, helping himself to a crabmeat-stuffed mushroom cap. 'While DHS was trying to figure out who Paul Sayers had become, I was busy trying to learn more about who he had been, back in the day. I figured the things he'd done twenty years ago in the Bay Area, operationally, might give us a hint about what he plans to do next. We know about two of his environmental attacks – on the lumber plant and the gas company – but I ran his name through different databases just in case he'd done other things that might be useful for us to know about.'

'Sounds like a good idea,' Tom said. 'Anything interesting pop up?'

'Nope,' Grant said. 'We had everything there was to have on him back then. Then I got pulled into the SWAT incursion on the Farley house, and I didn't come out of that too well with regards to my working relationship with Harris Carnes.'

'You've been taken off the case?' Tom asked.

'Not yet, but he's trying. I've been demoted and frozen out of the action till they figure out how to get me reassigned.'

'Sorry to hear it.'

'And I'm sorry I came down on your ass,' Grant said. 'To be honest, maybe I was a little jealous. I was Brennan's golden boy till you came along with your sixth sense about Green Man. It pissed me off. Sorry.'

Tom looked down and saw that Grant was holding out his hand, and Tom took it.

'Sounds like we're both in Siberia when it comes to this investigation,' Tom said. 'They want to bump me back down to computer analyst and reassign me, but – between the two of us – I'm interviewing in Silicon Valley.'

'And I am looking into a few new career tracks myself,' Grant admitted. 'High-end private security pays a lot more than Uncle Sam.'

'So, what brought you to the World of Dolphins?'

Grant glanced around, but no one was paying them any

attention. The other folks at the bar were watching a golf tournament as they sipped tropical drinks and dug into sumptuous fish dinners. 'Two days ago, I got a call from one of the computer analysts I'd used. Just the kind of nerdy and frustrated bottom dweller you would have been if Brennan hadn't yanked you onto the taskforce because of nepotism.'

Tom grinned at the good-natured insult. 'Have some respect for nerdy computer analysts. I take it something unexpected popped up on one of your searches?'

'Yup. And this analyst was so low on the food chain that he didn't know I was practically out the door, so he only told it to me.'

'Let me guess. Paul Sayers did something twenty years ago that we didn't know about, that might give us a clue about Green Man's next attack?'

'Not twenty years ago,' Grant said. 'Try two weeks ago.'

Tom looked back at him. 'What're you talking about? For all intents and purposes, Paul Sayers has been dead for twenty years. He's changed everything about himself, from his name to the way he looks. Don't you mean that Mitch Farley did something to show his hand?'

'A security guard in Texas filed an active report on Paul Sayers two weeks ago.'

'What kind of a report?'

'Just a routine sighting. No crime was committed. There wasn't even a suspicious action. It was so low priority that it's remarkable it got picked up by my search.'

Tom was quiet for a few seconds. 'How did this security guy in Texas even know it was Paul Sayers?'

'No idea.'

'Why was he on the lookout for someone who died twenty years ago?'

'That's one of the things I'm going to ask him tomorrow.'

'So you haven't talked to him yet? And I take it you also haven't shared this with your former pals at DHS?'

Grant looked uneasy. 'I don't know anything definite, so I'm not ready to make a report yet. Look, Carnes couldn't be more incompetent. Also, something happened last week to make me decide to go talk to the guy myself. I'm afraid this is bad news.'

Tom tensed and waited, watching the small colored lights that hung from the ceiling of the restaurant.

'Brennan had a full-on heart attack,' Grant said. 'He's in George Washington University Hospital. I went to see him. He's expected to pull through. But I decided to follow this up myself, for his sake. And seeing him reminded me of you. Every time there was something on this case that I didn't understand, you seemed to have a handle on it. And I don't pretend to understand this new wrinkle. So I'm here, and tomorrow afternoon I fly to Texas. Want to come? It's kind of on your way to Silicon Valley.'

'Neither of us is supposed to do this,' Tom said.

'Nope.'

'Did Brennan tell you to reach out to me?'

'Jim Brennan is not able to talk right now.'

Tom took a sip of beer, rolled it around in his mouth, and swallowed. 'Okay,' he said. 'Texas.'

50

Green Man skirted the Hanson Oil Field and drove his van to a bank of the Kildeer River. It was a warm and moonless night, and he was sweating in his lightweight black neoprene drysuit. A wetsuit would have been heavier and made it too hard to maneuver, but even this thinner drysuit clung to him like an unwanted second skin. The oil field was lit up and throbbing, just the way he remembered from his scouting trip. The flares that burned natural gas from the tops of the rigs were orange fires dancing in the night sky. He parked close to the riverbank and checked his watch. There were two hours till midnight, and he had much to do.

But Green Man was weary, and for a few precious minutes he sat in the van and did absolutely nothing. With the lights off, he watched the thirty-foot-wide Kildeer flow downhill to the fence and cut a gleaming path across the oil field. It was warm in the van, but he didn't dare doze off for even a few seconds. It was a real danger because he hadn't slept in the past three nights worrying about Sharon and the kids. He had seen footage on the news of their house blowing up and photos taken the next morning of the smoldering ruins.

If all had gone well, they should be in Ontario Province now, on a large private farm fifty miles from the Ojibwe township of Manitouwadge. The property was lovely, with a twenty-acre spruce forest and a lake stocked with bass.

But he could only imagine the conversations when Sharon had tried to explain to Gus and Kim why they were there and that they would never return to Michigan.

Green Man imagined himself with them, fishing with his kids in the lake. It had been more than two years since his first strike, and weary wasn't a strong enough word to describe his total exhaustion. He had done what he could, and it was time to stop. The moment had come to pass the struggle to save the earth to the next generation, and for him to make his way to Canada and be with his family.

But sitting in the silent van, battling the temptation to shut his eyes for a few seconds, he knew he had one more thing to accomplish – one final necessary strike – and there could be no more delaying. He took a pill to give himself energy and stepped out of the van onto the gravel bank of the Kildeer. First came the demolition equipment, which he had carefully packed into two waterproof dry-box containers. He lifted one box out of the van and laid it down gently on the bank and was pleased to see that the color of the heavy plastic exactly matched the basalt river stones.

A powerfully built African American man burst into the small security office on the run, and Tom and Grant stood. 'Jesus, I'm sorry. How long've they kept you waiting?'

'More than an hour,' Grant said. 'They said you'd be back in twenty minutes.'

'Hell, I was just over in Baines – that's a town right nearby. I was eating dinner at the bar and it was loud, so I didn't hear my pager. They should've just sent somebody to get me. But didn't we expect you seven hours ago?'

'Our flight to Midland was canceled. We finally got one

to Lubbock and drove like hell. Sorry for the mishaps on both sides, but we're here.'

'And you're with the FBI?'

Grant showed him his ID. Tom figured the more low profile he stayed, the better, so he kept his own badge in his wallet.

'Ray Mathis,' the security officer said, offering handshakes to both of them. 'Deputy chief of security at Hanson. What brings you gentlemen here?'

'Two weeks ago, you filed a report that you saw a man named Paul Sayers.'

'That's right. I saw him by the fence, when I was out on a night patrol. We said a few words. He turned and walked off.'

'How did you know that it was Paul Sayers?' Grant asked.

'I recognized his face from a wanted poster.'

'His face hasn't been on a wanted poster,' Grant pointed out, 'because everyone has thought Paul Sayers was long dead.'

'It was a poster from twenty years ago. Back then I was working security at a mill. He had hit a lumber plant nearby.'

'So you were guarding a mill in Northern California?' Tom asked.

'That's right. Up near Ukiah. That wanted poster was hanging on a bulletin board in our security office. It was on the bottom right corner of the bulletin board. Just above it was a pinup of Elle Macpherson in a red bikini. I have a good memory.'

'So you remembered his face all this time?' Grant asked dubiously. 'From a mill in Ukiah to this oil field in Texas?'

'And you spotted him here at night, in complete darkness?' Tom chimed in with his own doubts. 'But you were still able to recognize him from that two-decade-old wanted poster?'

Mathis looked from Grant to Tom and shrugged. 'I never forget a face,' he said. 'When I spotted him by the fence, I shined a flashlight on him and saw his face clearly. It took me a while to put a name to that face and figure out where I had seen him before, but I got it. That was Paul Sayers, right out by our fence. So how did you guys know I filed that report, and why do you care so much?'

'We were searching for any mention of Paul Sayers,' Grant said.

It was the security officer's turn to look a little confused. 'If you thought this guy died twenty years ago, why were you looking so hard for him?'

There was a silence in the small office. Different security-camera views of the oil field flashed on overhead viewing screens. A window was open, and someone outside was playing a car radio. Merengue music throbbed faintly on the night air.

'We think Paul Sayers is Green Man,' Grant told him.

'We think Paul Sayers *has become* Green Man,' Tom tried to clarify.

Mathis looked from one of them to the other. 'You're shitting me?'

'Wish I was,' Grant said. 'By the way, what we just told you is confidential.'

'The Green Man who blows up factories and yachts and dams?'

'And possibly oil fields,' Tom added softly.

Ray Mathis sat in a chair and crossed himself. He

350

thought it over for a few silent seconds. 'How sure are you about this?'

'There's no doubt,' Tom answered. 'He plans his attacks incredibly carefully, and we're almost certain that he scouts the sites he's going to attack – probably close to the time he intends to hit them. So that's what might have brought him to your oil field, and that's why we're here.'

'I get it,' Mathis said. 'But he could have been checking out a bunch of fields in this area, right?'

'Sure,' Grant said. 'That would make sense given that there are several large oil fields grouped closely together at the Permian Basin.'

'No,' Tom said. 'He came to Texas to see this one field.'

'Who is this guy?' Mathis asked Grant, studying Tom, 'and how does he fit in?'

'He's an irritating rookie who happens to be able to think like Green Man.'

Mathis scrutinized Tom carefully. 'You think he only came to see Hanson?'

'He doesn't waste time or take needless risks. If he came here, it was because he's planning to strike here. Did he know you recognized him?'

'Yeah, I said it out loud and drew my gun.'

'Why didn't you shoot him?' Grant asked.

'He hadn't done anything wrong. He just turned his back and walked away.' Mathis looked at Tom. 'You're so sure where he'll attack. Do you happen to know when he will attack?'

'There's no way to tell that,' Grant said. 'He picks his moments, and I'm sure the manhunt and what's happened to his family have thrown him off. The pressure might've sped up his timeframe or it could've pushed it back . . .'

'Do you have a computer that I can use to search the Internet?' Tom asked.

'Right over there.' Mathis pointed. 'The password is "FUCKTHEPASSWORD," all in caps.'

Tom walked over and started typing.

'What are you searching for?' Grant asked.

'The Östersund Clock.'

'What the hell's that?' The old security guard sounded nervous.

'It's an environmental doomsday clock, run by a group in Sweden. Two weeks ago, they moved the clock hand to eleven fifty-five P.M. Just five more minutes to doomsday.'

'What does that have to do with Green Man?' Mathis wanted to know.

Tom found what he was looking for. 'Last night they announced that after studying the latest satellite information, as of tomorrow at eight A.M., their doomsday clock would be moved the final five minutes. They say doomsday has arrived. The earth has just become unsavable. There's going to be a public funeral for the earth in Östersund. A youth choir is going to sing Nena's '99 Luftballons,' and at the last note of the song they're going to stop their clock and announce that it's over forever, and they're encouraging everyone in Europe and around the world to stop all watches and clocks. That's when Green Man will strike.'

'At five P.M. tomorrow?' Mathis asked. He glanced at the clock in the security office, which read twelve seventeen. 'So we've got plenty of time.'

'They're seven hours ahead of us,' Tom said. 'Eight A.M. there will be in forty-three minutes here.'

Mathis bolted out of the chair. 'Where would he strike if he hit this field?'

'He likes exploiting existing weaknesses,' Tom said. 'He'd use what's here to bring it off. He wants to teach the world a lesson, so he'd try to use something that's already on this oil field to cause the most possible damage.'

'The tanks,' Mathis said with dread. 'There's enough oil stored in the tanks here at Hanson to blow us all to fucking Sweden and back.' He ran to a radio, clicked it on, and began issuing frantic orders.

Green Man had just mounted the second drybox onto his diver propulsion vehicle when he heard the siren. He had heard it before, on his scouting trip, and he knew instantly what it was. He froze, shocked and momentarily terrified, and then he slowly stood and waited. Just like the last time he had heard the shrill warning wail, it was immediately followed by the switching on of powerful searchlights along the perimeter fence and by a fleet of security vehicles that roared to life and sped toward the front gate.

He was very close to the oil field, in a diving suit, with equipment unpacked. Even if he left everything behind and fled in the van, there was a good chance he would not be able to get away in time. He watched the security presence inside the field and saw how it was concentrating on the oil tanks. They were on the far end of the vast field from the flowback tanks. In a way, the fact that they were expecting him to hit the stored oil might be just the misdirection he needed. They would have electrified their fence, but he was planning to go in under it, through the river, to a target they couldn't anticipate. If he set off a tremendous explosion, there would be such damage and confusion that he might still be able to get away down the river to the far side of the field, where he had hidden his motorcycle.

Green Man made his decision. It was too late to turn back. He had come this far, and he would blow up the Hanson field right under the noses of their alerted security, and he would show the world the grave dangers that fracking posed. And then he would try to get away and rejoin his family, and if God willed it, so it would be. But he would not run from them. He would attack.

He had been weary, but suddenly he was flooded with strength. This was the greatest challenge he had ever faced, and he would meet it. Green Man had been willing to die for his cause since he was twenty-three years old, and now that that moment might be at hand, the flash of terror he'd felt when he'd first heard the siren was replaced by a grim determination. He had securely mounted both dryboxes on the DPV. He pulled his rebreather apparatus onto his back and adjusted the hoses and mask, and lowered himself into the cold Kildeer.

He had learned scuba with heavy air tanks on his back, but they would never do for this mission. A month earlier, he'd purchased a rebreather online for ten thousand dollars. The high-tech apparatus that was now strapped to his back could remove carbon dioxide from the breathing loop while adding the necessary amount of oxygen. It allowed him to rebreathe his own breaths and had two advantages for an attack like this. First, there were no bulky air canisters so it gave him a sleeker profile in the water. And since he would be rebreathing his own breaths again and again, there would be no telltale bubbles for guards to spot.

He switched on the motor, and the DPV's two plastic

propellers began to turn. He grasped the twin handles and the water scooter he had built from parts in his shed tugged him out into the Kildeer. There was no rudder, so he had to steer it with his body. He had practiced in a similar-size river in Michigan, and the key was finding the central channel. If he went in too shallow, he might be seen, and if he went in too deep, he could collide with the bottom, kick up mud, and possibly injure himself and his equipment. Soon he was gliding swiftly along five feet beneath the surface, a nearly invisible dark shadow against the black rocks of the riverbed.

He could see the spotlights on the fence as he got close to it. The wire mesh did not extend to the river bottom. They had probably wanted to avoid constant clogs as the current carried small and large debris downstream. As he dove underneath the fence, he pressed a button on his watch to start a countdown. Then he was skimming through the center of the oil field and could see the bright lights on all sides of him and sense the throbbing machines and frenzied pace.

Getting the distance right was absolutely crucial. The flowback tanks were a little less than a half mile inside the field. He was traveling at three hundred feet per minute, so he had calculated how long he needed to stay submerged. His watch alarm would vibrate after eight minutes and fifteen seconds. He gripped the twin handles and sped forward in the center channel, and every ten seconds seemed an eternity.

He wouldn't hit the oil tanks,' Tom said. He and Grant were alone in the security office, watching as views from different security cameras flashed on the screens.

'Why not?' Grant asked. 'That's the best way to blow up an oil field.'

'Because it would significantly damage the environment. And it would be predictable.'

'So what would he hit?'

'I don't know.'

The door opened, and Mathis hurried in. 'Local and state police are on the way. Meanwhile, my guys just found a van by the river, a half mile from the fence.'

'A black van?' Grant asked.

'Yes.'

'That's him.'

'I've posted men where the river flows under the fence.'

'Too late,' Tom said. 'He's already inside your field.'

'We don't know that. Anyway, it won't do him any good. The river doesn't go anywhere near the oil tanks,' Mathis said. 'To do any damage, he's gonna have to get out of the water and cross a mile of exposed field. I've deployed every guard I have to watch the tanks or patrol the field. Whatever he has in mind, he'll never make it.'

'He's not gonna hit the oil tanks,' Tom said.

Mathis looked back at him. 'The hell he's not. That's his best target.'

'If I were you,' Grant told the security officer, 'I would listen to this guy. He's been right every step of the way.'

Mathis got pinged and read a message on his cell. He looked alarmed and angry and fished his gun out of its holster with his right hand.

'Did your guys spot him?' Grant asked, excited. 'Did he hurt somebody?'

'I ran your names by the FBI when you first showed up,' Mathis told them, 'because I always cross all the T's. I just heard back from the Department of Homeland Security. They said you have no authority, you're breaking regulations, and I should detain you. I don't have any time to waste right now. I'm not sure what's going on, but I'm going to lock you in a room just down the hall, and I don't want any trouble.'

'Go ahead and detain us,' Grant said. 'You've got a world-class terrorist inside your oil field, and there's one person on earth who can tell you where to find him.'

Mathis's eyes flicked to the screens that were flashing different views of the oil tanks. Security officers with guns were in many of the camera angles. 'The Department of Homeland Security says I shouldn't trust you.'

'That black van you found had a Michigan plate,' Grant said, and it wasn't a question.

Mathis nodded slightly, studying their faces.

'This is the guy who first tied Green Man to Michigan,' Grant told him. 'He's done more to break this case than anyone else, and that's what got him frozen out of the investigation. You've been around high-level security and government bureaucracy a long time, so I guess you probably know how that works.'

'He won't come back to the van afterward, if that's what you're thinking,' Tom said softly. 'He's got another way out, downriver. Probably a motorcycle, because that's what he's used before. He knows we know about the van, and he's left it for us as a souvenir. He's going to blow up your oil field, and it won't be by igniting the oil tanks, and then he's gonna swim out downriver and disappear, and you've got about two minutes to make the right decision.'

There was a calm certainty in Tom's voice that seemed to convince Mathis.

He glanced at the screens one last time and then asked, 'Okay, hotshot, where do you think he'd hit?'

'It would be something near the river,' Tom said. 'Besides oil tanks, what else can blow up an oil field?'

Green Man's watch vibrated, and he switched off the motor and used his body to steer toward the bank. He reached the shallows, set an anchor that would keep the diver propulsion vehicle moored safely there, and lifted his head out of the water. The cluster of giant lime-green flowback tanks was less than a hundred feet away.

He peeled off the rebreather and his flippers and stashed them on the gravel near the anchored DPV. Then he dragged the dryboxes up onto the bank. Soon they were both open and he was methodically setting time fuses, using only a razor-thin beam from a penlight held in his teeth. He had practiced setting the fuses in his hunting shed in darkness but to do such precise work in the middle of an oil field, when he knew security was looking for him and every second could mean the difference between getting safely away and being shot, was a very different thing.

From one of the dryboxes he took a lightweight collapsible pole and extended it till it was thirty feet long – the height of the vents on the flowback storage tanks. He fastened a time fuse into an electromagnet bedding and then mounted the magnet on top of the pole.

Minutes later he was walking among the flowback tanks. The hulking cylinders cast monstrous night shadows that helped conceal him. He could smell the acrid chemical stench from the vents high above him. The water in each tank had settled to the bottom, but the volatile and highly combustible chemicals were floating near the top.

He started with a tank far from the river, to give him the best chance to escape. After the first tank blew, there would be a fast-building conflagration, and if he didn't make it back into the river in time, he would be roasted alive.

Green Man paused for a quick prayer. Once he set the first time fuse atop a tank, nothing could stop the firestorm to come. He thought of the roughnecks and roustabouts the explosion would kill instantly and those workers who might inhale poisonous fumes from the smoke and battle health problems for the rest of their lives. They were not bad people, and he knew he had no right to harm them. 'God forgive me,' he whispered.

He carefully lifted the pole so that the magnet at its top brushed the vent of the flowback tank. He clicked the current on from below, and the electromagnet was drawn to the nearby iron vent with such force that it audibly clinked against it. He retracted the pole and started walking quickly to another tank, this one closer to the river. He glanced at his watch. The time fuse he had just set atop the tank would blow in five minutes, and counting.

In the town hall in Östersund, the youth choir had almost finished. A young boy and girl stepped forward and with sweet, innocent voices sang the last haunting refrain of '99 Luftballons.' When their final note faded to silence, the founder of the radical environmental group walked onto the stage. He was a balding, middle-aged man, pushing a much older man in a wheelchair, who, at 103, was the oldest living resident of Östersund – a man well-known and much loved by the townspeople in the audience. In his teens, he had fought the Nazis. The old man slowly stood out of his chair to face a large clock that had been mounted on the wall. The centenarian reached out with his shaking right hand and pressed a button, and the big clock stopped, and the town hall was utterly silent.

Those are the flowback tanks,' Mathis explained, hurrying along the riverbank with his gun in his hand. 'Five of my guards are heading over here on the run.'

'How quick can they get here?' Grant asked, his own Glock out.

'A couple of minutes.'

'They won't arrive in time,' Tom said.

'Do you ever say anything positive?' Mathis asked. 'We don't even know if he made it into the field before I posted guards.'

'He's here,' Tom said. He had walked to the point where the river flowed closest to the flowback storage tanks and spotted two dark shapes half buried in the mud-and-gravel bank. The two dryboxes were side by side. Tom opened one of them. It was empty except for a few spare time fuses and some tools.

The three men looked at the drybox's contents and then at one another. There could be no doubt. He was here, and it was really happening. 'Fuck,' Mathis said, and then he turned toward the hulking cylindrical tanks in the near distance.

'The river was his way in, and it's got to be his way out,' Tom cautioned. 'If we wait here for him, we can surprise him when he comes back. If you try to walk up to those tanks, you'll have to cross open ground. I guarantee he's got a gun and night-vision goggles.'

'I can't wait,' Mathis said, and started up the hill toward the cluster of tanks.

Tom was left alone with Grant. 'The hell of it is he's right,' Grant said grimly, and took a step after the security officer.

'It's suicide to walk up there,' Tom told him. 'He'll just pick you off.'

'If he blows up those tanks, we'll die anyway.'

Tom grudgingly nodded and said softly, 'I don't have a gun.'

'Wait here for the guards who are coming,' Grant said. 'Tell them where we've gone.' He turned and started up the rise after Mathis, moving fast.

Tom stood by the river for a few seconds. Two shots rang out in the darkness. He found himself sprinting forward up the slope, madly disregarding the danger, wanting to help his comrades. He found Grant bending over Mathis. The security guard had been shot through the center of the forehead.

'Throw down your guns,' a voice ordered. They saw a tall man dressed in black walking toward them, his gun held at the ready.

Grant hesitated for a second and then quickly raised his pistol and fired off one fast shot. He grunted, his hand went to his chest, and he crumpled. Tom knelt over him and saw him die. They had never been friends, but Tom had grown to like and respect Grant, and he felt both shock and fury. He checked the carotid artery and then took the Glock from Grant's lifeless hand as footsteps approached.

'Tom Smith,' a familiar voice said. 'You brought them here.' It wasn't a question. 'You do think like me . . . God help you.'

Tom glanced up and saw Green Man less than ten feet

361

away. His right hand held his gun, and his left hand was pressed to his stomach.

Tom stood, and they faced each other. Tom raised the Glock till it was pointed at Green Man's face. 'You just killed two good men.' He wanted very much to pull the trigger – to avenge Grant and Mathis and the other innocent adults and children whom this man had killed, and to justify Brennan's faith in him, and because Warren Smith would have pulled the trigger with no compunction.

But they were looking into each other's eyes, and Tom didn't shoot.

'And I'm about to kill a lot more,' Green Man said. 'Those tanks are set to blow in two minutes. There's no way to stop it from happening. When they blow, this becomes hell on earth.' He grimaced in pain. 'One of us has a chance to get out. And it can't be me.' He lifted his hand from his stomach, and Tom saw the blood and the seriousness of the wound. Mathis or Grant had gutshot Green Man, and he was bleeding to death.

'There's no way out of here in two minutes,' Tom said.

'There's one.' Green Man stepped downhill, toward the river. He was slouching over, and every step was clearly agony. He pointed down at the bank. Dark metal gleamed in the moonlight. Something was anchored in the shallow water just below them. 'If you make it out past the fence, there's a motorcycle stashed by the first big tree, half a mile along.'

Tom looked back at him and hurled the Glock far out into the Kildeer. 'What's the point? It's doomsday. In Sweden and here and everywhere.'

Green Man replied haltingly, in tremendous pain. 'I would like to think that the people in Sweden . . . and God

362

himself . . . built in just a little extra time, if we use it wisely.' Then his face contorted, and he sank to one knee. He gasped out, 'Tom Smith, you wanted to live very much when you swam to shore from that ferry. Get going, and take this.'

He held out something, and Tom took it from his hand. It was a cell phone, in a protective sheath. 'What's on it?'

'A last message to my followers . . . and my kids. In case I didn't make it. Go now.'

Tom began walking and then running down to the water. He spotted the rebreather but didn't know how to use it, and there was no time. He waded over to what looked like a scooter anchored in the shallows. He switched on the motor, and the two propellers started to turn. But he didn't ride away yet. Instead, he took Green Man's cell phone out of its sheath and pointed it up the bank.

'Go,' Green Man told him again, and it was between a command and a plea.

Tom used the cell phone to start filming. Green Man seemed to understand, and he rose to one knee, and then struggled slowly to his feet. Behind him, up the rise, the first tank blew. A tongue of orange flame shot out of the top of it and then it exploded in all directions, and Green Man was silhouetted by the blaze. He made a sweeping gesture with his arm, as if summoning his followers, and then turned and stepped toward the explosion. A second tank blew, and the ground shook, and Tom put the cell phone in its sheath and tucked it away. He grasped the two handles and turned the speed up to full.

The motor roared, and the DPV shot out into the Kildeer, dragging Tom over gravel. Then he was speeding downriver, careening wildly off the bottom, nearly drowning till he figured out how to steer. He sucked in air when he rocketed to the surface and held his breath for minutes while the DPV roared back underwater toward the fence. Above him, the night sky was ablaze with clouds of orange and red fire while rocks that had been wrenched from rig base pits and pieces of twisted steel ripped from derricks were hurled up into the inferno's cloud by the explosion and rained back down on the river. And the earth itself shook so that it felt very much like the world was coming to an end.

51

Sharon had put the kids to bed and stayed with them till they were asleep. They had separate bedrooms in the cheerful little farmhouse, but they were both very anxious and preferred to sleep in the same room. She had listened as they said their prayers and asked God to protect their father, and then she had sung to them. In Michigan, when they were younger, she used to sing them to sleep every night, but when Gus had turned ten, he had declared that he was too old for it and she had stopped. Now, somehow, it seemed fitting and comforting, and she had summoned up a few of their favorite old songs and finished with the lullaby her own mother had sung to her, 'All Through the Night.'

When they were fast asleep, she went to her own bedroom and clicked on her computer and for the hundredth time she watched the brief clip that had become the single most searched-for video in the history of the Internet. No one apparently knew who had filmed it or how it had first been posted, but it had become a worldwide sensation. She could see her husband's agonized face clearly as he rose to his knees and then to his feet and made the sweeping gesture with his arm, inviting the world to follow him. And then he'd turned toward the inferno and taken a last brave step toward the flames as the video cut out.

Sharon cried, as she had each time she'd watched it before that. She cried for his pain and her loneliness. She cried because he'd wanted to stop and she had made him go on, and it had cost him his life and their future. Most of all she cried for her children, who would grow up with memories of a martyr but without a father.

But Sharon also understood that in his death, Green Man had achieved his purpose. His final letter about the grave dangers that fracking posed to the earth and especially the atmosphere had been received and published by the *Washington Post* and had generated a national outcry, particularly among the young. The idea of oil and gas as 'safe and necessary' bridge fuels was being debated from high school clubs to the floor of the Senate. Giant companies that fracked for hundreds of billions of dollars were suddenly defending their releases of methane and other dangerous gases and facing tough questions that even the sharpest lobbyists and the most creative scientific apologists couldn't seem to answer satisfactorily.

Perhaps even more important, Green Man's death and martyrdom had won him a larger-than-life status among the young who would decide the next election and the fate of the country going forward. He had become ubiquitous – his words and image were everywhere – in books, on the sides of buses, on T-shirts on college campuses. And it was no longer the image an artist had dreamed up. His real identity was known. Green Man had been Paul Sayers, and Green Man had become Mitch Farley. He had had two children and raised them in a small Michigan town, and the whole world knew that he had been married to a woman named Sharon. The FBI and the Department of Homeland Security knew it also, and she would never feel completely safe again, but at the same time it made her proud.

She dried her tears, walked to a window, and watched the moonlight forge the links of a golden chain across the lake. She'd have to tell the kids. Gus suspected a lot. They were lonely and wanted to meet other kids and to plug into the Internet. They had to understand why the family had to keep to themselves, at least for a few years, and why they would be homeschooled and spend so much time on this farm. They needed to know why their appearances would start to be subtly changed.

It was ironic that the whole world knew the truth except for them. But it was better that they should hear it from her. She would tell them the next morning, when they all ate breakfast together on the porch overlooking the lake. There would be tears and anger, but there would also be love and pride and a family secret that would become the glue of their special bond for decades to come, and it was the stuff of legends.

She would have to find the strength to show them his video – seeing was believing, and the truth was always the best. Green Man had recorded last statements to them that had somehow also made it out. They needed to hear what he said to them – how much he had loved them. He had not recorded a final statement to her. He had said it to her himself, after the last time they made love, in their house in Michigan in the bed that he had carved himself from a great oak.

Sharon trembled because she missed him so very much. It would always be like this. Or maybe it wouldn't. Maybe time heals all wounds and she would find peace and one day even someone else to love the way she had loved him. But she couldn't believe that. These were the hardest hours. She pressed her cheek up against the cold glass of the sliding door. Winter was still a long way off, but the night had bite.

She watched the moonlight on the lake and imagined him here, his strong arms around her. 'We made it, Shar,' he whispered. 'We turned the world, and now we have each other for forty years.' He was standing behind her so that she couldn't see him, but she knew he was right there. She could feel his solid presence, his breaths on her hair, the heat from his body. His lips touched her neck and his hands were loosening her robe, and then he was whispering that he loved her while his hands turned her to face him.

She turned slowly but saw only darkness. She pivoted quickly away from that yawning emptiness, back to the lake, and slid the porch door open. Three long steps took her to the edge, and she dived off the deck. She swam almost straight down to the bottom, where it was freezing and pitch dark, and she hid from the whole world at the bottom of that Canadian lake. But the moon wouldn't let her hide for too long; it spotted her and reached out, and she reluctantly followed the beckoning light back up to the surface. She swam home along its golden chain, and dried herself off, and put on her robe. And then she went into her kids' bedroom and lay down next to Kim, who stirred but didn't wake. And Sharon slept with her children.

52

Julie watched, a bit stunned. She had seen her mother speak at meetings before, and she knew the power Ellen could exert over an audience. But as the head of the Green Center, her mother had always been a polite, responsible, and cautionary presence, a brake on the more radical activists she worked with. This morning Ellen had left them all behind – even Richard was gaping at her – and she had done it without raising her voice or calling for any specific acts of destruction or violence. But there could be no doubt that she was striking a match and holding it to tinder with every bold, profane, and incendiary sentence.

'What I'm saying is that we as an organization can no longer afford not to embrace Green Man and everything he stood for,' Ellen told the forty employees in the Green Center's conference room. 'But it goes further than that. I'm also saying that we need to do anything and everything to carry his activist vision and agenda forward. And yes, if necessary, that means we need to fight.'

Her co-workers were watching her, but not slumped into their usual window seats, nor stretched out on beanbag chairs sipping kombucha. They were sitting almost rigidly, nearly at attention, as if their director's unexpected call to action had militarized this collection of hippies and dreamers into what could become the forward brigade of an undisciplined but potent army.

Lou got a little unsteadily to his feet and smiled at her.

'While I agree with a lot of what Green Man wrote and also with most of what you're now saying, Ellen, we simply can't condone violence. That's never been you, and that's also never been us.'

'Lou, it's not about violence,' Ellen told him. 'It goes way beyond violence. But if action is called for, we can't shy away. We need to lead and make tough choices. That's me now, and that's got to be us now, or we'll be left behind and meaningless.'

Listening, Julie was thrilled and a bit shocked to hear her mother repudiate her former caution and pacifism and stake out a new position that was even more radical than Julie's own. And Ellen did it so easily and forcefully that Julie realized this was in fact who her mother really was, and she wasn't transforming but actually revealing her true self. This was the young woman who had fired up rallies in San Francisco twenty years ago and gone on secret and destructive night missions with her lover and confidant.

'Don't you understand?' Ellen asked Lou and all of them. 'Green Man's death and the publicity it's generated is a game changer. Our struggle has now entered a critical phase. We're in a pitched battle to save the planet, and it's not a distance race anymore – it's a sprint. Sprinters can't worry about strategy – they just have to run as fast as they fucking can for ten seconds.' Her eyes found Julie's, and she held her daughter's gaze as she said, 'We have to throw out the rulebook and not be bound by what we've said or done before. It's time to forcefully lead, or we'll lose the support of the people we need most – the next generation. They have the most to lose, and we put them in this position, so we'd better not try to stall them or bullshit them.' Julie looked back at her mother and dipped her head slightly in proud acknowledgment of Ellen's new bluntness and passion.

Richard stood and said, 'Ellen, it's all very well to change your tune and talk about how we now need to embrace Green Man, but the fact is, you really embraced him –'

'That's a part of me that I'm not going to conceal anymore,' Ellen said, cutting him off. 'The whole world knows now that I was his partner twenty years ago. That's a giant plus for us, and I intend to use that legacy to lead. We need to put his face on our main screen, and I have photographs of Paul that no one else has seen. We need to use his words as part of the Green Center's dynamic message going forward, and I know what Paul said better than anyone. He will live through me, and he will speak through us, and together we'll lead the way forward.'

'That makes sense for you,' Richard said. 'You'll become a cult hero and a national figure as you plug into his legend. Given the degree of legal jeopardy you're in right now, it's probably a very smart strategy for you, but not for us. We do a lot of critical work here, especially right now, and we won't be able to continue it if our center is closed and we're all locked up. We're in a very unique and dangerous situation here . . .'

Ellen smiled at him. 'Richard, you've become so politically cautious I barely recognize you.'

'Now that's not fair,' he said angrily. 'I care about the work we're doing; that needs to be finished.'

Josie chimed in: 'Ellen, you hired most of us, and you founded and built this organization and we're grateful, but you're now under a bit of a cloud . . .'

'I'm not under a cloud,' Ellen told them. 'I'm under

371

investigation by several different governmental agencies, including the FBI and the Department of Homeland Security. If you can't handle having a director who may be arrested at any second, then either you have to leave or I have to leave, because that's where we are now and it's a strength, not a weakness, and I'm not going to back down one inch. Richard's absolutely right: if they arrest me, they'll make me a living martyr and I don't think they're quite dumb enough to do that. If they bust up our organization, it'll spawn a hundred like us and trumpet our message to the world. Let's take them on boldly, and if you don't want me to lead that way, I'll resign and build another organization that does.'

Julie got up and quietly left the conference room. She hated to watch her mother under attack as the organizational politics played out. She was pretty sure Ellen would win, but in a way, she didn't really care. It was time for the truth, and her mother was telling the truth.

Julie walked upstairs to her mom's office and sat looking at the photos on the wall. Many of them were pictures of her growing up, but there was a new one, right above the desk. It was a photo of Ellen and Paul Sayers, looking impossibly young in jeans, T-shirts, and boots. They were arm in arm on the deck of a small boat with cliffs in the background, and they looked happy and at peace together.

Julie studied the photo intently. Her mother was young and beautiful, and the two of them were clearly very much in love. Julie switched on her mom's computer and found Green Man's final message. She had listened to it many times before, but in this office, beneath the photo of the happy young couple on the boat, Green Man's words played with a new resonance.

He asked for forgiveness for the innocent people he'd killed. He told his followers that if they were hearing this message, it meant that he was gone. His struggle was now their struggle, and he was sure they would win it. One day soon they would live on a sustainable earth that had been saved. Near the end of his message, he described that healing future world a little bit for them, and Julie drank in his welcome words of hope.

Green Man ended by asking the world's forbearance as he said a few words of very personal goodbye to his own children, who were young and didn't yet understand why their father had vanished. His voice became intimate and taut with emotion. He said he was sorry he wouldn't be there for them, to watch them grow up. He knew his absence would cause them great pain. But he said that he loved them dearly, and when they were older and could grasp the totality of the dire situation, he asked for their forgiveness or at least their understanding.

In the second-floor office of the Green Center's brownstone, her eyes blinking back tears, Julie nodded her head and whispered back to her father, 'I understand.'

53

Lise taught her last class and biked home, and as she neared her house, a parked car blinked its lights at her, and she saw the driver open the window and wave her over. It took her a second to recognize him — he was growing a beard, and he seemed somehow different from when she had worked with him. He looked relaxed and unfettered, and he gave her a warm smile and said, 'Nice bike.'

'Tom? What are you doing here?'

'I was listening to country music. The songs are fun if you don't take them too seriously.'

'I meant what are you doing near my house? Are you stalking me?'

'I'm going camping in the mountains,' he told her. 'Want to come for a day or two?'

'Camping?'

'I bought a tent. I'm not sure how to set it up, but I figure with your engineering background we could probably figure it out. I'm actually driving cross-country to my new job in California.'

'I don't know if I should even be seen with you,' Lise said. 'The FBI has called three or four times with questions.'

'That's why I thought I'd try to intercept you,' Tom told her. 'Why don't you come into my car for a second so we can have a covert conversation.'

Lise hesitated, lowered her kickstand, and walked to the small electric car and got in. 'Camping?' she asked again.

'You look good,' Tom told her. 'Sorry about the FBI. They've been all over me, too. They think I posted the video of Green Man at the oil field, but they can't seem to prove it. Whoever posted it covered his tracks really well.'

'I should get out of this car and never talk to you again,' Lise said.

'You know I'm not much of a drinker, but on the off chance you'd agree to come, I bought a very nice bottle of Italian red,' Tom said. 'I can afford it on my new Silicon Valley salary. I'm not bragging, but I wanted you to know that I'm a bit of a player these days.'

She looked back at him. 'I have a conference call in half an hour.'

'I can wait.'

'It may be a long call.'

'When you drive cross-country, you go at your own pace. I'll be waiting here.'

She looked into his eyes and finally laughed despite herself. 'Why are you driving across country, anyway?'

'The long roads and big vistas are helping me deal with some of what I've been through,' Tom told her, and for a moment she glimpsed the pain behind his new bravado. 'Also, I've given up flying in planes. I'm trying to lessen my carbon footprint. As a scientist and a biker, I'm sure you'll understand that.'

'I understand that you're nuts,' she told him, and then she reached out and gently touched his cheek. 'Really?' she asked softly. 'Camping in the mountains?'

'Don't feel pressured. I was passing through and I thought why not invite you?'

'I never turn down a good bottle of wine,' Lise told him, and then she got out of the car and biked away up the block of fancy mansions, and Tom sat back and smiled.